David Rollins is a former adv............. .... creative director who decided to try to dig his tunnel out of that game by writing bestselling novels. Advertising is a long way behind him now, but he is still digging. And there are plenty of people who'll tell you he's still trying.

David lives in Sydney, Australia.

Also by David Rollins

Special Agent Vin Cooper series:
Death Trust ✓
A Knife Edge ✓
Hard Rain ✓
Ghost Watch
War Lord
Standoff

Collision series:
Field of Mars

Warrant Officer Tom Wilkes series:
Rogue Element
Sword of Allah

Stand-alone:
The Zero Option

Kingdom Come

David Rollins

For Sam and Ruby.

Acknowledgements

I'd like to thank Lieutenant Colonel Mike "Panda" Pandolfo, USAF (Ret.) for his time, knowledge and patience.

Thanks to Tricia and Jan for reading drafts and telling me when things were going off track. Essentially, if you don't like the book, they share the blame.

Thanks also to John for proof reading.

Thanks to Deonie who did an amazing job with the edit.

And thanks to William, from Bold Fox Designs, who crushed the cover design.

Finally, and I guess a little unusually, I'd like to acknowledge and thank Sam Harris and his excellent podcast series, Waking Up, for stimulating this idea.

One

Ronald V. Small @realSmall
America LOVES and RESPECTS its veterans. They are the best of us.

Lieutenant Colonel Arlen Wayne, my supervisor, leaned forward and tapped the letter on the table. "God knows you've had plenty of time to think about this. What do you want to do?"

"Order drinks."

"Vin, alcohol is not the answer to everything."

"It's not?" I nodded across the pool at Juan, the drinks waiter, my newest best friend, and indicated two. "You look good," I told Arlen. "Whatever you're doing, it's working."

He shrugged, a little self-conscious.

Something was going on. Arlen looked years younger. With a few post-adolescent pimples he could almost pass for lieutenant. Keeping company with Marnie, Anna Masters's younger sister, was obviously agreeing with him. Or maybe his paunch hadn't agreed with her and she'd put him on a diet or enrolled him in Bikram-Spartan-Zumba or whatever the current fitness fad was these days. And those gray tips showing up in his hair last time I saw him? Gone. Clearly he'd developed a Just For Men habit. Why is it that women want to change their partners into something better groomed and less sports-and-swimsuit oriented, whereas a man just wants his other half to remain that sweet non-judgmental hottie who told him she thought blow jobs were fun? It's one of the laws of the universe. Newton discovered it. Or was it Galileo? Hello, Venus, have you met Mars?

"You tired, Vin?"

"Why?"

"You keep slipping away on me."

I smiled at Hong, who chose that moment to strut past our table and throw me a knowing smirk. Her nickname for me was Hung. Hong and Hung. Cute. "Yeah, actually I'm exhausted." Arlen followed my gaze, which ended in a very brief bikini, a slender caramel-colored back and long straight black hair. "But that's vacations for you."

Admiring that bikini until it reclined on a sun lounge, Arlen said, "We were discussing your retirement. My question was, do you really want out?"

I was tired, which was why I'd written that letter resigning my commission in the United States Air Force that he was waving around. The last few years in the Office of Special Investigations had been tough, and not just physically. There was the mental strain. You can only save the world so many times before things take their toll, right? And I could hear the tolling.

"Assuming you actually do resign, any thoughts on what you might do once you're out?" he asked. "There's not much call outside the military for blowing things up."

"Balloon animals at kids' parties?" I reminded him.

"I mean it, Vin. The things you take for granted in this line of work would get you locked up once you're out in - let's call it the real world. Don't take this the wrong way, but your normal is kinda fucked up from pretty much every perspective except your own. People like you..."

"People like me..."

"People in your line of work... the thin blue line – outside of the military somewhere, some police department, is the nearest you're going to get to a world you can function in."

"You're saying I'm disabled."

"Emotionally, morally...yeah, that's a good way to describe you – disabled."

"Right."

"Look, if you want, I can make some calls. You're a decorated veteran with a Silver Star. That's a commodity you can sell. There's the US Marshals. I know people."

"I don't think so." The US Marshals? Playing nursemaid to convicted felons? Not my bag.

"Then what about the CIA?"

This one got the wry snort. "Really, Arlen? The CIA? You know how we feel about each other. Just my luck I'd find myself under Bradley Chalmers." That was not a place anyone wanted to be, not even Mrs Chalmers, assuming there was such a person these days.

"Chalmers has just been confirmed Associate Deputy Director."

"And you're suggesting I go there?"

"The Company is a big organization."

Chalmers running the CIA, or almost running it. Look out world.

"That's kinda your fault – him getting the number two job."

"Not my bad, Vin. Don't pin that on me. The President of Mexico lobbied hard for him after the work he did nailing Arturo Perez for the Horizon Airport massacre."

Another snort. There's irony for you. Arturo Perez, a.k.a the Tears of Chihuahua. He was the butcher who, in order to cover the smuggling of a planeload of blow onto US soil, slaughtered twenty-seven innocent civilians at Horizon Airport, a privately owned airstrip outside of El Paso. Chalmers didn't nail Perez. I did, and at great personal risk I might add. It was Arlen handing all the evidence I'd collected over to Chalmers that delivered the tool a gold-plated promotion.

"What are you snorting about?"

"Something's stuck up my nose. A glob of Chalmers."

"He owes you one."

"And I'm sure he'd just love some payback."

"The Company is not some personal fiefdom," Arlen reminded me.

"Someone should point that out to the CIA."

"Back to my original question. You gotta make a living."

"Well, I'm not going to make it doing police work." That right there was my problem: the gumshoe thing. No, thanks. Maybe I just needed a break; go do something simpler.

"Okay, so we've established that the Air Force isn't the problem per se. Is it the OSI?"

"Maybe." If I *were* saying that, I would be bucking the trend. OSI was the most desired job within the Air Force, other than pilot, with a long line of people wanting in.

"You're starting to sound like a millennial, Vin. Next you'll tell me you want to become an Instagram brand ambassador."

"Healthy sarcasm with a side order of stereotyping. Nice. I'm rubbing off on you." I watched Hong climb out of her lounge chair, sashay over to the pool and dive in. Arlen watched too and there was an appropriate thirty seconds of silence while we both appreciated the show, undistracted.

He gave a polite cough to restart proceedings. "You know, you're not being very helpful. There's always room in this man's Air Force for another fobbit."

Fobbit – Army slang for a soldier who didn't patrol beyond the forward operating base or FOB. Arlen was actually big noting himself here. Let's be honest, it had been a long time since he was anywhere near a FOB, let alone outside the wire. These days he was more the Power Point ranger type, a producer of slide presentations for meetings. But that's okay. The meat eaters can't do their thing without the plant eaters. We weren't getting anywhere. "You haven't come all the way out here for this."

"This and other things."

Right, it was the other things he was really here for.

"There's, um, something I wanted to talk to you about." Arlen looked almost sheepish. "Marnie."

"She's pregnant."

"No."

"You're getting a dog together." Juan returned with a couple of Glenkeiths and rocks. "Thanks, Juan," I told him, and got the chit to sign in return.

"Vin, I'm going to ask her to, you know … marry me."

That was my next guess. "Really? Arlen! Congratulations, buddy."

"A bit premature. I haven't asked and she hasn't said yes."

"Right, but that's the sort of question you only ask when you already know the answer." Marnie was Anna's sister. That's Anna Masters, my former partner and, well, partner. A picture of Anna formed. She was smiling at me, her blue-green eyes sparkling, the sun leaving highlights in her chocolate-colored hair, a gentle breeze playing with the halo of butterflies above her. But then the picture changed into the last time I held her, her limp body cradled in my arms and a ragged bloody hole in her chest. But I kept the grin on my face throughout the brief trip down memory lane because what else was I gonna do?

"I wanted to make sure you were okay with it," he said.

"Arlen, you don't have to ask my permission." And I meant that. Marnie was Anna's younger sister by fifteen months. Last time I saw her, she was the spitting image of Anna, her hair dyed the same lustrous dark brown as Anna's. But Marnie was not Anna. And I wasn't Marnie's father. "Go for it, fool. I mean sir." My best pal married to my deceased ex-significant-other's sister. There was symmetry in that. I picked up my drink. "To you and Marnie."

"Thanks," he said. "Means a lot."

We clinked glasses. "So, when's the wedding?"

"Don't know. Soon, hopefully. If she says yes, I'd like you to be my best man."

"I accept, as long as the best man's speech doesn't get censored."

"Deal!" Arlen's grin wavered. "Er ...wait ..."

"Too late," I told him.

He returned to the official business at hand. "Are we getting anywhere on this other thing?"

"Which one?"

"You. Your future. The other reason I've come all the way out here. Vin, c'mon. The service exists for people like you."

"So you keep reminding me."

"You're a violence junkie."

"And you mean that in the nicest possible way."

"I know you. Six months on the outside and you'll be climbing the walls, looking for shit to fix, only the most you'll be able to fix will be a leaky faucet."

"And that faucet had better watch the fuck out."

"You know I'm right."

Yes, he was right, but that wasn't going to stop me making him earn it.

Another respectful period of silence while Hong got out of the pool, strutted across the terrace, toweled off her hair and reclaimed her lounge chair.

"Vin, you want out, I get it. But after being in the service so long, you're gonna have separation anxiety about it. So why not leave, and stay?"

"Leave and stay... Have you changed your name to Major Major Major Major?"

"Whatever that means..." Arlen waved his hand at something annoying. Me, probably. "Look, your obligation to serve in the Air Force was up long ago, so you've got options. You can leave and enter into government civil service. Or you can transition without any loss of rank or status to the Reserves or National Guard, and still accrue points for retirement at age sixty, assuming you live that long. Five years ago I would have thought that unlikely, but here you are still breathing."

"I'm just a li'l ol' bullseye looking for an arrow."

"I've checked into this for you and, of all the options – and there are many – I suggest you separate and enlist in the Air Force Reserve as an Individual Mobilization Augmentee."

"Serve the standard one weekend a month and two weeks a year."

"Or serve 120 man-days per twelve-month period, but that would depend on which unit you joined."

"How does any of that make things easy for me exactly?"

"Like I said, you can leave, but stay. Out on the one hand, in on the other. You'll have left, but also stayed."

"As I said, Major Major Major Major."

"As an IMA, with your record of service, I can pretty much guarantee you'll have the run of the Air Force."

"I can run the Air Force? Now you're talking. There's this little country I'd like to nuke. Actually, it's several countries but they're all pretty much in the same sandbox. I think you know the ones."

"I can get you assigned to active duty units, organizations, combat support agencies, Unified Combatant Commands and even the Joint Staff... Whatever you want. The Air Force wants to keep its people engaged, doing the jobs that are essential in wartime and/ or during contingency operations, jobs that do not require full-time manning during times of peace."

"Jobs like whacking people."

"Be serious."

"I am. You said it – whacking folks is for people like me."

"I've got a job that will interest you."

"Is it whacking people?"

"No. Focus."

"Is there a bar?"

"No, there's not. In fact it's a no-alcohol gig and the government there is the opposite of stable."

"You're not selling it."

Two

Ronald V. Small @realSmall
Syria is a basket case thanks to my predecessor. If only he'd had
the guts to do more, like Russia. BIG MISTAKE!

And that's pretty much how I came to find myself serving as a
combat controller, leading a four-man-team that had HALOed onto
a hill in the north of Syria, surrounded by nutjobs and killers
otherwise known as jihadists. As Arlen suggested, I was in the Air
Force but also not in the Air Force. An IMA. I'd served in the
role of combat controller before, back when I was a youngster,
but things had changed. It was a new war, Afghanistan being so
yesterday. And there's a new name for this job – Joint Terminal
Attack Controller. Could be because our work is terminal to the
folks under the bomb runs we call in. Also could be that the T
in JTAC explains what happens at both ends of the pineapple, as
there were positions that suddenly became vacant in my old unit,
the 23rd Special Tactics Squadron.

My team and I had landed on the outskirts of Latakia, a Syrian
city close to the Turkish border, where we'd watched the Russian
bombers pound the skyline with high explosives and phosphorus
for three nights in a row. And, trust me, there's nothing precision

about the way the Russians go about their business. A jagged ridge of orange and yellow fires that stretched as far as I could see showed where the black starless sky touched the ground. The outline boiled higher at points where the flames were consuming gas cylinders and fuel tanks or when an unexploded bomb suddenly joined the party.

The road below us was clogged with refugees. Every now and again, they shuffled into small islands of smoky light from diesel fires ISIS fighters had lit in 55-gallon drums to ward off the cold. Some of the refugees drove vehicles, but most were on foot, a pathetic army of zombies shambling out of the darkness. Old men, women with crying babies, frightened children, wounded men, hospital patients and old folks on makeshift stretchers – all desperate to escape the hell that had devoured their homes and lives. People say if you see enough of this you no longer see it, so maybe I haven't been here long enough.

The jihadists, however, didn't appear to have any noticeable empathy towards the refugees. They swaggered like conquerors, even though they too had been separated from their spoils - the city - by the indiscriminate bombing.

I watched through a night scope as two men in those loose black ninja pajamas some of them favor stopped a white BMW. Why they stopped it I don't know. One guard sported a dirty blond beard and wore a *taquiyah*, a pill cap that was probably white once upon a time. The other was slight, his head shrouded in a light-colored turban. Foreign fighters. They ripped open the doors and pulled the occupants from their seats - a guy in a suit and a woman, presumably his wife, shrouded in a *khimar*, the black head-covering that left a slit for the eyes, and an *abaya*, the all-over black cloak. At a guess they were an upper middle-class Muslim couple. From the back seats, the fighters yanked out a stooped heavy-set woman, also covered head to foot in black; grandma, I figured. Along with her, they extracted a pair of young teens, both boys in jeans and T-shirts. I assumed these two Islamic State tough guys had drawn the short straw of guard duty and were gonna make someone pay for the fact they had to stand around in their jammies in the cold. The tall blonde-bearded guard dragged suitcases and boxes off the Beemer's roof. The luggage burst open when it hit the ground, the contents scattering across the dull gray grit that passes for soil in these parts. The scrawny one then picked through the debris with the muzzle of his AK, presumably looking for valuables.

The driver, the father, got down on his knees and appeared to be begging the fighters to stop, the column of refugees parting around the escalating danger the way a river flows around a boulder. I couldn't hear the father's pleas, but they appeared insistent. Gutsy stuff, given the reputation these ISIS killers have won for themselves. And just as I was thinking that, the scrawny jihadist lowered the weapon on his hip and fired a burst into the father that spun him around and ploughed him into the dirt. It happened fast. After a moment of disbelief, the boys attempted to run to their old man - who was face down on the ground as dead as dead gets - but they were held back by the mother and grandmother. The women gathered them up and held them close and tight. Blondie approached them, his weapon held one-handed and aimed casually at the wife. He pressed the muzzle against her head. She didn't move. The asshole then switched his attention to one of the kids. Grandmother's turn to sink to her knees, hands held to the sky, begging either him or Allah for mercy. Fat chance on either count. These guys were into mercy like they were into pork.

A large group of fighters strode from the building we'd been keeping an eye on, a decrepit warehouse adjacent to the oil-drum fires. One of the men was wearing what appeared to be a superseded surplus US Army combat uniform shirt, paired with the more conventional ISIS black pants. He gestured wildly at Blondie, who backed off a few paces, lowered his weapon and opened his arms like he was saying, "What? Who, me ...?". The guy in the combat camos had to be the leader, throwing his weight around, issuing orders. His squad reacted, two of them dragging the body of the dead husband off the road and dumping him under the lee of the warehouse. The boss then slapped the blonde fighter around the face while he made some point or other with a lot of gesturing at the newly minted widow huddling with her kids and the granny. The commander slid the turban off his head and wiped his face and beard with it, looking exasperated. It was a patchy, mostly red beard. What did we have here? The United Nations of Assholes?

A voice said in my ear, "Boss, we know this germ. Look at his hands."

Now that he mentioned it, we did indeed. He was high on the CIA kill list, a Predator drone with a Hellfire on standby just for him. According to his rap sheet, he had two noms de guerre: Abu Bakr al Aljurji, meaning Abu Bakr the Georgian - not the Peach State Georgia, the other one in central Asia positioned directly beneath Russia's asshole, Chechnya; and Al-Aleaqarab, the Scorpion, because he had eight legs and arms and scuttled around in the dirt. Okay, not true, but apparently he did have mutant claws instead of hands, or something like that. He was also, evidently, a murderous son of a bitch. "What is it with me and scorpions?" I muttered, keeping the scope trained on him.

"Boss?" One of my team asked.

"Nothing," I replied. "Stream of consciousness..." Scorpions were features of a recurring nightmare I'd been having for some time, since my first tour in Afghanistan in fact, which I had no intention of sharing with my guys. I'd also been stung in the face by a motherfucker of a scorpion the size of a house cat back in Africa. I didn't like them and they sure as shit weren't fond of me. This Al-Aleaqarab asshole wouldn't be any different.

I'd barely finished these unpleasant thoughts when the Scorpion produced a pistol from somewhere and emptied it into the mother, grandmother and the two boys. Just like that. No hesitation at all. Like it meant nothing.

The pistol jumped in his hand maybe a dozen times, the sound of it discharging inaudible at this distance. The river of humanity ran, scattering to get away from the violence. the Scorpion then walked casually back to the warehouse, job done, flinging further gestures at his men who then ran to the deceased and dragged them off the road, reuniting the family under the lee of the warehouse.

Fuck.

"Allahu akbar," said the voice in my earpiece. God is great. The sarcasm came courtesy of US Army Special Forces Sergeant First Class Bo Baker, a black guy from Tennessee, seated in the dirt beside me behind a spotter's night scope. "Just love to help those assholes marry their dark-eyed virgins," he added.

Me too. Unfortunately the whole area was crawling with retreating jihadists. There were at least a good fifty in number bivouacking in that warehouse down yonder. There was that, and also the fact that assassinating former ISIS leaders was not on our to-do list.

"Back door, five tangoes," said another voice in my earpiece, the tone low so as not to carry in the thick night air. That was Sergeant Jimmy McVeigh, US Army Special Forces. A white kid from Brunswick, south Georgia.

And now don't get all squirrely on me because I've brought color into the descriptions of Baker and McVeigh. I only mention it like I'd mention any distinguishing feature - a weird haircut or a neck tattoo, for instance. But since both are sergeants without neck tats, have their hair shaved to the skull, and are uniformly tall, athletic, good-looking roosters who speak with southern accents so thick you'd swear sometimes they weren't speaking English at all, frankly they could be twins. Except that one is white and the other black.

"Copy," I replied, getting my head back in the game. There wasn't much time for sympathy. McVeigh's warning wasn't a complete surprise. We'd seen a group of fighters leaving the warehouse ten minutes ago, packing AKs, RPGs, a light machine gun and plenty of belts. We figured they might be coming our way. "They ready to rumble?" I asked.

"Negative. Two are smoking, the others are laughing, out for a stroll."

Okay, so before things get real interesting, now's as good a time as any for a little backstory. The hill we occupied on the outskirts of Latakia afforded unobstructed views all around. My job was to recon and identify potential targets for our F-15Es. But the Russians have thrown a spanner in those works with their bombing campaign, which has left us free to execute the secondary part of our mission - to plant a TTS3030 TACAN on a high point. The TACAN is a man-portable navigation aid reminiscent of the Jupiter 2 on stilts. Why anyone needs a TACAN has me puzzled, given that satellites provide all the navigation grunt for our aircraft these days, but they do and their desire for it is paying my salary. Maybe someone up the chain was concerned about redundancy and a TACAN provided a little added insurance that no one would overshoot and drop their load on Tel Aviv. As for the three guys with me, all are experienced sergeants from the US Army 5th Special Forces Group (Airborne) and their job is to protect my ass. So far, at least their part of the mission was going to plan because, so far, ass intact. The beacon was also planted and functioning. But yesterday those retreating ISIS jihadists turned up, chased out of the city by the Russian bombing campaign. And since then we'd been stuck here. That was a problem because these ISIS fighters were seasoned, which meant sooner or later they would look up at our temporary home on the hill, realize it was the tactically astute place to be, and maybe pop over to borrow a cup of sugar.

"Got eyeballs on 'em?" I asked McVeigh.

"Yessir."

Though the sergeant was armed with a silenced M4, he would take some or all of them out with a ka-bar. Reason being he believed a blade paid more respect to the dead. I like a kid with values, though why he might have respect for these jihad shitheads was a mystery.

Nine of us on the hill. Four, once Jimmy dispatched our uninvited guests to their overdue rendezvous with the aforementioned dark-eyed virgins who, apparently, are waiting in Paradise for the arrival of fresh martyrs.

"Alvin?" I enquired over the comms link?

"Clear."

Sergeant Alvin Leaphart from Savannah, Georgia, the third member of the team, was down the hill a ways, guarding the front door - a sheer rock escarpment and an unlikely entry point to our temporary home. Alvin was a nugget, the human equivalent of a snub-nosed 38. Tough, brutal to look at and potentially lethal if you pulled his trigger. And rumor had it he was pretty handy with his fists, a rumor I would not personally like to verify. Seemingly at odds with his reputation, Alvin carried a picture of his mom and the Virgin Mary in the pocket over his heart. You might ask where the Army finds guys like these? It doesn't. Kids like Jimmy, Alvin and Bo find the Army.

So that leaves me, Vin Cooper: as you know, formerly Office of Special Investigations but currently US Air Force Special Ops, rank of major. Six-two, 230 pounds, thirty-four years of age, murky green eyes, a few identifying scars. And some of them on my skin. Interests: single malt and poor choices with the opposite sex. Or maybe it's me who's the poor choice. Been married once, divorced once, almost engaged a second time. That would have been to Anna, Marnie's sister. But my plans in that department never eventuated because, as I described earlier, she died in a perfect example of why I'm probably not the right man for anyone.

"Scratch tangos," Jimmy McVeigh announced calmly, having laid them all to rest without a single interruption to the crickets' chirpings.

Dropped behind enemy lines, we were supposed to keep a low profile. And, as I said earlier, engaging these jihadists directly was not in our job description. But icing the ISIS patrol just now, which had become an unfortunate necessity, meant the clock was ticking. No doubt someone in that warehouse, probably Mr Scorpion, would be expecting a signal sooner or later from his pals that all was copacetic on top of the newly occupied hill. When the signal wasn't forthcoming, another patrol would be tasked, and it would come with attitude. ISIS might have been fanatical in a religious sense, but it was not generally tactically or operationally inept in a combat one. That presented a problem, namely that there were already too few ways off this hill already that didn't involve body bags. We already knew an extraction option was not available to us until after dawn – hours away. The timetable had been made clear by Slingshot, our overlords back at Al Udeid Air Base in Qatar, before they set us down in these parts a little shy of thirty-six hours ago.

"Alvin, Jimmy. On me," I said quietly. I didn't need to state the obvious: that it was time to move. There wasn't a lot to pack – we'd already collected and bagged our shit, as well as all MRE wrappers and papers and other items of identification. There was the TACAN of course, which I would have to pack away and reposition elsewhere. So, even though we were pretty much good to go, the area had to be swept, like looking under the hotel bed before checking out.

"Major," said Alvin, his familiar voice in my ear, "more tangos on the way."

"Stand by," I replied, hoisting the M24 sniper's rifle to my shoulder. The night scope focused on the warehouse showed the Scorpion loitering with a bunch of his cronies who were pointing up at our hill. Half-a-dozen jihadists had already detached themselves and were pushing through the refugees on the road. I took in a deep breath and let it out with an expletive. "Jimmy, change of plan. Six tangos inbound. Hold position, we're coming to you."

"You hear that, sir?" said Jimmy.

Now that he mentioned it, there were new sounds competing with the distant low rumble of the wounded city. Rotary wing aircraft sounds. They were low, maybe 500 feet AGL and they were coming our way.

* * *

The noise was penetrating, even above the wailing of women and children and the shouts of men. Helicopters. Mazool Al Shamoun coughed to clear the dust from his lungs and the ringing in his ears. He could identify almost all aircraft by the sound they made, especially the ones that rained death. He stood back, wiped his bloody hands down the front of his pants, and let others more adept at healing attend to the screaming young man who had lost a leg and at least one testicle. Mazool's talents lay elsewhere. He turned around, right and then left, and then right again, trying to catch the sound. *More than one helicopter. But where are they coming from?* The thumping made by their rotors, which turned to a shriek with a shift of the breeze, suggested there were, yes – two of them. They were near, and drawing nearer.

"Bring rockets!" he shouted to his young fighters, beckoning them frantically, waving his arms. Two young men, both struggling to grow beards, flicked their cigarettes at the ground producing balls of orange sparks, and appeared from the darkened entrance of what remained of an apartment building. They hoisted the weapons, slung the spare rocket packs over their shoulders and raced toward Mazool as fast as the smashed masonry littering the road allowed. One of them stumbled, throwing his body beneath the RPG to protect it. "Hurry!" Mazool shouted, exasperation in his voice. The young fighter picked himself up and limped on.

One of the aircraft suddenly appeared overhead, presenting its vulnerable tail rotor. And just as quickly it was gone, obscured by a partially collapsed wall. Other fighters came out onto the street with whatever weapons they could find and began firing their rifles and pistols at the silhouette too late as it flew by low overhead.

"Taymullah! Farib! This way. Quick." Mazool pressed the button on his iPhone and held it up briefly so that Farib and Taymullah could see where he was. He turned and darted down a narrow alley and clambering over a pile of broken cinderblocks and shattered wood beams clogging the narrow space. Nearby fires illuminated a young woman's body smoking beneath live electrical wires. The smell of it, sweet and vile, filled his nostrils. Once it would have caused him to gag, but no longer.

Another glimpse of a helicopter maneuvering between shattered walls rewarded Mazool's agility, and he again broke into a sprint.

The Russians. Their bombs had murdered his brothers, his sister and mother. Assad's killers had come in the night and taken his father as well as his two uncles. Mazool was sure they were now lying silent in a pit, the cold earth having filled their mouths and lungs, keeping company with others who had spoken badly of the Assads or their followers, or who had merely been accused of this crime because of jealousy or some long forgotten family feud. The two young men who followed Mazool's orders were his only family now.

The Russians were outsiders who had come late to the fight and bombed Assad's enemies, who they claimed were terrorists. Terrorists? *Was my mother a terrorist? A woman whose passion was baking?* The Americans and their friends were unbelievers – that was true - but they fought on the side of God against the Baath Party and the Alawites, the true terrorists. From the back of his throat, Mazool dug up some mucous gritty with concrete dust and spat it. The Russians know of the killing and the torturing and the blood spilled by Assad, and yet they stand shoulder to shoulder with the Baathists. *One day, I will cut a Russian heart from its chest and squeeze it in front of his face and I will capture it on my phone and share it with the world. Allah bear witness, I will do this to avenge my own family and my country.*

Mazool ran into the square, an open space. It was dark, but the helicopters were in plain sight. Where were the rockets? "Here!" he called out, beckoning them furiously. "Both of you run like fat men up a hill. Hurry!" The RPG was not a guided weapon, but Farib and Taymullah had proven their aim true on many occasions with tanks and cars. Was a helicopter any different?

His two fighters stumbled into the square, fumbling their RPGs. But the helicopters continued on their path, once again hidden by the remains of buildings.

Mazool pulled the nine-millimeter from his belt and fired at the shadow in frustration as it slipped from view. The magazine was soon spent and he was left standing, the impotence like a fire on his skin, his lungs heaving, struggling with the taste of concrete dust and gas and blood and seared flesh in his nostrils.

"We need higher ground," Taymullah panted.

Mazool hunted the shadows and settled on a hotel, leveled except for the elevator shaft that was still standing, and three flights of fire stairs that clung to a partially collapsed wall. "There!" he said, and then ran across the square, sprinting around a large bomb crater. Arriving at the remains of the hotel, he ripped aside a door swinging on a single hinge and raced up the stairs, taking them four at a time, using his phone to illuminate the way. The staircase ended abruptly in smashed concrete and twisted steel reinforcing rods. But the view from the three-story vantage point yielded the helicopters outlined by fires.

Taymullah was next to arrive, gasping for air.

"You smoke too much. You are late again. See?" Mazool pointed at the disappearing aircraft, which was starting to climb toward the hills on the outskirts of the city.

"I can still hit one of them. I have a rocket loaded," replied Taymullah.

Farib panted up the darkness of the stairwell.

"They have gone," said Mazool, bitterly disappointed, shaking his head.

Farib pointed into the night. "Wait... Look! Do you see?" He punched the air and slapped Taymullah on the back. "Do you want proof that Allah watches over us? There, lighting up the sky!"

* * *

"They're running dark," said Bo, having suspended the task of stuffing gear into his pack to listen. "Can't see 'em."

"They ours?" Jimmy enquired.

Maybe someone up there looking down had seen just how shitty things were gonna get for us, decided to be a little proactive and do something about it. Which is about when I started to think an alien spaceship landing in Washington DC with a delegation of purple man-lizards would be more likely. "Russian," I ventured, squinting into the night. "Two of 'em." Russian helos made a different noise from Blackhawks, Lakotas and Apaches, which gave a low flat snarl. Russian jet engines were a couple of generations behind and screamed like ours used to.

"Boss, twelve o'clock low," Alvin's voice said in my earpiece.

A quick check on the warehouse showed it disgorging a hoard of jihadists like flies departing a disturbed corpse. The fighters swarmed out onto the road and gathered around the Scorpion. Quite a few were armed with RPGs.

Seconds later the Russian aircraft skimmed over our hill, engines shrieking, low enough that we could see their underbellies. Hinds, the heavily armed attack fuckers that even the unimaginative would agree resembled obese locusts. They'd come from the direction of the areas most heavily targeted by the bombing campaign. Perhaps they were doing recon, checking on the destruction, spotting for tomorrow's sorties. They climbed steeply overhead and changed course to the east, the general direction of Khmeimim, the Russian air base near the coast south of the city.

But then, as I watched, one of the aircraft seemed to explode from within, a gaping hole suddenly torn in the side of the fuselage between the main rotor and cockpit. Both engines began to spit gouts of flame from each end as if the aircraft had a dose of bad gastro. They'd devoured something that didn't agree with them, metal debris most likely.

"Anyone down there at the warehouse get off a shot?"

"Negative," came the unanimous reply.

Even so, I didn't need to ask to know that the jihadists would be cheering, patting each other on the back, owning the destruction in the sky. Instead I kept my eyes on the bird. It was spinning on its axis, pitching back and forth and yawing, out of control. Maybe the pilots were dead in their seats. By a miracle I'd survived several crashes involving helicopters and had good reason to hate the things. Half a mile away and drifting to the east, the wounded Hind staggered about the sky like a drunk.

I checked back in with the Scorpion and his men, just as one of them wearing night-vision goggles separated from the crowd and hoisted a long tube to his shoulder. This was no rocket-propelled grenade.

"Boss. Heads up. MANPADS," said Bo, incredulous.

A man portable air defense system – MANPADS. Or, to be clear, a shoulder-launched anti-aircraft missile system packing, presumably, a missile. Like Bo, I was surprised. Where the hell did they get *that*? I was only just getting my head around jihadists having NVGs. What other modern battlefield aces did these assholes have up their sleeves?

The shooter flipped up his NVGs and, a moment later, a missile jumped from the tube, ignited, and flew on its way. The wounded bird was a sitting duck, pirouetting on the spot, its engines coughing flames and sparks, smoke and more flames pouring from the rent in its side. And then a shadow orbiting around 500 feet above it began spraying decoys, a continuous stream of white-hot flares. The foundering Hind wasn't the missile's target, but the accompanying bird. It dove out of the patch of sky it had been occupying, clawing to get away from the killer punch closing on it at around three times the speed of sound. The bird never stood a chance. An instant later an explosion flared in the night scope, searing my eyes with bright green light. A direct hit. The Hind dropped out of the sky, a fireball of burning fuel growing in size and intensity. Seconds later, it smashed into a thicket of nearby trees with massive secondary explosions that rolled over our hill, stole the air from my lungs and punched into my eardrums.

Meanwhile the wounded aircraft had stopped spinning in midair. Its nose dropped and it appeared to fly with some limited control, heading generally further east. Maybe the pilots were still alive after all. I kept my eyes on the Hind until it disappeared behind a ridge between two and three miles to the east-northeast. No explosion, the aircraft was simply swallowed by the night. But I was as sure as I could be that, short of witnessing a fireball, it would ultimately crash.

I checked my watch. "I've got a few minutes before zero two hundred," I said to Bo. "Mark the time and call in those helos. And let Slingshot know we're moving to the alternate. Also call in a positive ID on the Scorpion."

Baker reached for his pack and pulled out the multiband multi mission radio, the MBMMR or Mumbles, as he called it, for obvious reasons. It was a box about the size of three stacked house bricks, with a separate SATCOM antennae. Mumbles sent and received encrypted messages of the top-secret kind to military comms sats in geodesic orbit. Two Russian Hinds downed in one go, with possibly significant loss of life - that would be something the folks who paid our salaries would want to know about.

The task would take the sergeant less than three minutes. There was time before the jihadist patrol arrived. Maybe.

Three

Ronald V. Small @realSmall
ISIS, America won't take its foot off your neck. GREAT VICTORY
AHEAD!

Known by some in Tbilisi as Temurazi Kvinitadze Sumbatashvili,
and in these parts as Abu Bakr al Aljurji, a.k.a Abu Bakr the
Georgian, a.k.a Al-Aleaqarab or the Scorpion, the jihadist
commander stared hard at the hill overlooking the road as if
attempting to penetrate its secrets. It was overgrown, rocky, and
crowned with a thicket of scrubby trees and bushes. Not much
to look at, but its crest was elevated enough to command the
road from both directions. For the military-minded, it was a hill
that needed occupying. A patrol had been dispatched there twenty
minutes ago, ample time to reach the summit, but they had not
returned the signal: a simple wave of a flashlight. Perhaps his men
had met with a wayward unit of Jabhat Fatah al-Sham, or the
Kataib Ansar al-Sham, or any one of countless others fighting over
the scraps of Syria. Some groups were hostile to Ad-Dawlah al-
Islamiyah, some others not. And allegiances changed, sometimes
overnight. As this war ground on, friends one day were enemies
the next. *I can imagine you up there sharing bread and cheese with*

friendlies, your flashlight set aside with their weapons. And I can also picture you slaughtered, ambushed, tossed into the bushes, a red smile cut across your throats.

Al-Aleaqarab had once trusted his instincts, but they had let him down too many times to be relied on. Had he not almost been killed twice by the Americans; once in an airstrike in Al-Shaddadah, northern Syria, and then again in a village south of Mosul, Iraq, with a drone strike? Only the will of God had enabled him to escape both times, although with major wounds. The ISIS commander was aware of his own grim smile.

Smoke from the drumfires and the dust kicked up by the shambling masses of refugees on the road came and went in waves.

If trouble was to be found up there, his men would not be unprepared a second time. He watched as the second group climbed the steep path that snaked up the side of the hill until they were lost in the night shadows.

"Amir, we are ready!" The call came from a lieutenant buried somewhere within the dust and smoke. The lieutenant, a minor one whose name was Abdullah Abdullah, ran up to him. Abdullah was a recruit from England, a fat man with a round face haloed by hair and beard. "Amir, please," he panted, "do you have instructions for the men staying behind?"

The Scorpion thought for a moment. "We need greater mobility, Abdullah. Gasoline, too. Requisition all passing vehicles for the glory of Allah and his caliphate."

"I will see to it, Amir," Abdullah Abdullah smiled, clearly glad of a task to acquit while the Scorpion was away.

A sky blue Toyota technical flying many black standards, a captured Syrian ZPU quad-barrel machine gun installed in the bed, drove by slowly and stopped ahead of the parked BMW. The rest of the column began to form up behind the white sedan. The Scorpion walked towards it and the passenger door opened for him. Inside, the black leather interior smelt new. It also smelt of a woman's perfume, he observed, as he placed his boot up on the dash. Yes, of all BMWs, this was his preferred model. Not too small, not too big. A five series, the four-door with turbo diesel, sat nav, self-driving, suspension that was both firm yet subtle ... He nodded with appreciation. Luxury *and* performance. If only the roads were in better shape. *If only life had taken another path. If only I had finished the engineering degree and become a builder of things instead of a destroyer.* He rolled his shoulders and allowed the firm seat to massage the tension from his back muscles. The car's interior was clean, antiseptic. Sitting in its comfort was like taking a bath. He felt cleansed.

Fifteen other vehicles, a ragtag mixture of stolen cars, utilities and trucks, lined up behind the BMW and the column rolled forward. Several vehicles peeled off early and headed for the Hind downed nearby, a forest fire marking the spot. The Scorpion kept his eyes forward. Surviving such a crash would be impossible. The prize was the other helicopter, the one that had disappeared into the hills. With luck there would be survivors. *Captured Russians...* He gestured at the driver, a young Chechen whose name was Ortsa. "Faster," he demanded and underlined it with a flick of his hand.

"Yes, Amir." Ortsa planted his palm on the horn and gave it several blasts, urging the technical with the ZPU ahead to pick up speed.

The Scorpion massaged his hands without realizing what he was doing. The skin on them was like melted wax, pink and fissured here and there with deep cracks which wept tears that dried a crusty yellow. As always, he picked at these scabs absently, ignoring the pain where there should be none. The fingers, the source of the ghost pain, were long since gone. *A downed Russian helicopter. Russian prisoners. A rich prize to turn the heads of even the fools that remained on the military council.* He glanced at Ortsa who quickly turned away as if caught in the commission of a crime. "Do you want to look, boy?"

"Look at what, Lord?" came the nervous reply.

The commander held up his left hand.

Ortsa's eyes left the road and took in the ruin and saw that only the thumb and forefinger remained attached to what was left of the amir's hand.

"A shard of stone," Al-Aleaqarab explained, "which an American drone missile turned into a butcher's saw. And this one?" He raised his right. "The work of a Russian detonator." The forefinger and middle finger were missing and what remained was even more misshapen than the left.

He knew Ortsa saw not hands but a pair of claws, the night-marish appendages of another creature entirely - the scorpion.

"And my face. It too is the work of the detonator."

Ortsa could not help but stare at the man who led them, the man about whom so many stories were told. He swallowed, a display of fear that he had no control over. The wreckage of the Scorpion's face was no less difficult to look at than those hands, the skin a collection of deep scars, nicks, chops, and melted tissue that prevented the growth of his beard. Instead, there was a patchwork of pink scarring amid islands of grizzled red and gray hair.

The young Chechen said, "When you arrive in Paradise, Amir, the virgins will fight over someone so gloriously wounded in the service of Allah."

The Scorpion continued to rub the round stumps of ruined flesh and bone with his remaining fingers. He growled, "What would you know of Paradise, boy?"

"I know only what is written in the Qur'an and the hadiths," the fighter admitted. "It is my ambition to serve Allah as you have served."

"Then I would hurry. We have little time left."

"It's true? We are retreating?"

We have lost Mosul, Abu Ghraib, Aleppo, Ramadi, Raqqa, Fallujah, Tikrit, Dabiq ... We have been chased from Iraq. And now we run from Syria. No one is being paid. We steal our supplies. We cannot use the radio. We cannot use the phones for fear that missiles will rain down on us when we do. We cannot receive orders. We do not know who among our leadership is alive or dead. The military council, what remains of it following incessant drone attacks, still talks of victory when all we do is show our backs to the enemy's bullets. Yes, there is almost nothing left to show from all the fighting. All that's left is the promise of Paradise. "We do as Allah wills," he said.

Al-Aleaqarab glanced at the young Chechen behind the wheel, concentrating on the road ahead, as they drove along in silence. It was easy to say what needed to be said when the conversation was only in one's head. Some jihadists were certain that the demise of Ad-Dawlah al-Islamiyah was the will of Allah and only temporary. Others whispered that Allah had deserted the caliphate. Was there even such a thing as a caliphate left? Or was a caliph, a successor to the holy prophet Mohammad, no more than a notion? It had been so different when the armies of Islamic State of Iraq and the Levant were winning. Women were claimed as prizes as they rolled from one victory to another in the deserts, ignoring borders, killing and raping, taking what was rightfully theirs - whether money or slaves - young men from around the world flocking to the black standard along with women willing to lie with the warriors of Allah and bear children for the caliphate. But those days were a memory. The west had woken from its torpor. Alarms had sounded. Now all that remained was to fill the hole created by killing. And when the killing came to an end, Paradise awaited.

* * *

Mazool ran to an ambulance that had stopped half way up a pile of rubble, one of its rear wheels off the ground, spinning slowly. The motor was still running, a cloud burbling from the exhaust pipe. The front windshield was smashed, as was the driver's side window, the driver slumped against the bloodied door, his head lolling out. There was enough light for Mazool to see that the man's eyes were open, gazing unblinking in different directions - the stare of death. Mazool pushed the man back inside the vehicle and checked inside. There was no one in the back. "We will take this!" he shouted. Taymullah and Farib stopped their own search for a vehicle, gathered up their weapons and ammunition and ran to the ambulance. Pulling open the door, Mazool cleared the airbag from the driver's knees, grabbed two fists of the man's shirt, dragged him out and laid him on the broken ground. Mazool closed the man's eyes and hurriedly said the common prayer for occasions of death, one that was now all too familiar to him. "O Allah, forgive this man and elevate his station among those who are guided. Send him along the path of those who came before, and forgive him and us, O Lord of the worlds. Enlarge for him his grave and shed light upon him in it."

"This is lucky," said Taymullah, regretting the comment when he saw the dead driver beside the front wheel.

"At least if we should be injured, an ambulance will be close by," Farib shouted as he flung open a back door.

Mazool clambered behind the wheel and put the gearbox in reverse. "It didn't help the driver. And it won't help you if you don't get in."

Farib jumped into the passenger seat and pulled the door closed behind him as the ambulance slowly backed down off the rubble. The interior air reeked of blood and antiseptic from a couple of heavy-duty black plastic bags full of soiled medical refuse. There were old, bloodstained clothes too. Farib picked up a pair of pants, a filthy T-shirt and a black niqab and stuffed them in the bags. He was about to close them up when the ambulance shot forward and caused him to bash his head against a railing. "Hey!"

"Hold on," said Taymullah too late as Farib clawed his way forward and wedged himself between the front seats.

Mazool wrestled with the steering wheel and the ambulance turned sharply, avoiding craters, potholes and fallen masonry that loomed as obstacles or deep shadows in its headlights. The black sky was tinged with an orange haze, the dust kicked into the air by the bombs reflecting the light from the many fires.

"Is this a good idea?" said Farib. "There will be others drawn to the Russians."

"Which is why we must hurry." Mazool glanced at the young man. "That flag around your neck. Take it off before someone shoots you because of it. Where did you find it?"

"I picked it up off the road."

"Take it off."

"I wish to burn it," said Farib.

"It is you that flag will burn if you do not remove it."

Farib found the knot under his chin and loosed it one-handed.

"It is dangerous enough fighting these criminals without having to worry about our own patriotic Syrians ending your foolish life, which they would do if they found that flag on you." Mazool continued. "And then I would have to answer to your mother, who I fear more than Al-Aleaqarab."

"Am I a child?" Farib asked.

Taymullah was smirking at him, enjoying his discomfort.

"You are always a child to your mother," Mazool pointed out to him, "no matter how thick and gray your beard becomes."

Farib removed the flag from around his neck and stuffed it inside his shirt as a building collapsed right in front of the ambulance. Mazool took evasive action, pitching their vehicle onto two wheels where it seemed to teeter for precarious seconds before righting itself with a jarring bounce. The building collapse triggered an unexploded bomb, which threw shattered concrete, cinderblock and tiles into the sky, smaller pieces of brick and masonry raining down on the ambulance, filling the cabin with stone chips large and small, and then a crash that almost caused Mazool to lose control of the vehicle as a solid chunk of brick-work slammed into the hood, crushing the metal like it was paper, before rolling off. A loud clatter screamed from the engine before it died. Mazool wiped the dust from his eyes with a dirty hand, his heart racing. Another foot and the missile would have come through what remained of the windshield and killed him.

You are already dead, fool. Do not think otherwise. The only thing that matters is to keep going. The ambulance, however, was going nowhere.

Four

Ronald V. Small @realSmall
Big thanks to our Military, the best in the world. You keep
FREEDOM SAFE!

The senior airman brought the message to the duty officer, Air
Force Major Jillian Schelly, who was deep in conversation with
another major about the rising cost of a latte.

"Five bucks!" said Schelly, looking into the disposable cup as if
the ring of foamed half-and-half deserved serious contemplation.

"I know. Ridiculous, right? I read somewhere the coffee plant is
temp sensitive. Gonna cost ten bucks a cup once global warming's
done with it."

"Excuse me, ma'am," said the senior airman hovering nearby.

"What is it?"

"A SPIREP, ma'am."

"Source?"

"Quickstep 3."

"You wanna put it on my desk?"

"I think it's important, ma'am." Otherwise I wouldn't be hovering nearby to hand-deliver this here special intelligence report, his
body language implied.

It's from Quickstep, the reason you're still here working at zero dark whatever. Focus, Major. Schelly took the paper, read the decryption and raised an eyebrow at it. "Thank you," she said. Then, to the climate change expert: "Duty calls."

Twenty minutes later, Major Schelly went to knock on the door of the Senior Watch Officer, US Air Forces Central Command Combined Air Operations Center. The door was closed, but she could still hear the conversation on the other side. The colonel was on the phone. She glanced at her watch, sighed and waited.

"Just get your lawyer to call my lawyer, why don't you?" Schelly heard him say. "And then they can bill us each another hour and further reduce the settlement to us both. You know crazy this is, right?"

Silence. Enough of it for Schelly to consider the call had ended and that it was safe to let her knuckles get on with the job.

"Come…" said the voice.

Schelly walked in. Colonel Desmond Gladston was moving papers around his desk, clearly not a happy camper, his unpleasant divorce an open secret. "Make my day, Jill, and tell me they've nuked Buckhead, Atlanta." Gladston paused for a moment, realizing he'd said more than he meant to. "It has been a day. Or, I should say, night. What you got there?"

Schelly pretended that she'd heard nothing untoward and passed him the SPIREP. "Sir, a Quickstep unit has observed two Russian Hinds downed in northern Syria. One was a definite missile shoot down, the other a probable."

"Probable as in a second missile strike?"

"No, sir. As in no confirmed impact."

"Nothing about survivors?"

"No, sir." Schelly didn't need to assure the colonel that Quickstep intelligence was reliable.

"The Kremlin will be thrilled," Gladston observed drily, unconsciously decoding the acronym stew in the report. "This is less than complete."

"Yes, sir. We've lost contact with the Quickstep unit."

"Why?"

"Enemy activity in the area, sir. They had to break off transmission."

Gladston took a moment to consider. "You worked up the appropriate due diligence on this?" he asked. "Map references and so forth?"

"Whatever we had prior to contact being broken off. Yes, Colonel."

"Cross sightings from other assets in the area?"

"None, sir. No other assets in the area."

"So supporting intel is on the thin side."

"I would say non-existent, sir."

"Well if we don't know where that second Hind came down, neither do the Russians, but they'll be running around like headless chickens trying to locate it. Kick it upstairs to the usual suspects. This is gonna brighten a lot of folks' morning."

The usual suspects meant the Joint Intelligence Center, Central Command at MacDill Air Force Base; Defense Intelligence Agency, Bolling Air Force Base; the Organization of the Joint Chiefs of Staff at the Pentagon; and CIA, Langley.

"Maybe we can get on top of this with a little help from a Reaper. I'll handle the request." Gladston shuffled Schelly's paperwork into an ordered stack, closed the folder and held it toward her. "That it, Jilly?"

"Yes, sir." She accepted the folder. *Jilly? How'd you like it if I called you Desie?*

"Damn. And I had such high hopes for a mushroom cloud over Atlanta."

* * *

The tangos came up fast and stayed off the path, strung out in a staggered line abreast. They appeared to be methodical, cool-headed and seasoned - a cut above the last patrol.

32

"Trouble's coming, boss," said Jimmy in my earpiece. Trouble – exactly what I was thinking when they came into view, creeping up the path, unfortunately not all conveniently bunched up for McVeigh's ka-bar to shish-kebab.

"Any of 'em got NVGs?" I asked.

"No, sir."

We did, so that would give us an advantage even though it was not an especially dark night.

"Gonna have to engage, sir," came Bo's quiet summation.

"Roger that," I replied. As I said, getting into firefights was not our job, but there was nothing we could do at this point to avoid one.

"Coming up on the tangos' six now, working around to the west. Acknowledge."

Alvin. He was approaching the bad guys from behind before clearing the kill zone. "Got it," I replied.

"Roger."

"Ditto."

The roger and ditto were from Bo and Jimmy respectively. I said, "We're firing west to east, our line twenty yards east of the path. Your ETA?"

"Twenty seconds to clear blue on blue," Alvin replied, voice low.

"Hold fire," I said, not wanting my guys taking each other out with friendly fire. Being experienced Special Ops assets of course they knew that too, but a few words on the obvious every now and then couldn't hurt.

Eight tangos moving slow but steady, with purpose. I could see five of them; four armed with standard AKs, one carrying some variety of squad automatic weapon, probably a Russian PK pried from the dead fingers of a Syrian army infantryman.

"Choose your targets. The SAW's mine," I said.

The tangos were equipped with body armor, quality Russian issue.

"Got a visual on you, Alvin," Bo informed us. "You are clear of the kill zone."

"Roger," he replied.

"On three," I said. The approach to the crest was through scrubby terrain – a mixture of stunted, water-starved trees, a type of poison ivy and dry grass. Plenty of cover for visual purposes though not much of it would stop a bullet. I had taken a knee behind a screen of shrubs, nettles and ivy, and could clearly observe the lead tangos walking stealthily, hunched over their weapons, concentrating, listening, taking in what smells hung on the night air. Our line was upwind of them and their rank, unwashed body odor, heavily mixed with acrid tobacco smoke, spoke of men long in the field. Maybe they'd been out here so long they hadn't heard the news that tobacco kills. "One, two -" I was about to say "three", when one of the tangos dropped to the ground and began yelling at the top of his lungs. An instant later that SAW blazed away on full auto, its tracer rounds etching a wide arc as the jihadist reached out blindly to kill. All his pals joined in, firing wildly, reacting as men do when they are armed and spooked. The sparks of Russian tracer rounds, green pencils of light that zipped through the night, flew briefly across the darkness, but none of them at us.

My infrared dot danced on the jihadist's body armor, jiggling around the region of his sternum. His feet had taken root and his body was crouched to take the forces unleashed by his machine gun as it chewed through a belt of ammo. My index finger squeezed quickly. Once. Twice. *Phut-phut.* The lightweight M4 jumped and two rounds of 5.52 millimeter steel-encased lead, sixty-two grams apiece, flew on their suppressed way. The tango went over backwards despite his feet placement, the barrel of his weapon spitting and cracking that tracer up into the night sky in a pretty arc. A slight shift of my head, eye line and arms, and my index finger squeezed again. Two suppressed shots. *Phut-phut.* Scratch tango number two.

The SS109 ammunition fired by the M4A1 rifle would penetrate three millimeters of steel plate at 600 yards. Tonight's range was closer to 100 yards. Quality Russian body armor or not, a pair of jihadists were now rolling up to the pearly gates, or whatever the architecture happened to be over their welcome mat.

The night was once again comparatively quiet with Bo, Jimmy and Alvin having also dispatched their chosen marks. I stood and stepped carefully toward the newly dead. Jimmy McVeigh was there before me. "Sorry, boss," he said.

"Sorry for what?" I asked him.

He motioned at the ground where one of the tangos had stepped on a jihadist Jimmy had knifed earlier. That's what had spooked the machine gunner.

A rustle of bush caused me to turn my head as the covered face of a jihadist dived at me with a short sword raised for the slash. My M4 was pointed at the ground and I knew I would be dead before I could raise it and shoot. Funny how a fraction of a second is all you need to process all the angles and the distances and consider the inevitable outcome of what's coming at you, but not near enough time to react in a positive way to defend yourself. A silver blur fluttered in my peripheral vision and the fighter with the short sword suddenly found his mouth full of ka-bar hilt, the blade protruding from the back of his neck. The guy was consorting with virgins before his body hit the weeds.

Alvin stepped over, put his boot on the deceased's neck and extracted his knife with a jerk, the blade coming free with that disturbing crunch of cartilage amplified by the cavern of the dead man's open mouth. "He worked his way round the back of the troop, sir. Couldn't get a clean shot." The shrug of Alvin's shoulders added apology to his words.

What can you do, right? "Better late than never," I told him.

A phone started ringing. One of the deceased jihadist's pockets was lit up. I reached down and extracted an old cellphone, the battery held in place with dirty scotch tape. There was a missed call on the screen. I pressed a few buttons and what I found was troubling. "Can you believe they got three fuckin bars of signal here? Looks like he made a call a minute ago. If we're lucky a guy on a pizza delivery bike will be turning up within ten minutes. If we're not, it'll be some more of the folks from down below. Bo, you get off the news about the Russian Hinds?"

"Yes, sir. The positive ID on the Scorpion too. Ran outta time when it came to the alternate."

"Break out Mumbles and let Slingshot know before someone comes along to investigate the racket. Alvin, keep an eye on the warehouse. Jimmy, let's get us some overwatch on the path. Keep it simple. Anything moves, kill it."

"Roger that, boss."

While Bo unpacked the radio transceiver and SATCOM antenna, I patted down the dead and confiscated half-a-dozen phones, all of them old tech. I pocketed the SIMs; a present for the intel folks back at the base, then stomped on the handsets. The task completed, I stood around and thought about … well, actually, in truth I didn't think about a hell of a lot, that being the reason I asked for this gig. I moved a little upwind of the freshly killed jihadists, where it was cool and clean and untainted by the smell of blood and torn intestines, breathed deep and took in the night air. Ah, the simple life. Nothing to figure out; no puzzle to unravel; no cunning ploy to thwart; no crime to solve; no evil genius to outwit. All I had to do was to make sure my shit was bagged and packed – check; all my guys were alive – check; I had clear orders – check. Everything was, as my Brit buddies say, tickety-boo – check.

Bo advised, "Major, comms are Tango Uniform." He held up one of the boxes and pushed a gloved finger into a ragged hole that shouldn't have been there. Tango Uniform for Tits Up, or, in other words, dead. The other side of the box was blown out. "Must have taken a ricochet."

Re tickety-boo. Uncheck.

Five

Ronald V. Small @realSmall
Syria's refugees. Who are they REALLY? Look what they did to
Syria! They destroyed it. Very sad.

The ambulance bounced as Farib pushed down on the end of a
wooden beam, using it as a lever to open the crushed hood. The
beam began to crack and splinter, but then a metal latch gave way
and the crumpled hood sprang ajar.

Refugees began to gather on the road, the night now relatively
quiet but for distant explosions.

Mazool helped Taymullah lift the hood, and glanced around self-
consciously, anxious to be on the move. Snipers. It was never safe to
be standing around in one place. The two men folded the hood back,
propped it open with the length of wood and peered into the engine bay.
"We're in luck. The noise was just the engine fan," Taymullah observed,
squinting into the darkness. "Half the blades are broken off."

"Any other damage?" Mazool enquired as several armed men
darted from one building and ran into another. "We must decide
what to do quickly."

Taymullah, the son of a motor mechanic who had wanted to
follow in his father's steps, but had been prevented from doing so

because of the war, reached down into the bay's bowels. He brought his hand out slick with blue coolant. "One of the blades cut the lower radiator hose."

"Can it be driven?"

"Yes, but how far I don't know. I can bandage it but it's a pressure system and it'll leak no matter what I do. With no coolant the motor will overheat. It will help if we can keep filling the reservoir with water, but we don't have any water and without a new hose..." He shrugged.

"We will risk it."

A short while later the ambulance was on the move again, hoodless and minus a windshield, joining the throngs of people on foot and in vehicles fleeing the city. The ambulance proved to be excellent cover. It was waved through multiple checkpoints manned by a variety of groups, some friendly some not, but all respecting the red crescent daubed roughly on its doors.

"Mazool, tell me again why we are chasing the helicopters?" Taymullah asked as they left the safety of the more familiar inner city for the open spaces of the outer suburbs.

"Hostages," Mazool replied.

"What need have we of hostages?" Farib chimed in. "We are not bandits or fanatics."

"Do you not want vengeance for what the Russians have done to our homes? Killing our families and friends?" Mazool examined the faces of the two supporters, young men who had become like brothers to him, and saw timidity. And in truth, the more he thought about what they were doing, the more he himself felt unsure about it. Taymullah had rightly pointed out that the downed helicopters would be magnets for trouble. But if they could manage to get to the Russians before anyone else ... Mazool laughed at the uncertainty lining the faces of Farib and Taymullah, but it was a laugh devoid of humor. "You are afraid of the dark, that's it isn't it? Afraid of the wide-open spaces and also the shadows that lurk in corners. Are you boys or men? I thought you were men. You have the beards of men. But perhaps they are not real." He moved to tug Taymullah's thin adolescent growth and found his hand slapped away.

"Out here we have no support," Farib pointed out. "Out here, it would be easy to disappear and no one would ever know what happened to us."

"You have listened to too many gossiping women," scoffed Mazool. He leaned forward and patted the dashboard. "And besides, as we have already observed, we have the best disguise."

"Yes," Taymullah said, "until someone asks us to remove a bullet."

Farib nodded. "Or worse, deliver a baby."

Mazool shook his head. "I am glad I chose to team up with lions."

The smell of a hot engine reached through the opening where the windshield used to be. Taymullah was the first to notice it. "We will soon need to find water for the radiator. What does the temperature gauge say?"

Mazool peered at the gauges. The needle was in the red. "It's okay, the needle is not yet in the red. We should keep going."

The ambulance turned a corner and, ahead, the night was lit up bright orange by drum fires clustered around the road. A handful of heavily armed fighters were setting up barricades against a warehouse, while a utility vehicle drove into place to form the other side of the barricade. Men were herding all vehicles off the road and inspecting them.

Mazool braked in the darkness, beyond the circle of light thrown by the fires.

"Are they ours?" Taymullah wondered aloud as a man was dragged from his car by two others and kicked repeatedly on the ground until he crawled away and became lost in the stream of restless refugees.

"I don't think so," said Mazool.

Black standards unfurled from the utility's windows confirming his suspicion.

Taymullah was puzzled. "They are Ad-Dawlah al-Islamiyah. With enemies all around, why do they advertise themselves so brazenly?"

"Because there are many of them," Farib concluded. "Perhaps they are looking for a fight."

"What do we do now?" Farib asked after a pause.

Taymullah didn't need to think about it. "We must go back."

"No," said Mazool. "They will let us through." He put the ambulance into gear and drove forward.

He caught Farib and Taymullah sharing a look as though they expected he would surely get them killed. They had scarcely advanced into the light when several Daesh fighters waved them off the road with flashlights, AKs and RPGs. Mazool felt the blood drain from his face. The feeling that he needed to shit was almost overwhelming. The fighters aimed their weapons at him, the driver. One of their number, a large fat man with wild hair and Arabic that sounded foreign, shouted, "Get out of the car. Hurry, before we shoot you in the face so that not even your mothers would recognize you."

"Are there weapons in your truck?" asked another. "If we find weapons we will shoot you! Out!"

Mazool, Farib and Taymullah clambered from the vehicle as ISIS fighters conducted a hurried but thorough search. "There are weapons, but they are not ours," Mazool protested.

"I do not believe you," replied the fat guard with the foreign accent.

"Abdullah Abdullah!" exclaimed one of the men holding up an AK and rocket launcher pulled from the back of the ambulance. "There's more."

"Take them," said the fat man – Abdullah Abdullah.

"You are mistaken, Amir," said Farib, reaching inside his shirt.

"Stop!" Abdullah shouted and shoved the muzzle of his AK in Farib's face.

"We are Ad-Dawlah al-Islamiyah, like you," Farib stammered. "We fight for the caliph and the glory of Allah the merciful."

"Open your mouth, dog fucker," said Abdullah in English.

Farib opened and closed his mouth.

"I said open your fuckin' mouth an' keep it fuckin' open!"

Farib did as he was ordered.

"You understand the Queen's fuckin' English, right? Well eat this." He shoved the muzzle in Farib's mouth, whose eyes were wide with terror. "Don't you fuckin' move. Now what do we 'ave 'ere? Better fuckin' hope it's not a shooter." Abdullah reached into Farib's shirt and extracted a black standard. The sight of it gave Abdullah pause. He looked at Farib slyly. "Where'd you learn to speak the Queen's fuckin' English?"

Farib mumbled, unable to speak with the muzzle in his mouth and his heart filled with terror.

"What? I can't hear you?" said Abdullah and pulled his rifle away.

"American…American movies. I, I learn little bit."

"What if I said you was an American spy?"

Farib's eyes went wider still. "No, no, Amir. No spy! No spy!"

"Hmm…" Abdullah seemed vaguely convinced. "American movies are shite, except for Iron Man. You want to learn English, watch movies made in England. Stands to reason, doesn' it?" He shook the flag in Farib's face. "'ow do I know this is not just some trophy you picked up along the way? Maybe you killed someone to nick it?"

"No, no, Amir," said Farib urgently, switching to Arabic. "Most of our brothers were killed by those dogs, the Jabhat Fatah al-Sham."

"Where are you from? What's your accent?"

"Syrian. My brothers also." He tilted his head at Taymullah and Mazool.

Abdullah grunted. "Don't have many of you Syrians fighting for the caliph." The Jabhat Fatah al-Sham – the Conquest of Syria Front – had been active in these parts recently and those apostates had wiped out several displaced units of Ad-Dawlah al-Islamiyah that had been separated from larger groups.

"Where are you going now?" Abdullah demanded.

"We have more brothers nearby. We hurry to join them and continue the fight."

"Well it's everyone for themselves now, innit? On yer fuckin' way, and count yourselves lucky. I'll be keeping this." He held up the flag. "And this." He motioned at the ambulance.

"Amir, please, we need transport," Mazool protested as Abdullah's men climbed into the battered vehicle and drove off.

"That's why Allah the merciful gave you those fings," he said gesturing at Mazool's legs, "wif feet on the end of 'em." Abdullah added with a sneer. "Now, fuck off."

Mazool insisted, "We can't fight without weapons."

"Didn't Abdullah Abdullah make himself fuckin' clear?" Abdullah cocked his AK and pointed it at Mazool. "On second thoughts, we've got foreign soldiers nearby, up on that hill. Could be American Crusaders for all we know. Maybe you'd like to go and take a peek for us."

Mazool saw a dozen men over by the warehouse, checking each other for weapons, getting ready for a fight. If he was not careful, he, Taymullah and Farib could end up being used as human shields. "We must rejoin our unit. If you need reinforcements, I will return with them."

Abdullah looked at the three Syrians, all of them sallow cheeked and under nourished. "No wonder we're losing this war. Count yourselves lucky. Now fuck off all of you." He jerked his thumb over his shoulder.

Mazool knew they might not get another opportunity to leave, so he turned and walked toward the column of refugees.

"We should go back to the city," said Farib, hurrying to catch up and put as much distance between himself and Abdullah as possible.

Taymullah agreed. "We can't get very far without a vehicle, Mazool."

"We don't give up that easily."

"Sometimes I wish we did," Taymullah muttered.

"I heard that," Mazool said over his shoulder.

Six

Ronald V. Small @realSmall
It's time for us to appreciate everything Russia has done for the world in Syria while the rest of the world stood back. Very brave.

"Show me," I said.

Bo shared the plasticized map. There was a red grease pencil circle around the hill, our current position, and a red cross on our new destination, the secondary around eight klicks to the east-northeast. No additional intelligence had miraculously appeared on the map. For all we knew, it might be hosting a jihadist convention.

So, the good news? First light was hours away. The bad news? Almost all of the ground we had to cross was open with little cover and more fundamentalists to the square yard than a public stoning in Raqqa. Also, there was the time issue. Our TACAN was supposed to have been transmitting by - well, by now.

"Boss, more tangos inbound," Alvin, having reassumed the observation point overlooking the warehouse, announced in my earpiece. "They got their Nikes on this time."

"Bo, Jimmy, on me," was my response to that. There was no need to brief the situation as our headset comms were open. We all knew the score. "Alvin, quickest way off this rock avoiding tracks and paths."

"Reckon it's here, boss. The north face."

I figured as much. North was not the easiest way down, but on the plus side it was headed in our desired direction. We would, however, be descending directly adjacent to our increasingly nervous Daesh internationals at the warehouse. But maybe that could be helpful; at least we'd be keeping an eye on them. "North it is. Jimmy, let's leave some best wishes from Uncle Sam."

Jimmy reached for a Claymore strapped to his ruck.

"And here's something personal from the former owners of a white Beemer," Bo said, offering the sergeant a second Claymore.

"You've got sixty seconds," I told Jimmy. "RZ at the rock shelf."

A short while later, standing with Alvin and Bo on edge of the sheer bluff that overlooked the road several hundred feet below, the reality of our tactical position revealed itself. The Daesh fighters remaining at the warehouse had set up a checkpoint and were confiscating vehicles and harassing any refugees in the column who looked likely to be carrying loot. The road had become a choke point, one we were going to have to cross. The orange light provided by the oil-drumfires was potentially to our advantage, robbing the jihadists of their night vision. The shadows looked gratifyingly deep, but US combat assets had distinctive and well-known profiles, especially because of the helmet and NVGs. "Alvin, after you," I told him as Jimmy rejoined us.

The sergeant traversed to the right of the bluff and disappeared down a narrow chute, using outward pressure on his arms and feet to lower himself down. I went next, the weight of my rucksack not making the descent easy. The chute was at least seventy feet straight down and a little over three feet wide. We assembled on a ledge and Alvin found the crack in the next sheer face that angled downwards at around fifty degrees. It wasn't an easy task, but that's why they pay us so much money, right? We assembled again at the base of the rock, which was shrouded in scrubby bushes and stinging nettles of the type we were all familiar with. From there it was a relatively simple climb down to the road.

Two loud explosions somewhere above us on top of the hill punctuated the night, and a ripple of fear went through the refugees on the road. The anti-personnel Claymores had been tripped and sprays of 700 steel balls apiece, lethal up to a range of about 100 yards, had ripped into anyone within an arc of around sixty degrees. "Sorry," I said, looking back up over my shoulder. "Not."

The explosions activated the jihadists at the warehouse and yet another bunch of them ran across the road, checking that their AKs were locked and loaded, and launched themselves at the path up the hill.

"A suggestion," I said. "Take off your helmets, clip 'em to your rucks. Got a scarf, wrap it around your head." I explained my thought about our distinctive silhouettes. "Won't stop a bullet, but might stop a second look. We'll separate and RZ in the shadows a hundred yards east of the warehouse, beyond the firelight." I indicated the general direction two hundred yards up the road.

Cunningly disguised thus, we joined the sad parade of the unfortunate dispossessed. I shuffled along beside a family group, a toddler with a bloody bandage covered in flies around her head and another around her arm, riding on her father's shoulders. She was bawling her eyes out, her mother limping beneath a full niqab while she herded three young girls in front of her. They were all covered in filth, one of the kids wearing only one shoe. I kept waiting for someone to call out "*Amriki!*" but there was too much misery around for anyone to notice a man hunched over like all the rest, dragging his feet. It was the same for Sergeants McVeigh, Baker and Leaphart, and the next RZ was reached without incident.

Helmets back on, we double-timed it because the Air Force does like to keep to its schedules. There were plenty of shadows about and very little ambient light to speak of - no streetlights, no starlight, and even the firelight from the city reflected off the cloud base was diminishing. After several uneventful klicks jogging through the scrub away from the road, we took a breather behind a deserted shed. The road had forked some way back, the refugees taking the other fork. Up ahead, it appeared that the two roads merged again into one, which was once more clogged with fleeing humanity.

"Boss," said McVeigh, motioning down the road with the tube attached to his Camelbak. A single headlight approached. "Motorcycle."

It wasn't. The NVGs revealed a beat-up van flying black flags from the passenger window, one of its headlights smashed. The flapping flags said it was ISIS.

"More of our favorite peeps," said Bo.

"Gonna ask nicely if there's room for four more," I said and opened fire on the driver. Three more silenced M4s joined in, clattering like muffled castanets, and the van slowed and most helpfully rolled to a halt near us.

"Shit," said Alvin, when the red crescent daubed on the side of the van became apparent. "That's gonna be bad karma."

"Yeah," I gestured at the ISIS flag hanging from a well-punctured door. "And we delivered it."

There were five deceased in the vehicle, plus a bonus - a twelve-pack of bottled water, six of which hadn't been shot up. We kept the water, ditched the bodies and hit the road. The ambulance itself, though, was badly wounded with no hood to speak of and no windshield. The bodywork was riddled with bullet holes and the interior smelt of blood, shit, urine and gun oil.

"Shotgun," I said, and slipped into the passenger seat. The blood on the vinyl and the cloth inserts was already sticky. Jimmy took the wheel, Alvin and Bo climbing in back.

"Any tunes available?" Bo asked, doing his bit to keep it light.

There was a radio, but it had been blasted into its component pieces. I pulled out some wires and broken plastic from the hole in the dash. "I can sing," I said.

"Best not, boss, I'm armed and dangerous," Bo replied with a grin.

"So we're heading east, but we gotta go north. Where's the turnoff?"

"Coming up in a klick or so," he said.

Alvin emptied a water bottle into his Camelbak. "Maybe we'll come across a Russian helo on the way."

That was a point. The Hind we saw flying away with a hole blown in its side was headed in the general direction of our secondary, and would be a magnet for jihadists of all persuasions. "Maybe," I said. We had to ignore the additional risk of running into tangos. The mission – planting that TACAN – was all that mattered. Our orders were clear. Check.

So I sat back, swung the NVGs into place, and kept an eye out for assholes who might attempt to commandeer our ride, as we had done.

But no sooner did I get comfortable than the engine died. No warning. Not even a splutter. We'd covered maybe half a klick, no more.

"What's up?" I asked Jimmy.

He shone a flashlight across the instruments. "We got gas, unless the gauge is Tango Uniform." He tapped the Perspex. "Oil temp's in the red. Something vital took a bullet."

"Like I said, karma," Alvin pointed out.

I reached back, took one of the bottles of water and passed the remaining one to Jimmy. "We should stay off the road anyway," I said. "Avoid the checkpoints."

* * *

"Fuck me," said Abdullah as he poked through the darkness on the hilltop with the flashlight. There were deceased everywhere, some shot, some stabbed, others ripped apart by mines. It was the scene of a major skirmish, or several minor ones, and his men had come off second best. There had either been no enemy casualties or they'd been carried away.

Abdullah had already dispatched men on a thorough search of the area, as the Scorpion would have commanded. The jihadists' anger was sky high.

Several men approached him, one wearing NVGs flipped up on his head. "Amir, the area is secured," he said. "There are no more traps. We found flattened grass on the northern end of this rise. We think this is where the enemy retreated."

"You mean snuck away like dogs," said Abdullah. "How many?"

The jihadist shrugged. "Three or four at the most."

"No, I don't believe it." There had to be more – Abdullah was certain of it. "We have lost fourteen men. There are no wounded." The eyes of one of the dead stared at him. "Verily we belong to Allah, and truly to Him shall we return." He pointed to one of his fighters. "Take four men. Cover each martyr with a clean sheet, say the Dua, and bury them. They have gone to Paradise and are welcomed into Allah's presence." He shifted his frown to the jihadist with the NVGs. "Gather the men. We must find these godless criminals and take our revenge.

Seven

Ronald V. Small @realSmall
Daesh, ISIS, IS, ISIL. They can't even settle on a name, but they
want to run a country? BIG JOKE!

All but one checkpoint, intimidated by the many Daesh black
standards, waved the Scorpion's column through. The one that
did not, a barricade recently overrun by Syrian Army troops
not ten minutes before the Scorpion arrived, had audaciously,
foolishly, opened fire on them. The Toyota technical with the
ZPU had performed an immediate 180, pulled to the side of
the road and the four, .50 caliber barrels were unleashed,
annihilating the checkpoint. A ZPU-4 was not the sort of
weapon that took kindly to resistance, especially when the range
was point blank.

The roads were congested with fleeing traffic, but they cleared
readily enough ahead of the ZPU and the column behind it honking
horns, its fighters firing bursts at the sky from AKs.

But now the column had left the highway behind, the road
becoming dirt as it climbed through dusty abandoned farms
overrun by poison ivy and scrubby thicket. With no clear picture
of where the Russians had come down, the Scorpion was beginning

to think they may not locate the helicopter. "How many kilometers have we been driving?" he asked Ortsa.

"Five, Lord."

The Scorpion peered out the window at the darkness. They had seen the damaged Hind fly off in this direction, barely under control. It was impossible to imagine that the pilots had nursed the helicopter to safety. The terrain had changed markedly with the steady climb. Ahead were towering hills and ridges, and the slopes were planted with either olive trees or ragged copses of pines.

"Shall I slow down?" Ortsa asked.

The Scorpion gestured with a claw to keep going. "Where are you from, boy?" he asked to pass the time.

"From Aldy in Grozny, Amir."

"I have been there. I have heard a rumor that your father was among the brave hearts that raided Beslan. Is that true?"

"Yes, Amir. Spetsnaz killed him. They burned him alive."

"How old were you then?"

"Seven, Amir."

"Seven. Around the same age as the children in the school."

Ortsa remained silent.

Many died in the school: children, Chechens, Russians. Allah had willed it, thought the Scorpion. And more than likely it was the Russians who had also willed it. The attack on the hostage-takers was merely an excuse to shoot Muslims and wage war against the faithful in Chechnya and elsewhere on Russian soil. "The Russians made your father a criminal. But the truth is that he was a hero with very large balls."

Ortsa appreciated the compliment. "The Russians got what they wanted, Lord."

"I am sure when you get to Paradise, Chechen, that you will see your Pappa sitting close to Allah, on his right, a beautiful new bride on his lap."

"They would not return his body. I was happy when the Russians announced that they would be joining the fight to stop our liberation of Syria. I dreamt that I would one day have the opportunity to take an eye for an eye."

The Scorpion saw the smile flicker on the young driver's lips. *Yes, few emotions are as self-sustaining as revenge.*

Ahead, the Toyota with the ZPU had pulled off the road and stopped. The doors flew open and men jumped from the cabin with their AKs and pointed excitedly up the hill, into the trees.

"Stop!" the Scorpion pressed the switch on the door that lowered the window. It was only then that he heard the crackle of small arms fire. The soundproofing of the BMW was excellent, the Scorpion noted, perhaps a little too excellent. The column of vehicles had also pulled over and his men were gathering, keen for orders, the sound of gunfire exciting them. Battle, fighting, pain, misery and adrenaline sustained them. Al-Aleaqarab opened the door and removed himself from the seat's embrace. He stood in the cool of the night, many pairs of headlights blazing in the dust cloud raised by their arrival. The sounds of familiar and distinctive gunfire told the Scorpion much - a fight was going on between no less than ten AK-47s and other rifles which brought back memories of battlefields in Georgia: specifically AK-9s, the assault rifle favored by Spetsnaz. He called to Ortsa, "That day you have been wishing for, Chechen, I think it has come." Mostly, the Scorpion felt little, his senses dulled by so many years of war, but at that moment he felt joy. His men had already spilled from the vehicles. "Dawar," he called out, pointing to the *Amriki* jihadist with the blond beard.

"Lord!" Dawar stepped into the light, an aura of dust swirling around him and others.

"Take five men and remain behind to guard the vehicles."

The Scorpion could see that Dawar was annoyed and disappointed at being left behind. "This is not a punishment," he told him in English, the accent thick.

"I wanna fight, Amir," Dawar replied.

"And I wish for our vehicles not to be driven off by thieves and opportunists," he snapped. "This country is alive with criminals.

There is no redemption required by you, Dawar." He flicked a glance at the BMW. "If not for you, I wouldn't have this car. I thank you for it. Go now." Dawar bowed and backed away, into the dust.

The Scorpion turned his attention to the men close by and spoke without raising his voice. "Pass the order. Assemble in your fighting units, protect each other and go forward quietly until you fall upon the rear of the fighters making all the noise. It is possible that a prize awaits in these trees – Russians. Do not kill any of them unless you must. They are worth less than dust if they are dead. Wait for my signal to advance." He raised a crippled finger to his lips to impress the need for stealth upon them, and said, "Allahu akbar."

The men quietly repeated, God is great, before running off to pass along the Scorpion's orders.

After many previous battles and skirmishes, the men were ready. Al-Aleaqarab raised a hand and the men rushed the hill silently, the units on either end of the line moving to form a wider encompassing arc to ensure they were not outflanked.

"Be on your guard," the commander told Dawar, pulling the Glock from the holster on his hip, checking the magazine and the chamber. Dawar nodded, "Yes, Lord."

The Scorpion lowered the pistol by his side and walked up into the trees, feeling almost light-headed with expectation, the sound of gunfire ahead intensifying with every step, the shouts of surprised men being attacked from behind drifting down through the trees. The Scorpion did not have far to climb before he stepped onto the crest of a false peak. Already his men had swarmed into the low depression between the hills and he gazed down on the scene with satisfaction and expectation. Resistance from local opportunists had effectively been wiped out within minutes. The last of the opposition, two men in filthy jeans and shirts and ammunition vests, were dispatched by a single burst of submachine-gun fire. At the base of the depression was a battered Russian Hind, lying on its side at a forty-five degree angle. A large hole had been blown in the fuselage, its tail boom was snapped off and four of its main rotor blades were broken off close to the hub. The cockpit windows were smashed. Flashlights flickered over the fatally wounded machine as his men encircled it. Black and white smoke drifted skywards, and the cowling area over the engines was heavily blanketed in fire retardant foam.

Several of his men advanced warily on the downed aircraft, shouting at unseen occupants to surrender and throw out their weapons, several of which were tossed toward them, clattering against rocks. Above the edge of the fuselage, a rifle displaying a white shirt was raised and waved - surrender. The fighters around the helicopter held their AKs above their heads and cheered in celebration, shooting into the sky.

The elation the Scorpion had felt was still upon him. "Secure the area," he shouted and his men spread out, having learned through hard-won experience that there were always opportunist rats nearby. "Do we have dead and wounded?" he asked a jihadist, a Turk with thick black hair and beard. "None dead, Amir. Two wounded." the Scorpion nodded. His men had done well.

The air was heavy with the smell of burning kerosene and scorched tree sap. Al-Aleaqarab strode down the incline toward the Mi-24, pausing to put a bullet in the head of a man who was on the ground, screaming, a pilot from the look of his uniform, his shaking hands attempting to push the white bone of a shattered femur back into a leg pumping blood in thick powerful squirts. A Russian – but he was as good as dead anyway. Fighters dragged survivors from the wreckage and made them kneel on the ground, hands on heads, fingers interlocked.

The Scorpion took a flashlight from one of his men and approached the bewildered captives. There were four in total. Two deceased occupants of the Hind were laid on the ground, the co-pilot and another man wearing a combat uniform.

Al-Aleaqarab played the flashlight over the line of captives. All were covered in blood, gore and scorched oil. One of the men immediately caught his attention, three stars on his shoulders clearly visible. "Good evening, Colonel General," he said in fluent Russian, but the general refused even to acknowledge him. "I see you are wounded. This I regret. A foot wound. I will have someone see to it. Now, I count five passengers - the four of you, one dead Spetsnaz, and two dead pilots, as was the will of Allah. But a Hind carries eight passengers. Are we missing some?"

"You are Georgian," the general replied.

"You have an ear for accents. Yes, I am Georgian."

"I do not speak to Georgian scum."

The Scorpion handed the flashlight to one of his men standing nearby and indicated that he wanted it pointed at the first Russian in line. "You are fortunate this Georgian scum has come to your rescue, General..." he read the man's name off the tag on his flight suit, "Yegorov." The name came with excited recognition. "You are Colonel General Nikolai Yegorov, Commander of Russian Forces in Syria."

The general glared at him and turned away.

"Do you know who I am?"

"You are a piece-of-shit Georgian. I do not know your name, but soon there are people who will have your name and the names of your family members and that is all I shall say."

"I am but a humble jihadist fighting for the glory of Allah and these men around me are my family. You can call me Al-Aleaqarab, the Scorpion, or al Aljurji, the Georgian. Either will be suitable." He then cracked the general on the back of the head hard enough with the pistol so that the man slumped to the ground, barely conscious.

Al-Aleaqarab stood back and regarded his prisoners. This was an extraordinary haul. *No Russian soldier of any rank has yet been captured in any of our occupied lands, and here is an officer with three stars on each shoulder!* One of the most senior officers in the whole Russian military had literally dropped into his lap. The Scorpion moved to the next man in line. He was breathing hard, hyperventilating, obviously terrified and possibly wounded or injured from the crash. He was of middle age, a little overweight with jowly cheeks latticed with broken spider veins. The face of so many Russian men with a thirst for vodka. A big man, and strong once. More interesting than his face was the object chained to one of his wrists. "And what do we have here?" The Scorpion toed the scorched briefcase in the dirt with his boot. He received no answer. "It is burnt. I see that your hand is burnt also. Most unfortunate. You must be in pain," he said. "What is in the briefcase that you would try to burn it, and injure yourself in the attempt?" The man on his knees, sweating profusely, was silent. "It is okay. There will be plenty of time for us to have its secrets revealed."

Next in line was a man in his late twenties or early thirties who wore webbing over his body armor and shooter's gloves protecting his hands. He looked fit, and was certainly angry. "Spetsnaz?" Al-Aleaqarab enquired of the man presenting him with silent loathing. *A man like this has his uses.* Shining the light on the fourth man in the lineup caused the ISIS commander to blink. *No! It cannot be!? Surely not?* Here was a man of supreme power, his face as well known to Al-Aleaqarab as that of a movie star. The man stared up at the Scorpion with hard hateful eyes.

"Bozis shvilo!" Al-Aleaqarab exclaimed aloud in Georgian. Son of bitch! The men around him drew in their breaths and whispered among themselves when the flashlight beam illuminated the Russian's face. A shiver of expectation ran up Al-Aleaqarab's spine. *What have I done to deserve such bounty as this?*

He ducked involuntarily as two fighter-bombers roared by almost overhead, obscured by the trees. Russian? Possibly, but they could also be American, French, Australian, Syrian or indeed any one of a number of the foreign air forces patrolling the skies. The shriek of jet blast reverberating through the hills reminded the Scorpion that time would be short. A massive search and rescue effort would already be under way, and soon it would descend to scour every centimeter of this part of the world, looking for the downed Hind and its priceless cargo.

"Allah has presented us with a great gift," the Scorpion announced to the hillside. "Search the Russians, ensure they have nothing secreted within their clothing or elsewhere. Search the helicopter for weapons, phones, computers, maps and other intelligence material, and bring it to my vehicle. Photograph the crash scene, the helicopter and the dead. Do it fast. We must leave immediately. All of Russia will soon arrive on this hill."

He stepped past a man with a shotgun pointed carelessly at the ground. "Do you mind?" He held out his hand.

The jihadist snapped, "Amir!" and presented the weapon to the Scorpion who took it and examined it quickly, ensuring that there was a shell in the chamber. There wasn't, so he pumped one in.

"You found this in the Hind?"

"Yes, Lord," the jihadist replied somewhat nervously.

Al-Aleaqarab strolled back along the line of captives whose hands were on top of their heads, the general now struggling back onto his knees with the assistance of a jihadist. *No, these are more than captives. Much, much more...* "I am familiar with this," he said. "It is a Russian KS-23. A fine weapon utilizing, so they say, cut-down anti-aircraft barrels. Issued to Spetsnaz." He pointed it at the elbow joint of the man with the briefcase and pulled the trigger. The weapon jumped with tremendous recoil and a mighty boom rolled up the hill. The Russian lifted his hands off his head in shock, his fingers interlocked, and found that one of his arms - the blackened and burnt one still chained to the briefcase - was amputated. "Yes, a fine weapon," the Scorpion said, using the muzzle to prize the man's interlocked fingers loose from one another. "I no longer have any questions about what your briefcase contains." He chambered another round as the one-armed man began to shriek. The shotgun boomed once more, ripping a hole through the man's back and chest, silencing him. The Scorpion kicked him down onto his face as the blast echoed around the hill. "A warning to you all," he said softly in Russian. "You will remain among the living only as long as keeping you alive serves Allah, for as unbelievers you have no right to live, only to spend all eternity in hell for denying His greatness." Al-Aleaqarab tossed the shotgun back to the fighter who had found it.

"*S kazhdym biyeniyem ya obeshchayu, chto ya budu vam,*" a voice familiar to him said. *With every heartbeat, I promise I will kill you.*

The Scorpion shone the flashlight beam directly into the face of the man who had spoken and saw the cold eyes harden around black needlepoints. "It is true what they say," the Scorpion said in Russian. "You wear blue contact lenses." A corner of his mouth flickered with amusement at this vanity. "You want to kill me." He bent down, picked up the severed limb and the briefcase and tucked them both under his arm. "In another time and place," the Scorpion told the Russian, "you and I could have been comrades." He patted the man on the shoulder and told him, "I bid you welcome to your worst nightmare, Mr President."

Eight

Ronald V. Small @realSmall
ISIS is on its knees. Time for us to move on to more important
things. Like GOLF.

The firefight was close, though how close it was difficult to say as
the hard cracks and larger explosions rolled around the hills and
valleys. It was either an assault or an ambush, though probably the
latter as the hills seemed pretty much devoid of infrastructure. As
long as it wasn't at our alternate, I thought. The rattle and crash of
small arms fire petered out and silence filled the void.

As for traffic, there wasn't any to speak of on the dirt trail
snaking up through the trees. According to the map, this was a
lesser track that led to an arm of the lake. I was keen to stay
away from roads, but decided this one was worth the risk as the
only other route involved slogging it out through a sea of stinging
nettles between groves of unkempt almond trees clinging to the
steep grade. A significant boom echoed through the trees. A twelve-
gauge? No. Something bigger.

"So, here we are in Syria," I said between breaths, in case anyone
thought I was getting us lost. We had reached yet another four-way
intersection; there was a tangle of trails all through these hills.

"The secondary has gotta be close," Bo huffed.

We'd been double-timing for around forty-five minutes and had to be closing in on the hill's summit, the black-orange sky visible through the tops of the trees further up the trail, unless this was yet another false peak. "Yeah," I replied. "Half a klick or less. We can cut left off the road any time from now."

The designated Plan B for the TACAN was not a commanding rock like the one we'd vacated, but ours was not to reason why. And I've never liked the second half of that catch phrase. I was about to suggest we leave the road when the engine noises of multiple approaching vehicles forced my hand. No one needed me to say take cover, and moments later a motley convoy of speeding trucks, utilities and sedans arrived at the intersection. They were either in a hurry to get somewhere or get away from something.

"Gotta be our pals from the warehouse," observed Alvin, noting the blue Toyota technical with the quad-barrel ZPU option tailed by a white Beemer, black ISIS flags flapping from many of the vehicles.

Yeah. There couldn't be many ZPU-BMW pairings running around.

"Odds on they're out here looking for Russians," Jimmy said. "That Hind came down somewhere in these hills for sure."

"Could be that's what all the noise was about," I supposed. Mr Scorpion had sped away from the warehouse in the direction taken by the stricken Hind. Most likely he would be hoping to recover useful hostages. Maybe he'd gotten lucky.

At the intersection, the convoy split up, two thirds of the cars and trucks – around twenty of them – kept going straight ahead while a third split from the main convoy to take the fork down the hill, toward the main road. As we watched, more of that grouping diverged, taking other roads. Maybe what they wanted to get away from was each other, but I could care less. More important to me was the requirement to take a leak, which I did. With my own personal emergency settled, we moved on.

"This is the place," Bo announced not long after as we arrived on the crest of a hill covered with the ubiquitous stinging nettles.

The weeds seemed to have taken over, the farmers either fighting or fleeing.

Jimmy, Alvin and I swung our packs off our backs and liberated the various parts of the TACAN. They then went into overwatch mode along with Bo, which left me to assemble the flat-packed gizmo and run it through the various sat-nav positioning and self-diagnosis programs to ensure all was working properly. The lights all came up green, my favorite color when it comes to electronics, and I stood back to inspect my handiwork. The entire unit was painted a drab green, a color scheme that blended in well enough with the surroundings, but its shape was utterly man-made and therefore easy to spot. So I draped a little netting off the saucer, tossed some light twigs and nettle leaves over it and stood back to gauge the effectiveness of my camouflaging handiwork. "Yeah," I said to myself - better.

I sucked some water from the Camelbak. Elsewhere in this country, other teams of Special Ops were planting similar beacons, thus setting up a triangle of radio sigs. Assuming those teams had also switched on their TACANs, this part of Latakia would now be wired up better than O'Hare for approaching aircraft, and our F15s could now go ahead and deliver hell through a mail slot. Turning on the TACAN also triggered our extraction from the nearest LZ, so the lack of unit comms was no great handicap providing things stayed nice and simple. I took another slurp from the Camelbak hose and gave my balls a scratch, there being not much else to do at this point. A shower would be nice, and maybe a glass of single malt. Make that two, and make 'em doubles. I licked my lips.

A branch cracking unexpectedly gave me a start from this pleasant daydream, and caused my hands to reach for the M4 on my chest webbing. But the barrel of a pistol in the back of the head has a certain feel about it that tends to make you stop what you're about to do.

"*Podnimite ruki. Ne shevelites'.*"

A woman's voice.

"Podnimite ruki."

Same words, but this time harsher and more insistent.

I raised my hands slowly. The words weren't familiar, but the attitude was.

And then another voice joined in. "Drop the gun, lady."

Jimmy.

"You're good, boss," he said, so I turned. Jimmy was standing behind the woman, the point of his ka-bar in the side of her neck a convincing argument for her to go with the flow. And on either side of Jimmy, Alvin and Bo had their carbines trained on her. None of them had made a sound that wasn't supposed to be heard. Jimmy peeled the pistol from her grasp, handed it to me, and then patted her down. Nothing else came to light. A nine millimeter Yarygin – no spare mags - was the sum total of her baggage.

"Jimmy, cover the road," I told him.

He melted into the bush and I turned my attention to our unexpected visitor. She wore a flight suit slicked in blood and, if I wasn't mistaken, bits of flesh. She was also shaking. Her build – slight; height – medium; skin - green; eye color - green. What? Wait... I flipped up the NVGs. Amend hair color to covered in oil; skin, also oily. Eye color - too dark to see.

And then, before I could do much else, a substantial weight crashed noisily through a succession of branches before hitting the ground with a heavy thud less than ten feet away.

"What the hell was that?" said Alvin.

Well, it wasn't a coconut. Approaching the lump on the ground with some caution, I peered down at it and caught a whiff of something. Alcohol?

The lump groaned and then belched.

I glanced at Alvin. "I think it's Russian."

Nine

Ronald V. Small @realSmall
RUSSIAN PRESIDENT CAPTURED. ISIS has bitten off more than they can chew. You don't scare us!

The briefcase on his lap, Al-Aleaqarab sat in the back seat beside President Valeriy Petrovich. The president's hands were bound behind his back with duct tape, the shoes removed from his feet. His ankles were also tightly bound with tape and there was tape across his mouth. The General Yegorov, who was by the far door, was tied more leniently, his hands taped at the wrists, and his feet left unbound. He was clearly in considerable pain from the gunshot wound in his foot. The Scorpion had seen many battles and much torn flesh and foot wounds were among the worst. *Feet. And hands...*

The general's eyes were closed, his head tilted back. His face, sweating profusely, was locked in a grimace. The lines in his forehead were deep and knotted together as he tried to deal with the pain. He made no sound, but when the car hit a bump or a pothole, or Ortsa braked hard or swerved to avoid a collision, he cried out involuntarily, the sound coming from deep within him, uncontrolled. The wound had only been received within the hour.

The pain would intensify once the man's body had taken stock of the damage and tried to deal with it.

In the front passenger seat, Dawar sat turned towards the back seat with a Yarygin pistol in hand, hammer cocked and a round in the chamber. Ortsa drove, his eyes continuously roving to the rearview mirror with the excitement of a child who cannot tear his eyes from a stack of gifts wrapped for Eid.

The Scorpion noted the young man's distraction with a degree of amusement. *I feel it too, Chechen. My heart races and my scalp prickles as if charged with electricity. We have been given weapons of immense power. And we will use them to Allah's best advantage.*

Directly in front, shrouded in a veil of boiling road dust, the ZPU led the column. And in the utility immediately following the Beemer a contingent of jihadists guarded the Spetsnaz bodyguard.

The convoy raced along the trail, shedding vehicles from the main column until just the ZPU, the Beemer and two king cab pickups remained. The Scorpion leaned closer to Petrovich and ripped away the tape covering his mouth. "Mr President, you are thinking that your Spetsnaz will arrive soon to pluck you from this unfortunate situation."

President Petrovich did not respond, choosing instead to focus on a point in front of him.

"But do your people know where you are? No, they do not. For if they did surely these hills would right now be swarming with rescue teams. We will melt into the earth, protected by the grace of Allah's will."

Still no response from Petrovich.

The Scorpion continued, "Would you like to tell me why you are here in Syria? How is it that your helicopter exploded?"

Nothing.

"I wish to thank you for this great gift." He patted the briefcase.

The Beemer came to a dusty stop behind the ZPU. They had reached the intersection with the main road. Through the window, Al-Aleaqarab could see hundreds of refugees, the slow-moving river of humanity heading east, away from the dangers of Latakia. "Do you see the effect of your air force, Mr President? But you do not feel for them, do you? And neither do I. Why should we? They are no better than cattle and like cattle we feed off them - Russia, the caliphate, Assad, all of us. Even the Americans, if they were honest with themselves. These Syrians pay tax and have a value as bargaining chips with all parties, and they are worthy human shields for the glorious warriors of Ad-Dawlah al-Islamiyah. But that is their sum total of worth. Look at them. Right now they have the will for nothing other than movement."

The Scorpion knew that it was impossible to hide a large cohort of vehicles from eyes on the ground and in the sky. But reduced as they were now to a column of four, they would draw far less attention.

"Which way, Amir?" asked Ortsa. "Do we return to Latakia?"

Al-Aleaqarab considered the question and looked right and left. "No. Turn left, Ortsa," he said, "toward the end of days."

* * *

The column moved slowly. Not even passing truckloads of fighters raised the refugees from their lethargy. Everywhere women and children cried, some of the men too, lamenting a lost child or family member. Mazool, Taymullah and Farib trudged along with the human stream.

"If you were truly concerned about my mother, Mazool, we would turn around now and head back to the city."

"It's true, I *am* scared of your mother, Farib. Even Assad would give her plenty of room, but we must find the helicopter," Mazool said.

"Walking along on foot?" asked Taymullah.

"We will find a vehicle and steal it. Allah favors the bold."

Farib continued, "You've told me about the Russians and the necessity for revenge, but I don't understand why we need to find this helicopter."

"What have you gained from this war, Farib?"

The young man shook his head. "Nothing."

"Taymullah?"

"Nothing."

"Me also, nothing. And, despite all the sacrifices, where is Assad? He still rules over Syria's carcass from his palace. We have lost our families, our futures, our wealth, our jobs. All Syria is in mourning. And why do we keep fighting? Because we can't stop. We have no other choice. Assad will not stop bombing us. And we will not stop fighting because how can someone who thinks nothing of killing his own people and destroying everything just to stay in power rule us? If we stop now, all our losses will hold no meaning. What would have been the point of the sacrifice? But somewhere close by is a helicopter full of Russians. If we can get to them, and if they are still alive, we can take them prisoner. And what might we gain from that?"

"What might we lose?" Farib replied. "As you yourself have said, everything to do with war is loss."

"We can take them hostage and that will give us power," Mazool assured him.

"Power to do what?"

"Who knows? Power to stop the barrel bombs for a few days. Perhaps delivering the Russians to others will bring opportunities. At the very least we will be noticed."

"Noticed enough to be killed."

"Mazool is right, Farib," Taymullah said. "We live from day to day, firing the ammunition we can borrow or steal, and then we run away like frightened dogs. These Russians are like treasure. Who knows what having them in our possession will buy us? Who knows what we could trade them for?"

"Let us leave it in the hands of Allah," Farib suggested.

"Allah helps those who help themselves," replied Mazool

"Well, we will not find them along this road," Taymullah pointed out. "I am sure they came down further to the north, closer to Tishreen Lake. And the only transport available is owned by armed gangs with more guns than us. In fact, we have no guns." He suddenly pulled Farib and Mazool to one side, out of the march to nowhere. "Look," he whispered, motioning secretively at the darkness beyond the side of the road. "Our ambulance."

"What about it? Daesh took it," said Mazool.

"No, look there," said Taymullah. He pointed into the darkness beyond the side of the road. "Daesh is too impatient, and they don't understand engines." Across the road abandoned, shrouded in darkness, was the distinctive hoodless ambulance. Taymullah found a pathway through the darker night shadows and ran to it, Mazool and Farib following close behind him.

"It smells of burnt rubber and grease," said Mazool, looking into the engine bay.

"Leaking bottom hose, remember? They would have driven it till it overheated." The engine was still hot, ticking as it cooled.

"Smells ready for the junk yard."

"Perhaps, and perhaps not."

'You think you can get it going?" Mazool asked.

Taymullah turned on his phone's flashlight and checked some of the more critical gaskets. He wiped a finger along the seal. No oil. "Maybe," he replied. "These newer vehicles protect themselves from damage with all kinds of cutoff switches. If the engine gets too hot, the switch cuts the ignition and spares the engine. Once it cools a little, it might start again."

"You would have made a good mechanic," Mazool told him.

Taymullah opened the cap of the coolant reservoir and saw that it was empty. Next, he checked the bottom hose. The bandage he'd applied earlier had come loose. He moved quickly to the back of the ambulance. The bags of used bandages were still there. He pulled out the niqab, the T-shirt and the pants and threw them on the floor, then took one of the used, bloodstained rags and dived under the vehicle's front end. A short while later, he climbed up onto the fender and unzipped his fly.

"What are you doing?" Mazool said.

"There's no coolant. This will have to do until we can find some." Taymullah urinated into the reservoir, some of it splashing and sizzling on hot metal.

Farib screwed up his nose. "What have you been eating? Your piss stinks."

"Your turn next." Taymullah shook off the drops, zipped up his fly and jumped down.

Mazool shrugged, climbed up and unzipped, followed by Farib.

"They left the key," Taymullah called from inside the ambulance, finding it in the floorboards. He turned over the ignition and on the third attempt, the engine fired.

Mazool jumped in through the passenger door, Farib climbing in through the double doors at the back.

"We need water," Taymullah told them.

In the back, Farib picked up an empty water bottle and squeezed it, the plastic crackling like distant gunfire on a cold morning. "Go to the lake," Farib suggested. "It's close."

Exactly what Mazool was thinking. *It's in the right direction. With luck we'll find some Russians there too.*

Ten

Ronald V. Small @realSmall
BMI is a failed measurement. It is fake science.

"Geneva Convention. Name, rank, serial number. I give you nothing more. Serzhánt Nadezhda Novikova, number K14878049."

First impression, winter in Siberia, but I held out my hand anyway in the usual welcoming fashion. "Numbers aren't my strong suit, Sarge. Major Vin Cooper, United States Air Force." She didn't take it. "Natasha, is it?" No comment, so I guessed that was close enough. She was shifting her weight from foot to foot, her eyes flicking between me, Bo and Alvin. I stated the obvious: "You're Russian."

She nodded. The woman seemed nervous and pretty shaken, but I knew from experience that falling out of a moving aircraft would do that. "As for the Geneva Convention, relax." I hit my Stars and Stripes shoulder patch with some red flashlight beam. "You and us – we're allies." At least we were three days ago before I'd HALOed into this shithole.

"Then I go." The fact that we weren't about to shoot her gave her an instant shot of confidence.

I checked the safety on the Yarygin, a catch on both sides of the weapon, ejected the chambered round and handed back her pistol and the round. "Sure. Where are you going to exactly?"

"I must find helicopter. Do you know where is?"

"No." It had to be somewhere in this vicinity though. Russian nationals dropping from the heavens told me that if nothing else.

A groan came from the bulk lying on the ground. Was that because of the fall or because he needed another shot? Maybe both.

"Anyone got smoke?" Natasha asked, wiping her filthy hands on her soiled coveralls.

Alvin shrugged. "Only the grenade variety, ma'am." He tapped a canister on his webbing with his ka-bar.

"So, your helicopter," I asked. "What happened? We saw an explosion."

"It was missile."

It wasn't a missile, but I let it go.

"There was much blood. Helicopter, it began to ..." She made a spiraling motion with her hand. "I wake up in tree."

The reality of her evening seemed to strike the serzhánt anew and she swayed as her legs collapsed from under her and she sat heavily on the ground.

"You sure you're okay?" I asked her. "There's a lot of blood on you."

She looked down, dazed, at her gore-studded flight suit. "This not mine. Not wounded."

I offered her my Camelbak tube. "Water?"

She accepted and slurped several mouthfuls.

"Your English is good," I said, being the super affirmative type that I am, and helped her to her feet.

"My father was teacher."

"What did he teach?"

"English."

Okay, so here's my question. Why the hell don't Russian teachers of English ever include articles of speech in the curriculum? What's so hard, right? Y'know, *a* teacher, *the* helicopter, *a* smoke. "What do you do in the army?" I asked her instead, keeping it business-like. "What's your unit?"

"Now, or before?"

Odd answer. "Now. But you can give me the before too, if it's relevant."

"I make poster for recruitment."

At the moment, covered in the remains of someone else, she was hardly poster-girl material, though I did detect the waft of French perfume. "You were on a promo tour, visiting the troops?"

"Something like this." That's what she said, but it sounded more like "Somesing like zis."

"And, before?"

"I drive T-90."

"A tank?"

"*Da.*"

Chanel No. 5, armor plating and a big gun. Had to be a male fantasy in there somewhere.

"What about your friend?" I asked. A groan morphed into snoring as the man rolled onto his back. Waving the red flashlight beam over him, I picked up a well-known insignia on his battle jacket. "Spetsnaz," I said to myself, more than a little surprised. If you don't know, Spetsnaz are Russia's finest – Special Forces, though there wasn't a lot that was special about this particular specimen at the moment. But with my own fine regard for Glenkeith, I could hardly throw stones.

"Drunk Spetsnaz is useless Spetsnaz," she sneered like she'd happily run over him in her tank.

"Do you remember how you came to be here?"

"Is this interrogation?"

"Nope, just trying to work out how come it's raining Russians."

"No more question. You have radio. Make call. My people come."

Was I supposed to snap to attention? I thought I was the officer here. Maybe it works differently in the Russian military.

"Love to, ma'am, but our radio's Tango Uniform," Bo told her, saving me the trouble. It seemed to me that he enjoyed telling her.

Natasha looked at him, comprehension eluding her.

"Tango Uniform. Tits up," he grinned. "It's broke."

When a bird hits the dirt, standard operating procedure is combat search and rescue races to the scene, recovers survivors, attends the wounded and secures or destroys the downed aircraft. Like I said, that's SOP. The only reason Russian CSAR wasn't here already had to be that they didn't know where "here" was. That onboard explosion we saw must have wiped out the Mi-24's comms, transponder – everything – in an instant. "What happened to your helicopter?" I asked again.

"I must find wreckage."

"Well, it's gotta be somewhere close by, right?" I glanced around. Maybe it was perched on a nearby tree like Boris had been. For her part, the serzhánt seemed to be looking for an escape avenue. Was it shock?

"There was an internal explosion," I repeated. "We know because we saw it. Blew a big hole in the Hind. Y'know, from the inside ..."

"I must go," she insisted.

"As I said, no one's stopping you. What about your friend?" I motioned at GI Joseph at my feet. "You gonna carry him?"

"You do not understand."

Nope. I didn't. Something was going on here. I would have thought that stumbling into friendly forces after a helicopter crash in country crawling with folks who made a habit of decapitation, would have come as a relief.

"President Petrovich ..." She was moving around like she needed to pee badly, shifting from foot to foot. "He was in helicopter."

"What?" Okay, she had my attention. "Valeriy Petrovich?"

"I must find helicopter."

"The President of Russia, *your* president, Valeriy Petrovich – he was in the helicopter with you?"

The serzhánt nodded. Her eyes were big and wide and scared.

My mouth was probably open. Bo gave a silent whistle and Alvin shook his head. "Shit," I said, because I felt I needed to say something and that was the only word that stepped forward to volunteer.

A moment or two for the shock to subside and Bo said, "Boss, all those Daesh vehicles we saw …"

I knew immediately what he was getting at. While we couldn't be certain, in all likelihood ISIS had already found the crash site and looted it. That would explain the vehicle convoy out here in the middle of nowhere vacating the area in a hurry. Maybe it also explained why those same vehicles had dispersed. A smaller number of them traveling together would attract less attention, a point to be mindful of when you're spiriting away high value hostages and there are things like Predators and Reapers flying around that can see from 10,000 feet whether you've washed behind your ears. Those jihadists at the warehouse had witnessed the same thing we had – a bird partially ripped apart by an internal explosion, which flew off on an erratic course to the east-northeast. The Scorpion's crew had then blasted the accompanying aircraft out of the sky, jumped in their vehicles and raced to these hills. Had we known we were all heading in the same direction, maybe we could've hitched a ride.

My body language must have troubled the serzhánt. "What? Tell me!" she insisted.

"If your president's alive, he's been captured by a killer known as Al-Aleaqarab."

"Who, who is that?"

"The Scorpion, an ISIS commander. A very very bad dude, as our Commander-in-Chief would say. He comes from your neighborhood back home. He's Georgian." The Russian warrior spread-eagled on the ground farted loudly. "Wake him up," I told Alvin. "Do what you have to do to get him sober."

Alvin checked the man over, patting him down, feeling his pockets and the rest of his clothing. He found some loose change, an empty hipflask and a wallet with various cards – credit and ID. Grunting with the effort required, he dragged the comatose Russian across the ground to a tree, propped him against it and slapped him around the face a few times. "Wake up, Boris," he whispered. "Places to go, people to fuck up."

The man said, *"Пошёл на..."* the words appearing to dribble out of his mouth, along with some drool.

"What'd he say?" asked Alvin over his shoulder.

"Fuck off," I said.

Natasha was surprised. "Oh, you know Russian?"

"I know hangovers."

Alvin retuned to the business at hand. A drink of water, a few more slaps, a noisy vomit on all fours into the dirt and the Russian was back with us. Did he even know he'd been spat out of a helicopter before it spun into the ground?

"His name Igor," the serzhánt informed us.

"Boris. Got it," I replied.

"Boris?"

"English translation of Igor. Your father never told you that?"

Okay, so I lied, but Boris and Natasha had a ring to it that Igor and Natasha didn't. You gotta get your kicks any way you can in today's Air Force.

"Boris? I do not believe this. His name Igor."

In my worldview, Igor had a hump on his back and walked with a sideways limp. The noncom with a skinful didn't fit the picture and I'm the type that needs to make some kind of memorable association to get a name fixed in my head.

"His name. It is Igor Rostov Ivanovich Astaninnovich."

Okay, I thought, no chance of remembering that. "What caused the explosion inside the helicopter," I asked, hitting the subject for a lucky third time.

Natasha stared at me for a few seconds. Then she wiped her cheek with the back of a hand and I realized it wasn't to remove the caked blood but her own tears.

Eleven

Ronald V. Small @realSmall
It's a lie. I do not cheat at golf. Golf cheaters are the worst people.
I would never do that. Never.

The serzhánt sat alongside the man with the briefcase. There was
a dry retch in the back of her throat brought on by the stench
of roasting people that was coming through the air vents. The
"perfume of victory" President Petrovich had called it.

General Yegorov sat on the other side of cabin, on one of the seats
against the bare metal skin and framework of the aircraft, his head
gently rolling in small circles with the motion of the Hind. Natasha
liked him. He talked straight and acted the same way and he had
not tried to sleep with her. He had warned her about the president.
"Remember the bear?" he had said, referencing the animal the bare-
chested president had wrestled for YouTube cameras. "Beware, pretty
young tank driver, or you might wake one morning and find your
mouth strangely chaffed, your asshole stretched and a gap in your
memory. My advice to you: keep an eye on everything you drink from
a cup." And with that, he had toasted her.

The general had passed along this advice after she had confided
that the president was one of her heroes, a man to rival even Stalin

in greatness. "All I would say is that it is an essential truth of life," he told her, "that meeting one's heroes is rarely a rewarding experience."

Beside the serzhánt, sleeping it off, his helmet pushed low over his face and with one boot crossed over the other, was Starshina Astaninnovich, a career non-commissioned officer in Spetsnaz, a man who, the general had told her, had won the Hero of the Russian Federation medal. Such awards were handed out rarely, and the deeds that had won Astaninnovich the medal were secret. The general had refused to divulge any details other than he had killed many enemies. The Russian newspaper *Pravda* had nick-named him *Kapitán Rossiya* – Captain Russia, the motherland's own Captain America. Why was he here, in this helicopter? Was it purely because the president liked to be seen with such types, the ideal Russian with broad shoulders, big muscles and a thirst for vodka? Astaninnovich seemed to sweat alcohol on a daily basis. "But it is good Russian vodka, so that makes it okay," she had heard the president comment to General Yegorov that morning, when the starshina surfaced from his cabin on the *Admiral Kuznetsov*, his balance affected and his breath a fire hazard. Yegorov had joked that his liver must be the size of a Trabant.

The helicopter lurched and the saliva bridging Astaninnovich's chin with his collar collapsed as his helmet-encased head fell on Natasha's shoulder. When she went to push his helmet away she instead found the back of his close shaved head, soft bristles damp with alcohol sweat. Another sudden movement woke him, but only long enough for Igor Astaninnovich to let out a belch, a sudden hiss of air like a stabbed car tire, audible through the headsets. He went back to his snoring, just as he had done since they had lifted off forty minutes ago from the carrier out in the Med.

And then it happened.

It was Arkady Geronosovich, one of the president's two body-guards. Natasha glanced across in time to see him reach inside his jacket. There was something about his face, blank and trance-like.

She knew then that something was wrong. When his hand came out, his fingers were gripping something tight, a small round object. A grenade. *A grenade!* The pin must already have been removed because when he released the spoon, it sprang off and looped up over his arm. A loud popping sound came next, a small explosion, and the grenade head emitted a plume of white smoke.

No one moved and no one yelled. Because no one saw it, except for her. But she did not move, either – there was no time. It had happened so fast, but also slowly, each second stretching like elastic. And then Arkady stood. He glanced at her and shouted, "Allahu akbar!"

Natasha did not hear the explosion, but felt a blast of wet heat cover her.

Twelve

Ronald V. Small @realSmall
Europe needs to get its own house in order. Especially Germany. Their immigration policy is causing big, big problems for the rest of us. Big.

Well, that's what Serzhánt Novikova told me as we stood in the clearing. She concluded with, "And thirty minute ago, I wake up on forest floor."

"Hmm," I said, nodding. A fascinating story with a familiar ring. The bodyguard did it. Bodyguards and butlers must be cut from the same cloth. How much of it was true? Then again, why would the woman lie? What I did know from my gumshoe days was that people with long and intricate statements usually give them in order to hide something. Truth is more often than not provided in brief, sweeping explanations. Question: "How did you fall out of a helicopter and end up covered in gore, alive and in one piece on the ground?"

Answer: "Dunno."

A statement like that I could swallow whole. How much of Natasha's interesting and detailed story would Boris support? How much of it *could* he support given his pickled state? Was she lying? If so, why was she lying? And what part was she lying about? All of this assumed I gave a damn, which I didn't, because none of it was the new Vin's business. Check. "Jimmy, on the way to you. Your position?"

"Down by the intersection, sir," his voice replied in my earpiece. "Got traffic coming and going."

That figured. The Russian Hind would have been a beacon for every hostage taker with a keen nose for a business opportunity for miles around. "Jimmy, muster us a vehicle."

"Roger that," he said.

"Alvin, how's Boris?"

"Don't know, Major," he replied, "But slapping him around sure is entertaining. Wanna try?"

"Only if it will get him on his feet."

Natasha planted herself in front of me. "Where you going?"

"Home." Well, not exactly home, more a shipping container in the desert with a cot, WiFi and a bottle of single malt. Close enough.

"And Igor and me?"

"You mean Boris. That's up to you, but I would come with us."

"No."

That was a surprise. "I can leave you here if that's what you want, but you have no supplies, no comms – nada. We've got the opportunity to dust off at 0730 and I don't want to miss it." I checked my watch. "And we gotta hustle. Once we're airborne we can call in the situation with your president. I can guarantee you there'll be keen interest. So what's it gonna be?"

"We must find president now," Natasha insisted, "before is too late."

Clearly, this woman had a problem listening. "We as in us?" I gestured back and forth. "Firstly, he's not our president, so *we* don't gotta *do* shit. Secondly, how are you going to find him? And even if we found him, what then? We've got four carbines, a sniper's rifle and Boris's breath against who knows what else, but I guarantee it'll be substantial."

"Igor," she reminded me, "not Boris." And then, with a pout, "You must help."

"No," I replied, leaving even less room for interpretation. The pout turned into a glare, which she fixed on me for lengthy seconds, and I was reminded of that scene where Darth Vader pinches his thumb and forefinger together and uses the Force to throttle a minion. "Let me say again, the best thing we can do for Mother Russia, Serzhánt, is get you out of here. We'll hand over what little intel we have and let the people in higher pay grades work it out. This area is crawling with jihadists. We're gonna move now while we still can. Come with us or stay. Decide." For added effect, I glanced at my watch like I was in a hurry, which I was. Again, that frosty silence and the feeling of something tightening around my throat. Clearly, this was a woman used to getting her way.

"Okay, we go with you," she blurted.

Good decision. "Right."

Alvin had Boris on his feet, finally. I noticed for the first time that the Russian was a big man – I'm talking Redskins defensive-end big. I hoped he was a happy drunk, because he could do some serious damage to his surroundings without even thinking about it.

"Bo, give the area a sweep," I said, not forgetting the SOP of ensuring we hadn't left anything behind that announced "USA". Even the TACAN was stamped all over with "Made in Taiwan", just in case. The SFC gave me a nod, lowered his NVGs and commenced a quick grid search. "We'll rejoin at the intersection," I informed him.

"Got it," he said.

Alvin herded Boris down through the nettles and the almond trees. The Russian moved well, all things considered; those things being that he weighed close to 260 pounds and was still halfway to blind drunk. As we moved, terse words in Russian were exchanged between Natasha and the starshina. I gathered the feeling between them was mutual dislike. Mental note to self: ask Natasha if they were husband and wife.

I took point. The trip down through the stinging nettles was quicker than the one up and I brought us back to the trail just above the intersection. A screen of young trees and poison ivy obscured it. Dust hung in a thick curtain over the track, which was clearly now alive with vehicles.

"Got a loner coming this way," said Jimmy somewhere on the track below our position. "One headlight – could be a motorcycle."

"Unless it's got a minibus for a sidecar, let it pass. We're fifty yards north of your position," I told him.

We crouched in the bushes and waited, Bo rejoining us. And then Jimmy announced, "One vehicle commandeered, Major. An old acquaintance."

"What do you mean?" I asked.

"Come take a look."

The red crescent on a side panel solved the mystery. The ambulance, the one that had broken down on us earlier, was nosed into the bushes by the roadside. Two men were moving a log Jimmy had placed in its path. A third man was under Jimmy's supervision, the muzzle of his M4 pushed into the guy's back. "This one speaks English – kinda," said Jimmy with a shrug. "Claims they're medics. From Latakia. Checked the vehicle for weapons, found none. No medical supplies either. They say they were robbed of this vehicle at an ISIS checkpoint, but found it again some time later, abandoned."

I guessed that was possible. "They're a long way from home. What are they doing driving around up here?"

"Said they saw the helicopter come down and came to offer assistance."

"With no medical supplies?"

Jimmy shrugged. "Shoot 'em?"

Leaving people in our wake that could identify us as Americans was a problem, but the driver and his friends were unarmed, which placed them in a category the ROE said we couldn't shoot. Of course there are all manner of instances in the past where letting "civilians" loose has ended in tragedy for our guys and I had no wish to write our own scene in that movie.

The two fellas moving the log out of the way finished the job and rejoined their buddy by the ambulance, their hands on their heads with fingers interlocked, as directed by Alvin and Bo. The oldest of the three, the one with Jimmy's carbine tickling his ribs, was perhaps in his mid-twenties, covered in concrete dust and grime, with dark but intelligent eyes sunken in his malnourished face. He seemed strung out yet strong, afraid and also confident. I pointed to him, and said, "Al Qaida."

"No, no, al Qaida, no! SDF! SDF!" he insisted, almost shouting it, apparently taking monumental offense at the label.

"Keep your voice down," I told him. "So, not medics."

"You are American! Friends! We are friends. Long live America!" And so forth.

"Quiet!" I hissed. The Syrian Democratic Forces were one of the larger anti-Assad groups operating in northern Syria. That much I remembered from the intelligence briefings I had been made to attend but largely ignored given that contact with the local population was to be avoided at all costs. If these guys really were SDF, then they were allies; the TACAN was in place largely to support them fighting al Qaida, Daesh, the Assad regime and a shopping list of other groups. Except that the other snippet I remembered from the intel briefings was that lying pretty much happened to be the national sport in these parts, and folks took pride in playing the game. While I was weighing all this up, one of the other two, who had been eyeing Boris and Natasha suspiciously, said, *"Kunt alrrusi?"* And then the guy I was questioning, suddenly realizing that some of us weren't all the way with the US of A, spat on the big Russian starshina, and then jumped on him and started pounding on his head like this was a horribly mismatched UFC cage fight.

The testosterone levels in our little band soared a few thousand feet in an instant, the two other Syrians yelling what was probably encouragement at their boy, while Jimmy, Bo, Alvin and I raised our M4s as a matter of security, covering all of them, Natasha included. This could turn ugly.

But then Boris managed to get a handful of the Syrian trying to chew on his ear, Tyson-style, and peeled him off. Holding the guy aloft in midair by what appeared to be the scruff of the neck, the Syrian's legs twitching and kicking, Boris swung him in a half circle into side of the ambulance so hard that the sheet metal buckled. This took the wind right out of him, the fight too. Boris let him drop to the ground and the Syrian's buddies fell silent. I felt sorry for the ambulance.

"I guess that settles the al Qaida issue," said Bo, lowering his weapon.

"Yep," I agreed. Al Qaida and Russians probably wouldn't have had the same explosive reaction rubbed up against each other that we'd just witnessed, and neither would a jihadist from any one of the murdering fanatical bands operating in the area, such as ISIS, the Khalid ibn al-Walid Army, the Islamic Muthanna Movement, and a bunch of others the Russians were supporting in a de facto way by targeting the anti-Assad folks. Confused? Us too, but that's how the locals roll around here. In short, maybe the ambulance crew was, in fact, who they said they were. At least I was convinced enough that I didn't feel we could legally shoot them.

The guy on the ground, whom the big Russian had just rearranged the ambulance's kidneys with, groaned, lifted his head and said, "You want someone to kill Russians, we will do this."

That was a kind and generous offer, but our guys back at Incirlik wouldn't approve of that either. Not this week anyway. "Thanks. I'll consider it. Meanwhile, you're driving. Bo – shotgun. Everyone get aboard the freedom bus." I motioned at the ambulance. "Tell your friends," I instructed the designated driver as he climbed painfully up off the ground, with assistance from Alvin. It would start getting light soon and I figured a Syrian behind the wheel would attract a little less attention than an American soldier. To keep everyone honest, I said to my boys, "Keep an eye on 'em."

The Syrian, gingerly checking himself over for serious damage and finding none, held out a hand ingrained with dirt. "I am Mazool." He pointed to the teens. "Taymullah and Farib."

I couldn't leave the guy hanging so I shook his hand. "Cooper," I told him and filled him in on who was who in the rest of our zoo.

"Americans. Allies," Mazool said.

"Allies," I replied. "Unless you prove to be otherwise."

"Okay."

The Syrian called Taymullah, really no more than a kid, began talking rapid-fire to Mazool, who translated. "Taymullah says the ambulance is, er ..." he searched for the word. "It has thirst. Do your men need to make piss?"

* * *

There was more motorized traffic on the road and it was moving east, away from Latakia, in a hurry. There was almost no room on the road for vehicles headed in the opposite direction, towards the city, and a great reluctance to clear out of their way. Ortsa kept his palm planted on the horn, but it made little difference. All people cared about was putting as much room between themselves and what they'd left behind, which was mostly deafening, earth-shaking and lethal.

Thunder shook the Beemer. More jets passing overhead. And even lower, beneath them, were many helicopters. Everything was heading in the one direction. Al-Aleaqarab tilted his head and peered at the sky out the side window.

"Announce that you have rescued us from the crash and I guarantee that you will live," said Petrovich, his voice firm and commanding.

"Keep your mouth shut, Mr President," the Scorpion replied, "and I guarantee I will not remove your head from your shoulders right here and now." The aircraft appeared to be converging on the outskirts of the city. The Hind that had been blown out of the sky, The Scorpion reasoned, must have had time to call in the problems with the first helicopter before it was reduced to a ball of flaming metal. Those coordinates would be ground zero for a thorough search. He had wanted to enjoy firsthand the panic spreading among his old foes, but it was evident now that the risks of such an indulgence were too great. The Russians had mobilized with impressive speed. Two more Hind gunships covering a third transport helicopter flew by at treetop height. The Scorpion watched them pass. Spetsnaz. Large numbers of them would be deposited on the ground to secure the area and question possible witnesses. The Russians would make countless martyrs as dawn came to the battlefield, chief among them his fighters left behind at the warehouse, close to the burning helicopter wreckage. Russians would soon be manning checkpoints ahead and, as the frantic search widened, also behind, cutting off retreat.

Ortsa, sweating anxiously, watched the sky up through the windshield. In the ZPU, the jihadist in the passenger seat was hanging out the window, also looking skywards, his apprehension clear.

"Are you afraid of dying, Ortsa?" The Scorpion asked.

"No, Amir. When I die, I will be in Paradise. Finding a death that's most pleasing to Allah is what concerns me. And in the meantime, we have the most valuable property in Islam. I wish to make good Allah's purpose in this, whatever it is, but I am sure it is not to hand him back to the Russians."

"What I could do with a thousand jihadists like you, boy," the Scorpion said. "You will find martyrdom if Allah wills it." The president seemed smug, emboldened by the presence of so many Russian aircraft nearby. It was clear that a change of plan was required. "Signal our escort, Ortsa," the Scorpion commanded. "We will turn to the east." It would soon be light. He examined his prisoners. "Let us see if you have anything to take pleasure in when the sun rises."

Thirteen

Ronald V. Small @realSmall

I love Germany. Greatest country in Europe besides our friends in England. I have many golf courses in Scotland, which is part of England.

"Weight divided by height," President Ronald Small muttered to himself as he finished the calculation on his phone, "equals 31.6 ..." He checked the scale. "Obese?" *Obese? Me? No way!* He yawned as he stood and examined his image in the full-length mirror installed beside his portrait, a far slimmer and more flattering version of himself, and held up his shirt. *I can't even see my own dick. It's all those lunches and dinners. You sit down every day with some foreign bum from a place you've hardly heard of, make nice and eat, and you're gonna pay for it bigly. And all the time the jokes from nasty washed-up two-bit actors.* He sucked in his gut and regarded the figure in the mirror. *That so-called washed-up actor, Whatshisname, with the stupid wig. What did he say on that show the other day?* Small relaxed and a white, gray-haired hairy bulge slid over his belt. *Said I was having a baby. Said it was too bad with the changes I'd made to the federal court I couldn't get an abortion. And then those media assholes get a hold of it and the next day it's all over the Internet. And then nasty jokes get made about the jokes. No respect. It's very bad. You'd think people had something to get on with, like maybe working for the good of the country.*

There it was again, the knock on the door, sharper this time, more urgent. *Dammit!* Small shook his head. *Twenty minutes peace in the Oval Office at the end of the day to do a little putting practice, that was the deal. Everyone agreed to it. Not too much to ask.* Another knock.

"Mr President?" said the muffled voice on the other side of the door.

"What!" he called out. And then, sighing heavily, "Come!"

The door swung open and people surged in like fish through a net suddenly holed. "It's my private time and you all know that. The day is done. All I ask for is a lousy twenty minutes. This better be good."

Secretary of Defense, Margery Epstein, early sixties and pencil thin, with a voice like a coffee grinder, the legacy of a long-time diet of Johnny Walker and Chesterfields, stepped to the front of the scrum. Her makeup was Kabuki thick, applied so that it would last the day without too much maintenance, wearing down layer by layer like an archaeological dig. "Mr President," she announced, "you're not going to believe this."

"There's a UFO parked over the roof."

"The Russians, Mr President."

"The Russians have parked on the roof?" Small said without humor. Experience told him something unpleasant was about to land on his desk. *The Russians ... Something nuclear? An accident, maybe?* No, there were a whole set of protocols for that kind of thing. This, he sensed, was something else.

Epstein exchanged a glance with the asthmatic Secretary of State, Edward Bassingthwaite, and Andy Bunion, the short, permanently red-faced National Security Advisor known behind his back as Rumpelstiltskin, or Rumples for short.

"Do you want me to guess?" Small said, his impatience showing.

"Sir, the Russians have lost Petrovich," Director of the CIA, Reid Hamilton, announced, concern pushing his thick gray eyebrows together so hard it seemed the hairs were tangled.

"What? What do you mean 'lost'?"

"Mr President, this could be a game changer," Bunion interrupted. "In a good way."

"Well, I'd love to agree with you, Andy, just as soon as I know what the hell you're all talking about. Did he wander off at the mall or something?"

"Mr President," Hamilton continued, "NSA has intercepted traffic on multiple levels, government and military, that Russian President Valeriy Petrovich has gone missing in northern Syria."

"You're kidding."

"No, sir."

The president grinned. "Is it my birthday?"

"Your birthday?"

Epstein, Bassingthwaite, Hamilton and Bunion stood before the president like children who had lost their tongues.

"Well, no, but..."

Small suddenly got up out of his chair and busted a churn-the-butter move, cleared his throat and did his best to project concern. "Has this been announced in their media, or anywhere else?"

"No, sir," Bassingthwaite advised him. "Our guess is that they're hoping to locate him before the Kremlin is forced to make any kind of announcement."

"Do we know what happened?"

"We believe his helicopter came down on the outskirts of the city of Latakia," said Bunion.

"That's in the north of Syria, near the Turkish border," Hamilton added, knowing that his president's sense of geography was more a Monopoly board view of the world defined by the number of hotels he had once owned there, and he had never owned hotels in Syria. "Petrovich was making a surprise visit to the battlefront to review Russian armed forces."

"Then I guess Valeriy was the one who got surprised. You'll never catch me doing anything so tremendously stupid. When did this happen?"

"Around 2 am, local time in Syria. 7 pm our time."

Small grunted, looked at his solid gold Patek Philippe. *Seven minutes past ten. Just over three hours ago.* "And it's not some kind of stunt?"

"By whom, Mr President?" Bassingthwaite enquired.

"The Russians. Who else?"

"Sorry, sir. No, sir. Not a stunt," the SECSTATE assured him.

"Unlikely," said Epstein, backing up her colleague, somewhat surprised that POTUS was accepting this news with such a light heart.

"I know what you're thinking," Small told Epstein. "Geniuses can do that – read minds. Einstein could read minds. Did you know that, Madam Secretary?"

"No, Mr President," Epstein replied, clearing her throat. "I didn't."

"He was a tremendous mind-reader. There's a lot you don't know. You're thinking I'm pretty relaxed about this, right?"

"Yes, Mr President," Epstein agreed.

"I knew that. Well, we want Russia to play ball with us on a number of trade and defense deals. And anyone who knows anything about how to structure a great deal will tell you – and if there's one thing I know it's how to make a fantastic deal – you gotta have leverage."

"What leverage do we have here, Mr President?" asked Hamilton, apparently at a loss.

President Small underlined the point with the usual hand gestures. "I'll tell you once you've told me everything we know about this. Do we have intel of our own?" the president asked the room. "Of course we do. Give me the headlines, no need to dig around in the weeds. We have the most fantastic intelligence in the world, everyone knows that."

"Yes, sir. We have a SPIREP from assets –"

Exasperated, the president stopped him. "A what? Spare me the initials for things, General."

"Acronyms, sir?"

"Don't try and *seem* clever by using words no one knows. What did you say? Acro ... acro ... You want to use words everyone knows – *that's* clever. Now, can we get on with it? You people were handpicked to make me look good. That's your job, but so far you're not giving me confidence. Next time come into my office better prepared."

"Yes, sir," Bassingthwaite wheezed.

"We don't have much, but it's something, Mr President," Bunion told him. "Yesterday evening, local Syrian time, we received a Spot Intelligence Report from our assets on the ground over there that two Russian Hinds had crashed outside Latakia – as I said, that's on the Syrian side of the border close to Turkey – the very vicinity in which, it turns out, we believe the Russian president has gone missing. It's yet to be confirmed, but I'd bet that Petrovich was aboard one of those helicopters."

"And you think he may have been killed in the crash."

"We don't know as yet, but it's a real possibility, sir," said Epstein, relieved that the president was at last joining the dots.

Bassingthwaite, mopping his face with a hanky, added, "The thing is, Mr President, the Russians will make it our problem."

"Why do you say that, Ed?"

"History, Mr President. That's what they do."

"Despite that," said Epstein, "I wouldn't be surprised if they ask our help to find him, assuming he is still alive. As I said, we've got people incountry. Not many, but more than the Russians do, and they know it."

Bunion agreed with a grunt.

"Back to leverage." The president made a steeple with his fingers beneath his chin. "Let's see if we can't find a way to turn this to our advantage. You know, when the stock market goes up, people make money. When the stock market goes down, people make money.

You with me? Up, down, it doesn't matter. You can make money out of bad news too, no problem. If the Russians ask for our help, we'll provide it. We're America, the greatest country in the world. But there will be payback. That's the way it works."

"Our concern is that it could have been one of the anti-Assad groups we secretly support who shot these choppers down," said Hamilton.

Bunion paced, arms folded. "Just think where this will go if our missiles took him down. The Russians will have a field day."

Small had an answer. "If that turns out to be the case, it would be a shame, because you know President Petrovich and I have an understanding." *Or I should say* had *an understanding. Right up to the time he said I wasn't the genius he thought I was and that I "Forest Gumped" my way into the White House, blundering across the right thing to say at the right time. He called me a five-year-old. And plenty of other nasty things besides. And all because my people wouldn't support his claims in the Baltic States. So I called him President Golum because, let's be honest, there's an incredible similarity there with that bony head and those ears.* "But America has to come first and if it looks bad for us, we'll just take a leaf out of the Russian handbook on handling bad publicity, and deny, deny, deny."

SECDEF Epstein gave the president the glimmer of a smile.

"Meanwhile, what of those people you mentioned? Are we talking, like, Special Forces or whatever? Personally, I like the SEALs. Can we change their mission? Give them a new one? Get the SEALs to go take a look at least?"

"They're not SEALS, sir," Bunion replied. "And we've lost contact with the team who made the report. Communications with small units on the ground there are always difficult."

"I'm sure you can fix the problem, Andy. You know I have the most tremendous faith in our armed forces. The American military is the best in the world – everyone knows it. Those SEALs are one of the many reasons. No doubt you'll all keep me well briefed on developments." The president picked up his putter by the handle and gave it a flick so that it spun rapidly in his hand, and sized up the SECSTATE. "What's your BMI, Ed? Do you know? I would say that, technically, you're obese. Mine? We're talking the high side of normal. I think it's something I should tell the media. Body image is important, right? Gonna get my press secretary onto it."

Fourteen

Ronald V. Small @realSmall
ISIS, you don't scare us. You are a failed movement. If you were a
TV show, you would be axed. Russia will make you pay unless
you release my very very good friend.

It was 0725 hours, but no one told the sun that. It beat down on
the open dusty field like it was noon, the air thrumming with insect
joy. Whoever had selected this RZ had chosen well: over a hundred
square yards of open space with plenty of room to accommodate
whirling helicopter blades, shielded from prying eyes on all sides by
groves of adolescent olive trees, the gaps between them filled with
low scrub, and no poison ivy for a change.

The area was accessed by a minor dirt road, which fed onto
a slightly wider dirt road that was empty of the usual traffic
hereabouts – refugees and horn-honking jihadists shooting people
whose stuff they coveted. "Who bought the picnic basket," I asked,
taking in the idyllic surroundings. All we needed to complete the
picture was a babbling brook.

"Good idea, boss. A meatball sub and a Bud coming up," said
Bo, holding the map in one hand while he scoured the sky with a
pair of compact binocs in the other.

"Where is helicopter?" demanded Natasha.

Behind her, Farib popped the top off a hissing, steaming radiator. Boris stood by to piss into it.

"It'll be a CV-22 Osprey and give it a minute. We're early and the US Air Force is always on time," I told Natasha. That was mostly true, unless poop had hit the rotor blades for a reason that couldn't be communicated to us because our radio was literally shot. In all of recorded history, to my knowledge, there wasn't a single Special Operations mission that had gone off without a hitch. Whatever could go wrong, did. *That* was something you could always rely on.

Alvin handed me a packet of cheese and crackers from what was left of our MREs. "Sorry, boss," he apologized. "The Bud is warm and the meatballs are cold."

I ate the cheese.

0729.

Duly relieved, Boris retired under a tree and swished the flies out of his face with a small olive branch.

Natasha stood around with her arms folded, either looking up into the sky or glaring at me like it was my bad that her president was in Shitsville.

Mazool and Farib were cleaning out the ambulance while Taymullah worked under the vehicle, legs protruding from beneath the front bumper. Better him than me, given what was leaking out of the radiator.

0731, nothing.

And, of course, once the appointed time came and went, Natasha became impressively impatient. Her attitude pretty much fell off a cliff once 0830 rolled around. But Jimmy, Alvin, Bo and I knew something was wrong long before then. Our tilt-rotor's no-show probably had something to do with the many contrails overhead. And you didn't have to be a combat air controller to know those trails had everything to do with the fate that had befallen President Petrovich.

"What now, American?" Natasha demanded, glaring at me, making the word "American" sound like "asshole".

Fair question, tone aside, so I told her, with more patience than she deserved, "Gimme five and I'll get back to you."

"No! You kidnap me. I wish to do duty for President Petrovich, but you stop this."

I said, "Please back the fuck off so that we can work through how to get outta here." Or at least that's what my face told her.

"Americans!" There was that euphemism again. She spat on the ground, but I suspected the preferred target was me.

"See up there?" I said to her, and motioned overhead at all the white crosshatching the blue. "That's your people. By now, both crash sites have been secured and there'll be Russians all over them – Russians on top of Russians on top of Russians; a babushka doll of Russians. What could you – or us – possibly do that they're not?"

Natasha glanced over at Igor, who was still sitting under an olive tree, swishing, out of earshot. She took a step closer to me and said, quietly, "Look, you want to know why must find him?"

No, in fact I hadn't given it any thought. But I took a guess at it anyway: "He's your president?"

"We were lovers."

I blinked. Bo cleared his throat and Jimmy and Alvin shared a smirk and turned away. So Natasha and Petrovich were thrashing the mattress. I supposed that did explain her heightened concern to find Russia's number one citizen. I tried to rustle up some empathy. "Does Mrs Petrovich know?"

Storm clouds drifted across Natasha's face.

Okay, so maybe I was empathizing with the wrong party. But my ex-wife had done the same job on me, only with our marriage counselor. A little sidebar: I walked in on them. They enjoyed showering together, saving water, while she scrubbed his very small limp dick with her mouth. And, unfortunately, once you see a thing you can't un-see it, right?

She assured me, "He said he would make divorce."

"Right." Of course he did. Natasha was, what? Maybe twenty-four? I wondered if she knew that she was as much a victim as Petrovich's wife. Big swinging presidential cocksuckers were given to spraying their tadpoles around. We'd had a few of them in the White House ourselves. Perhaps on some level Natasha knew this, but her own considerable ego wouldn't let her accept the possibility that she could be anything less than Petrovich's main game. More than likely, and unknown to Natasha, her hairy-chested president kept a harem of Natashas. But, as interesting as this *Days of our Lives* contemplation was, we had more pressing fish to fry. Namely, getting out of here and back to our comfy shipping containers in one piece.

Natasha pressed her demand. "You can see it is important I get to crash site. Also, I must report."

For some reason I couldn't put my finger on, and perhaps in spite of everything she'd told me, her demand didn't seem to make total sense. Petrovich was either barbecued in the wreckage, or abducted by jihadists. And as for rendezvousing with her comrades, I was reasonably sure that she wouldn't be reporting *everything*, right? But I let it all go 'cause, as I think I've already stated, that's the new Cooper way. And besides, perhaps thumbing a lift with the Russians was our easiest ride out, too. "Let me discuss it with my team," I told her, ladling on some infinite patience. She walked off to find a vacant olive tree to stew under.

I went into a huddle with Jimmy, Alvin and Bo.

"Looks like the Russians aren't letting anyone in," said Jimmy, glancing skyward, avoiding mention of Natasha's newsflash – a true diplomat.

"As you know, there is no plan C," I reminded them. "We'll have to leg it. Turkey's just over there." I pointed north.

"Thirty klicks as the crow flies," said Bo, finessing it. "And that crow would be flying over some 2000 foot peaks in these parts."

"Molehills," I said.

"Not to mention jihadists," added Jimmy.

"Not if we stay off the roads," Alvin said.

"And embrace the poison ivy." I threw in.

Jimmy scoffed. "I ain't scared'a no salad, boss."

"Of course not," I said. Then added, "We make for Turkey, and if we come across a Russian patrol we can drop Boris and Natasha off. Maybe also bum a ride out if everyone's okay with that."

Alvin was onboard. "Works for me. As they say, keep it simple, stupid."

That's my cue. Check.

"Well, we already got us transport," Jimmy pointed out, the ambulance still receiving some TLC from the Syrians. He grinned. "Question is, do we have enough urine 'tween us to get the sum-bitch to the border?"

"Someone cough up a roll of duct tape and fix it," I said. "We move when it gets dark. Rest up until three. Bo, Alvin, your watch. Get some eyes on that access road. I'll relieve you in two hours. I'm gonna take Jimmy and find us some water."

"Map says there's a brook at the treeline," said Bo, gesturing in the general direction.

"You're kidding."

"Nope."

"Will it babble?"

"Huh?"

"Forget it. Camelbaks," I motioned to hand 'em over.

"What about our pit crew?" Jimmy asked, meaning the Syrians and whether or not we were going to take the M4A1 option.

Alvin gave his Camelbak to Jimmy and scratched his jaw. "There's always that question. We let 'em loose, will they give us away?"

I glanced at Mazool, Farib and Taymullah – was that their names? They had everything out of the ambulance, doing what they could to clean it up. "Who wants to shoot 'em?" I asked. "Shall we draw straws?"

Bo, Alvin and Jimmy went quiet and looked at me like they were seeing me for the first time.

"Okay, in that case, I volunteer to do it if they give us the slightest provocation, right up to the time we let them off at a vacant cab stand on the border. Agreed?" This was met by a mixed sense of relief, mostly because the decision was made. No one wanted to kill someone they'd shared a ride with, but at the same time there was always the risk that this generosity might turn around and bite us on the ass. Remember SEAL Team Six in the 'stan? But our Syrians had given us no reason to suspect that they were anything other than who and what they said they were – the national hobby of lying notwithstanding. It was something that couldn't be said with confidence about Natasha. The jury was still out on Igor, though he was Spetsnaz *and* traveling in Petrovich's helo. I figured there had to be a reason for that.

I went over to the ambulance. "There's water down by those trees," I said to Mazool who was bagging a handful of old bloody bandages. "We could use any containers you've got, and maybe do a couple of runs."

"Your helicopter has not come," he observed.

"I hope not, otherwise we missed it," I replied on the basis that one dumb observation deserves another.

"What do you do? Do you wait?"

"Turkey. We drive out."

"That is dangerous. You need guide. The main roads, they are not safe."

"We've got Google Maps and Colt is coming along with us." I patted my carbine.

"America help us. We help America."

That's the spirit.

Mazool threw out a couple of sentences at Farib and Taymullah, who fetched two empty bottles and put them in a large heavy-duty plastic trash bag we could use as a bladder. He handed it to me. "Thanks," I said and both replied with nervous grins like they wanted to trust these Americans, but weren't convinced that we wouldn't turn on them and hose them down. All in all, sensible Syrians. To Mazool, I said, "I'll think about your offer."

Igor was racked out, snoring, a large hairy caterpillar moving slowly across his forehead. On to Natasha who was sitting in the shade against a tree, flapping the two halves of her flight suit material together to get the air captured within it circulating. "We'll be back shortly," I told her.

"You are going?"

"Get some water." I presented the trash bag by way of filling in the picture.

She perked up immediately. "There is water? Where?"

I motioned in the general direction. "A babbling brook."

"What?"

"Like a stream, with babbling."

"I come," she insisted.

I didn't have a problem. Natasha seemed the type who needed to be kept busy and distracted and she could help me carry the bladder, leaving Jimmy unencumbered to provide security. So there were two good reasons to say yes.

And then a third and possibly best reason of all presented itself when we arrived at a fast-flowing ribbon of silver splashing over and around smooth black rocks and boulders. Natasha, delighted, immediately kicked off her boots, tossed the Yarygin on the grassy bank and stripped down to her underwear. I pinched myself while she grabbed one of the empty bottles and picked her way over the rocks and settled into a deeper pool in the middle of the stream. "Cold!" she called out, and then leaned back, held her nose and put her head underwater briefly and came to the surface – there's no other word for it – squealing. She then removed her sports bra, wriggled out of a G-string that was more string than G, picked up handfuls of river sand and began to scrub herself all over with it, standing occasionally to ensure the scrub was thorough. She did all of this like no one was watching, though of course Jimmy and I were staring as hard as our eyeballs allowed.

"Thank you, Lord," Jimmy said for the both of us.

I've seen some women with extraordinary figures in my time, but Natasha's nudged the dial to eleven. Nothing was too big or too small, her smooth skin was the color of milk coffee and the curves were all just where Hugh Heffner said they were meant to be. And, as far as I could see, all of it was natural, except for down in the southern states, which had been totally deforested. In fact, she was utterly hairless. In truth I always find that a little surprising, and even oddly wrong for reasons I'm not prepared to put my finger on. But I believe in diversity and I'd happily fight for a woman's right to laser her sausage wallet. That's what freedom and democracy are all about, and if it's not, it should be.

"Come!" Natasha called out and gestured with one hand as she poured water from the bottle over her breasts with the other, washing away the black sand. The water formed dual waterfalls around nipples that were pink and large and standing out like a couple of volunteers. There was no doubt in my mind that this was a show put on for a reason. Nudity? Breasts? Nipples? It's just the human body, right? What's the big deal? Okay, I get it, but I also get that Jimmy and I were being manipulated by a master. Or, I should say, mistress. Maybe knowing what was inside that flight suit would make us a little more amenable to suggestion.

The sand on her belly was next to be sluiced. Knowing I was being manipulated didn't mean I refused to buy into it. I am, after all, just a man with all the pathetic inconsistencies that come when the head dangling between your kneecaps takes over the decision-making. In fact, at that moment, my one hope was that she would turn around and waterboard her ass.

I gave her a wave that said, "No, we're good. Just happy to stand here and watch you turn around and wash your tush, if you would be so kind." It was a complex sort of a wave.

Natasha shook her head, disappointed, I convinced myself, because I had declined to join her in a frolic. It didn't even occur to me that the invitation might have been for Jimmy.

Jimmy said, "On a mission in Iraq one time, we saw a guy giving it to his goat. Crazy. You never know what you're gonna see incountry." He cleared his throat, adding, in case there was any question, "This is way better."

I was too engrossed to weigh the comparison, but I knew what he meant. I thought I was coming here to fill a trash bag with water.

Natasha thrashed her flight suit on a rock, rinsed it and wrung it out a couple of times, the muscles working in her shoulders, legs and arms. Nice muscle tone, too. Okay, Petrovich, assuming you're still with us, you're a lucky son of a bitch. This is what I was thinking as I crouched and filled the Camelbaks, the remaining bottle and then the trash bag.

Natasha managed to wriggle back into her wet flight suit, which resulted in more great viewing as the motion involved quite a lot of topless jiggling. Finally dressed, she picked her way back across the rocks and rejoined us on the bank, grinning like she'd forgotten that she'd fallen out of a helicopter in the middle of Jihadland. She squeezed the remaining water from her underwear and draped the pieces on a shoulder.

"I feel better," she told us.

"Me too," I said and Jimmy agreed.

"You should bath. You need to."

I informed Jimmy, "She means you. I smell like roses."

Natasha put her socks and boots back on, checked the Yarygin and pocketed it. She flicked her hair back over her head. This squeaky-clean Natasha was a big improvement over the previous one, who could have been a fugitive from *The Walking Dead*. Now that her hair wasn't plastered against her head with dried blood and bits of intestine I could see that it was brown to golden with lighter streaks, cut fashionably short but with a long jagged fringe that swept across her unlined forehead. Her skin was smooth with a light tan, a sprinkle of freckles over the bridge of a strong, straight nose. Lips? Yeah, she had them too – on the full side and, because of that fullness I supposed, always slightly parted. While I found it a stretch when she first told me, now I could believe the Kremlin would choose her big green eyes to feature on recruitment posters. No doubt adolescent Russians in their thousands jerked off to her poster hung on their bedroom walls. Sex sells, and Natasha was hard sell. Problem was she knew it. No one's perfect.

"You wanna give me a hand with this, Sarge?" I asked her. The water-filled bag weighed a good sixty pounds.

A voice in my earpiece announced, "Boss, tangos inbound." I dropped the bag while Jimmy dropped to a knee. I pulled Natasha down beside us.

"Hey!" she squawked, or tried to, my hand tight around her mouth.

Fifteen

Ronald V. Small @realSmall
ISIS, we are coming to get you. Be afraid, be very afraid.

Abdullah Abdullah prowled out of the trees with five fighters as two vehicles carrying the balance of his men converged on the ambulance. They circled it, kicking up clouds of dust that filled the airless morning. The jihadist counted four silhouettes in the dust cloud, one of them an American soldier caught out in the open, his hands raised.

"Allahu akbar!" Abdullah shouted. *Americans! Fuckin' jackpot!* "Hostages! Take hostages!" he said in Arabic and urged his men to follow as he advanced in a crouch at the double. "You are surrounded! Drop your weapons!" he yelled into the choking dust. His men were excited, adding their own demands in Arabic, and the noise and the sense of victory filled Abdullah with elation. *The Amir will surely reward me for this.* He headed straight to the big black American sergeant, kicked his rifle away, ripped out the earpiece and tore the mike off his head. "We can't have you communicating, can we, Sunshine? Where are your friends? Nearby?"

The sergeant said nothing.

Abdullah directed one of his men to search the American. He patted him down, removing an M9 from a thigh holster, a smaller

102

caliber Ruger from behind his back, a ka-bar from a scabbard between his shoulder blades, some smaller throwing knives from a belt around his left arm and a set of knuckledusters attached to a small blade inside his webbing. Impressed by the haul, Abdullah said, "A boy scout, eh? Come prepared, have we?"

The American glanced at him and looked away.

"Hands on your head, fingers interlocked. You know the drill." The soldier was slow to move. "C'mon, you 'eard me." The American did as he was instructed. "There you go. Wot's your name? Don't be shy. Out wif it." Abdullah pulled and tugged at the sergeant's webbing until the nametag beneath was revealed. "Baker. Well, Sergeant Baker, as they say back home, you're nicked."

Abdullah ran his eyes over the other hostages – three men. Syrians. He recognized one of them instantly. "I know you, don' I?" He turned back to the sergeant, a black man like himself. "You're on the wrong team, mate. Your ancestors were children of Allah. The Crusaders have poisoned your mind. Not much I can do about that. A little late to be embracing the Merciful One now." He instructed two of his men to tape the American's hands behind his back and called out to the fighters patting down the Syrians, "Bring 'em here."

The three men were brought before him, shoved along by AKs. Abdullah coughed, the thick dust catching in his throat. "So, you find our fellow jihadists you was lookin' for?" he asked Taymullah.

"Why are our hands tied?" Mazool said in Arabic. "These infidels captured us, stole our transport."

"It's true, Amir," said Farib. "We were about to counterattack and take back the ambulance."

Abdullah was doubtful. "I fink you is SDF. 'At's the troof, innit?"

"No, no," Taymullah implored him. "We are Ad-Dawlah al-Islamiyah. You took our flag. Do you not remember?"

"I remember, fool. An' all you Syrians are fuckin' liars." He lifted his AK and rested the muzzle on Taymullah's sternum. "I fink I will kill you and let Allah decide the troof. If you are who you say you are, you'll be welcomed in Paradise. An' if not?" He shrugged.

"No, no, Amir. We beg you. We want to enter Paradise as martyrs."

"You must fink I came down in the last shower," Abdullah told them as a flicker of movement in the corner of his eye proved distracting. Or was it an unfamiliar sound? Whatever, it caused him to glance over his shoulder where he saw, in a pall of choking dust, a huge man holding a jihadist over his head like a set of dumbbells. As Abdullah watched, the giant dropped the man onto his massive thigh and a crunch was heard that reminded Abdullah of snapped breadsticks. The man then tossed the corpse aside, dusted off his hands and took several steps toward Abdullah.

Huh? Realizing his peril, Abdullah remembered the AK and started to raise it, but it was suddenly and expectedly kicked out of his hands by ... *Wha...?* A long serrated blade slick with blood was pressed hard against his jugular. *Jihadists! Where, where are you?* And then Abdullah saw that they were all on the ground lying still. Dead. *How? Er ...*

Baker read Abdullah's amazement and explained, "It's what we do, asshole." The sergeant's hands might have been tied behind his back, but not his forehead. He crashed it down onto Abdullah's cheek, which burst apart like a snowball hitting concrete.

* * *

"Ooh, that's a real nasty shiner you got there," I said when the man's eyelids fluttered open. In fact, it looked like he had a small polished black and purple bowling ball for a cheek. "Gonna be hard claiming you walked into a door with that one, buddy."

"Fuckin' 'ell," the jihadist swore quietly as tweety birds and pain did a little synchronized swimming around his head.

"What's that accent? Sounds English."

No answer.

"You're not the famous Jihadi John, are you? You're not the guy I've seen beheading folks on YouTube?"

"Fuck off," he replied with some discomfort.

"Nah, Jihadi John was a runt. But you, you're a fat bastard. You been living on donuts?"

"His name is Abdullah Abdullah," said Mazool before the jihadist could swear at me again. "He is Daesh."

The vehicles confirmed it, hung with so many black flags they looked like bat colonies.

"Abdullah Abdullah ... Are you one of the London Abdullah Abdullahs? Is Abdullah Abdullah hyphenated, by the way?"

The man glared at me.

"You weren't born with that name. Who'd do that to their kid? Abdullah Abdullah, just in case you didn't hear it right the first time. Your real name has gotta be Simon, or Nigel, or maybe Ian. Abdullah's just your asshole name, right?"

The man fired off a barrage of Arabic.

"What'd he say?" I asked Mazool.

"He speaks with difficulty. I heard dog and pig and something about your mother."

"Lucky for him I don't have any of those," I explained. "Took off when I was in diapers – the mother, that is." I addressed the captured jihadist directly. "So, Abdullah – mind if I abbreviate? Saying it twice sounds like I'm stuttering. How'd you find us?"

Silence.

"As I said, nice shiner. Is it sore? Looks like a bit of pressure building up there. Would it help if I lanced it? Here." I pulled my ka-bar and brought the point in close.

He blurted, "We just asked the cattle on the road, didn' we? Not fuckin' rocket science. Found out we was looking for an ambulance." He lifted his chin at our vehicle. "That fucker there sticks out like Niagara Falls."

"What?"

"Niagara Falls."

This guy had a thing about repetition, obviously. "Who?"

"Orchestra stalls."

"Huh?" What the hell was this guy saying?

105

"Orchestra stalls, Niagara Falls – fuckin' balls, innit!" the Brit said, exasperated. "Are you stupid? The ambulance. It sticks out like fuckin' balls."

Right. Note to self: ditch the ambulance.

Igor and Natasha came over to get a look at our prisoner. Their presence caused a flicker in Abdullah's face, the way a card player reacts after he has drawn, sees the card, and realizes he should've folded. "Yeah, look at that – Russians," I said. "You found yourself some Americans *and* Russians. Almost a mixed dozen of us. Imagine. I'm sure Al-Aleaqarab would love to get his hands on this little haul, am I right?"

Abdullah said nothing.

"Major," Alvin called out, squatting by a dead jihadist, holding up a set of night-vision goggles. "They're Russian. Found one pair only. No phones."

I was relieved to hear that about the NVGs. A single set among ten fighters suggested they'd most likely been lifted off a dead Syrian government soldier. Spreading tech like that around ISIS would take away one of our biggest advantages. As for the lack of phones, that wasn't surprising. Each one was a potential bullseye for a Reaper Hellfire. Even playing a round of Words with Friends between killing infidels could get you blown to atoms around here. Back to Tubby. "So, your boss, tell me about him. Al-Aleaqarab, Al Aljurji, Old Lobster Claws. You know who I'm talking about." I showed him my hands and made sinister pincer movements with them.

"You're a cunt."

"Sticks and stones," I countered.

"You fink you're bad ass," he scoffed, "but the Scorpion would eat you lot for fuckin' breakfast."

"There you go. Now we're getting somewhere."

"Wot are you? Some kind of suicide squad?"

"We got missiles for that, dumb-ass. No, we're just looking around for a good place to build a casino, a southern barbecue joint, a Hooters and a nice southern Baptist church. Once we evict you guys, of course."

"Allah damns all filthy kafirs. May the blood freeze in your veins."

"In this place?" Heat induced sweat was already running down my spine and into my shorts. "Unlikely. So, focus, Nigel. We were talking about Al-Aleaqarab," I reminded him.

"The Scorpion is halfway to Raqqa by now. So, you lose, motherfucker."

"What road did he take?" I asked.

"Fuck off."

It was clear we weren't going to get far with Abdullah, at least not right off the bat. It was also clear that the Scorpion wasn't going anywhere near Raqqa.

"Why you do not kill him," Natasha said as I stood.

"I agree it's tempting." Crows were already circling overhead, beckoned by the piles of bloody rags dotting the dirt. "But a swift trip to the hereafter is probably what he wants. Why oblige him?"

"He is scared. This is not someone unafraid of death."

I told her, "He's scared only because it's a sorry ass who turns up to face Allah without dead infidels to his credit. Life on this earth is just preparation for the main event – eternity. They really do believe that shit." I glanced at Igor whose forehead was swollen and raw, one eye half shut. I remembered the caterpillar. "He okay?" I asked Natasha.

"It was bug," Igor said.

That took me by surprise. "Am I understanding Russian or are you speaking English?"

He reassured me, "Little English speak."

Good thing I hadn't insulted him earlier. Wait, there was that whole Boris thing ...

"You Americans." He wagged a finger at me. "No like."

"What about Elvis Presley?"

"He okay," Boris replied.

"See? We're not all bad, right? What about terrorists?"

"Hate terrorist."

Having at least established that the super bad guys were further down the negative end of the friendship continuum than the entire US of A as far as King Kong here was concerned, I returned to the business at hand. Bo was re-equipping himself, tucking a small pistol into the holster in the small of his back. "You good?" I asked him.

"A great day to be alive. Always is when you're reminded there ain't no promises," he said, tucking away the knuckledusters. "FYI, when the chips were down, the Syrians claimed they were Daesh. Abdullah there didn't believe 'em."

"Well that's good enough for me – at least for now. You?"

He shrugged. "I guess it kinda confirms their shit."

"Strip some of the dead. Put the Syrians to work on it. We might need to move around cunningly disguised. Also, check those vehicles over." I motioned at the ISIS utilities. "We'll be here till nightfall. We need to post some eyes on the turnoff and get us some perimeter defense."

"On it, boss," he replied.

To Abdullah I said, "You're coming with us, Fatso. Just remember the great words of Jesus the Prophet – 'Duct tape can't fix stupid, but it can muffle the sound.'"

"First chance I get, gonna kill ya," he said.

"Don't like Fatso? How about Ian?"

"What of president?" Natasha demanded for the world to hear. "Maybe jihadist can lead us to Scorpion and Petrovich."

"Well, it's pretty clear to me Abdullah here couldn't lead kindergarten kids to candy."

"You is so fucking dead," he piped up.

"Right." Was I mistaken or was the zip on Natasha's flight suit a half-a-dozen inches lower than it had been a few moments ago? Maybe I was right about the game I thought I was in for – not that I was complaining, mind.

"'Ang on a second," said Abdullah, realization dawning, "Petrovich was on that 'elicopter wif you? You sayin' we shot down the Russian fuckin' president?"

Natasha's face gave away the answer, which delighted Abdullah no end.

"Un-be-fuckin'-lievable. Well, don' you worry, lovey. If Abu Bakr Al-Aleaqarab has your fearless fuckin' leader, he'll be well taken care of."

"I thought you fundamentalists didn't go in for swearing," I said.

"Only swear in English."

"Because Allah doesn't speak it?"

"Fuck off."

I left them to it and went on a scavenger hunt. I had two full mags plus the one in the M4 with maybe three rounds. On my webbing I had one AP frag grenade, and one smoke. I also had a ka-bar and a sharpened HB pencil for when a quick drawing might suffice to get us out of trouble. "Ammo check," I said over the comms. It was soon clear that we were all sucking fumes ammunition-wise. I picked up an IS AK from the dirt and gave it a shake. A stamped receiver, rather than a forged one. Russian-made. Next to useless if accuracy was required. It fired 7.62 x 39 mm rounds incompatible with the M4, which consumed smaller, lighter ammo. An AK could pack a hefty punch and kill as well as any other rifle, but you had to get close. "Inferior goods going cheap in aisle nine," I told the unit. "Get 'em while they're hot."

Alvin sauntered over. He motioned at Abdullah with a tilt of his head. "What are we gonna do with him, boss?"

Yeah, the Brit's survival was kinda inconvenient. Carting the guy across country would not be easy. There was also the chance that he may take the opportunity to give us away if a suitable moment presented itself. But there was the troubling reality of the Unified Code of Military Justice, which frowned on killing in cold blood, even the enemy. "He might be useful to the intel types across the border," I said, reaching.

"He's a grunt, boss. Not gonna be much he can give anyone, except maybe the shits."

True. He seemed good at that. "Lemme sleep on it."

Sixteen

Ronald V. Small @realSmall
I never said I liked Germany less than England. And I never said
Scotland was part of England. Fake news!

The two young Arab fighters stood by, Jalil and another fighter
whose name he did not know. Their beards were long and unkempt,
their skin deeply tanned and filthy with fire soot. They could be
brothers. Both were of slight build but Jalil was tall, well over six
feet. They said he was a high jumper at Cairo University before
answering the call of jihad.

"What is your name?" the Scorpion asked the short fighter.

"I am Imad bin Askr, Lord," he replied.

"Where are you from?"

"From Saudi, Lord."

"Imad and Jalil. I need you to do something."

"Yes, Amir," said Jalil, eagerness in his eyes. "What are we to do?"

"When we are finished editing the video later in the day, after
Durhu prayers, you will take the USB stick to Raqqa. You will not
draw attention to yourselves. You will find an Internet café and you
will upload videos to YouTube. Go only to Raqqa and return. This
is a sacred task that I entrust to you."

"Allah, may his name be praised, will watch over us."

"He will." Al-Aleaqarab could see that they were in awe of him. It was pleasing, if only because it guaranteed effort and commitment. "Now, stand over there," he motioned to them. "You are in the shot." The Scorpion turned and readied himself for the task ahead.

* * *

They were on their knees, heads covered with black hoods, hands taped behind backs, ankles also taped. The Scorpion stood behind them dressed in a black loose-fitting top and baggy black cargo pants, flanked by a pair of black standards hanging limp in the still, mid-morning air. His head was wrapped in a black scarf so that only his eyes were visible, hands hidden in black gloves.

The setting chosen for this most important video was a barren, flat and featureless desert. A metaphor, in the Scorpion's mind, for the end of hope. It would also be impossible for the West to place the location. It could be anywhere in Syria or Iraq.

Men adept with technology fussed over the DSLRs on tripods, three cameras covering the scene from different angles, muttering to each other like uncles discussing family scandal.

"I am waiting." The Scorpion snapped, his impatience flaring.

"Amir, apologies. But now we are ready," said a camera operator.

"Then begin."

The operator raised a finger and counted down, "*Thlatht, athnan, wahid…*" and then pointed at him.

With the tape running, the Scorpion's first action was to remove the scarf from his face and the gloves from his hands, much to the consternation of his men. *They would uncover my identity soon enough. But I will embrace the light of the desert and not cower in the shadows.* "My name is Abu Bakr Al-Aleaqarab. I stand before you with no concealment so that you may know the face

112

of deliverance." He raised a mutilated hand holding a long curved blade, pointing it at the camera and the millions who would hear his voice.

Seventeen

Ronald V. Small @realSmall
The world is a terrible place and that is why we have America.

Schelly reached for the ringing handset beside the bed and resisted the temptation to snap, "What!". Instead she mumbled into the plastic, "Hello," her brain groggy with sleep as she glanced at the bedside radio, the numbers rolling over to 0932.

"You were asleep?" Colonel Gladston asked. "Lucky you, Jilly," he said before she could reply. "Wake up, Major, you've got things to do."

"Yes, sir. I'm up, sir." *Four hours sleep. Thanks a bunch, boss.*

"Hamilton has called an urgent briefing in DC. You've been invited."

Hamilton, Hamilton... The name was familiar, but not enough to penetrate the remnants of sleep. And then, suddenly. *Oh, shit!* "You mean CIA Director Hamilton, sir?"

"Do Hamiltons come in mixed dozens, Major?" Gladston asked dryly.

"Um..." *No wonder your wife left you.* Schelly sat up, put her feet on the carpet and rubbed the sleep from the corner of an eye.

"Forget it. Pack for a four-day turnaround. I'll see you at base ops in sixty-five minutes in Class As. The SECDEF will be

114

in the meeting along with some other brass. You wanna make a good impression."

"Yes, sir." Schelly was already on the way to the shower, naked, grabbing a towel from the back of her bedroom door. *The SECDEF? I've been specifically invited? What the hell's this about?*

"Have someone pull together all available material on Quick-step 3."

Okay, there's a clue. Kinda ...

He continued, "Get it forwarded to our liaison in the Pentagon. We'll need ten copies, appropriately stamped with classification and handling instructions. Old school. No electronic devices where we're going. Old school. Also, get whatever you can on Temurazi Kvinitadze Sumbatashvili."

"Sir?"

"The Scorpion. C'mon, Jill, wake up. Make that shower a cold one."

"Yessir," she replied as the line went dead. *Asshole.*

Eighteen

Ronald V. Small @realSmall
ISIS, we have SEALs, so many SEALs. Remember that …

The distant ridge soaring high off the desert plain. Here and there it glowed in the late afternoon as might rivers of molten gold. Night was only hours away, but every jihadist knew the darkness was more perilous than daylight. Helicopters, drones and bombers could see clearly where the unaided eye could not. The Scorpion's jihadists had only one set of night-vision scopes amongst them, but the fighter this was entrusted to was not among them, left behind at the warehouse – a regrettable oversight. It was said that there were caves in these hills, some carved by Allah and others by man, and none of the West's technology could look inside them.

The roads here were heavy with ruts and potholes that made the going slow, but there was no traffic, only the occasional goatherd and, insha Allah, one had been abducted to provide guidance to the lesser known caves. The Scorpion took in the fading light through his window and was relieved to see that the skies above were clear of contrails.

In the rear seat the general dozed fitfully, struggling to remain conscious. He had lost much blood and his skin had the familiar gray pallor of intense pain, infection already beginning to gather in his wounded foot. They had driven most of the day, which hadn't helped the general's condition, but at least there was room in the Beemer. The headlights swept the dust ahead, the ZPU technical appearing occasionally, bouncing on the roads, the two badly wounded fighters laid out in the bed on either side of the guns, and a goat stolen from an untended flock tied to the guns' pillar.

Valeriy Petrovich, President of the Russian Federation, seated beside General Yegorov, had said almost nothing since their capture, choosing instead to fix an unblinking stare on the Scorpion, pure in its hatred and condescension. "My hands are numb," he announced suddenly. "The circulation is cut off."

"Mr President, you will be fortunate if that is all we cut off," replied the Scorpion.

"I need to take a piss," Petrovich said.

Al-Aleaqarab passed him an empty water bottle.

"How do you expect me to use that with my hands bound behind my back?" replied Petrovich.

"Then relieve yourself into your pants. Or wait. Our day's journey will soon be over."

"Where are you taking us?"

"To the end of the world as you know it."

"Spetsnaz will find you and kill you."

"I am a devout Muslim engaged in jihad, so death for me is a welcome blessing. It holds no fear." The Scorpion turned his back on Petrovich. *There will be plenty of time for talk.*

The goatherd pointed the way from the front seat of the technical, and brought the vehicles hopping and struggling along various trails deep within two twisted fingers of rock at the base of a high plateau. The small convoy eventually stopped beneath a copse of gnarled and dusty sun-scorched trees as the last rays of the sun dipped below the horizon and the first stars appeared in the evening sky. Ortsa parked the BMW beside the Toyota, beneath the thin canopy provided by the trees, as the third vehicle in their convoy, another black Toyota utility, pulled up behind with a squeal of dry brakes.

"Cut their bonds," the Scorpion told Ortsa, motioning over his shoulder, adding, "Where can they run?"

"Yes, Amir," the Chechen replied. He got out of the car, pulled the Russian president from his seat and sliced through the tape binding his hands and his ankles.

Petrovich massaged his wrists and stumbled immediately to a tree where he wrestled with his fly and stood there for an age, swaying, groaning occasionally, one hand holding a low bough for support.

"You and you," the Scorpion said, pointing at two of his men standing near Thalib, a doctor from New Zealand. "Remove the general to the cave. Be careful with him. And help Thalib see to our wounded." The rest of the men prepared the vehicles, draping engines and exhausts with space blankets to hide the heat signatures from thermal scopes. Mines were also set to provide a perimeter defense as weapons and other essentials were transferred to the cave.

The Scorpion called to the goatherd, who was entranced by the ZPU, staring up at it in awe, sensing the power of the anti-aircraft guns. The boy, the Scorpion noted, was on the edge of a gangly adolescence. A large open sore on one of his cheeks was festering, weeping. The Scorpion had seen this before, the disease that ate the flesh. "Do you have any more of these, boy?" The Scorpion asked him, motioning at the ugly abscess. "No, Amir. My younger brother has one on his leg. It is hard for him to walk."

"What is your name, boy?" The Scorpion asked, brushing flies away from his face, warning others away with a wave of his hand.

"Zuti."

"Are you devout, Zuti?"

"I pray five times a day, Amir."

"Who was Abu Bakr?"

"He was Mohammad's best friend and the first caliph."

The Scorpion put his hand on the boy's shoulder and sensed the recoil, the boy's eyes fixed on the wreckage of his fingers. "Do not be afraid. You have been well schooled, Zuti. Do you know the Ayah al-Kursi?"

"I know it," he said, his voice cracking into a higher register.

"Tell me then, if you know it."

"Allah! There is no God but He, the Living, the Self-subsisting, the Eternal. No slumber can seize Him, nor sleep. All things in heaven and Earth are His. Who could intercede in His presence without His permission? He knows what appears in front of and behind His creatures. Nor can they encompass any knowledge of Him except ... except ..."

"Except what he wills," said the Scorpion, prompting him. "Go on."

Zuti continued, "His throne extends over the heavens and the Earth. And He feels no fatigue in guarding and preserving them, for He is the Highest and Most Exalted.

Alah, the Most High, speaks the truth.""Very good. It is beautiful," said the Scorpion. "Words from the mind of God, given to Mohammad." He gazed up and willed there to be a crescent moon, but there was none, though the stars were becoming visible in the fading light. Soon the night would glow with the brilliance of a billion stars sprayed across the darkness. "Tell me of your ambition here on God's earth."

"To prepare myself for eternity, Amir."

The Scorpion found himself admiring the boy's piety. For him, the world was as simple and as pure as it ought to be. "Thank you for sharing the knowledge of this cave with us, Zuti. How many people know of it?"

"I have come here with my uncle," he said, brushing the flies gathering around his sore and at the corners of his mouth. "I have two brothers. They know of it. And perhaps my father, too."

"But no one knows that you are here now?"

"Only my goats," he said, grinning.

"Again, I thank you for showing us this place. We fight for the glory of Allah. But you should go home now. Your father will be worried.

Assalamu Alaikum warahmatu Allahi wa barakatuhu," said the Scorpion. *Peace be upon you and Allah's mercy and blessings.*

Zuti replied, "*Assalamu Alaikum warahmatu Allahi wa barakatuhu.*"

The boy turned and picked his way back down the road. His head occasionally bobbing from sight behind rock outcrops.

"Ortsa …" The Scorpion beckoned and the Chechen offloaded the goat he was carrying to another fighter and joined the Amir. The Scorpion pointed at the AK slung over the fighter's shoulder and Ortsa passed it to him. Burying the stock in his shoulder, checking that the safety was off, and resting the magazine on his knee, the Scorpion took aim.

"It fires low and to the left," the Chechen advised.

The crack of a single shot rolled through the hills and Zuti's bobbing head disappeared in a red mist. The Scorpion handed the carbine to Ortsa and said, "The boy is with the Highest and Most Exalted and he shall praise me for his introduction to Paradise." He waved away the flies. "See that his earthly body is properly bathed and shrouded before burial."

"Amir," said Ortsa and chose two men to accompany him.

* * *

The animal's incessant bleating was stopped only when its mouth was held closed. "*Bizmillah,*" the butcher said, *In the name of God,* and cut its throat. Barely a twitch animated its muscles as the knife severed arteries, veins and windpipe. The spinal cord required some concerted sawing, but the head soon came free and the carcass was drained of blood and gutted, the jihadists eagerly awaiting the day's main meal. The smell of roasting meat soon filled the cavern, firelight dancing on the walls and smoke rolling against the high ceiling.

The Scorpion sensed the mood of his men. Their morale was excellent. Food was coming, they had won a brief but intense skirmish and the spoils of this small victory were two of the most powerful enemies of the caliphate. Every now and again, the jihadists turned furtive eyes on the president, set apart in a natural alcove. How was it possible? How could the Russian tsar and his top general have fallen into *their* hands? Only one conclusion made sense – that Allah must have personally bestowed on them this great and special bounty. This certainty awed them, and they felt privileged to have been singled out amongst all of the faithful. And surely this was proof, if further proof were needed, that they were destined to be favored in heaven. The Scorpion could see in their faces and hear in their voices – *we* are Allah's chosen ones.

Nineteen

Ronald V. Small @realSmall
Bad guys - we have many aircraft carriers and generals and they all do whatever I tell them. Your DAYS ARE NUMBERED.

"First chance we get I say we let these Americans and Russians dig their own grave," said Farib, leaning far into the engine bay of the Toyota utility. "When the night is darkest, we should look for the opportunity then."

Mazool pulled him back, off the fender. "What are you talking about?"

"I do not want to die here with these people," Farib hissed. "And for what, eh? They are dangerous – all of them. I think the American officer, the one called Cooper, is the most dangerous of all, although the big Russian scares me."

"I don't trust the Russians, but only because they are Russian. I do not know them as people. I have not made my mind up about the American."

"Good, then it is settled. First chance we get."

"No."

"Why do you say no, Mazool? Perhaps they'll push us ahead of the vehicles to clear mines, or use us as human shields."

"The Americans are not soldiers of the caliphate."

Farib snorted. "Do you know this for sure? I have no wish to find out. We have families back in Latakia to think about. They will be worried about us. Surely we have done enough."

"Forget about your mother, Farib. I told the Americans that we would guide them to Turkey."

Farib's voice rose in pitch. He ran both hands through his short hair. "Why did you make this offer? And on behalf of Taymullah and me? It does not take three of us to guide them over the hills. And my fear has nothing to do with my mother."

"So you would be happy to leave us behind? Is this the Farib that Taymullah and I have fought beside these last months? It takes three of us because we each know different paths over the border and this might prove useful."

"Admit it. The truth is that we are the Americans' prisoners, no different to that one." He gestured at Abdullah Abdullah sitting against an olive tree, his wrists and ankles cuff-locked.

"We are not bound like he is, or have you not noticed?"

"So we are not bound, but they would still shoot us if we tried to leave. Are we allies or not? If we are allies, we should be able to walk out."

Taymullah wriggled out from under the radiator and stood, well pleased with himself. "Yes, it is the same hose – the same engine. I can exchange them easily."

"You should ask the American leader first," Mazool told him. "There was talk the ambulance would be left behind."

"Ask this one?" Taymullah motioned at the American lying on his back in the shade. Was he asleep? It was impossible to tell with sunglasses hiding his eyes. The black soldier was also resting, both Americans having come off guard duty while the other soldiers took their place, patrolling somewhere out of sight. The Russians, too, were resting in the shade.

Farib dropped his voice to a whisper. "We don't have to wait till night. We could go now. No one is watching."

"Where are we going?" Taymullah wiped his grease-covered hands on the ground.

"Where have you been, Farib?" Mazool shook his head. "After all this time fighting in the streets of Latakia, how are you still alive? Did you not see what happened this morning when the caliphate tried to overrun us? The Americans were nowhere and then they were everywhere. Four against twelve – that was my count. And yet within moments," Mazool clicked his fingers twice, "the jihadists were no more. I think it will be safer to stay with these people than take our chances on the road. Also, you have not considered weapons. We have none."

Farib stood his ground. "These Americans and Russians will attract trouble, like they attracted the caliphate. There are many more jihadists out there. The whole world is looking for these Russians."

"Do you not have eyes and ears, Farib? The President of Russia could well be in the hands of the caliphate. Do you not see what will happen? We believed the war against these foreign barbarians was nearly at an end, but there are many crazy people who will look on the capture of President Petrovich as a sign from Allah. How many will flock to the black flag? Thousands? Tens of thousands? Hundreds of thousands? The war we had will be nothing compared to the war we will have."

"The Americans are going home," Farib countered. "They do not care about all of this."

"And we should be trying to change their minds about it, not running away."

"I am not running away."

"Then what do you call it?"

"Retreating, that's what I am doing. What do you think, Taymullah?" After a moment's consideration, Farib shook his head and added, "No, forget it. I know whose side you are on."

Taymullah peeled the grease from beneath one fingernail with another. "We have fought Assad and Daesh and all the other madmen with Mazool for six months, Farib. We have fought hard and we have seen things no one should see. Do you remember Hazim?"

Farib glanced away, reluctant to acknowledge the memories that haunted all three of them.

"Hazim the carpenter," Taymullah continued. "We found him in his shop, remember?"

"Stop," Farib demanded. "I do not want to remember."

Taymullah took Farib's face between his hands. "They sawed off his legs and arms and used them as the legs on a table. They put the rest of his body on the tabletop. We found him, the three of us."

"Please ..." Farib pleaded.

"The caliphate used his own tools to dismember him. Hazim made furniture for your family and for mine and for Christians and others, and so the caliphate made furniture out of him."

"Taymullah!" Farib swept aside his friend's hands, tears moistening his eyes.

"And the children they burned," said Mazool, "pouring gasoline on them and setting them alight, threatening the parents of other children with a similar fate if they would not point out the Yazidis, Christians and Shiites amongst us. Our neighbors. Our friends. So many atrocities. Like you, I also do not want to remember what I have seen. And now, when there is just a little light, with the caliphate on the run, disaster threatens to turn this around. Perhaps we can make a bigger difference here with the Americans than we ever made with bullets and rockets."

"Hey!"

Mazool glanced over his shoulder. It was the American officer calling him – Cooper. He was coming toward them, rifle attached to his chest, one hand in his pocket. But for the rifle, Mazool thought, he could be crossing the road, greeting a friend.

"Everything okay?" the American asked them. "You want someone to settle the argument?"

"Don't touch my face with your hands again. They stink of piss," Farib said to Taymullah and walked away, heading for the ambulance.

"What's the problem?" Cooper asked.

Mazool told him, "Farib believes you will kill us."

Cooper looked around the open field – at the bloody vehicles full of bullet holes, and the dead piled under a tree. "Mazool, we don't know you and you don't know us. So I guess a little mutual mistrust is expected, and maybe helpful – keeps us all on our toes. But I meant what I said. Do right by us and we'll return the favor and send you home with a balloon animal and candy."

"I am sorry?"

"We're good – you and us. Let's both work to keep it that way. You help get us to within sight of the border, as agreed, and we'll take it from there – that's the deal and that's all we ask." Cooper removed the shooter's glove from his hand and held it toward him.

A bargain was a bargain. They shook. The American's hand was large, dry and hard, like shaking hands with the bough of a tree warmed by the sun.

Cooper motioned in Farib's direction. "Your boy cool?"

"Yes, he is cool."

The American nodded. "I was thinking we would leave the ambulance behind. The duct tape didn't work and none of us has enough pee-pee to keep her going. Gonna take these two pickups here. Noticed your mechanic has been digging around underneath them. There a problem?"

Mazool translated for Taymullah and a brief exchange flew between them. "Taymullah says we should take the ambulance. He can fix it."

"Why's he so keen on the ambulance?"

"Because most fighters, no matter who they fight for, hesitate before shooting at it. Perhaps they think they may need it for themselves one day."

Cooper thought about it. "Sounds reasonable ... Okay, do what needs to be done. Prep the ambulance and those two," he said, motioning at the pickups, "and leave the others. Maybe pack away the black flags for a while until we get the lay of the land."

"And you will not go looking for President Petrovich?"

"No."

"Why not?"

"One, because it's not our mission. Two, because where do we start? And I have a three, four and a five, but they can wait."

"I would look where Sunni tribes have sympathy for the caliphate; where they can get food, water and gasoline. There is an area between the village of Al Bukamal on the Euphrates River and the village of Baa'j, which is north. There are villages in between."

"How do you spell that?" said Cooper squinting in the late afternoon sun. "I know an Al Bookerman. He owns a deli in Queens. Makes a hell of a Reuben sandwich. These villages. They far apart?"

"Two hundred kilometers."

"Right. That's like giving your home address as Maryland. With a bit of luck, we might stumble across Petrovich given fifty years of searching."

"There are not many people in this area. The villagers know if there are strangers around."

"Like armed Americans and Russians searching for their pals?"

"Yes," said Mazool, delighted that Cooper understood the plan instantly. "Daesh cannot resist a challenge, especially one from foreign infidels."

"You mean we should advertise our presence and let a force of unknown size, backed by unknown numbers of sympathizers, find us at a time when we have limited ammunition, no communications, no intelligence and no backup?"

Mazool knew he probably had the look of a man whose feet had just slipped out from under him.

Cooper continued, "Alternatively I hear Istanbul is a great place for a steam bath at this time of year. We leave once it's dark."

"For Istanbul?" Mazool asked, confused.

"I wish."

* * *

I left the Syrians to get the vehicles in order. I still wasn't sure about them, but I was equally sure I wasn't going to waste them without probable cause. Igor was next on my rounds. He'd stirred and was drinking from one of the bottles we'd filled at the stream. I fully expected him to spit and say, "Water, that stuff'll kill ya!" but not everyone's a comedian, right? I stepped under his tree and said, "I wanted to thank you for helping out earlier."

"Is okay."

"We're leaving soon. Heading for Turkey."

"No. Must find president."

"It's a big haystack out there, fella," I told him. "And there are others with more resources searching for that needle. Like half the Russian Air Force."

"Sleeping when helicopter crash. Failed duty to president."

Sleeping it off was more accurate, but, as I mentioned earlier, glass houses, stones, and so forth.

Rising to his feet, he continued, "I not protect president."

Okay, here we had yet another Russian assassinating the article – *my* duty, *the* president – but Igor was clearly linguistically challenged, more so than Natasha. He was also twice my size and three times hers. I looked up at him, blocking the rays of the sun, and decided to cut him a break.

"If we run into your countrymen, you can join them in the search." He grunted in response to this, either not understanding what I said or rejecting it. "Natasha also wants us to go looking for him."

He gave another grunt and went over behind a nearby bush.

"Fuck ambulance," he told me over his shoulder, watering the tree instead of our transport's radiator.

Right. I would be happy to drop both of these Russians off at the first opportunity. Their missing president was maybe a problem for the world, but not for good ol' Keep-It-Simple Cooper.

Check.

Twenty

Ronald V. Small @realSmall
The fake news only reports on bad things. If it had something nice
to say maybe more people would listen.

Schelly arrived in DC somewhat shattered from the 15-hour flight
from Al Udeid aboard a C-17. Those web seats are killers. But
exhaustion had given way to excitement, awe and trepidation on
arrival at Andrews Air Force Base, the Secret Service meeting her
and Colonel Gladston and escorting them to the White House.

The emotional roller-coaster ride continued when, seated in the
vast underground Situation Room, she had watched the Scorpion's
latest sickening YouTube video.

As it concluded on a still frame of the ISIS black flag, Schelly
realized that she had been holding her breath. *Jesus! Did I just see
what I thought I saw? What chain reaction of shit will this unleash?*

Looking around the room, it was clear everyone was equally
stunned by what they had just seen. This was not why she and
Gladston had been rushed to DC as the video had been launched
on the Internet while they were somewhere over Germany, but the
video and its content had changed the situation drastically. *Now
things are gonna get seriously fucked up.*

Looking around the table, this meeting – these people – was a new experience for Schelly. She was a backroom person, a "mushroom". A couple of the attendees she recognized, mostly from the news. There was SECDEF Margery Epstein and Edward Bassingthwaite, the Secretary of State. And the Director of the CIA, Reid Hamilton – his face was familiar, being a reasonably public figure. The President's Senior Strategist, Andy Bunion, was also a controversial personality almost never out of the press. But the others were a mystery: their roles, their responsibilities. And no one wore nametags, except for the military types in uniform – herself, Colonel Gladston and Admiral Kirby Rentz, the Chairman of the Joint Chiefs, whose nickname, Angry Kermit, was supposedly based on an enlarged pair of eyeballs coupled to a legendary gruff manner. She had yet to witness the manner, but there was no mistaking those eyeballs.

SECDEF Epstein was clearly agitated, like she was sitting on something sharp and unpleasant, and moved constantly in her chair. "Thank you all for coming here on such short notice," she began in her signature hard, dry voice, "but now you've seen the video I'm sure you would agree it was necessary. Clearly, this is going to motivate every crazy on the planet to do something vile in support. And that's just the fallout." She paused for effect. "But before we jump in, some housekeeping. Your job here today is not necessarily to come up with answers, but to share what information you have so that we can expedite a fulsome brief to our Commander-in-Chief. To that end, we have a stenographer who'll provide a written draft of this meeting." She motioned to a middle-aged African-American woman sitting at a separate table who did not look up from her machine. "It's also being video-recorded." The secretary pointed at the pod in the ceiling above the main table, bristling with lenses and antennae. "I'm sure I don't need to remind everyone that whatever's discussed in this room is classified Top Secret. So, Debbie," she said, motioning at a petit Vietnamese woman, "before we get underway here, and for the benefit of those who don't know you, give us the executive summary on you. Please keep it brief."

"Doctor Debbie Ng, NSA, Director of Media Analysis, Middle East section," she replied in a quiet, firm voice. "I speak Arabic and have lectured at NYU on the Qur'an and the hadiths and their place on the secular world. I've been heading up my section at NSA for five years."

Schelly assessed the woman: *You're Vietnamese-American ... were your parents refugees? No discernable Asian accent so you were probably born here. Pleasant face, tiny lips and nose. Pale skin. Rimless glasses – far sighted. You look thirty, but are probably closer to forty. A ring – you're married. You look and speak like the bookish quiet type. Stereotyping bookish quiet types says you're probably an animal in bed, especially after you've had a couple of drinks – your limit. I'd guess you have one child, because two would split your focus and you seem a very focused person. Your husband – my guess, a university professor. You're confident, used to giving opinions and having them listened to.*

Epstein said, "We can't keep a lid on this, can we, Doctor?"

Ng shook her head, looking over the top of her glasses, which were low on her delicate nose. "We're already half a step behind the networks, Madam Secretary. As you know, IS has over sixty media companies disseminating information. Conversely, as the organization loses men and territory, this number grows. According to SITE Organization that video was uploaded to YouTube a little over an hour ago, posted on jihadology.org, a clearing house for Islamic State ideology, along with multiplicity of other sites, and it appears that links were copied and emailed to all major news services in the Middle East and Europe, as well as to a range of sympathetic Facebook and Twitter bloggers. Unfortunately, we received it when the public did. We can shut down all of the sites, but, after years of practical experience, these people know what they're doing and they would simply shift to new servers and addresses. So, in short, no, Madam Secretary, we can't stop it. This one simply has too many leaks for us to plug."

Epstein clearly knew it would be a pointless exercise, but had to ask.

"Do we have a read on the reaction of the news services yet?" Admiral Rentz asked.

Ng continued, "Sir, I'll get a summary on that as soon as this meeting is concluded and pass it through the normal channels. Obviously, though, this is big news – the biggest. The media will dissect the video, extend their news programs, pull in various talking heads for discussion and opinion – anyone they can find. I imagine the reaction of the network and cable news services won't be too dissimilar to our own, sir – horror, pure and simple."

"What about from our Islamic friends? They condemning it with the usual this-has-nothing-to-do-with-Islam gusto we've come to expect?" Bunion snorted, clearly derisive.

"Yes, sir. Of course it is early days, but the moderate response is unequivocally one of condemnation," she said. Then, moving along to safer, more PC ground, she added, "So far, the world seems to be holding its breath, waiting for the Russian reaction."

A knock on the main exit door. Bunion, the closest, got up and opened it. A young female airman walked in as rigid as an automaton, made a b-line for Bassingthwaite, passed him a note, turned and walked out. The SECSTATE read the note and said, "Speak of the devil. We won't have to wait long." He raised the note. "Russian ambassador's private secretary. The ambassador's on his way over. Apparently not a happy camper. Go figure."

"What about the Russian media?" the admiral asked, returning his attention to Ng.

"Up to the time this meeting began," the doctor replied, "nothing from Tass or the government-owned or funded sources like Rossiyskaya or Izvestiya. Even the Russia Today channel is silent on anything substantial – other than outrage."

"Not surprising. There's no precedent for something like this," Epstein commented. "Don't even think we've got simulations covering this contingency. Have we modeled anything even remotely similar to this, Andy?"

"I believe the Pentagon has a situation based on the Russian president's assassination," Bunion replied, "but ..." he shook his head, "nothing like this."

"Admiral?" asked Epstein.

Rentz shook his head. "No, not in our wildest dreams."

DCIA Hamilton gave the woman beside him the faintest of gestures, indicating that it was her turn to speak. "Professor?"

"I am Professor Kiraz Başak," the woman announced. "A civilian contractor, currently on secondment to CIA from the Defense Intelligence Agency. My area of expertise is terrorist profiling, assigned to the CIA Middle East bureau. I have doctorates in international relations and Middle Eastern history. Also, I am a Muslim."

She smiled and paused, perhaps waiting for any objection. There was none, Schelly observed, unless she counted Bunion noisily choosing that moment to shift in his chair. The professor had taken the seat opposite her. Schelly assessed her the way one woman notices another who she believes is more attractive: with a mixture of admiration and envy. *Gorgeous black hair, shoulder length, fashionably cut. And you have that olive skin that never gets sunburned. I hate you. Are you forty? It's hard to tell. Eyes – gray-green and just the right amount of mascara to make them pop. Eyebrows, professionally shaped – those things don't happen naturally. Your arms have muscle tone – you do light weights. Maybe you play tennis. You're a C-cup. I bet they bounce when you run to the net."* Schelly was conscious of her own chest, which barely filled an eggcup. *"Lucked out in the gene pool, bi-atch. White blouse – silk, probably. Dark navy skirt, tight at the waist, but flouncy. Heels, too. Successful, smart, sexual.* Schelly wondered which part of her own body or appearance the professor didn't like. She couldn't imagine what it would be, but every woman had something. As for the Muslim thing, that surprised her. *Where's your headscarf?*

"If I might say," the professor continued, "if we were dealing with the assassination of the Russian president that would generate a markedly different reaction to the situation presented here where Petrovich has been captured, threatened, shamed." She consulted a pad with notes, and put down her glasses. "There'll be mass anger, a feeling of national humiliation, which will engender a desire for revenge and retribution. I would not be surprised if there was an attempt to shift the blame – that will be the Kremlin's own need for self-preservation. I do not doubt that heads will roll." She cleared her throat, somewhat embarrassed. "Excuse me – no pun intended."

Schelly noted that the professor's voice was serious and considered, but with the singsong lilt of somewhere exotic. And the *faux pas* about decapitation? Given what they'd just seen on the monitor, the misstep was somehow inexplicably charming. But the professor's clear embarrassment at having been accidentally disrespectful suggested a measure of self-deprecation, which Schelly found likeable. *I bet you drive the boys wild.* When Professor Başak spoke, the major had an excuse to look at her more closely, without being accused of staring: *full lips, clear lip-gloss. No foundation. Designer cat's-eye glasses you'd rather hold and use to accentuate your points than wear. Long fingers, long nails – professionally manicured, clear lacquered. A man's Omega watch. Diamond earrings, maybe one and a half carats apiece. Expensive, but unobtrusive. And that perfume ... Coco, by Chanel, isn't it?*

"It's just more of the usual senseless fanatical butchery," Bunion said to no one in particular.

"Mr Bunion," the professor addressed him, "if you would please excuse what I am about to say – yes, this is butchery and it is also fanatical, but it is in no way senseless."

"Yes, yes," Bunion said with what appeared to be impatience at academia, or perhaps *female* academia, and waved away the debate. "I get it, the Russian president is a powerful symbol; ISIS is on the ropes. They have him and this will raise them from the ashes. Cutting off Petrovich's head will carry all kinds of powerful symbolism."

"I agree with you on many points, especially the symbolism. Its potential for the rejuvenation of ISIS is undeniable, but you misunderstand me," said the professor. "Are you familiar with the Islamic term, '*fitrah*'?" She directed the question politely to the table, rather than at Bunion specifically.

The advisor responded gruffly, "Is it relevant to what will end up in the president's briefing? You know he doesn't stand for mumbo jumbo."

"Possibly, if you will allow me?" she said with a gentle smile that exerted its own pressure.

"Go on, then," Bunion insisted with another wave. "We live in a world of affirmation."

Where everyone has to be listened to and valued ... Even you, jerk, thought Schelly.

The professor ignored the disrespect and continued. "The term 'senseless slaughter' – we keep hearing it in relation to the acts of jihadists. But what this says is that we truly do not understand what we're dealing with. ISIL, ISIS, IS, Daesh, whatever you choose to call it, indeed all Islamic fundamentalists, believe that we come onto this world instilled by Allah with *fitrah*. *Fitrah* is the natural ability to distinguish between good and evil. But the West, with our secularism, atheism, a religion that worships symbols and saints and a holy trinity, and what Islamic fundamentalists see as our idolatry of wealth and pleasure ... They believe that all this has corrupted our *fitrah,* our ability to recognize Allah as the one true god. You must understand that, to an extremist, the single evil that rises above all others is the denial of Allah. It's because the West has done exactly this – insult Allah with our unholy ways, and mock Him with denial – that we face eternal damnation to Hell. Apostasy, not politics or oil: this is the reason they hate us and want to kill us. They don't envy our freedoms, as a former president once said. In fact, they want nothing to do with the freedoms we have. They see these freedoms as symptoms of apostasy and therefore an insult to the God who created all beauty. This is their 'sense', if you like, justifying the slaughter of those who we consider to be innocent bystanders. To them, they – we - are not in the least innocent. Murdering us is a true act of faith. So, we either believe in Allah, or we die. By killing non-believers, releasing us from our folly, the faithful are helping purify the perfect world that Allah made. And if you are one of the faithful and you are killed while enacting this sacred rite of purification, then because you were doing the work of God you will be welcomed into Allah's presence a hero and a martyr and enjoy all the rewards of Paradise."

"Raping virgins," said Bunion, shuffling paper, impatient. "Being a Muslim, is that also what you believe, Professor?" he asked.

"If you mean that apostasy deserves a death sentence, no, Mr Bunion, of course I do not."

"Because?"

"I am a Muslim, not a religious extremist. Like the vast majority of Muslims, I believe that the Qur'an is the word of God given to humankind as allegory and metaphor, not a literal path that cannot be strayed from.

You go, girl, thought Schelly.

Bunion grunted. "So, what you're saying is that the random attacks on civilians have had little to do with our invasion of Iraq and Afghanistan."

"Well, I do not doubt that those actions may have helped to radicalize more Muslims, but it is not the reason behind the fundamentalists' desire to see us all dead one at a time, or by the cinema or planeload full. The destruction of the World Trade Towers by jihadists occurred *before* our intervention in Afghanistan and Iraq. It is my opinion that the terror visited on us by these jihadists will not stop until there are no more terrorists because *that* is their divine duty: to kill us all, or be killed in the attempt and thus be rewarded for all eternity. Returning to my starting point, there is nothing at all senseless about their reason for wanting us all dead, as far as they are concerned. Perhaps we might be able to deal with the threat they pose if we were to accept this simple truth."

Schelly had heard similar views to the professor's expressed in the past, but she had never heard them delivered quite as forcefully or convincingly.

Epstein asked her, "Do you think it's possible that these ISIS thugs will negotiate for President Petrovich's release?"

"No, Madam Secretary, I do not. No matter what these terrorists say, Petrovich is as good as dead unless he is liberated."

That gave everyone something to think about. Into the brief silence came a new voice. "If you don't mind me asking, Professor, what flavor of Muslim are you? Shia or Sunni?"

DCIA Hamilton interjected, "For those of you who haven't been introduced, this is my new Associate Deputy Director, Bradley Chalmers."

"If your real question is to ask whether I have any jihadist sympathies, Mr Chalmers, that is the question you should ask."

These two are off to a good start, thought Schelly.

"Okay, do you?"

"Sympathies, no. Understanding, perhaps. And I am Sunni, as the Scorpion and ISIS professes to be."

Various eyes darted around the room, including Schelly's, looking for a safe place to be.

"And you don't believe in the Qur'an's call for jihad?" asked Chalmers, pushing on into the abyss.

Epstein assured him, "No one here questions the professor's allegiances, Associate Deputy Director."

"I am just curious, Madam Secretary," he replied. "And I mean no disrespect, Professor."

No, of course not. Schelly felt the discomfort in the room for the academic, but she was nonetheless mesmerized by the exchange. *Wow, these Washington types really eat their own.*

"You are curious because there are so few Muslims addressing the issues of Islam, so you wonder what I am doing here?"

The major looked from one to the other. They may have only just met, but it was plain that neither liked the other.

"That is not a question for me to answer." She turned to Epstein. "And as for offense, please, I do not take any. Conversation is what takes the place of conflict." To the table more generally, she said, "Fortunately for the prospects of world peace, the vast majority of Muslims have no love of war. I am one such Muslim."

"There are the passages in the Qur'an that call for jihad. Do you just, what? Disregard them?"

Schelly couldn't help but glare at Chalmers. *Boy, you don't let up, do you?*

"No, I do not disregard them," the professor replied. "They are the words of God. The hadiths also call for jihad. But like many Muslims, *my* jihad is not fought with bullets and bombs. It is my own personal internal struggle, a struggle of reason versus faith. This is a battle I fight every day. And if one side should eventually win a victory over the other, I believe I would thereafter be less than I am."

Chalmers gave the half-hearted smile of the outmaneuvered and covered his retreat with an apparently important note he had to make on the pad in front of him.

Pussy, thought Schelly.

"What's this – what did you call it? The hadiths?" Chalmers asked lamely, trying to prove that he had at least been paying attention.

"The Qur'an is the word of God. A hadith, of which there are many, cover the words and deeds of the Prophet Mohammed and were written many years, perhaps hundreds of years, later."

Chalmers nodded, ticked something unseen on his notebook. "So, unreliable."

"I believe much of the Bible was authored hundreds of years after the events it describes."

Chalmers ticked his pad again, a little more aggressively.

The professor confessed to the table, "I am married to a Jew, who follows his religion as I follow mine. And it's funny, you know, we argue about almost everything *except* the nature of God."

This small intimacy caused a ripple of laughter, even from Chalmers, though it seemed to Schelly that his response was somewhat pained. *Certain women, conventional types, would probably find you handsome, Mr Associate Deputy Director. But I'm not conventional. Do you not like women? Or Muslims? Or is it women with brains you don't like? Or all of the above? You're early forties, so given you're the ADD of the CIA, you're a high achiever. You're well groomed and you carry a slight paunch. You live a mainly sedentary lifestyle, punctuated with bursts of fitness and dieting when vanity dictates. I bet you're a wine snob.* She further observed that he was blessed with the kind of thick, salt and pepper hair that people voted for, or at least used to before the current occupant of the Oval Office made bizarre comb-overs fashionable.

"If we could return to the problem at hand," said Secretary Epstein, "what are the current figures available on the numbers of Islamic extremists?"

Professor Başak waited for someone else to speak.

"I would say, considerably less of them after Syria," said Bunion with a grin, which he exchanged with Chalmers whom he no doubt saw as something of a kindred spirit. "Thanks to Petrovich and his support of Assad."

Epstein ignored the thoughtless quip. "Anyone? Professor?"

Professor Başak leaned forward to answer. "We all know the estimates on the numbers who follow Islam – roughly a quarter of the world's population, around 1.6 billion and change. But there are still no reliable, consistent findings on the subset who are extremists, even less on those who might be given to extremism if pushed."

"It's true," said Doctor Ng. "We just don't know."

"I've seen research that estimates the numbers of jihadists as high as twenty-six percent of the global Muslim population, and potentially as low as one percent," said Hamilton. "One poll asked British Muslims if they thought the Charlie Hebdo cartoonist should be imprisoned and sixty-eight percent said yes. What percentage of Muslims would have said yes in Saudi Arabia, or

Egypt? And what about the figure that said seven percent of the world's Muslims thought the 9/11 attacks were justified? That's 112 million Muslims who thought it was fine to burn and crush thousands of innocent people."

"I wonder if that sort of reasoning is not helpful," Epstein cautioned.

"But that's the point, isn't it?" Hamilton responded, "We just don't know where this will go. How many Muslims could be induced to take up arms, given the right stimulus? If we take that twenty-six percent figure as the mark, we'd be looking at a potential army of around ..." he doodled on a pad, "Four hundred and sixteen million people. Okay, that sounds absurd. But so does even just one percent – 16 million potential jihadists making their way to Dabiq."

"You seriously think the Scorpion can carry off this 'End of Days' baloney?" Bassingthwaite snorted. "Surely not."

"He will if he gathers an army of 16 million," said Hamilton. "Just to remind everyone, ISIS has successfully crowd sourced terrorism, recruiting over 27,000 foreigners to fight in Syria and Iraq, mostly by posting videos on YouTube of jihadists separating non-believers, mainly westerners, from their heads. What's gonna be the reaction to images of the leader of a major world power meeting a similar fate, linked to a prophecy in the Qur'an?"

Twenty-one

Ronald V. Small @realSmall
Everyone wants to be an American, but it's just not possible. But America can be everyone's friend, if they play ball.

Zuti had not returned, but Hakim, his father, was not overly concerned. This happens, he told himself as the sun dipped and the stars rose. Perhaps one or more goats had become lost, or had fallen between rocks and Zuti had needed time to rescue the animals. When Zuti had not returned at Fajir, the dawn sunrise, Hakim was still not in his bed. He had spent most of the night awake, reassuring himself that Zuti would come back.

Fear for his eldest son bloomed in his chest when he rolled up his mat and heard the sound of familiar bells, several of his goats having found their way home unaccompanied. The goats were the family's only wealth. Zuti would give his own life before leaving them unattended. What had happened to him? Surely an accident had befallen him.

Hakim secured the goats in their pen and woke Labib, his second eldest, and Nur, his youngest son. He sent Nur to an uncle who lived nearby, while he and Labib searched for Zuti.

All day and into the early evening they searched, calling Zuti's name, but he could not be found. Zuti had not told him where he would be taking the herd and there were many places he could be. And so Hakim had gone to the village. Zuti was well liked, a clever boy who knew the Qur'an almost as well as any imam. Many people offered to join the search, but the desert was vast and the boy had disappeared without a trace.

Twenty-two

Ronald V. Small @realSmall
When things get very bad, you want America in your corner. But you'd better open your checkbook because there are no free rides. Period.

The secretary of state breathed in audibly and let it out between her teeth, as if she herself had only just grasped the scale of the situation now facing the world. "Okay, what have we got to go forward on?"

Colonel Gladston suddenly found his voice. "I am Colonel Desmond Gladston, Senior Watch Director, Central Command Combined Air Operations Center," he began.

"Colonel," acknowledged Epstein.

"Among other things, our organization manages forward combat control for air assets in the Latakia region of northern Syria," he continued. "We show the assets where to lay it down. We are here because roughly this time yesterday, we received a spot intelligence report from one of our special ops teams on the outskirts of the city. At this point I'll hand you over to my Deputy Chief for Intelligence, Major Jillian Schelly."

Lord, don't let me fuck up, Schelly told herself, feeling all eyes on her. She opened the folder stamped SECRET/NOFORM -

SECRET being the Quickstep program's classification and NOFORN, an acronym for No Foreign Dissemination, its handling instruction – drew out a sheaf of satellite maps of northern Latakia and handed them around. Superimposed on the map were four glowing blue triangle idents. "This is the northeastern edge of the city of Latakia. The idents are Quickstep 3," she began.

"You want to enlighten us about Quickstep, Major?" Bunion asked.

"Quickstep 3 is a Joint Tactical Air Control Party, sir. Three Army Special Forces personnel supporting one Air Force special tactics officer. Specifically, they were inserted several days ago to recon potential targets, and also set up a temporary ground-based navigation aid."

"And?"

"This was the unit's position when they called in the downing of one Russian Hind by a MANPAD, with another severely damaged in flight. Included in their report was the positive identification of Temurazi Kvinitadze Sumbatashvili, alias Abu Bakr Al Aljurji, alias Abu Bakr Al-Aleaqarab, otherwise known as the Scorpion – someone the whole world is now familiar with. It was his men who downed at least one of the Hinds. What ultimately happened to the damaged aircraft was unclear to the unit. The Scorpion is one of the few surviving quality veteran commanders ISIS has left in the field." She passed around various photos of the younger red-bearded solider in the uniform of a Georgian sergeant and more recent shots of him as an Islamic State fighter. There was no question that this was the terrorist in the video.

"So, let me get this straight," SECSTATE Bassingthwaite summarized. "One of your units actually witnessed the Russian aircraft being shot down, and saw this Scorpion guy, too?"

"We're getting somewhere – finally," Bunion added.

Bassingthwaite continued, projecting boundless hope, "Are the assets still in contact with this Scorpion? Are they equipped to take him out, and his men? Can they effect a rescue of the president?"

Whoa, you're getting way ahead of the curve there, cowboy. "Sir, unfortunately I'd have to say no – they are no longer in contact with the Scorpion."

"Why not?"

"Did your assets eyeball Petrovich?" Chalmers interrupted.

Can you let me finish? "No, sir. Quickstep 3's SPIREP did not include any mention of survivors or fatalities. They observed one helicopter severely disabled by an explosion, and a second Hind destroyed after being struck by a shoulder-launched anti-aircraft missile. The disabled aircraft flew off. They were sure it was a probable kill, but didn't observe this helicopter actually crashing. From the SPIREP, it seems unlikely there would've been survivors from the aircraft struck by the missile."

"So it's speculation on our part that Petrovich was in that second chopper," Chalmers said.

Why are you splitting this particular hair? Is this about impressing your boss? And we don't call them "choppers" anymore – that's a motorcycle. In today's AF we call 'em birds, okay? "I would say it's a reasonable assumption, sir. The Russians haven't lost any other assets in Syria that we know of and, as we can see from the video, it is this Al-Aleaqarab – the Scorpion – who has Petrovich hostage. *Duh.* It's a reasonable conclusion that Quickstep 3 did in fact witness the final moments of the Russian president's aircraft. That means what we do have is a rough approximation of the president's position – at least, his whereabouts approximately twenty-four hours ago. The terrorists can only move so far in so many hours in a country like Syria, though it will still be a large search area."

Chalmers conceded with a shrug.

"Major," said Admiral Rentz, "can we assume that President Petrovich, General Yegorov and this bodyguard, whose identity is still unknown, were the sole surviving passengers of the Hind? That aircraft carries eight passengers, plus crew, doesn't it? Is it possible that there are additional unaccounted for PAX? Were they killed? Captured? Do we know who usually travels with Petrovich?"

"Those are important details we'll be looking at after this meeting, Admiral."

Hamilton had been examining Schelly across the table and appeared to like what he saw. "Bradley, you can be our point man on this. Anything the major needs, okay?"

"Yes, sir," said Chalmers, pasting Schelly with a sloppy grin.

Great. Then I need someone different to your ADD. "Thank you, sir." Major Schelly then addressed the room more generally. "Quickstep 3 has had some technical problems with their comms. We're out of contact with them, but the unit is due to exfil shortly and we'll know more then."

"So, assets that could have expedited a resolution to this situation before it had time to get up a head of steam have broken off contact with the terrorists?" said Chalmers, a *tsk-tsk* in his voice.

Really? "Sir, on their initial sighting of those two Hinds coming to grief, Quickstep 3 was not aware that the President of Russia was onboard. But even if they did have this information, they have no latitude to do anything about it. They are on the ground in a limited and covert capacity, with no resources for much else."

"Bradley," Colonel Gladston said, weighing into the discussion, "I sense you think Quickstep 3 might have dropped the ball here. The officer in charge of the unit, Major Cooper, is very experienced as are the Army Special Forces soldiers who –"

"Wait, wait a second ..." Chalmers leaned back in his seat, hands on his head like he was witnessing a horrific accident he could do absolutely nothing to prevent. "I'm sorry, did you say Major Cooper?"

"Er ..." Colonel Gladston appeared suddenly hesitant.

"Major *Vincent* Cooper?"

The colonel deferred the question to Schelly with a glance.

"Yes, sir. That's correct." Schelly consulted the material in her folder, shuffling through it. "Major Vincent Cooper, special tactics officer, Silver Star won in Afghanistan for gallantry, two purple hearts, a couple of citations and other commendations, former OSI special agent. He's had an interesting career if all the redaction is any indication." She flicked through the papers. "Seems he recently separated from active duty. Luckily for us he transferred to the Reserve as an IMA."

"You did say luckily, didn't you?" Chalmers asked, as chalky and white as a dusted marshmallow.

She pulled a slab of paperwork and slid it across the table toward the ADD, extracts from Cooper's service record with a photo of the man paperclipped to it. In the photo, he was wearing light tan chinos and a navy polo shirt, the non-uniform of the OSI. Cooper had an intriguing face, Schelly thought. Vaguely handsome in some non-specific way. A trustworthy face, but with some lines that suggested either cruelty or pain. She couldn't decide. Maybe both. *Unusual for a service photo, you're not smiling, either, like you know this photo is never going to stand in a frame on a desk or a mantelpiece and be admired by a loved one. You're a loner. I think I'll like you, if we ever get to meet.*

Schelly glanced up at Chalmers. He didn't look so good, which quietly pleased her. *What is it about this Cooper guy that makes you look like you just found a turd in a sub you've already taken a bite out of?*

"So we can't contact this unit," said Epstein, "but can we at least get some eyes on them? Colonel? We don't want anything of ours shot down by the Russians."

"Madam Secretary," Gladston informed her, "we're on top of that. A Reaper has a pretty low radar cross-section and Russian fire control radars wouldn't trouble it none. I've spoken to a ..." he checked his notes, "... a Lieutenant Colonel Josh Simmons commanding the 42nd Attack Squadron at Creech. They're operating Reapers out of Incirlik so we should have additional intel on Quickstep 3's condition presently."

Gladston shared a look with Schelly and the major took notes.

"I've heard of Simmons. A good man," said Admiral Rentz.

The door opened following a gentle knock. The head of a young office type popped in and caught SECSTATE Bassingthwaite's attention. "Right, gotta go. Russian ambassador's sitting on my doorstep. Margery, you coordinating?"

"Looks like," she replied.

"I'll let you know how it goes with Rodchenko."

"See you when you're done."

"Got it."

Twenty-three

Ronald V. Small @realSmall
America and Russia share many interests in common. Mostly, that is other countries. We need to share and share alike.

"Come in, come in, Mr Ambassador, please." Bassingthwaite held the door open for Mikhail Ivanovich Rodchenko, the 68-year-old former GRU colonel, Russia's most senior diplomat in the United States. "This is a most terrible situation," Bassingthwaite continued. "President Small is outraged, as are the American people."

Rodchenko held up his hand for the SECSTATE to stop.

He looked angry, Bassingthwaite thought, but he wasn't sure. The man's face had been badly broken years ago in an auto accident, which had left it permanently set part way between a sneer and a scowl. He walked into the office, rolling his shoulders, reminding Bassingthwaite of a boxer who had hit the canvas too many times, the smell of vodka trailing him like steam from an old locomotive. The SECSTATE's next move was reflexive. It was early, but never too early for a true Russian to drink, the former military intelligence chief had once advised him at some frozen dawn service in remembrance of the battle of Stalingrad, as he passed around a hipflask stamped with the GRU's odd Batman emblem. "Please take a seat, Colonel," said Bassingthwaite, opening one of the panels in the wall to reveal a compact wet bar with a selection of exclusive spirits, wines and variously sized glasses.

"Yes, a drink. Good idea," the ambassador growled, lowering his body onto the sofa with an extended grunt. "I myself have had several good ideas already this morning. It is that kind of a day. You will drink with me, of course."

"Can't have you drinking alone, can we?" Bassingthwaite opened the compact freezer and removed the bottle of Iordanov, a most expensive vodka, made with water collected from an obscure northern European spring and kept on hand especially for the ambassador's visits. Pouring two fingers into a couple of heavy crystal tumblers, Bassingthwaite added rocks and passed a glass to the Russian. "How are the knees? Did the operation go well? You're walking better, I see." No more than a month ago, Rodchenko had had complete knee replacements performed at John Hopkins, quietly convinced the American hospital would deliver more certain success than the orthopedics at Moscow's Burdenko General. "They are still a little tender, though I continue with the exercises. You should see the physiotherapist. She is Russian. I am sure she is one of your spies – she is too willing not to be." He smirked privately. "I am hoping for a hip operation next so that her treatments may continue."

Is the physio one of ours? Bassingthwaite wondered. "Well, anything we can do to help, just ask." The leather armchair sighed as the secretary of state settled noisily into it while pretending to sip the vodka. "And Mrs Rodchenko?"

"As demanding as ever. But we are not here to talk about the wrecks that are my skeletal system, or the resistance to my wife's needs. Of course you have seen the video …"

"Yes, yes. Appalling. If there's anything we can do, you will let us know. It is times like this that true friends stand up for one another."

The ambassador examined the vodka in his glass, moving his hand in a manner that made the rocks spin. "We are confident that the situation will be resolved quickly."

"Oh, so you know where the terrorists have taken President Petrovich?"

"Our military has assured us that Russia's first citizen will not remain long in the hands of these scum."

Rodchenko's statement meant the opposite to Bassingthwaite's ear, honed as it was by a lifetime of diplomatic service – it was the word *assured*. "I am well aware of the sensitive nature of this situation for the Kremlin, and, forgive me for reading between the lines here, Ambassador, but perhaps you are less than certain of your president's whereabouts."

"We have the best people working on it."

In short, your people have no fucking idea, do they? Certainly Rodchenko appeared to be rather more stressed than a man sure that this emergency would end soon, and well. "What do you know of the situation that the media does not yet know?" Bassingthwaite enquired.

"Are you saying that your intelligence is running behind the media? Come, come, Mr Secretary. Your intelligence is omnipotent. I suspect you knew of this situation before even we did."

Bassingthwaite smiled and tried his best to inject some warmth into the expression, while his mind went to the fact that CENTCOM did have a team in the area. "We both know that our intelligence agencies don't know everything – Hollywood fiction. 9/11 should have dispelled that."

Rodchenko shrugged and polished off his vodka.

"Freshen that for you, Mr Ambassador?" Bassingthwaite asked, aware of the answer before he asked the question. *At least some things are known quantities.* He got up, went to the bar and poured the last of the bottle into the Russian's glass, adding fresh rocks.

"We have secured the sites of both crashed helicopters," said Rodchenko.

Both? Well, that's something we didn't know. "That was fast. Do you know what caused these crashes?"

"Terrorism," the ambassador said with a hint of irony. "Investigators are en route to determine the factors that brought them down.

When they have answers then perhaps we will share. Or perhaps not – neither of us are good at that."

Bassingthwaite examined the Russian as he sipped his drink. Rodchenko was being cagey and that suggested there was more going on here. "We have known each other for many years, Mikhail Ivanovich, which is why I am invoking our longstanding mutual cooperation and friendship to say –"

"No bodies were recovered from the aircraft accompanying our president's helicopter. However, several bodies were identified at the scene of the second crash – the president's helicopter. One of these was missing an arm."

"Lost in the crash?"

"No. It was amputated by a shotgun blast. There was a skirmish at the site. After the crash, the survivors were attacked."

"By ISIS," said Bassingthwaite.

"It is reasonable to assume is was ISIS, because it is they who have our president. The man who lost an arm –"

"Wait ... They shot it off?"

"To remove the Cheget chained to his wrist." The ambassador examined his glass. "Even in distasteful circumstances, I still enjoy this vodka." He took a mouthful and pushed it from one side of his mouth to the other. He swallowed. "You know of the Cheget?"

In fact, Bassingthwaite had gone into a momentary state of mild paralysis in order to process the enormity of this development.

"Mr Secretary?" Rodchenko prompted him.

"Mr Ambassador, I –"

Rodchenko cut him off. "Tell me ... What part did the United States play in these unfortunate events?"

That caught Bassingthwaite completely off guard. "What? I'm sorry? Did you say –"

"The hand of your CIA is all over this. Who shot down our helicopters? Our own experts believe it is unlikely that these two Hinds should be targeted and taken out by jihadists. Only two aircraft have been lost to ground forces in the entire conflict

– these two. What are the chances that the very helicopter transporting our president would be targeted? It doesn't, as you Americans love to say, add up."

"But, but this is ridiculous. We would never –"

"No, no, of course you would *never* seek to take advantage." The ambassador's words dripped with sarcasm.

"We would not deliver the President of Russia into the hands of killers. You know that. That's crossing a line. I wouldn't lie to you."

"Our spheres of influence, they constantly overlap. It is again almost like the old days. And now with our two presidents trading insults like schoolboys ..."

Oh God! "No, c'mon." Bassingthwaite shook his head vehemently. "What you're suggesting ... it's utterly unthinkable."

"The attempt to assassinate our president was cover. It was the codes, wasn't it? You wanted them."

"The codes?" *The Cheget.* "Look, that's absolute madness."

"We agree, then. Complete madness." Rodchenko levered himself up off the couch with the usual grunt and placed the empty tumbler on a side table. "You will hear from me again once our investigators are satisfied they have enough evidence to take to the United Nations."

"Mikhail Ivanovich –"

"Do not Mikhail Ivanovich me. The Russian Air Force has placed an unofficial no fly zone over Latakia. I would advise your air force of this. We do not want further incidents between our countries at this delicate time."

"I can assure you, Mr Ambassador, there wasn't a first incident. So how can there be a further incident?"

"Good day, Mr Secretary," said Rodchenko, swaying slightly on uncertain knees. "One last thing. You should know that we have raised our alert level to 'Danger of War'." He walked to the door, opened it and picked up his private secretary on the way out, while Bassingthwaite stood in the middle of his office feeling like a man on a holed rubber dinghy circled by sharks. "Danger of War" was the Russian equivalent of DEFCON Two, and meant its nuclear arsenal was being readied for launch.

"Fuck." Bassingthwaite tossed back the vodka he had been determined not to drink, and reached for the phone.

Twenty-four

Ronald V. Small @realSmall
Terrorists! You have no idea what you are dealing with. We have so many great options. And some of them are nukes.

The figure, dressed all in black, stood behind three men of varying age who were kneeling in the dirt, their bruised heads bowed, their clothes torn, scorched and bloody. The horizon was empty and lifeless, the desolate plain endless and baked the color of kiln sand. Wind ripped and snapped at the loose-fitting clothes of the figure in black. It seemed that the world was empty, save for the captor and the captured kneeling at his feet. Then the figure in black unwound the scarf obscuring his head, revealing a man in his forties with a scarred face and grizzled red beard patchy with scarred skin and gray hairs. He removed the black gloves covering his hands – raw hands, mangled and misshapen – and, raising a long knife blade that caught the brutal sun, he pointed it at the camera and spoke in heavily accented English. Arabic subtitles dissolved onto the bottom of the screen. "My name is Abu Bakr Al Aljurji. I am known as the Scorpion. I stand before you with no concealment so that you, the faithful, may know the face of deliverance."

President Small leaned in a little closer to the monitor. "This asshole. Wow. I mean, he's like for real, right?"

No one said a word. The video would answer the question.

"As you can see, I have captured a Roman Caesar, one of his supreme generals, and a bodyguard. Allah delivered them into my hands."

The film cut to a close-up of President Petrovich who ground his teeth, far from meek. He was on his knees, bent forward, his wrists tied behind his back and trussed to his ankles. Beside him, head bowed, was General Yegorov, clearly in pain. He leaned heavily against the Spetsnaz bodyguard, now identified by the CIA as Lieutenant Vladimir Leonov – thirty-two years of age, a qualified sniper.

The terrorist continued, "Only by the will of Allah could such a thing come to pass. Caesar and his general will be released when the armies of Rome arrive at Dabiq to fight the holy warriors of the caliphate. The age of the Mahdi is upon us. This I swear on the blood of a non-believer. I call on all true Muslims to submit. Wage war against the kafirs. Shoot them, stab them, slaughter them, for they defile the world's purity with their unholy ideas."

Abu Bakr Al Aljurji adjusted General Yegorov so that he no longer leaned but sat up straight. Satisfied that the Russian would not topple over, he kneeled behind the bodyguard, positioned the blade under his chin and began sawing it back and forth across his throat as he held the man's head in the crook of his arm. The bodyguard's eyes popped wide open and his mouth opened in a silent scream. He offered no resistance, blood gushing from the ever-widening slice. It began to spurt in thick pumping streams, the video cutting to another view of the dying man, his body convulsing. The Scorpion kept sawing until the head came away in his hands, the fountain of blood ebbing quickly. He tossed the severed head on the ground and it rolled to a stop in front of a camera lens, big and grotesque on screen, the muscles exposed in the neck slaked with desert grit but still fibrillating. The video focused on this image for several long seconds until the screen went black.

"Jesus ..." exhaled the president. "That's disgusting. I'm disgusted. That is why we need to wipe these people off the face of the Earth. This guy, the Scorpion. A seriously bad dude. Seriously. Why haven't we taken him out already?"

"There were a lot worse on the list ahead of him, Mr President," Admiral Rentz informed him.

"I can believe it," said the president, still coming to grips with what he'd just seen. "This is really bad. It's terrible. We need to smoke his ass."

"We have to find him first, sir," DCIA Hamilton said, hands clasped in front of him. Hamilton had seen the Situation Room in the basement of White House West Wing humming on many occasions, the room alive with people, its many video monitors and computer feeds spewing out information from assets stationed all around the globe. But today the room was almost empty. This was Russia's crisis. But for how long would it remain so?

"Well, what are we doing about that?"

"At present, nothing, Mr President," Bunion told him. "We don't know exactly where he is, on top of which the Russians have placed a no fly zone over the area."

"Did we agree to that?" asked Small, the bags under his eyes blowing up like pasties, a familiar tell for his stress levels.

"No, Mr President," Bunion continued. "We figure they did it to keep us out."

"Why would they want to keep us out? Maybe they've got something to hide."

"In fact, Mr President," said SECSTATE Bassingthwaite as he walked in, "they believe it's because we shot Petrovich's helicopter down, or at least had a hand in it."

"Stop," said President Small, infuriated by Bassingthwaite's sudden appearance. "You're late. Why are you late? I'm a busy man, you know that. I don't have time for you to be late."

"It was unavoidable, Mr President. I just had Ambassador Rodchenko in my office and he –"

"I didn't hear an apology for your lateness. I think I'm owed an apology."

"I'm sorry for being late, Mr President," said Bassingthwaite, appearing chastened as he took a seat.

"Okay. In the future, don't be late." The president waited, visibly impatient for the secretary of state to settle. "Now, did you say Rodchenko said we had something to do with this? He accused *us*?"

"Yes, Mr President."

Small was suddenly livid. He thumped the table with his fist, but not too hard. "Where do these people get off attacking us like that? It's tremendously disappointing." A sudden thought seemed to occur to Small and his tone went 180 degrees in the other direction. "We didn't, right? We, er, we didn't have anything to do with shooting Golem down?"

"No, sir," said Bunion. "We don't breathe unless we have your signature on it. That's the way it works."

"Good. I don't like mistakes." Small returned to his former bullishness. "Can we make a deal with this Scorpion? How much would it take?"

"Mr President, bargaining with ISIS has proved futile in the past. All these fanatics are interested in is fulfilling their prophecy from the Qur'an. We know how their minds work. Unless Petrovich can be rescued, he's as good as dead."

"You're saying there's nothing we can do … Well, Petrovich was becoming difficult anyway, right?" He checked Bunion for reassurance.

"A little vacuum in the Kremlin might be a good thing, Mr President."

Small grinned, his blue-white teeth sparkling against pale lips.

"Now if we could just organize for Chinese Premier Xi to be dropped into Syria too, that would free up a little space in the world,"

Bunion added, feeding off the boss's mood, enabling his whims, especially if he could use them to nourish his own agenda.

"See if we can arrange it, Andy," President Small asked with a chuckle.

"There is a complication, sir," Bassingthwaite said, his mood far more subdued.

"Oh c'mon, Eddy, why the long face?" asked Bunion and grinned at the president.

Bassingthwaite was reluctant to be the bearer of bad news, the president having a habit of blaming the person who delivered it, but he had little choice. "According to Ambassador Rodchenko, the terrorists have…" Bassingthwaite's throat tightened and he felt both hot and cold. "Sir, ISIS has acquired the authority codes for the launch of Russia's nuclear arsenal."

"What?" Bunion couldn't help himself. It just came out, his voice cracking in the middle of it.

"Most of which is still aimed at the United States, as you know," the SECSTATE continued. "The Russians recovered a body from the crash site of one of the helicopters. The terrorists shot the man's arm off to recover what the Russians call the Cheget, a briefcase chained to the deceased's wrist that contained the codes."

"The Cheget is the Russian version of the football that travels with POTUS," Admiral Rentz explained to the president.

"Are you … are you saying the terrorists now have nukes?" asked Small, all color drained from his face. "Is that what we are talking about here?"

"Mr President, it sounds a lot worse than it is," Bassingthwaite ventured, taking two shots from his puffer.

"Well it sounds real bad to me."

"The secretary of state is correct, Mr President," the admiral soothed. "The Cheget carries the Russian presidential authorization codes for a nuclear strike, not the actual launch codes for the missiles themselves. So we've caught a break there."

"What does that even mean?" asked Small, blinking back his own confusion.

"ISIS can't launch missiles at us, Mr President, nor do they have access to them."

"At least that's something, right? Am I right?" said Small, relaxing somewhat.

Rentz answered, "Yes, sir."

"Thank god. Still, this is crazy."

"Loath as I am to extinguish this ray of light," said Epstein, her voice rasping more than usual, "but merely having these codes gives ISIS a lot of power, especially when they also have the Russian president."

Small frowned. "But, if I'm hearing correctly, the codes are worthless, right?"

"Technically, yes – and the Kremlin will have changed the codes already," the admiral pointed out.

"But it will be our spin against ISIS's," said Hamilton. "We can raise any number of experts who'll say the codes are useless for the reasons pointed out, but now the terrorists know *the form* of the codes. And no matter what we say, you can be sure the media and the Internet will dredge up any number of experts who'll assert that merely having the codes will give ISIS vital clues that could help them hack into the Russian nuclear command and control computers. Whether it's true or not, this is an enormous psychological windfall for ISIS, Mr President."

Epstein squared up to the president. "Sir, we just sat through a briefing with the best minds we have on this and the consensus is that the situation will play directly to the percentage of the world's Muslims on the edge of being radicalized. Coupled to the news of the president's capture, having the nuclear codes in their possession will turbocharge the terrorist's recruitment message. We could potentially see millions of newly radicalized Muslims arriving in northern Syria to fight the armies of Rome – the West, us."

"I suppose we could just let them, Mr President," said Bunion with a smirk. "You need two sides to make a war, right? What if one of them doesn't show up?"

Small nodded, an eyebrow raised, impressed with this reasoning.

"It's not as simple as that, Andrew," Hamilton countered. "How many recruits do you think will choose to make a contribution to the ISIS war effort by wearing suicide vests to their local Walmart?"

Bunion's smirk vanished.

"Mr President," Epstein continued, "this is about the End of Days battle. Apparently it's foretold in the Qur'an. Getting their hands on Petrovich and the Cheget are like gifts from heaven. As the Scorpion said, 'Only by the will of Allah could such a thing come to pass.' This is exactly what ISIS needs to reinvigorate its cause and kickstart the flow of volunteers for jihad."

"So, give me some options," Small said. "You gotta give me options. What needs to be done to put an end to this?"

"President Petrovich would need to be rescued," said Hamilton. "Nothing else would prove to potential ISIS recruits that his capture was not Allah's doing, something foretold."

"The Russian no fly zone over the area means we can't get in there in a meaningful way without risking an incident, and tensions are already way too high to risk it," said Bassingthwaite, who added the news about the Russians ratcheting up their preparedness to "Danger of War".

"And what could we possibly do to help locate President Petrovich that the Russians aren't already doing anyway?" Epstein pointed out.

"We got that SEAL team on the ground, right?" the president reminded them. "SEALs can do incredible things. They're the best. The best of the best."

"There are no SEALs, Mr President," Admiral Rentz corrected him.

"No SEALs? Who told me there were fucking SEALs?" Small's temper flared. "How can you expect me to make good decisions if you give me bad information?" He thumped the table again.

"It's the big league here, people. Are you telling me I have to sit on my hands? That is not what the American people expect from their Commander-in-Chief. Not impressed."

"Sir, we do have a small joint Air Force and army special ops unit close to where the terrorists shot down Petrovich's helicopter," Epstein told him, feeling desperate for a smoke and wishing to god she hadn't kicked the habit. "But my understanding is this unit is under-equipped and under-manned. They can't be expected to make any meaningful contribution to the situation. They happened to be in the area, putting up a navigation beacon."

"What are you saying, Margery?" asked President Small.

"That I don't see what we could reasonably expect them to achieve."

Admiral Rentz agreed.

"Fact. One of ours is worth four or five of theirs," the president asserted. 'So you tell our team on the ground I said their Commander-in-Chief wants the Russian president found and liberated at all costs, and they're the boys I'm counting on to do it. Petrovich is a man I respect. He's also a friend. We have, from the first, had a mutual understanding. And if we have to kick some Russian butt along the way to get the job done, then we gotta do what we gotta do."

Admiral Rentz reminded him, "Mr President, we're talking about a four-man unit in a part of Syria swarming with jihadists, radicals, Assad loyalists, and now with pissed Russians who apparently believe we shot down their president."

"I think the Commander-in-Chief has given his orders," said Small in an imperious end-of-discussion tone. He considered for a moment. "We got any aircraft carriers in the area?"

"The *USS Dwight D Eisenhower* carrier strike group, sir."

"What else we got?"

"There's the Sixth Fleet, Mr President. That's in Italy."

"Well, let's get 'em on standby."

"Yessir."

"Andrew, you make sure that unit on the ground knows I am taking a personal interest."

"Yes, Mr President," said Bunion, his nose redder than usual. "I'll see to it."

"How's the little shit gonna do that?" Bassingthwaite muttered sotto voce to Epstein.

"Carrier pigeons," the SECDEF replied.

Twenty-five

Ronald V. Small @realSmall
Everyone knows there is only one heaven and one hell. It's the one
ruled over by God, the God who blesses America.

Schelly felt exhausted, but though the suite at Henderson Hall, Fort
Myer, was clean, spacious and the bed was large and firm and just
how she liked it, she just couldn't sleep. So instead Schelly sat glued
to the TV, sipping V8 juice. *You don't need the NSA's Director of
Media Analysis to provide an overview. Just turn on the television
and the parade is non-stop.*

On screen was an Islamic cleric, a self-styled moderate. He was
a heavily beaded man in his early fifties with droopy eyes that made
him look vaguely sad. He assured the reporter, "The demands of
these terrorists have nothing to do with our religion."

"But aren't there passages in the Qur'an as well as certain
hadiths that call on Muslims to kill the unbeliever?" An English
reporter from the BBC said.

"As there are similar passages in the Christian Bible," the
cleric countered, adjusting his charcoal-gray waistcoat over
flowing white robes. He seemed less certain of himself. "I could
quote them ..."

"But unlike the Bible, the Qur'an was dictated to Mohammad by the angel Gabriel, am I right? So this book is the actual, unaltered word of God commanding believers to kill non-believers."

"Yes, but –"

"And the hadiths are the accounts of what Mohammad said or did."

"That is true, however –"

"Muslims aren't going to argue with God, are they? You know, re-interpret *His* words? And Mohammed, they're not going to go against his views?"

The moderate swept away this uncomfortable line of questioning with a wave of his hand. "I can assure you, no one will travel to Dabiq. You do not understand Islam. It is a religion of love. All this is nonsense."

"Uh-huh," said Major Schelly to the television monitor and changed the channel. The Internet was already exploding with many voices calling on the faithful to take up arms, pledge allegiance to the caliphate and make Dabiq their pilgrimage instead of Mecca.

An hour of channel-surfing told her that broadcast network commentators and experts – religious and secular – were mostly being careful not to be inflammatory. The questions on the capture of the Russian president also generally followed a similar pattern: would the terrorists ever be inclined to hand over Petrovich? Could he be ransomed? What would a president of Russia be worth? Who would pay such a ransom? Russia? The UN? Wouldn't paying ransom money only encourage terrorism, which was the reason why governments claimed they never paid ransoms? Would Petrovich's capture alter this position? Was the West prepared to accept, as this Scorpion terrorist preached, that it was at war against Islam? Did the Qur'an actually foretell of a battle between Islam and the West? Did the prophecy predict a winner? Could anyone win? Could a prophecy be altered? Was fate etched in stone?

Schelly's head swam.

Many of these networks, she noted, had done their homework and were taking it upon themselves to educate the public with questions put to numerous experts such as: was it true the Qur'an also foretold that Islam would be on its knees as a result of this great confrontation? Why would Islamists want to bring about this calamity upon themselves and their religion? Did the Qur'an really foretell that, after the battle, Jesus would again walk the earth with the dead? Was this the same Jesus from the Bible? The same loving, peaceful Jesus of Nazareth? The shepherd of men? One network following this angle, with a panel including a priest and an imam, broadcast graphic footage, borrowed from various movies, of corpses digging their way out of graves on Judgment Day to join Jesus. Preppers everywhere were storming Walmarts for extra ammo and tins of tuna fish. Doomsday cultists were ecstatic.

The more practically minded commentators asked whether the Pentagon had modeled any estimates of casualties and wounded should the Scorpion's End of Days battle be fought. Were estimates of a million or more Muslims turning up to fight the so-called Army of Rome in any way accurate? And so forth.

Some experts aligned with the sad-eyed cleric and believed the confrontation would never happen. Others opined that the reference to Dabiq as the End of Days battlefield was not a literal one, and that if just a small percentage of Muslims decided to wage war against the West, the front lines of such a battle would be suburban schools, shopping malls and amusement parks, and, if that were the case, security forces everywhere would quickly be overwhelmed.

The one-line summary: the airwaves were in meltdown. Schelly changed the channel and saw that one enterprising news service had managed to land a reporter on the plain outside Dabiq. Drone footage showed that it was a very large plain stretching beyond the horizon, and the reporter, kitted out in a combination of battle armor and Armani, reasoned that it would certainly hold a couple of million soldiers. As Schelly watched, the report segued into

Google Earth style overhead shots of the plain with detailed *Game of Thrones*-like title sequence animations showing the clockwork movement of tanks, aircraft, and men around the plain. War porn. And, the icing on the cake, archival footage of President Small saying he would consider using nuclear weapons against a pressing adversary, as if this presaged their use: "That's why we have the things, right?" the commander-in-chief, dressed in bomber jacket and ball cap, had pronounced to cheering, newly graduating officers at the Naval Academy, Annapolis.

Another channel change. A masked demonstrator in New York threw a Molotov cocktail, its wick scribing a delicate parabola in the darkness before exploding against riot shields. It was a similar story in capitals around the world: Muslims demonstrating against Muslims; Shiites opposing Sunnis; rednecks versus liberals; Muslims marching in support of ISIS; moderate Muslims and non-Muslims marching in opposition to the jihadists. At a demonstration in New York, right-wingers waved placards pronouncing, "I told you so!"

Even the non-violent demonstrations held the promise of physical confrontation. Police were nervous. Containment was already an issue. One anti-terror law enforcement officer voiced everyone's fear: "How long before we get a truck driven into a crowd here, or a suicide bomber there?"

Schelly changed channels again and finished her tomato juice as Chris Matthews shuffled paper and chatted informally about the effect all this was having on the New York stock exchange. Stocks for Priceline and the Flight Centre Travel Group were through the roof, due to anticipated windfall revenues. Made sense, he said. All these combatants making their way to northern Syria would have had to book their flights *somewhere*, right?

Vaguely in disgust – why, she couldn't articulate to herself – Schelly was about to turn the monitor off when Matthews interrupted some other inane observation mid-sentence and touched his earpiece. Experience told anyone who consumed these shows that breaking news was coming. Matthews didn't disappoint. He cleared his throat. "Okay, well, news has just come to hand ... Seems there's another video from the terrorist who calls himself the Scorpion. It has been uploaded onto numerous websites. I have to warn you on behalf of the network that viewer discretion is required. I'm told this video is disturbing. If you're at all squeamish, folks, now might be a good time to go tuck the kids into bed."

The screen went to black with a title that read, "Viewer discretion advised". A bar dissolved into place at the base of the black frame with the words, "Latest ISIS video". A picture materialized in the black frame – the Scorpion dressed in black. Only his head and shoulders were framed. Behind him, the same endless sky, the same flat, baked-biscuit expanse of desert Schelly remembered from the first video, though the light was different this time. Harsher, more overhead.

A breeze tugged at the terrorist's beard. "Sons and daughters of Allah the Merciful, whose wisdom and perfection is sublime," he began. "As you know, Allah has delivered unto the faithful the President of All Russia. And many other bountiful gifts have been delivered into our hands along with him. I showed you his general, a great prize. And now I would show more of Allah's promise to us that he smiles on jihad and is warmed by its fires."

Schelly turned up the volume. *Why do these criminals always use language that makes them sound like they're delivering a sermon written by a corny B-grade screenwriter? Why can't he simply say, "I've got your president. I showed you that yesterday. And now I've got something else I'm going to shove up your ass."*

The Scorpion produced a compact but slightly scorched leather briefcase that looked incongruous in his mangled hands. A chrome chain dangled from the briefcase's handle.

What the ...

"This is no ordinary briefcase," the Scorpion pronounced. "It is the Cheget. As your military will confirm, the Cheget possesses the codes for the launch of Russia's nuclear arsenal."

Oh shit!

"Tremble in fear if you have no belief in Paradise, for this is truly a weapon for the End of Days. And do not listen to your leaders who might say we do not speak the truth. The Cheget always travels with the president, wherever he goes."

The Scorpion retrieved the chain and pulled into view an amputated forearm, faintly green in color, manacled at the wrist to the chain's other end.

Schelly unconsciously sucked in a sharp breath as her hand flew to her mouth, aghast. She was aware that the arm's fingers were black, but couldn't immediately figure why.

The Scorpion took a step toward the camera and, cradling the black fingers in his own scarred digits, pressed the dead finger pads against a pane of glass in front of the camera lens. The Scorpion rolled the fingers from side to side in such a manner that clear prints were left on the glass, which the lens of the camera did its best to focus on. The Scorpion then retreated to his previous position a distance from the camera, still holding the briefcase and arm, his image blurred by the black prints on the glass. He turned to face another camera. "I say again, I have no doubt that your own corrupt governments will attempt to lie to you about the truth of the weapon Allah has delivered to us. Do not allow yourselves to be deceived. The prints of the Cheget's carrier are proof and can be easily confirmed. I have spoken to you of the End of Days. And now you know that it can be delivered. An eternity in Paradise will be the reward for all who accept Allah's perfection. But for those who deny him, an eternity burning in hellfire awaits."

The video flickered and ended.

"Jesus Christ," Schelly murmured. The screen cut back to Matthews who was visibly shaken. Words were failing him. He looked off camera a couple of times at unseen people, like he wanted some help or perhaps some reassurance.

He cleared his throat. "Well, I … That's …That's probably, you know … probably one of the most shocking things I have ever seen."

A tone sounded, a tweet come through on Schelly's Twitter feed. The screen said it was from President Small. She swiped it open. "Barbarians. Very, very horrible. We will wipe you from the face of the Earth." And then another one. "If anything happens to Petrovich, we will send incredible devastation your way like you have never seen before." Good threat. Love to know how we make good on it, she wondered, still dazed by the images that had played out on the television.

Schelly's cell rang and vibrated – a call this time. Half in a trance, she answered, "Yes … um, Major Schelly."

"Major, Secretary Epstein," returned the dry, oddly masculine voice on the line. "Where are you at this moment?"

Schelly snapped out of it. It wasn't every day a major received a call from the SECDEF. "Fort Myer, Madam Secretary."

"Can I presume you caught the video released just now?"

"Yes, ma'am."

"I'll see you in my office at the Pentagon in thirty minutes. Have you received your credentials yet? You'll need them."

"No, ma'am."

"They should have reached you by now. I had them sent over personally."

There was a solid knock on the door. "Oh, wait," said Schelly. "Maybe they've just arrived."

"I'll see you shortly, Major," Epstein said, ending the call.

Doesn't anyone ever sleep in this town? Schelly opened the door on a US Navy Yeoman First Class. His nametag said Goldman. *Big soft man, big soft brown eyes…*

A few moments later, she said thank you to the yeoman and closed the door. The envelope he left with her contained various badges for access to all required areas in the Pentagon, and an encrypted government phone plus passwords and a charger. She did as the yeoman instructed – memorized the passwords and then burned the card.

"What's your take?" Epstein asked Schelly with no preamble other than a gesture for her to take a seat on a sofa parked behind a coffee table. "On the video."

The question surprised Schelly, the broader strategic questions being beyond her pay grade. *Maybe it's just a conversation starter.* "Ma'am, I think it couldn't get much worse."

The SECDEF scoffed and got up from her desk to join Schelly in the breakout area of the spacious office. "You haven't been around long enough, Major. It can *always* get worse." She sat in an armchair, leaned forward and lifted a cut crystal jug to a glass. "Water?"

"No, thank you, ma'am."

Epstein poured some for herself, picked up the tumbler and rolled it back and forth between the palms of her small, bird-like hands. "The more responsible media will soon come around to reporting that ISIS won't be able to use the codes to launch missiles."

"Can I speak freely, Madam Secretary?"

"Of course."

"The people who'll be most influenced by the Scorpion won't see the distinction. The Scorpion has the Russian president *and* his nukes. He has won a massive public relations victory."

"I agree. Which is why we need to do what we can to stop this before it goes any further. And that brings me to the substance of why I asked you here this evening. Your special ops unit in northern Syria. The commander-in-chief wants your assets to locate and rescue President Petrovich. Colonel Gladston has been briefed and you run that unit."

Whaaat? "Yes, ma'am."

"Then get it done. Whatever resources you need. Your orders are being cut as we speak. We've allocated you an office here with the Joint Chiefs."

Schelly's mind was already crammed with issues and problems, primary among them the plain fact that Quickstep 3 was spectacularly underprepared for the task it was being ordered to execute.

"Something the matter?" Epstein asked.

Where do I begin...? "No, ma'am," Schelly replied.

"You know where your team is currently?" Epstein asked.

"We're working on pinpointing them as we speak, Madam Secretary."

Epstein took a moment to sip her water and gather her thoughts. "Major, this cannot be a zero sum game. I know we're asking a lot of your people, but if there is the slightest chance that we can positively affect the balance, we have to take it. This End of Days thing ... If it happens ... Well, we just can't allow it to happen, that's the bottom line." The SECDEF's phone sounded. She plucked it off the table and scanned the screen. "Do you follow the President on Twitter, Jill?"

"Yes, ma'am."

"He has just now tweeted, 'Mr Scorpion we have the very very best military in the world. We will bury you...'" Epstein looked hard at Schelly. "The commander-in-chief has put the shovel firmly in your hands, Major. Any questions?"

Jesus Christ, where do I start! "No, ma'am."

An alert on Schelly's phone. She glanced at the screen - the president's latest tweet.

"We'll need your update and operational thoughts by 6 pm this evening," Epstein continued. "You'll join us at the Situation Room."

Jesus! "Yes, ma'am."

"Not a lot of time, I know. Tell me ... What did you think, generally speaking, when you saw this latest video?"

"Ma'am, I was thinking that the Scorpion knew he had the Cheget when the first video was shot. He held back that information so he could take another opportunity to turn the screws, raise the terror stakes ..."

"And."

"Both videos were shot at the same location, though in today's video the sun was higher overhead, which means it was shot later in the day. Could be the Scorpion wants us to believe he's, y'know, bivouacking out in the desert – marking time, staying in the one place. He knows the world is looking for him, and he wants the hunt concentrated on the sand between Syria and Iraq, where the video was probably taken and where we know ISIS has some support from Sunni villages. But I think that's the last place he's gonna be right now."

"According to the NSA, the videos were uploaded from an Internet cafes in Raqqa. The CIA's got eyes on that café, along with two others still functioning in the city, but frankly we're not expecting any hits. ISIS knows how to hide in plain sight and they know how to use the net."

"The videos are being examined?"

"Frame by frame by the Defense Imagery Management Operations Centre."

"And the fingerprints, ma'am?"

"The NSA and CIA have confirmed the prints on the video within a certainty of eighty-nine percent, which is to say, there is no doubt. They belonged to one Vassily Borinkachov, the official holder of the Cheget." The SECDEF paused to let it sink in. "I'll see you this evening." She stood.

Schelly also stood. *They blew his arm off...*

Walking away from the SECDEF's office, Schelly was aware of her own heartbeat and the feeling of wanting to run somewhere. But where? The Scorpion's possession of those codes was unthinkable. And somehow America's effort to stop WWIII had come to rest on her shoulders and those of a four-man special ops squad lost somewhere in a corner of Syria where chaos and the fog of war were the only certainties. She slumped against a wall, feeling utterly out of her depth.

Twenty-six

Ronald V. Small @realSmall
Terrorists beware. You haven't met our SEALs. They are the best soldiers in the world. AND THEY DON'T LIKE YOU!

"Never seen so many BTRs," Jimmy observed.

"Maybe the Kremlin's decided to annex the joint," I suggested. BTRs were the Soviet-era armored personnel carriers still being used by Russian ground forces. I crouched with Jimmy behind a cluster of adolescent trees on the side of the hill overlooking the main access road to these parts, a patchwork ribbon of broken asphalt and dirt that wound through the dusty olive-green hills. Much smaller than a highway, it was still a significant east-west access road, and that made it popular with anyone in a hurry as the main thoroughfares were clogged with refugees. Now that Jimmy mentioned it, there were a lot of the Russian troop carriers on the move, another two rumbling around the bend. "How many you counted?" I asked him.

"Twenty, give or take."

"Headed both ways?"

"Yeah, like they don't know whether they're coming or going."

"It's the vodka," I said.

I heard a noise behind me, Igor and Natasha moving through the scrubby undergrowth toward us. They took a knee either side of Jimmy and me as another BTR drove by, spewing noisy plumes of diesel smoke into the dust-cloud kicked up by its six chunky tires. "I'm sure I said stay with the vehicles," I reminded them.

"You are not commanding officer for me," Natasha said.

"You're with my unit, you do what I tell you. Both of you. That's how it works. There's a lot of Russian activity on the road. You're welcome to go join it." I motioned at the BTR disappearing around a bend. "There'll be another one along any minute." Natasha stared at me, and I stared back, wondering what was going on behind those photogenic eyes. She blinked first, which meant I won.

Igor grumbled, although it could have been his stomach. None of us had eaten much lately.

Two Russians who would rather hang out with a handful of despised Americans than hook up with their own who were hunting high and low for their president. One and one usually adds up to two, but this wasn't one of those times. The old Cooper would have scratched this itch. But the new Cooper? Well, let's just say the new Cooper was aware that the old Cooper was starting to make his presence felt.

"Make that twenty-one," Jimmy offered as yet another BTR, this one in a hurry, made an appearance.

"What I tell you?" I said to Natasha.

"Ruskies look a mite jumpy," Jimmy observed.

He was right about that. Desperation was in the air, the kind that clouds judgment. The Russian military probably wasn't aware of an American Special Ops team being in the vicinity when the sky shat out their top banana, and experience told me that it would be in our best interest for them to continue in that ignorance. The Russians do like to tell the world that Uncle Sam is capable of anything, maybe even of shooting down their first citizen. "We're going to hold our position and reassess later," I told him.

"Roger that, boss."

"I'll send someone to relieve you in an hour." I edged back from the road, ushering Natasha and Igor ahead. We needed the cover of darkness to move about in open countryside, which meant another whole day to kill. But movement would only get more difficult as more Russian resources were brought in, so there was that to consider also. I wondered where the sweet spot of that particular Venn Diagram was. I was not keen about us staying in the one place, especially when the place in question offered no height advantage.

"Where do we go?" Natasha asked.

"We go back," I said. "And sooner rather than later, you're going to tell me what the hell happened inside your helicopter and why." There it was – Old Cooper. I knew it was only a matter of time before he lost patience and announced his presence.

* * *

It was pointless returning to Fort Myer - Schelly knew that sleep would elude her anyway. The offices of the Joint Chiefs of Staff weren't far from the Department of Defense and so, five minutes later, she walked into the clean but uninspiring box set aside for her with a desk, a chair and a sofa. Importantly, there were two computer terminals on the desk, one called SIPRNet and the other NIPRnet, known colloquially as sipper and nipper, the former for secured information and the latter for everything else. The air smelt of new carpet. Framed side-by-side photos of President Small and Admiral Kirby Rentz, each trying to outdo the other in the serious expression stakes, hung on the wall.

Schelly eyed the sofa with longing but instead took the seat behind the desk. "Right." She opened her mouth wide a couple of times so that the skin around it stretched, and patted her face lightly to get the blood circulating. "Let's get this party started."

A gentle knock on the door. It opened and a familiar face appeared – the yeoman who'd dropped off her credentials

"Mr Goldman," said Schelly, reading his nametag again.

"Thought you might be paying us a visit, ma'am."

"Seriously, doesn't *anyone* sleep around here?"

"Insomnia is part of the deal, ma'am," he replied. "Bathrooms are 30 yards down hall. Turn right. Help yourself to coffee and cookies. There's fresh cream in the fridge. And if you want something more substantial, there's a cafeteria on Corridor 8, our level, at the C ring. Can't miss it. Open 24 hours."

"Of course it is," said Schelly, grinning.

"Like I said, ma'am, need anything, just call."

"Thanks…"

"My name's Idris, ma'am."

"Thank you, Idris." *Those big soft brown eyes - you I can trust.* The door closed.

Right. To work. Schelly unpacked her briefcase and spread Major Cooper's records across the floor. Knowing what kind of a man he was might be helpful. *Cooper…Cooper… Your name is vaguely familiar… Why is that?* Touching the space bar on the nipper keyboard revealed her Common Access Card needed to be scanned prior to use. She swiped it through the gate and the screen welcomed her. Access gained, next task was to tap "Vincent Cooper, USAF" into the search bar. The window loaded with multiple hits on the OSI Special Agent and almost all of them were surprising. *Whaaat?* People Magazine's *World's Most Sexy People issue?* She followed the link and read the article. Cooper had provided close protection in the Democratic Republic of Congo for a rapper whose music she'd never liked – Twenny Fo – and his former fiancée, Leila. *She's cool – her, I like.* Schelly read the article. The rapper was captured by one of the DRC's warring factions, but somehow Cooper had managed to effect a rescue and get everyone out alive. *Is that what really happened? Sounds like tabloid nonsense.*

Shifting to his records, she located the mission report. It neither confirmed nor denied as most of it was redacted. *Back to the computer with you.* Schelly read aloud the article's closing para: "Cooper was not only defending freedom, he did it with rock hard abs. What's not to like?" *Right.*

Schelly shook her head. *As for the abs, where's the proof? Where's the shirtless pic?* There wasn't one accompanying the article – just a reportage photo of Cooper in combat uniform beside a CV-22 tilt-rotor. *Ho-hum.*

She checked images associated with her search. There were shots of Twenny Fo and Leila, but also good clean images of Cooper in Air Force blues from a very public court martial connected to the mission in Africa, which had found the OSI special agent not guilty. There were other photos, but no images that proved the existence of the alleged rock hard abs. One image showed Major Cooper in a navy polo shirt and tan chinos talking to an attractive woman similarly dressed. Her name? Schelly clicked through. *OSI Special Agent Anna Masters. Your name is familiar too. Why is that?* She returned to Cooper's file. *Masters ... Masters ...*

The answer was found in a mission rep, which she held up to catch the light. *Here we are. Anna Masters, also OSI, partnered Cooper at Ramstein Air Base, Germany, where they investigated the murder of the Commander-in-Chief, United States Air Force in Europe, General Abraham Scott.* Schelly skimmed the pages anew, again, most of them redacted. *And here – another case Cooper and Masters worked together.* She skimmed it, the gruesome murder of the US Air Attaché to Turkey, Colonel Emmet Portman. Once again, plenty of redaction, but the investigation eventually led Cooper and Masters to the Department of Energy's depleted uranium storage facility at Oak Ridge where Masters was fatally wounded in a gun battle. *Two tough, violent missions, the latter ending in tragedy.*

Aside from the photo of Cooper and Masters together, the search engine could only find one other image of Masters, an official portrait of her in Air Force dress uniform lifted from *Airman Magazine*, where she was one of a number of contributors to a feature on activities for US airman newly posted to Ramstein. Even with her hair pulled back in a severe bun and wearing a flight cap, Masters was super attractive: dark hair, olive skin, piercing blue-green eyes ... *Were you single? What about you, Cooper?* Schelly again checked his stats and service photo. Some women considered danger an aphrodisiac and Cooper had danger written all over him. And while he wasn't Hollywood handsome ... *There is definitely something about you. Divorced, too, I see.*

Turning to sipper, Schelly went hunting for Masters's service record. Sealed. Access denied for some reason. *Hmm, interesting, but you're a rabbit hole I don't need to go down. Focus – back to Cooper.* There were other photos of him in combat uniform somewhere in Afghanistan, and a particularly striking shot of Cooper's face covered in white concrete dust, his eyes black and cavernous, bloody stripes across his lips. It was a famous photo. She remembered it splashed across the news for a time. *So you're* that *guy...*

Another reference, a news article. She followed the link to the page in *The Washington Post*. The headline read, "Silver Star for Jungle Hero" and the article featured the horror movie portrait shot she'd just looked at. The article outlined the action in brief – Cooper, under intense fire during an ambush, had single-handedly cleared a two-story building of Taliban fighters. He had further risked his own life to save a wounded buddy, carrying him to relative safety during the firefight, and then stayed behind to cover the battered and bruised unit as they drove off to safety. Schelly glanced up from the screen. Purple hearts, jungle rescues against the odds, controversial courts cases, top-secret murder investigations, rubbing shoulders with celebrities, the *People* magazine thing, the Silver Star ... There was another report from the MPs. It was a while ago. Cooper had assaulted a colonel. And then there was the court martial – another assault, this one on a US contractor. A colorful service record to say the least. Randomly sifting through reports, Schelly came upon another almost wholly redacted case. Her eyes jagged on a name – Bradley Chalmers. There was not a lot to go on other than Chalmers was involved as the Deputy Director of the CIA Tokyo station. There was criminal activity and somehow the CIA had been caught up in it and clearly Cooper and Chalmers had gone head to head. They had a history, one that somehow played into the CIA's new Associate Deputy Director's animosity. *What happened between you two?*

A performance report revealed Cooper's most recent supervisor, one Lieutenant Colonel Arlen Wayne, was stationed at Andrews AFB, serendipitously around twenty minutes drive from Fort Myer ...

Schelly's encrypted cell suddenly buzzed, startling her. *Who's this calling?* "Major Schelly," she said.

"Morning, Jill."

Colonel Gladston. She checked he watch. 0210. *Yep, morning.* "Morning, sir."

"You've heard from Secretary Epstein?"

"Yes, sir."

"Good. Seems the ball's now firmly in our court. Don't let me down."

"No, sir." *Three bags full, sir.*

"The folks at Creech took their bird for a few passes over Quickstep's secondary when I called them yesterday. A good result, apparently. I've been informed the intel has been uploaded to the CAOC Quickstep mission server. You might want to take a look."

"Great, sir. I'll do it right away."

"Where are you?"

"OJCS – at the Pentagon, sir."

"I don't know how you do it. Get some sleep, Jill. That's an order."

"Yes, sir." *Sure, I'll just tell the world to go away.*

"I've requested continued surveillance on Quickstep 3 until further notice. Waiting approval on that, but given the priority I'm pretty sure we can count on it. SECDEF Epstein told you whatever you need ...?"

"Yes, sir."

"She means it. Assume you have your orders. Officially, they'll be with you later today. Major?"

"Sir?"

"Good hunting."

The call ended.

Well, at least he didn't say, "Good luck." Now, where was I? Returning to sipper, she cruised through the various levels of digital security, arriving first at the Quickstep portal and then Quickstep 3's files. Burrowing into them revealed a folder titled, "Operation Smirnov". *An interesting coincidence given the names for these things are chosen from a pre-existing list... Perhaps someone out there has a sense of humor...* Additional clicks showed a range of other folders including a recently added one titled "Imagery". From this she extracted a range of scans converted to PDFs and pulled them up in a preview program. According to the numbers, the Reaper had loitered over the secondary RZ at a height of 39,000 feet for around half an hour, utilizing scanners in the thermal and visible light ranges.

At just over 0930 yesterday morning local Syrian time, the first pass picked up the reflective strips on the helmets of four US assets – Quickstep 3. *Gotcha!* But, right off the bat, things got weird. Additional thermal imaging showed that five additional persons accompanied the unit. Still higher power photos captured one of these extras, a naked woman apparently splashing around in a river, with two Quickstep members present. *WTF?* Other images showed a dark-haired man standing up in the engine bay of an ambulance with a red crescent on the roof. Schelly was perplexed. *Are you pissing on the engine?* Two other males, and a third member of Cooper's team (or Cooper himself), were standing nearby. Another male was shown to be lying under the canopy of a tree, his identity obscured by the canopy. The fourth Quickstep asset was some distance from everyone. *I would say you're keeping watch on the only road in – that makes sense at least.*

The story changed dramatically, though, when a large mobile force in four vehicles showed up. Photographs revealed these vehicles flying black ISIS flags. *Shit.* The vehicles stopped briefly to disperse armed men in a manner designed to outflank Quickstep 3 and company. Subsequent visible light photos of the immediate area around the ambulance were obscured by a localized dust cloud, probably kicked up by the incoming ISIS vehicles, but subsequent thermal images showed the smaller Quickstep force hidden by the cloud rapidly overpowered the attack. The final pass identified persons lying on the ground, presumably dead or wounded, none of which were US personnel, as all were accounted for standing around.

Ultra power magnification photos in the visible light spectrum captured high angle portraits of all the survivors with phenomenal resolution: Cooper, whom Schelly identified immediately, and the other three she recognized from their service records – US Army Special Forces Sergeants Baker, McVeigh and Leaphart. *But who are these others?* From their dress and features, three of the unidentified persons were more than likely Syrian, and they weren't restrained or under guard so unlikely to be Daesh or other unfriendlies. So who were they? Also, there was a man cuff-locked and seated on the ground. It stood to reason he could be a captured Daesh fighter. *Was there only one survivor from the attack? And who are these other two? One female – you have to be the river nymph. And one male, probably the person lying under the tree now walking around.* And then it hit Major Schelly. *Oh Jesus - this guy, the one walking around. He's wearing a fucking Spetsnaz uniform.*

Quickstep 3 had made contact with Russians. But which Russians? Was it feasible that they had located the president's traveling companions? No, surely not. More likely was that these persons were part of the Russian response. She re-examined the photos and the more likely scenario didn't seem to fit. Why just two Russians? And why were neither of them carrying rifles or machine guns? Clearly, though, whatever was going on down there, Cooper and his men were in control of it. Schelly made a snap decision.

It's gonna take some coordination with Creech, but didn't someone say, "Whatever you need to get it done"? She checked her notes – Lieutenant Colonel Josh Simmons – and dialed Al Udeid.

Twenty-seven

Ronald V. Small @realSmall
To all those people who think they are fighting for God, let me say
this. When you meet him, you'll be very very disappointed. He's
not your guy – he's ours.

The small fire flickered in the darkness, its feeble yellow light fighting
a losing battle against the cave's shadows feinting back and forth
against the dry rock ceiling above. Here and there flashlight beams
swept the area as men cleaned weapons or played sheesh-beesh on
pocket boards with dice the size of milk teeth. The men were
comfortable here, relaxed, though the Scorpion was anything but.

"Ortsa," he called to the Chechen, and the man rose and came
to him.

"Yes, Amir."

"I do not trust the media, any of it. Find two reliable men.
Send them to Turkey for news. I want to know if our army is
growing. How many of the faithful have answered their pledge to
the caliphate? How fast does the army grow? Are they bringing
weapons? We cannot stay here long. It would be ideal to join
our fighters and beckon the Crusaders to do battle. If we have
momentum, we need to use it."

"I will do it now. Which vehicle should they take?"

"Not the BMW and not the ZPU."

"Yes, Amir."

The Chechen turned into the smoke from the fire and it rolled in behind him as he left.

* * *

President Petrovich watched the Scorpion and the younger man in discussion and wondered what they talked about before the younger man was sent away on an errand. Petrovich sat with his feet facing the flames, the soles of his slowly roasting shoes giving up wisps of smoke, his back clammy with cold sweat, his hands numb below the cords that bit hard into the raw and bloodied skin of his wrists. Comfort was something he had ceased trying to find, his unsupported back aching, the bones in his bottom feeling like they were trying to push through the very muscle and skin. The backs of his legs were about to cramp so he thrust his feet forward, to one side of the flames. His empty gut ached from lack of food. He was filthy and, yes, scared. But the President of Russia does not show fear, he told himself, and so he worked hard to transmute the anxiety into bitter defiance, at least outwardly. But how long could he keep it up? He still had hope that somehow they would be rescued. The army, the air force, Spetsnaz – somehow they would know how to find him. The whole world would be looking for him, and the Cheget. It *had* to be. All he needed to do was hang on and *believe*. But how would he cope when hope was dimmed? Would he beg and snivel for freedom, to be allowed to live? Fellow countrymen who this monster killed had gone to their graves without a whimper. Could he too call on hidden reserves of strength? Or would his bowels and bladder loosen when a butcher's knife was pressed against his jugular and the red light on the video camera blinked?

How long had they been captive? When had their Hind crashed? It was difficult to know for sure. Was it two days ago? Three?

More? With no sunlight, his wristwatch stolen (and his wrists tied behind his back anyway), there was no way to judge the passage of time. And the Scorpion and his men slept and ate erratically – when they felt like it. Petrovich felt utterly abandoned. The same questions ran through his mind anew. How had the world reacted to the terrorist's demands? Would the ransom be paid? How had the West responded? And Russia? What about the Muslim world? Things he felt certain about one moment deserted him the next. He fought against feelings of helplessness, weakness, defeat. Short of rescue, survival was hopeless. And so the cycle of hope and despair went around again.

Cramp contracted his leg muscles without warning and he stretched out, kicking the fire, its embers scattering. Several fighters shouted at him, annoyed.

The Scorpion rose out of one of the deeper shadows and spoke to several of his men who came at once to attend the president. While the fire was reorganized and the stones around it replaced, Petrovich was offered goat's milk from an old plastic water bottle and some unidentified meat was stuffed in his mouth, along with a variety of undercooked grain that was too dry to chew properly. But it was food, and Petrovich was hungry and thirsty and he could do nothing other than accept it. The food helped to fight off the cramps, and Petrovich found himself looking at the Scorpion, now seated on the far side of the fire.

The ISIS commander tossed a small stick with dried leaves into the flames. It cracked, the fire brightened and the air was filled with an unknown fragrance. "Your general is strong for an old man," the Scorpion said. "The fever has broken, along with the infection. He will live."

"So that you can murder him for the video cameras," said Petrovich, his voice somehow even, unflinching.

"I admire your courage, Mr President. His life will serve Allah's purpose, as will yours."

"You have no intention of freeing us."

"As it is written, so it will be."

"Your riddles betray your ignorance. You are nothing but a filthy murderer. Do not pretend otherwise."

The Scorpion gave the president his warmest smile. "What use have I for pretense? I am Allah's servant. I do his bidding. That is why I am here. And that is why you are also here."

"You are a religious whacko."

"A whacko who has the Russian president, his top-ranking general and the Cheget in his possession. And with them I will reshape the world for God's greater glory."

"As I said: whacko." Petrovich stared at the Scorpion. "And what will this new world of yours look like?"

"I do not know. Neither the Qur'an nor the hadiths say. Only Allah can know the future. As he wills, so it shall be."

Despite aching in every part of his body, Petrovich found himself drawn into the mad discussion. "Fools and charlatans have been predicting the end of the world since the beginning of the world. And, like all who have come before, you too will be disappointed. The day will come and go and the sun will still rise in the east and set in the west."

The Scorpion shook his head, showing his adversary a deep well of pity. "Let me help you to understand."

"What choice do I have?"

"You can choose to accept God. The Qur'an is the perfect word of God. The laws written within it are God given. Its prophecies have come directly from God's all-knowing wisdom. Allah has seen all, sees all and knows all. He has seen what has come, what is now and what will be. And what will be, he tells us in His book, is that the armies of Rome will ultimately be defeated. Not at first, but at the end. Your deliverance to me, tells me that I am chosen by God to be instrumental in the end of the world. You and I will lead this earth to apocalypse and return it to perfection."

"Whacko."

"You are godless, Mr President of All Russia, and because of that you believe everyone is godless. Such is your arrogance and your blindness. We have God and you do not and that is why you must die. Denying God his existence is the height of apostasy and the punishment for the crime of apostasy, according to the word of God conveyed to man in the Qur'an, is death. That is what I know to be true."

"You can't win, you must know that. The caliphate is dead, your fighters are being killed off one by one. Your dream of prophecy is no more than that – a dream."

"Before victory, the armies of Islam will near obliteration, so says the prophecy. Being pressed from all sides, having our numbers so reduced makes us happy. The Qur'an and the hadiths also promise that we shall receive succor from Allah. And what are you and your general and your Cheget if not the means of that succor?"

Petrovich realized that argument was pointless. A reasoned discourse would not change this deluded mind. And he was aware that the Scorpion viewed him in identical fashion, each both impossibly beyond reach of the other's argument. "Untie my hands. Let me stand. Where can I go? This is a prison and you have many jailers."

The Scorpion hesitated before coming to a decision on this. He called to some fighters who came over to him. He spoke to them, after which they hauled Petrovich to his feet. The ISIS commander also stood. "The Qur'an says that the armies of Allah will defeat the armies of Rome," he told Petrovich. "The caliphate will spread and rule over Constantinople for a time. But then the anti-Messiah will come and another great battle will see the destruction of our fighters until only 5000 remain, cornered in Jerusalem. Just as the anti-Messiah prepares for the final annihilation, Jesus will rise with the dead to defeat him. And until that time, and at every opportunity, we shall kill your men, rape your women and sell your children into slavery, for that is merciful."

"How is that merciful?" Petrovich grimaced. The cord that bound his hands cut deeper into his flesh.

"To frighten into submission those who would oppose the will of God. To do otherwise would be to prolong war, which is forbidden."

Petrovich glared at the man, unable to find the words that spoke his mind, except for one. *Whacko.*

"I know what you are thinking. You kill our women and children with your bombs. You tell yourself that it is to shorten the war."

Petrovich had no answer other than to grind his teeth. "My hands …"

The Scorpion appeared to have come to another decision. "You say they are numb. If that is true, you will thank me for it."

Thank me for it? What does that mean?

"Take him," the Scorpion told his fighters.

Twenty-eight

Ronald V. Small @realSmall
Hang in there, Mr President. America hasn't forgotten you!

Abigail Diamond-Travis, Director of DIMOC, the Defense Imagery Management Operations Center, thumbed a button on a remote. "These frames were lifted from the second video."

Schelly had never met this woman, or heard anything about her, but she was clearly an important cog in the Washington intelligence machine. *You look somewhere in your forties but could easily pass for thirty-something. Snappy dresser. Fitted dark navy twin-set with an emerald green shirt and push-up bra. White-blonde hair cut fashionably short to accentuate a slender neck. I'm thinking American* Vogue. *I'd like to know what happened that put you in a wheelchair.*

Diamond-Travis aimed the remote at the screen and circled what appeared to be a white scratch on a blue background. "It's small, almost impossible to see with the naked eye. And if you do notice it, you could mistake it for a scratch on the tape, except this is digital so there's nothing to scratch," she said with some measure of triumph. "The weather patterns weren't conducive to the phenomenon at that time and place, and that's why it's only visible for a few seconds." The frames advanced and the scratch became a smudge that disappeared.

The room was silent, intrigued.

The blue became the sky behind Al-Aleaqarab's head. Director Diamond-Travis continued, "From around the middle of 2016, commercial flights were diverted around the airspace of what is known as the 'Chaos Triangle', the skies over southern Turkey, Syria and Iraq. But military flights are another matter and all of them are logged by the Air Force for deconfliction purposes." The picture rewound several seconds, stopped, and she circled the now tiny white fleck above and behind the terrorist's head once more. "So the appearance of this contrail is a real break. It could only be one of three possibilities – one of ours, a C-17 out of Aviano bound for Perth, Australia; a Royal Air Force tanker heading for a rendezvous with NATO fighters over Somalia; or a Luftwaffe Jaguar on a training flight. Working with these three possible options gives us three possible locations for the terrorists on the ground at the approximate time this video was made."

She pressed a remote and the image on screen became a high altitude shot of northern Syria and northern Iraq, the borders highlighted. The Euphrates writhed like a green snake on a hot plate as it curled across the almost featureless light brown desert plain. "Here, here and here," Diamond-Travis said as three small solid yellow triangles appeared on the image. The altitude decreased slowly and the triangles became areas on the desert floor, roughly evenly spaced in an arc between the Turkish border and the Euphrates. "Each line of these triangles is roughly five miles long. Unfortunately, we can't be more precise than this because, while we know the speed and direction of each of these aircraft, the precise time that this video was shot is a guestimate."

"Can we get any real-time surveillance on those areas?" Bunion asked.

"That's a question for the Air Force, sir. I would say possibly, but the Russian Air Force is making things difficult for us."

"How far are those triangles from the estimated position of Quickstep 3's first sighting of the Scorpion near Latakia?" Epstein wanted to know.

"Roughly 280 miles to the area designated Position Charley in the south, Madam Secretary, close to where the Euphrates crosses the border into Iraq; Position Alpha, 220 miles to the triangle in the north; and around 250 miles to Position Bravo roughly equidistant between them."

"This information forms the backbone of the briefing prepared for the Quickstep unit incountry," Schelly reassured the room.

"Is it possible the Scorpion could have covered the distance required in the time available?" SECSTATE Bassingthwaite asked.

"Forget Position Charley," Rentz replied.

"Yes, sir. Agreed," said Schelly.

"So that reduces the possible locations by thirty-three percent," he said.

"Yes, sir," Schelly agreed.

"How many people in this unit?"

"Four, sir."

"Right," the admiral replied, dubious.

Following several seconds of silence, Epstein asked, "Any other questions?"

None came forward. "Thank you, Abbey," Epstein said, adding, "Good job," to reassure her.

The director gathered various items into a briefcase, which she placed on her lap. "We have to get this son of a bitch," she said, reversing from the desk, wheeling about and then motoring to the door, her wheelchair motor generating a slight hum.

Admiral Rentz opened the door for her.

"Thank you, Admiral," she said

Schelly watched the director glide around the corner before the door closed behind her.

The insights from the DIMOC were something of a breakthrough, albeit a minor one. They reduced the search area substantially but,

Schelly knew, the task of finding the Scorpion, his hostages and the Cheget was still near impossible.

Doctor Debbie Ng, NSA's Director of Media Analysis, spoke. "As we know, this situation has spooked Wall Street, the 'footsie' jumping all over the place. We understand the downward pressure, but the upswings were what intrigued us. It seems the Scorpion's actions have turbocharged the dark web and all kinds of schemes are being offered, financial and otherwise. There are even crazies offering to develop algorithms that will allow the Scorpion to use the Cheget codes he has to launch nukes. We don't believe that is possible, by the way."

"Why would the threat of blowing up the world cause the stock market to go up?" asked SECSTATE Bassingthwaite. "That makes no sense to me."

"It wouldn't, sir, not specifically anyway. But markets love uncertainty. With chaos comes opportunity. The wild swings up and down take on a life of their own. It's interesting that ordinary people, not just hackers and Internet criminals, are flocking to the dark web to buy into some of the money-making schemes on offer." She gave an amused snort. "But this is sooo unnecessary. Some of the craziest barely legal schemes are no further away than a call to a Wall Street broker."

"What about those algorithms you mention?" asked Rentz.

"We are working with the NSA and the FBI," CIA Director Hamilton replied. "Keeping tabs on potential buyers."

Schelly's attention returned to the screens on the wall, glowing with activity. A billion or more smart phones around the world, in the hands of diligent amateur reporters, were feeding news services with almost real-time reporting and had supplanted the CIA, NSA, MI6 and others in the role of primary real-time intelligence gathering. These news services and selected Twitter feeds were already reporting on more than a dozen apparently ISIS-inspired "lone wolf" stabbings and hit and run attacks on civilians in London, Paris, Madrid, Berlin and New York. In Sydney, Australia, two terrorists had hijacked a harbor ferry during the morning commute and rammed it into a passenger ship. The ferry had sunk and many passengers drowned. Many more were injured. There were revenge attacks going on, too. Ten Muslims in Brussels had been struck by a delivery van in a predominantly Muslim neighborhood. The media consensus: this was just the beginning.

Screens showed maps of countries and borders drawn in fine lines of green and blue, while numerous on-screen digital counters reeled away the milliseconds and seconds. Others showed the swooping orbital tracks of relevant satellites across a flattened Earth.

SECSTATE Bassingthwaite wiped his nose with his ubiquitous handkerchief and threw his news into the bleak discussion. "Ankara reports large movements of people to its southern border with Syria. There have been riots, mostly because there is no food or shelter. Towns are being looted. There have been skirmishes. Potential combatants are arming themselves with weapons from deserting police and smaller army units. Our own agencies in Lebanon are reporting similar issues, as are the Saudis. What border protection there is around Syria is being overwhelmed with movements in and out of the country. Populations in northern Syria are being displaced. There's a new refugee crisis building by the hour. We've got a different kind of Haj here. In short, this is now very real, people. An army is already forming."

Schelly registered these concerns, but only abstractly. She had her own more immediate issues, noting the time. Not a lot of wriggle room. *Twenty-two minutes ...*

Folders with summaries on Cooper and his team, mission reports, FITREPS, and some of the explosive images captured by the Reaper revealing the presence of Russian personnel lay scattered across the table.

"The contrail is a break, but we can't bring it in any closer?" Rentz wondered.

Reid Hamilton shook his head. "Not at this point, Admiral. But you can rest assured every resource we can call on is working on it around the clock."

"We have been looking into the Scorpion's motivations – the tools he will use in the coming days and possibly weeks and months," said Professor Başak. "In the first video, he says the age of the Mahdi is coming. There are some scholars who believe the Scorpion may believe that *he* is the Mahdi. Or that his followers will proclaim him the Mahdi."

"What the hell is the Mahdi?" Bunion wanted to know.

"He is the messianic caliph foretold in the Qur'an who will lead Muslims to victory. Whether the Scorpion believes he is this Mahdi or not, it plays well to potential fighters who join believing they will personally be involved in an historic struggle far bigger than their own lives. I stress – this is a large part of the appeal. I have a written brief on the apocalyptic eschatology of the Qur'an." She pulled a stack of folders from a briefcase and slid them across the table. "It may help us understand what drives this man and the people who will follow him."

"I think the word you're looking for is power, Professor," said Bunion, accepting a folder passed to him. "That's what drives him." He opened the folder and skimmed the notes. "Really ... The Antichrist, whose name is Iblis, has red skin and lives chained on an island in the Red Sea. He has one good eye. The other droops and is covered by a wrecked eyelid." He glanced up. "Oh, c'mon. People actually believe this crap?"

"Which part upsets you, Mr Bunion?" the professor enquired.

"It's a collection of B-movie clichés. Does this antichrist carry a pitchfork? And what about this island in the Red Sea he supposedly lives on, and has been living on for, what, the last 1500 years give or take?" He removed his glasses and looked up from the notes. "If you want to be literal about it – as they seem to be – someone would have spotted him by now, don't you think?"

"He is not yet visible to humans, not until the last thirty-seven days of his life."

"You're kidding, right?"

"This is religion, Mr Bunion – faith," the professor reminded him. "Does a virgin birth make any less sense?"

Bunion grunted.

"The dream of the struggle for the establishment of a caliphate is an apocalyptic drama," said Professor Başak, continuing her briefing. "ISIS fighters see themselves as players in this drama. The belief in a higher meaning is perhaps one reason why bored, well-educated young men and women, born in western countries, are radicalized and take up jihad – they sense a pointlessness, an emptiness in their current existence. Taking up the fight for a grand purpose, fighting for no lesser being than God, gives an aimless existence significance."

Bunion gave another grunt.

Schelly watched the clock.

Chalmers looked around the table, nothing to add.

SECDEF Epstein sipped a glass of water and placed it on the coaster displaying the seal of the President of the United States of America. She tapped it with a fingernail. "Okay, crazy thought. We give the Scorpion what he wants – the grand battle. Send a United Nations coalition of ground forces to Dabiq to take on ISIS. We throw everything at it, and, of course, so will they."

Admiral Rentz's perpetual glower brightened. "I like it. In one engagement we could roll up the whole shebang. Annihilate ISIS in its boots. They'd never recover." Rentz brushed his hands together a couple of times to emphasize the point.

Başak countered, "Perhaps. But this would also fulfill important aspects of the prophecy and perhaps convince many more Muslims that the age of the Mahdi is upon us."

Bassingthwaite agreed. "Also, it would be a bloody admission that the West really is engaged in a crusade against Islam, and desires an excuse to crush it. I would think another galvanizing influence on otherwise peaceful Muslims all over the world to take up jihad. Ultimately, we'd end up facing the biggest army the world has ever seen. And you're also suggesting slaughter on an unprecedented scale."

"And what's this Mahdi army going to fight with?" Bunion asked. "Spears?"

"The most technologically advanced military force in history unleashed on human waves armed with a few chapters from an old book," quipped Hamilton.

Secretary of State Ed Bassingthwaite breathed deeply, the picture sobering. "Let's be honest, our policy directions in the Middle East have lurched from disaster to catastrophe for two decades or more. Personally, I don't think we want to go there. A head on military confrontation?" He shook his head. "It's not worth the risk."

Admiral Rentz glared at the SECSTATE, his eyes doing their signature bulge, and Schelly pictured a spoilt child who'd had all his toys suddenly confiscated.

The door opened, a welcome distraction. An Air Force officer excused himself as he walked in. He was in his early forties, silver oak leaves on his shoulders and with lines across his forehead suggesting a conservative nature prone to worry. *Not bad looking, though*, thought Schelly. His eyes met hers, after flicking to the nametag on her chest, and there was acknowledgement in them. "Good evening, sir," Schelly said, and then addressed the room: "This is Lieutenant Colonel Arlen Wayne. I thought it might be useful to have the colonel share his impressions of Major Cooper, given that he has been Cooper's supervising officer for the last few years."

"Good idea," said Epstein, who was somewhat grateful for the change of pace. She gave the Air Force officer a courteous nod. "Colonel Wayne."

"Madam Secretary," Wayne replied.

"There seems to be a lot riding on your man, Colonel," Hamilton informed Wayne.

"Sir," the colonel replied, in the time honored way a subordinate responded to a statement from a superior for which there was no suitable reply. "Happy to help." He then gave the Chairman of the Joint Chiefs a deferential gesture. "Admiral."

Angry Kermit eyeballed the man over his bifocals, giving his military bearing the once-over. "Colonel Wayne."

"Please take a seat," Epstein beckoned the colonel.

"Thank you, ma'am," Wayne settled in the chair tangentially opposite Chalmers, beside Professor Başak.

Schelly completed the introductions and then pushed a folder across the table toward him. "These are briefing notes on Cooper and his team already shared with those present, Colonel. I believe you've authored some of them."

Wayne opened the folder and removed a photo of Cooper in combat uniform, leaning against a Black Hawk.

"And I've done my own digging into Cooper's military career," Rentz interrupted. "My two-word assessment – rabble rouser."

"Mine's loose cannon," Chalmers replied, interrupting, his moment arrived. "Expanding on that, I'd add wise guy, along with unpredictable and uncontrollable." Chalmers continued, "The world's in a bucket of trouble if you think this guy's going to save it."

"If I may," said Wayne.

"Please, Colonel," Epstein replied. "It's why you're here."

"I've known Major Cooper a long time –"

"You two are pretty thick," Chalmers interrupted. "I don't think you're capable of impartiality where this man is concerned."

"Let's hear what the colonel has to say, shall we?" said Epstein in a voice about as smooth as eighty-grade sandpaper.

"I have been Cooper's supervisor," Wayne continued, "and we worked alongside each other as special agents in the OSI."

"He's an iron major, Colonel, his rank rusted on," Rentz said. "You are contemporaries, but there's a reason you progressed up the ladder and he didn't."

"Admiral, I'll grant you Cooper is unpredictable and at times uncontrollable, and that hasn't helped him in some quarters, but it's those same qualities that made him one of the most valuable assets in the OSI. As someone who has been his commanding officer, yes, I'm the first to admit there are times he has metaphorically shot himself in the foot. But Cooper always gets the job done. Iron major he might be, but he is also a highly decorated one, and for good reason."

"If I could paraphrase, Colonel Wayne, you're saying he's a risk." Admiral Rentz ran his eyes over a FITREP and then flicked it onto the pile in front of him.

"A big risk," Chalmers added.

Rentz turned to Epstein. "Look, if we were going to vote on it, mine would be no. I say we stay out of it. Minimal intervention. Let the Russians take care of it. It's their president, not ours."

"I'd agree, Madam Secretary," Chalmers said.

"Sirs," continued Wayne, "Cooper is an unconscious master of asymmetrical warfare. He's resourceful, he thinks on his feet, and the decisions he makes under pressure are usually the right ones. If you don't know what you're up against, Cooper's your man."

"Usually? You're saying his decision-making is erratic," Chalmers paraphrased.

No he's not! Chalmers's point of view was getting under Schelly's skin. *Clearly you only hear what you want to hear, oaf.*

"No, sir," said Wayne, covering his exasperation well. "What I mean is, he gets it right more often than not."

"It's the 'not' that concerns me."

"You know he assaulted a bird colonel," Rentz said to the room. "How he got away with that says a lot about problems in today's Air Force. Should've been dishonorably discharged." He earned nods from Chalmers and Bunion. Hamilton frowned, arms folded, sitting on the fence.

"There were mitigating circumstances, sir," Wayne added.

"For beating on a superior officer? This I gotta hear."

"Sir, the colonel in question was having an affair with Cooper's wife. I believe he caught them together in the shower, if you know what I mean. At the time of the beating, the colonel was not in uniform. It's also worthwhile noting that the colonel in question was acting as Major and Mrs Cooper's relationship counselor at the time."

This last point clearly caught Rentz off guard. An embarrassed, "Well ..." was all he could muster.

"If I may enquire," asked Wayne, "why is Major Cooper's fitness under scrutiny?"

Schelly glanced at the screen. *Five minutes to abort. Keep your cool – don't come across desperate.* "I believe Cooper and his team have already made contact with at least two of the party accompanying President Petrovich when his helicopter was shot down."

Wayne gave a snort. "Well, if trouble's looking it'll find Vin Cooper."

Schelly continued. "We have the opportunity to give the major and his team the green light to try and rescue the president, whoever remains alive in his party, and also secure the Cheget. There's some resistance to that."

"I would remind everyone," said Epstein, "that the commander-in-chief has himself demanded Cooper and his team rescue President Petrovich. There's no democracy here. The decision has been made."

"Madam Secretary, I think letting Cooper loose is a bad idea," said Chalmers. "Surely we can insert assets that are far more competent into the picture. What about SEAL Team 6?"

"What is it with the SEALs?" said Epstein with some exasperation. "As we know, the Russians have locked everything down, so what is on the ground at this time is pretty much the only option available. On top of which, we don't know if Petrovich is alive. But if Cooper is already in touch with members of the president's party. That, at least, is *something*."

"One other point," Bassingthwaite said. "The Russians are on the verge of claiming publicly that the United States was complicit. They believe we helped ISIS capture Petrovich."

"That was ridiculous the first time I heard it. And it still is." Admiral Kermit glared over his glasses at the messenger.

Bassingthwaite shrugged. "Unfair and unreasonable, but there you have it. So whatever we do, it had better be done with discretion."

"A discrete Cooper is an oxymoron," warned Chalmers.

Hamilton counseled his deputy, "I think you're made your point, Bradley."

Schelly examined Chalmers in an effort to penetrate his reluctance. *What is it between you and Cooper?* She faced Epstein. "Madam Secretary, we have less than sixty seconds to abort."

"Admiral?" Epstein enquired.

Rentz sighed, somewhat annoyed. "What choice do we have?"

Chalmers sucked in his lower lip and shook his head.

Bassingthwaite raised a hand. "Let's do it."

Epstein summarized, "As I said, this is not a democracy."

Epstein motioned at Schelly. "Do what you have to do, Major."

"Yes, ma'am." Schelly turned to a keyboard, tapped in the confirmation code and pressed enter. The countdown on screen said fifteen seconds. *We've cut it pretty fine. Hope the servers aren't overloaded …*

Twenty-nine

Ronald V. Small @realSmall
Today I shot an amazing 74. Thinking my handicap should be 2.
It's time!

I woke in the late afternoon, the sun soon to disappear behind the hills. The Syrians were stretched out in the shade of the ambulance. Our ISIS captive, Abdullah, lay some yards from them, on his side and cuff-locked to a smaller tree. Jimmy and Igor were crouched over a portable stove. I could hear Jimmy running Igor through what was in the pot he was stirring. I didn't like the sound of the ingredients, at least the combination of them, but we were a long way from Spagos and food is food.

Into the comms, I said, "Alvin, what you got?"

"All quiet, boss. Traffic's light. No BTRs for some time."

"Take a break. Dinner's on the table."

"Roger that."

I yawned, walked over to Bo racked out on the ground, and tapped the sole of his boot with the muzzle of the AK. "Rise and shine," I told him.

The sergeant's muscles spasmed. His eyes flashed open and flicked left then right. I knew that reflex, the senses coming online to check everything was as you left it.

"What's up, boss?" he asked, sitting up.

"It's serious. We're out of coffee."

Bo blinked a couple of times and wiped a grimy eye with the back of a dirty gloved hand. "Shee-it! You drop your guard for just a moment ..."

"But luckily there's still plenty of carbohydrate-fortified beverage powder."

"Goodie," he said without enthusiasm. That stuff was poison.

Coffee was only a short drive to the north, just over the Turkish border, a good incentive to move out, aside from the one that being on Syrian soil was seriously dangerous to the health. "Go grab some chow," I told Bo.

He grunted as he stood, which made me feel good – nice to hear young muscles also creaked and groaned. "Smells like tuna, refried beans, peanut butter, strawberry Jell-O, hot sauce and sweet sauce."

"You got it," I said, "plus whatever MREs you can throw into the mix."

"Two packs of Spaghetti with Beef & Sauce."

"Been saving the best till last?"

"Yeah."

"Offer it to our Russian friends instead."

"Good idea, boss. That's why you d'officer."

Spaghetti w/Beef & Sauce was, in fact, more accurately described as Inedible w/Unspeakable & Unbelievable, and mostly the first meal to go in the trash before departure, should you be unfortunate enough to score it in your rations allocation. On the positive side of the ledger, it also came with a large portion of dried fruits, which, as the name suggested, were fruits, dried, nothing added or subtracted other than air and moisture. You gotta take the rough with the smooth.

"Load out?" I asked him.

"Going with this piece of shit." Meaning a well used ISIS AK-47 resting against his ruck. He readjusted his webbing. "Got six mags and half-a-dozen F1s. No choice. Gone black on ammo for the M4 – only one mag left. Gonna save it. You in the same boat, I see."

"Uh-huh," I confirmed, checking his straps. Everything was tight and secure.

He did the same for me. "You good, boss," he said, slapping my webbing with the check completed.

My M4 was strapped to my ruck, which was leaning against a tree, so pretty much useless. I was black on ammo, too – almost out. As for the F1, that was the museum piece Soviet anti-personnel frag grenade first issued in World War II. It still did the job, though the weapon's timing could be a little off and had been known to be equally lethal to the person pulling the pin. The fuse delay topped out anywhere from zero to thirteen seconds. I had a few of them too, tucked into webbing pockets, but hoped I wouldn't have to call on them. "I'll join you in a minute," I told him as, out of the corner of an eye, I saw Natasha stand up, stretch, and brush down her clothes. "Pass the word along. We're leaving when it gets dark." That was in around forty minutes or less. I went over to the Russian.

Before I could open my mouth, she informed me, "I told you what happened in helicopter. I have nothing to say. You are right, we have best hope of finding president with Russian military so we are leaving."

"Right. I was gonna say go get something to eat. Why the sudden change of heart?"

"What is change of heart?"

"You've changed your mind."

"Then why not say this?"

I shrugged. I had nothing, except maybe a few expletives to throw at her.

"Will you help find president?"

"No," I told her.

"So there is reason why we go. So ..." She gave me one of those annoying shrugs that says, "so fuck you", and walked away, drawn, apparently, by the delicious aromas of countless dietitian-approved long-life artificial colorings and flavorings bubbling in Jimmy's kitchen.

I watched her go. Women: can't live with 'em ... can't live with 'em. Or however that goes.

Alvin appeared, jogging back up the access road. He gave a wave that said both "hello" and "don't panic, I'm not running coz there's a problem". He slowed to a walk when he came adjacent to the ambulance and stopped beside Abdullah. I watched him say something to the terrorist lying on his side on the ground. Then he crouched next to the Brit and poked the guy with his M4. A heavy sleeper, I figured.

"Boss ..." Alvin said over the comms, "the Brit's dead." Okay – that was unexpected. I walked over. Abdullah seemed asleep except for his lips, which were forced apart by a swollen black tongue, a sure giveaway something else was accounting for his reluctance to wake. I crouched, removed a glove and put my fingers next to his trachea, feeling for a pulse in his carotid. A tongue the color of boot leather and a fly standing on it rubbing its front legs in a fashion that said "Oh, goodie!" told me not to bother, as did the cold, clammy skin. But there are protocols for this kind of thing. There was no blood and no injury was immediately visible. But when I moved Abdullah's head from side to side I felt vertebrae move, grind and jag against each other. "Neck's broken," I said, standing.

"Solves a problem," the sergeant volunteered.

It did, if he meant that now we didn't have to kill Abdullah or lug him around with us. Except that in our midst was apparently someone prepared to kill in cold blood, which I wasn't especially pleased about, however much I disliked the terrorist and his world view.

"But who, right?" he asked.

Yeah, who? And why?

"You're ex OSI, aren't you? Something like this would be, you know, like, memory lane."

I eyeballed the Syrians ending their siesta in the lee of the ambulance and coming to their feet. None appeared to display any concern that Alvin and I may have come across a stiff in our midst, suggesting that they were either cool customers, or oblivious. My money was riding oblivious. The killer wasn't Alvin, who had been on watch for the duration. And I'm in the clear, right? But what about Jimmy or Bo? No, too much discipline. They killed folks who shot at them and neither had shown any particular malice toward Abdullah. Killing in cold blood wasn't their style no matter how bad the person stank, and Abdullah was seriously ripe.

"Takes a lot of strength to break a man's neck." Alvin looked straight at Igor.

"Maybe you should transfer to OSI," I suggested.

He shrugged. "That'd be a pretty cool gig, sir. No doubt."

I crouched and took a closer look at the Brit's neck. Whiskers and grime was the sum total of what I could see. Nothing outwardly suggested violence or a struggle. Whoever had done the deed had positioned the body in such a way that it wouldn't attract attention. For all intents and purposes, Abdullah seemed to be having a rest, unless you were up close. His skin temperature and general pallor indicated death had tapped him on the shoulder several hours ago, which was right about the time I'd come off watch and hit the hay. "Gonna move him into the shade, out of the sun," I said.

"Good idea," Alvin agreed. "The guy's got some serious animal musk going on."

I cut the cuff locks with a Leatherman. "Get his feet." I grabbed a couple of handfuls of clothing around Abdullah's shoulders, grunting as I hoisted him up. I wondered what his weight might be in donuts. And then I wondered where do you even get donuts around here, all of which reminded me of a joke. "So, where does an Englishman hide his money?" I asked.

"No matter what they say, your jokes really lighten the load, sir."

"Under a bar of soap."

"Right."

"I got that one from an Aussie. And just to balance the scales, here's one about the Aussies I got from a Brit …"

"Not necessary, sir."

"Don't want anyone saying I'm biased. Anyway, an Englishman wants to become an Irishman, so he visits a doctor to find out how to go about it. 'Well,' says the doctor, 'that's a tricky operation and there's a lot that can go wrong. I'll have to remove half your brain.' 'That's okay,' says the Englishman, 'I've always wanted to be Irish and I'm prepared to take the risk,' so the operation goes ahead. But when he awakes, the Englishman's eyes open to a look of horror on the doctor's face. 'I'm so terribly sorry!' the doc says. 'I told you it was risky. Instead of removing half your brain, I accidentally took it all out.' To which the patient replies, 'No worries, mate. Any beer in the fridge?'"

"We gonna carry him all the way to Turkey, sir?" Alvin asked, looking around.

"Put him over there." I motioned at a nearby tree. "Australians say 'mate' a lot, and they like beer. Get it?" I explained as we put him down.

"Great joke, sir."

"I've got others."

"Smells like they're serving Spaghetti with Beef and Sauce, sir. Don't want to miss out on that, no, sir. I'll save you some." Alvin jogged away to join the general assembly milling around Jimmy and Igor.

I was considering saying something indignant to his departing back, but was prevented from doing so by the growing wail of approaching jet engines. The others around the pot had also noticed it, and were checking the sky. The noise was not the rotary wing thump-thump of paddles slapping the air, nor was it the unmistakable shriek of a fighter jet, which sounds like the very fabric of the atmosphere tearing. There was plenty of iron flying around the skies, but this sound was somehow different. I cocked the AK, just in case. And then, in my peripheral vision, a couple of sets of navigation lights winked on in the fading light. Two aircraft – small – coming in low and hot. I took aim as they skimmed over the trees on the edge of the field and banked hard overhead, one hundred yards or so behind the other. MQ-9s. Reapers, a pair of them, pushed along by turboprops, which accounted for the unusual sound. Jimmy, or maybe it was Bo, let out a whoop. Uncle Sam hadn't forgotten us after all, at least that was my take.

The MQ-9 was primarily a stealth weapon. It had a radar cross-section about equal to a dime, whereas a Black Hawk showed up like Dumbo in pink sequins on primary radar screens. With half the Russian Air Force flying CAPs in the area, maybe Reapers were one of the few options our Air Force could sneak in. All this filtered through my mind as the drones flew another half circuit with their flaps down, wings waggling, the aircraft equivalent of a friendly wave. I resisted the temptation to wave back, and then they were gone as quickly as they arrived, banking hard and climbing. I walked back towards Jimmy's kitchen, a little disappointed. But what was I expecting, right?

"What the hell was all that about?" wondered Alvin, beating me to the question.

"Boss," said Bo, pointing back over my shoulder, "look …"

Thirty

Ronald V. Small @realSmall
Americans don't become terrorists. Remember that when we send
you back to wherever your parents or grandparents came from.

Yousef Ali turned the radio on and searched for the news. There
was a lot of news around at the moment so it was easy to find, and
much of it thrilled him. A man had just killed two random tourists
walking along Hollywood Boulevard in Los Angeles, according to
the newsreader. The man had pulled up beside them in his car,
calmly got out and smashed them in the back of the head with
a tomahawk. An off-duty Los Angeles City police officer shot
him dead before he could attack other passersby. Police had not
confirmed that this was a terrorist attack, but what else could it be?
Yousef smiled to himself. Of course the man with the tomahawk
was a jihadist. The love he must have had for God ... Right now he
would be enjoying the first fruits of Paradise, the reward for having
sent two apostates to an eternity of fiery hell.

Elation turned to excitement, and then it became fear. Yousef,
too, would soon be with God, celebrated for his bravery and
devotion, provided, of course, he had the nerve to go through
with the plan he'd been considering for some time. Yousef had

been thinking about it for months, and then working through the practical details for weeks. He had even come here on several prior occasions, always by himself, sometimes taking a bus, other times just walking, checking timetables and other factors like weather and traffic density, wondering if he would ever have the guts ... He never shared the plan, never told a living soul, trusting no one but Allah, may his name be praised. And then the President of Russia fell into the hands of devout jihadists in the holy lands. It was a sign, and Yousef knew that he must follow through.

Yousef's love for God was beyond question. But it was also true that he was afraid. It was difficult to know the emotion, to recognize it, but fear was always there, a hand around his heart and his throat, squeezing. Was it fear for himself? Or for his family? If he did what he planned to do, what would they do to his mother, to his younger brother and sister – "they" being everyone from the government to their neighbors? Would his family be imprisoned, hounded, made scapegoats for his choices? Or did his fear come from another place? Was he afraid of failure? When the time came, would he have the courage?

His watch said eight-thirty, the appointed time nearly arrived. Yousef reached into his jacket and felt the butt of the pistol. There was no going back and so he concentrated hard on banishing all doubt. When he stood in front of Allah, his devotion must be pure. The realization that he would soon be in the presence of God suddenly filled him with ... joy. Yes, that was the only word for it – joy.

Across the road several school children gathered with their mothers. Yousef checked up the street. The traffic was minimal. 8.31. The school bus was late, but it had been late before. He was aware that his forehead and back were damp with sweat, though the morning wasn't hot. No one looked at him, but why would they? Yousef, or Frank as his mom called him, was just another skinny fair-headed guy with an unkempt beard.

He glanced up the street again, impatient. And there it was, coming slowly around the bend, the streetlights green. On the other side of the road, mothers kissed their children goodbye. Perhaps only a minute later, the yellow bus arrived at its stop opposite as a gap conveniently appeared in the traffic. Yousef jogged over casually as the last child climbed aboard. And just as the door began to close behind a small girl wearing a fluffy Minion backpack, he muscled his way in, squeezing through the gap. Pulling the pistol from his pocket, he shouted, "Allahu akbar! Drive!" and buried the muzzle of the barrel hard into the side of the infidel's cheek so there would be no argument.

There was a moment of hesitation as the woman behind the wheel processed the nightmare that had just forced its way onto the bus.

"I said drive!" Yousef yelled and raised the weapon as if to strike her with it backhand.

"Okay, okay," she said. She glanced at the door mirror and then pulled away from the curb as the situation dawned on the mothers gathered at the stop. They began to scream and cry out the names of their children and beat at the side of the bus as they ran beside it until the old relic picked up speed and outpaced them.

In the bus, the kids, who were all less than seven years of age, began to cry and wail.

"Keep goin' till I tell ya otherwise," demanded Yousef.

The driver said, "Don't hurt us none, mister. They just kids."

"They belong to God," Yousef told her. "C'mon, faster." He tried to stay immune to the mounting distress in the seats behind him. He glanced back to see what was going on. Some of the children stared wide-eyed at him, and then at the pistol, unable to process the situation. Others were pounding at the windows, shouting at the world outside, and some were simply bawling, their faces screwed up as tears of fear and uncertainty streamed down their cheeks.

Checking the street, Yousef was pleased to see the traffic still moving with no sign of panic, the air free of police sirens.

And look, not far ahead, in the same lane as the bus, a sheriff's vehicle even turned slowly into a side street, oblivious. Yousef was pleased that his action had not yet reached the dispatch desk, but he knew that ignorance would not last. Soon there'd be law enforcement all over the bus, including anti-terror and tactical response units. How long did he have, he wondered? Thirty seconds? A minute? Maybe two? Yousef knew that death was assured, whether by police bullet or by the means he had planned, and his scrotum tightened with the thrill of it. Soon his life would end, and a new blissful existence would begin where he would be important, valued, special.

An intersection approached, a turn to the left was the bus's usual route. And then he heard it – a siren wailing. No, two of them. "Turn right here," Yousef demanded, indicating the street, gesturing with the pistol.

The driver wound the big old worn steering wheel hand over hand, the bus lumbering around the corner. Yousef felt relief – they were nearly arrived at the intended destination. The sirens were closer now. But how close? They had responded quicker than he'd anticipated. He bent down to look in the side mirror. There, maybe 200 meters behind, a police car – lights flashing – on the wrong side of the road, closing fast. And Yousef knew he would never make it. The gas station. It was too far. More sirens. They were closing in from all directions. A brace of red and blue flashing lights bounced out of a street some distance ahead. Yousef's own anxiety flared. And that's when he saw it coming toward the bus on the opposite side of the street. Perhaps Allah, may his name be praised, had intervened here, providing Yousef with an even better end game. Perhaps this was already written.

The woman looked at him. "You ain't gonna make it, no."

Yousef smiled at her and then discharged the weapon into the base of her skull. His noise in the confined space deafened him. The window beside her was shattered, blood everywhere. She slumped away from the wheel, which Yousef grabbed with his spare hand,

and he pushed it a quarter turn away from him. The bus veered across the road, into the path of the B-double hauling heating oil. "Allahu ak –"

Thirty-one

Ronald V. Small @realSmall
As far as I am aware, not a single Republican is a terrorist. I can't speak for the Democrats.

The cell phone in the truck finally ceased its muffled ringing.

"Do you think God will care that we were late with Shorook?" Mohammad asked, coming up on his knees.

Hafiz stood and bushed the desert dust off his knees. "Allah, may his name be praised, has special forgiveness for his soldiers."

The CB radio in the cabin crackled into life. *"Chuck. Where you, bud? Not ans'rin' yer phone. You got a mechanical or somethin'?"*

"Better get moving. Help me get him out." Hafiz balanced with one foot on the footplate, reached in and grabbed Charlie by the belt. He pulled as hard as he was able, but Charlie wouldn't budge. "He is a fat pig," said Hafiz reconsidering the situation. "Leave him. It doesn't matter. There's enough room for us. We can push him down into the floorboards on your side."

Mohammad shrugged. Dead is dead and Charlie was in no state to complain about it with three bullets in his head, or what was left of it. Mohammed jogged around the front of the cement truck to the passenger side and vaulted into the cabin.

215

Charlie, the driver, an old guy in his mid-fifties with a red face and a beer barrel for a gut, lay in a pool of his own blood and brains across the width of the old dusty cracked seat. A photo of two young children, maybe seven and eight years of age, a boy and girl, both redheads, was taped to the chipped dash. Mohammed assumed they were grandchildren. Charlie had to be too old to be their parent. He looked at the dead man covered in blood and thought with a measure of amusement, "See? You're a redhead now too." Mohammed took a hold of the grab rail over the door, brought his feet up, placed one on the body's neck and the other on his shoulder, and pushed. Finally the man moved, sliding onto the floor.

"Good job," Hafiz told him. The engine was still idling, surging in a regular pulsing rhythm. He grabbed the shift lever, stepped on the clutch pedal, found a gear and the truck moved forward, the cabin bucking, the engine's torque wrestling with the weight of the concrete mixing in the bowl behind.

"Do you really think we will succeed?" Mohammed asked.

Hafiz had no doubts. "Yes, of course. Don't be stupid. Why wouldn't we? How much time do we have?"

Mohammed glanced at his watch and tapped the glass to make sure. "We have ten minutes."

"We're late." Hafiz shrugged, "But there are plenty of trains."

The CB crackled again. *"Okay, Chuck, well, I have to assume you got some kinda issue. The GPS says you goin' the wrong way. If you can't answer, just click the mike twice if you're in trouble, three times if you're not and we'll take it from there."*

"Stupid kafir," said Hafiz. He reached forward, took the mike from its cradle and thumbed the "talk" button twice.

"Right then. Click twice for mechanical problems, three for something else."

Hafiz clicked twice.

"I'm guessin' your phone's out of battery, otherwise you'd call. Let us know what the problem is when you get the chance and we'll send out a rescue team."

Hafiz clicked the button and said, "Your friend Charlie has gone to hell. You can thank Islamic State and the caliphate. Allahu akbar!"

"What? Who are you? Answer me. Put Charlie on!"

"What did you do that for?" Mohammed demanded.

Hafiz wrapped the microphone cord around his hand, wrenched it from the transceiver and threw it out the window. He then grabbed another gear and planted his foot on the pedal. "A little fun. There's nothing they can do. I want the glory of God known to all."

Mohammad kept his eyes on the road ahead, expecting to see flashing blue and red lights of law enforcement vehicles swooping on them. "It was unnecessary. That's all I want to say."

"Relax. Paradise awaits and we are almost there." Lining the highway now were a few homes and small businesses, the occasional gas station, a fast food outlet, a car yard or two. "We are making good time."

"When we meet Allah, who will do the talking?" Mohammad asked.

"You can, if you like. Or me. Or we can both talk. It won't matter."

"What will Allah look like?"

"I asked the imam. He said the Lord of the Throne cannot be described, and that His perfection is beyond mere words."

"'He ... Allah is a man?"

"What are you suggesting? What else would He be? I am not an imam. Don't ask me. All I know is that we will be with Him soon. Look." Hafiz gestured ahead.

The boom arms of a railway crossing lowered, blocking the roadway in both directions, pulling to a stop two smaller vehicles directly in their path.

"There it is," Hafiz shouted, motioning ahead, "right on time." The speedo read just over sixty miles per hour with his foot hard against the firewall. The truck could go no faster even though it was running downhill. Ahead, the commuter train approached the crossing fast as it was between two stations.

"I am excited!" Mohammad shouted over the roar of the engine and the drumming of the tires on the roadway.

"Me too. I shall see you in heaven!" The two young men reached out for each other and held hands as the concrete truck careered into the parked cars waiting for the train to pass, and all three vehicles slammed into the leading train coach speeding through the crossing.

Thirty-two

Ronald V. Small @realSmall
Turkey is a great nation, and its people are great people. I mean that sincerely.

Two parachutes drifted downwards, a canister swinging beneath each. Supply drop, I figured. That made sense of the MQ-9s' arrival. "Bo, Alvin – special delivery," I said. "Gonna see if they need a signature."

The payloads hit the dirt not far from one other, thirty yards or so from the ambulance. Someone somewhere cared enough about our situation to dispatch those Reapers, which, I figured meant someone somewhere wanted something. If we couldn't be airlifted out, CENTCOM would have expected us to find our own way out. That was SOP. So what was the deal here?

Bo and I went to one canister, Alvin headed for the other. "What do we have here?" I asked the universe. Unfastening the clips cracked open the tube and revealed a treasure trove of warfighter essentials: four M26 shotguns, enough twelve-gauge double-ought shells to finish anything we started, boxes of 5.56 millimeter rounds, additional magazines, a brace of M67 AP grenades, claymores, MREs, plus a mysterious separate black case with the figures RQ-11 stenciled in dull yellow on one end.

"All right! A fuckin' Raven," Bo exclaimed when he saw the case. "That is some sexy ass shit right here." He rubbed his hands together, lifted the case out, placed it on the ground and worked the latches like a kid opening a present on Christmas morning. Flipping the lid revealed several parts to a small aircraft painted air force low-viz gray. "Oh, man!" he exclaimed. "Ain't no one gonna sneak up on our ass with this motherfuck covering our six."

"Sir!" Alvin called out, holding something above his head.

Was that a phone?

"You got a call."

Yeah. Who was calling? And what did they want? I guessed I was gonna find out. I jogged over and took the sat phone. "Cooper," I said.

"Major Cooper. Colonel Wayne here."

Arlen! Whiskey Tango Foxtrot, right? What was my favorite fobbit doing on the line? But *Major* Cooper? *Colonel* Wayne? A phone call delivered by Reaper? Had to be official business. "Sir," I said, playing along. "Who do I thank for the resupply? You?"

"Me? Hell, no. Send the commander-in-chief a thank you note."

* * *

Arlen was aware that everyone's expectation was turned toward him. *Vin, don't say anything that's gonna embarrass me, or you for that matter.* Getting in quick, he said, "Major, I'm in the White House Situation Room with a number of heavy hitters – Secretary of Defense Epstein, Secretary of State Bassingthwaite, the Chairman of the Joint Chiefs Admiral Rentz, CIA Director Hamilton, Associate Deputy Director Chalmers and others and we are –"

"Sounds like a fun crowd," crackled the voice on the line.

Jesus, Vin. "We're on speaker."

"Right… Wait. Hey, did I hear it right? Did you say Chalmers? Not the former Head Buffoon of CIA Station, Tokyo?"

"Vin, we're on speaker," Wayne reiterated.

Chalmers's face had screwed itself into a complicated expression that was part embarrassment, part hate and the rest revenge. Wayne swore at himself for pure stupidity. Chalmers. Waving that name at Cooper was always going to be a mistake.

"Good. Mustn't let a good insult go to waste," said Cooper.

"See? That's what I'm talking about," Chalmers announced, red faced.

"Major Cooper, Andrew Bunion here, Chief Advisor to the President. If we could stick to the business at hand? Intel photos reveal you and your unit traveling with Russians."

"It's the other way around, sir. The Russians have come along for the ride, but I think we're about to part company."

"Who are they? What's their unit?"

"They were with the Russian president when their helicopter came down. One is Spetsnaz and holds the rank of starshina, the other a sergeant. Doing some promotional work for the motherland's troops here, so they told me."

"Major Schelly forwarded us the image files of all persons in the company of Quickstep 3," said Hamilton. "We'll have positive IDs on both before the day is out."

Heads around the room were nodding, all except Chalmers who glared at a small stack of papers almost hard enough to move them.

"Major, Secretary of Defense Epstein here. You say you're parting company with the Russians. Why is that?"

"Our mission is complete, exfil aside, ma'am. Theirs is just beginning. We're headed in different directions you might say."

Bunion cut to the chase. "So do you know where President Petrovich is being held captive or not?"

"No, sir. Our mission was confined to recon and planting a navigation beacon."

Bunion shook his head at General Rentz who seemed equally disappointed, hope fading that Cooper and his unit might be able to perform some kind of useful service.

"Major Cooper, this is Major Jillian Schelly. I run Quickstep out of Al Udeid."

"Jill," Cooper replied.

"What more can you tell us about the Russians in your party?"

"Not much other than what I've already said. We stumbled across them. They were expelled from a Russian Hind as it crash-landed in the vicinity of our first alternate. They're lucky to be alive. As for the Russian president, I have no knowledge about him at all – where he is, whether he's alive or dead or somewhere in between."

"I can tell you that, at least as at this time yesterday, President Petrovich was alive," Schelly informed him, "held captive by the ISIS commander your unit correctly identified in an earlier SPIREP as Al-Aleaqarab – the Scorpion. The jihadist holds several other hostages, including one of Petrovich's top generals. And he has in his possession the Cheget. Do you know what that is, Major?"

A gentle whistle was heard. "Yeah, I know what it is. You mind if I ask how you know all that?"

"The Scorpion has posted videos on YouTube since the crash – graphic videos."

There was a pause on the line, Cooper digesting this news. "What's the ransom?" Vin eventually asked, breaking the silence. "What does the shitbag want?"

"Basically, what all these crazies want – an eternity in Paradise. But this lunatic has put a twist on it. He wants to die in the mother of all battles against the armies of Rome, as he calls them – presumably NATO or the Turks." Schelly outlined the terrorist's request in more detail.

Cooper asked, "And you think he'll give Petrovich back if we oblige?"

"Unlikely."

"Agreed ... So I guess the world has gone into the toilet."

"As of this moment, Major, I think you could say it's on the edge of that figurative seat. Homegrown ISIS sympathizers are using Petrovich's capture as a pretext to grab whatever weapons come to hand and use them on innocent bystanders, and we don't know how many thousands of potential combatants are already on the move to Dabiq, supposedly in preparation for this so-called End of Days Battle." Schelly took a breath. "Look, I don't know enough about what you may have seen, or any intelligence that you may have come across to ask the right questions, but can you tell us anything that might help us locate Al-Aleaqarab? Anything at all? As far as we know, you and your unit are the only assets – American, Russian or otherwise – that has had any contact with Al-Aleaqarab, no matter how remote, in the last forty-eight hours."

The line went quiet.

"Do you understand the importance of this, Cooper?" Angry Kermit growled.

"I'm sorry … Who's this?"

"Admiral Rentz."

"Admiral, I have nothing solid," said Cooper, "but I can give you an educated guess."

Loud enough to be heard, Chalmers said, "Educated? Really?"

"Do you need a drum roll, Cooper?" asked Rentz impatiently.

* * *

What is it with squids? Maybe too much salt hardens the brain. I took a walk away from the speedballs as Natasha and Mazool were coming over to inspect them. I told the CJCS, "Admiral, at the point where Al-Aleaqarab's fighters shot down one Russian Hind and crippled another, the Scorpion was seen to get into a white 5 Series BMW in company with a late-model blue Toyota technical, armed with a quad ZPU. Those are unique vehicles, especially traveling in a pair. Both departed the area as part of a larger convoy. We were reasonably certain at the time that the Scorpion was giving chase to the wounded Hind, which, as I said, must have come down close to our mission alternate. Later, when departing the alternate, we observed a white BMW and a blue

Toyota technical with a ZPU option in the bed traveling together, moving away from the area at speed. It makes more sense than less that these were the same two vehicles we observed earlier. And the way they were shedding other vehicles in the convoy, it must be they decided that fewer vehicles drew less attention than a column of them. They did that for a reason."

"We could get Wide Area Aerial Surveillance operating in the target area," Schelly suggested, addressing the SECDEF. "Major Cooper's right. Those two vehicles traveling in tandem would be pretty unique. If they're still moving around out there, we've got a good chance of picking them up."

"Do it," Epstein replied. "Whatever it takes."

"CIA Director Reid Hamilton, Major Cooper. At that point you had no idea President Petrovich may have been in the downed Hind?"

"Affirmative, sir. Not at the time."

"But now you think the Scorpion and other captives were in those two vehicles?" said Rentz, pushing in.

"Does make sense of what we saw. But, like I said, we can't be sure."

From his body language, the admiral seemed rather less convinced than more, and he confirmed as much saying, "Sounds like goddamn sketchy rumint to me."

Rumint, the combination of rumor and intelligence. Schelly wondered if this secret squirrel op would do her career more harm than good. But Epstein gave her the glimmer of a reassuring smile, which Schelly interpreted as, "You done good." The SECDEF then leaned forward as if to make herself better heard. "Secretary of Defense Epstein here, Major Cooper. We don't have much time left on this satellite … What was your intention before resupply?"

"Head for Turkey, ma'am."

"Change of plans, Major. We want you to locate and liberate President Petrovich. And, of course, secure the Cheget."

Silence.

More silence.

"Major?"

"Ma'am, with respect, there are more Russians here right now than Arabs. They're climbing over each other to find Petrovich and his launch codes. Even assuming we knew where to start the search, we're more than likely to get in the way and start some kind of incident."

"We believe Al-Aleaqarab shot the videos he posted roughly 220 miles to the east-northeast of your present position, in the region known as the Al-Hajarah. There are Sunni tribes in the area sympathetic to ISIS."

"Where Al Bookerman lives."

"Who? I'm sorry?" Epstein shrugged at Schelly and mouthed, What?

Al Bookerman. That's familiar ... Schelly grabbed a map of the Al-Hajarah and pored over it. "Here. It's here. Al Bukemal. Madam Secretary, one of the villages in the target area potentially sympathetic to Al-Aleaqarab."

Epstein glowed. "Impressive, Cooper. So you're already on the case."

"Oh for god's sake," muttered Chalmers.

"We've sent you what intel we have along with the resupply," Schelly said, "and we can see that you're mobile. Also, we can tell you that there aren't many Russians, if any, searching in the area we propose."

"Maybe they're not searching because they know Petrovich isn't there?" Cooper asked.

"Different intel can lead to different conclusions, Major," Schelly observed.

Cooper conceded the point. "You said the Scorpion has uploaded videos. How many?"

"Two."

"When did the first video hit the interweb?"

"At 1004 this morning, Syrian time."

"So roughly seven hours after the president's bird did a face plant. Let's say it took the Scorpion another hour and a half to secure his prisoners. That would give him a maximum of five and a half hours of traveling time. I guess it's possible to drive two hundred miles, but not likely. Not here."

"You might be right, but it's *something*," Schelly said. "Vin, can I call you Vin? Look, I sense your difficulty with this."

"Vin is fine. I'm guessing you think Al-Aleaqarab may be in that area because there were indications in the videos posted?"

"We have positively identified three areas. You'll find an intelligence briefing in one of the canisters."

"Wherever you think he was, the Scorpion would be long gone by now."

Schelly glanced at SECSTATE Epstein. She believed much the same.

"Have you thought about Istanbul, Jill? Everyone's going there this time of year."

"Istanbul?"

Chalmers sent a plea to the room: "What did I tell you?"

"Istanbul is not in the picture, Vin," Schelly replied. *I hope Chalmers is wrong about this guy.* "But we know the Scorpion's going to be on the move. The Sunni tribal areas of the Al-Hajarah are our best bet, unless we get some fresh intel which, we're hoping, you'll provide."

"Right," said the voice over the speakers. The way he said it conveyed a gulf of uncertainty.

"Major," Schelly said, reverting to more formal tones, "if there's a chance we can prevent a global meltdown, we're taking it. And given that you've already located passengers who were in Petrovich's party, that puts you way ahead of anyone else on the scoreboard. The Scorpion has styled himself a messianic figure. He's going to attract attention. We believe he *demands* attention. With luck, he generated some of that in the desert among people he knows are supporters, if not outright followers."

Silence.

"Luck has got nothing to do with it," said Rentz, losing patience. And then to Cooper, "Orders are orders, Major."

Silence.

"The satellite," Schelly said, assessing the telemetry on screen. "We lost it." And then she caught a glimpse of a screen monitoring a number of Twitter feeds and the words, "Oh my god" escaped from her mouth before she could prevent them.

A click on the link caught the reporter at the scene mid-sentence. "… hijacked the school bus, the local community devastated. This neighborhood, the most populous municipality in Jefferson County, is all about families, schools, restaurants, shopping …"

A pull-through at the bottom of screen announced, "Hijacked school bus rams oil tanker. More than twenty children dead. A terrorist attack suspected."

The reporter's voice was heard over pictures that showed various angles of a smoking, steaming pile of metal, with other fires dotted around. The area was a sea of emergency vehicle lights, fire trucks, law enforcement vehicles and ambulances. A montage of devastated parents followed.

"At the time of the hijacking, the bus was packed with school children under seven years old – an appalling target that authorities believe was no accident. Specific numbers in the bus have not been confirmed.

The tragedy of the scene was writ large on the face of the reporter whose head and shoulders filled the screen. "Witnesses say that the bus came down this street and veered across the road into the path of an oncoming oil tanker. The ensuing explosion smashed windows for two blocks and caused a number of other vehicles to catch fire. We'll bring you an update when more information comes to hand. As for the motive, local law enforcement isn't saying, but in an unconfirmed report, the hijacker was said to yell, 'Allahu akbar' as he stormed the bus, which means 'God is great' in Arabic."

"Police are yet to confirm the identity of the suspect. We'll bring you updates on this tragedy throughout the day. Tracey?"

"Jesus H Christ," Bunion exhaled.

Schelly switched to CNN to see if more information was available.

"The concrete truck ploughed into vehicles waiting at the crossing," the reporter said, facing the camera. Behind him a zigzag of train coaches lying on their side, strewn around as if thrown there by an angry giant. The reporter continued, "...which in turn cannon-balled into the 9:47 Tucson to San Diego, causing a derailment."

"What the hell?" said Bunion. "When was this?"

"Police have been quick to call this an act of terror, and have already identified two suspects."

Photos of two young men in their early twenties, smiling at the camera, were presented to the president's chief advisor. "These guys? Fuck. Why the fuck haven't we sent fuckers like this back to where they came from? This is what keeping America safe is all about."

The journalist continued, "Both men were born in the United States and attended the Tucson Art College. They are believed to have been only recently radicalized –"

"Jesus," muttered Bunion.

Schelly felt dizzy. Sick. Hot tears ran through her nose and over her top lip. "My god," she mumbled, her brain incapable of putting any other coherent words together.

* * *

I looked at the handset. Had I maybe switched it off accidentally? Nope. I put it to my ear. I'd get more from a seashell. I pocketed it and returned to Bo who, in the meantime, had assembled the drone and was trying to get it to speak to the control center, a screen about the size of an iPad mini set into a khaki-colored plastic case with two small control sticks either side of the screen.

"What gives, boss?" he asked me, preoccupied.

"They want us to wander the dessert, looking for a messiah. For around forty days and forty nights I think they said."

"Sir?"

"Just kidding," I told him. "Actually, they want us to locate and rescue President Petrovich, stop the world blowing up, and prevent a few hundred thousand people from killing each other. And if we could do it before lunch, that would be handy."

"Damn Steve Jobs," he cursed, not hearing me, his attention focused on the drone. "Damn piece of shit don't wanna do its thing." But then what I'd just said to him must have sunken in because he glanced up and said, "How they expect us to do that?"

"Not sure," I replied. "But they've given us a model airplane that doesn't work."

I kneeled beside the canister, listening to Bo curse the UAV while I ditched the AK mags from my webbing and replaced them with rattle for the M4, fitted the M26 shotgun to the barrel and grabbed a bunch of MREs. "Forget it," I said to Bo, who was still cursing the drone. "You can have the shits with it on the road. Let's go."

The iPad suddenly came to life, as did a red LED on the top of the aircraft's fuselage, which then turned green.

"Have I told you that green is my favorite color with electrics?" I said.

"Okay, now I get it." Bo gave a minor fist pump. And, continuing to talk to himself, "The passcode goes in the *other* slot."

"They do it that way to confuse the enemy should it fall into the wrong hands," I said, absently, taking in the general ambience of our bivouac. Alvin and Jimmy were stuffing their rucks and webbing with various items from their canister while Igor wiped a finger around the inside of the cooking pot, savoring the last morsel, which was the most unlikely thing I'd seen in a long time. Natasha was not far from him, re-doing her ponytail so it was nice and high, an important detail not to be overlooked. Mazool was coming toward me, something on his mind.

"I went to make a piss. Found the terrorist behind a tree," he said conspirator-like when he was close enough that the conversation wouldn't be overheard by anyone other than Bo. "He was dead."

"I hope so," I replied, kinda hushed. "People have a nasty habit of coming back to life in this part of the world, right?" Not the slightest flicker of a smile animated Mazool's lips. Nothing. Maybe he didn't get it. Maybe he'd heard that one before. Maybe there was a language problem. Maybe they just take religion far too seriously in this part of the world for their own good, or anyone else's for that matter. Maybe I just hit on a self-evident truth. "He was murdered," I said. "Did you murder him?"

"Me?" Mazool was shocked by the accusation. "No!"

"One of your boys maybe?" I motioned at Taymullah and Farib.

"No! They are still childrens, not murderer," he said, doing a little butchering of his own. "Igor? Was it him?" he asked, pointing the finger elsewhere.

"Maybe," I replied.

"I am sure he was deserving of it."

I knew he meant Abdullah was deserving of being murdered, not Igor was deserving of doing the deed. "Perhaps," I agreed. It was close to dark, with only the faintest memory of the sun visible in the sky above the hills, the temperature also cooling noticeably. "If you need to get organized, now is the time. We're outta here."

"We are ready."

Mazool moved off toward the ambulance and I headed over to my ruck, dumped an armful of necessities on it, and then made my way to Igor and Natasha.

"Spaghetti. Is good," Igor exclaimed looking up at me, sauce dribbling from either side of his mouth so that he seemed to be frowning and grinning at the same time.

"It's the Jell-O that makes all the difference," I told him. And to Natasha, I said, "You murdered the prisoner. Wanna tell me why?"

Natasha smoothed the hair on each side of her head, feeding errant strands into her other hand to wrangle inside the elastic. "How do you know was me? Why not them?" She motioned at the Syrians with the point of an elbow, her hands behind her head. "They have many reasons to kill this man."

"You broke his neck," I said.

"Is this how he was killed? Broken neck?" She smiled pleasantly. "It takes strength to do this." Using that same elbow, she motioned at Igor whose back was to her.

"Strength leaves bruising, but there wasn't any," I said. "Good technique doesn't leave marks. Why'd you do it?"

She looked at me, still with that smile. It was the kind of smile that could live happily with a statement like, "Sure, I'd love a vodka martini. I thought I was gonna have to buy my own drinks tonight." Or similar. But instead she said, "You are Sherlock detective or something?"

"Nope, just a guy who likes to know who he's traveling with."

"Well ... this man was terrorist. What was plan? Carry him to Turkey? It was parting gift from me to you."

How thoughtful. There were other things I'd have preferred. Cuff links, a nice tie ... In truth, I didn't care for Abdullah. The asshole got what he deserved. The Brits had several hit squads operating in Syria taking out their citizens before they could return from the caliphate and bring home a little jihad with their duty free cigarettes. Same with Australia, New Zealand, France and a host of other countries. Abdullah was a marked man – his sudden death was only a matter of time. Nevertheless, I like to know who and *what* I'm traveling with.

"I hear you are leaving," Natasha said, motioning at the activity around the bivouac. Abdullah's murder was of far less concern to her than a particularly recalcitrant strand of hair that refused to be controlled.

Igor stood.

Given that our mission had changed, I was rethinking the benefits or otherwise of us parting company with the Russians, and that made resolving who killed Abdullah important. None of my guys spoke any Arabic worthy of mention and neither did I, so that gave the Syrians a place in our squad, aside from their local knowledge of trails and roads. And if we came up against any

Russians with a particular dislike for Americans, which seemed to be their national disposition, particularly at this moment, I was thinking that having Natasha and the Incredible Hulkovich in our corner vouching for us would be helpful. But, at the same time, I was leery of having a cold-blooded killer looking over my shoulder. There were other considerations on my mind also. Traveling with such a large party, for example, had its drawbacks. Like, forget stealth, right? In our current configuration, we couldn't sneak up on road kill. Mentally, I put everything in the scales – and, just so you know, Natasha's spectacular rack wasn't one of the items, even though it was on display at every opportunity. In the end, I gave them a choice. "My president wants your president found, and he seems to think we're in a good position to do that. You killed the one opportunity we had to maybe find out where the Scorpion has taken your guy."

Natasha was less than convinced. "He would not have talked," she said with a flick of a hand.

"Maybe," I replied, "but you'd be surprised what people give up when you ask them nice."

She shrugged a load of obstinacy at me.

"Look, our mission has changed, but whether that alters your plans is up to you. Come with us or not, that's your choice. But if you're with us, no more killing unless I green-light it." Granted, as counter offers go this wasn't much of one, but I didn't want these two Ruskies thinking they had us by the pubics.

Natasha examined me as if trying to discern what I was really thinking, given that this was a complete about-face on my part on the question of going after Petrovich. They'd done this to me and now I was doing it back at them. A Canadian two-step without Canadians. I watched her eyes scanning my lines and features, hunting for nuances, subtexts, unspoken plots and so forth. After a moment, she seemed to decide I wasn't smart enough for such subtleties and put a full stop on the probing with a shrug. "Okay, is deal," she said. "We go with you." She checked this with Igor.

Igor belched, which I read that if we had more Inedible w/ Unspeakable & Unbelievable he was all in. "Find yourselves an AK each that's not too bent out of shape, and some magazines," I told him and Natasha. "We're gonna need all hands. We leave in two minutes."

"I have nothing to pack," Natasha replied, and then added, "except for an unfeasibly spectacular body tucked into this here flight suit."

Okay, she didn't say that, but the way she was standing, one hand on a hip swaying slightly, daring me to try something, the zip of the flight suit just so, I knew what she was thinking. In fact, what she more accurately said was, "We look for president ... where?"

Good question. I waved a hand in the general direction of the northeast. "There," I said expansively and went off to my ruck to pack away those MREs.

When it was time to go, I put Mazool behind the wheel of the ambulance, Natasha riding shotgun, and I rode with Alvin in back. Ahead, riding in the Toyota's tray, Bo, Igor and Taymullah were dressed up like ISIS fighters, their heads shrouded, waving AKs just for show, Farib and Jimmy up front at the controls. We'd stowed the ISIS flags for now. Under the right circumstances, they could be a free pass, but more than likely they could get us wasted by zealous Russians or the special forces of half-a-dozen countries including American, Australia, France, New Zealander, the Netherlands – in fact, the elite soldiery of pretty much the rest of the world.

Alvin handed me the intelligence pack, a typewritten set of original documents that included notes and maps. I'd scanned it earlier and considered it to be roughly half a pound of hooey. The material and its conclusions and assumptions were thin, clearly put together on the fly by people under pressure. It was about as convincing as a carnival toupee. The three areas – Alpha, Bravo and Charley - in which the Scorpion had been "pinpointed", were around 220, 250 and 280 miles respectively from our current position. These areas weren't exactly adjacent to each other and each was roughly twenty square miles. That made it a job way beyond my little search party's capabilities, no matter how awesomely cool the drone was. Another consideration: the roads. The highway east wasn't exactly Route 1 on a Sunday morning. In this part of the world the roads – even the lesser ones – were either clogged by refugees or bands of militias, and often both, the latter more than especially trigger happy with their leadership gone and all their allegiances either breaking down or broken. "Fact is, despite what this says, the Scorpion couldn't have covered 280 miles, shoot a video and upload it all by mid-morning coffee break." I said to Alvin, considering the maps and notes spread out on the gurney.

The sergeant was likewise unconvinced. "ISIS fighters lately are in the habit of slipping away when the going gets tough. No way is this guy going to be hanging around out in the open, waiting to get pinned down."

"He's going to make sure he's got a back door."

"The border." He pointed his ka-bar at the triangle. "The only option for this guy's hideout has to be this one designated Position Alpha."

The target triangle was 230-plus miles from the Hind's crash site. That was a long way to drive in a handful of hours. Being in convoy with a mobile ZPU would help – it would give Al-Aleaqarab a reasonably free passage, unless he came up against organized elements of more heavily armed infantry, or an airborne threat. Perhaps that was where the Al-Hajarah and its Sunni-centric support came into the picture. Or maybe not.

"What about these Sunni villages? Are they really gonna help the Scorpion?" Alvin wondered, thinking along the same lines.

"I was thinking … What would someone like Petrovich be worth as a hostage?"

"Depends on who's buying," said Alvin.

"He'd have to be worth, what … maybe a hundred million? Five hundred million?"

"Really? That's a lot of coin."

"He's the President of Russia … So you're the Scorpion and you roll into town with this famous guy wearing a big fat price tag around his neck, and I'm living in a mud house with a dirt floor and no air-conditioning…"

"Five hundred million is gonna buy a lot of floor boards and air-conditioning."

"If you had hostages worth that much, and the world knew you had them, who would you trust in northern Syria? Where would you go?"

"Somewhere quiet. He's not going to be anywhere near a village. He'll be hiding under a rock."

"Right," I said, "like a scorpion."

Thirty-three

Ronald V. Small @realSmall
If you are an American and you fight on the side of terrorists who
hate Americans, we will hate you right back.

Night had fallen, the day well and truly done. And that meant time
to go to work. Sam Nanaster rode in the Desert Patrol Vehicle,
an open-wheel desert racer powered by a dual, turbo-charged V6,
a healthy shot of NOx available in the event of a tight squeeze.
Nanaster removed the NVGs strapped to her head to better review
the picture relayed to the tablet on her lap. "We're close enough.
Pull over up there," she said with a gesture ahead.

The DPV growled to a stop on a flinty bluff overlooking a wadi
cutting through the desert, the V6 burbling at idle. "Kill it," she
said to Ronan, her RTO – radio, telephone operator - and driver
of choice. The motor died, imposing a momentary silence until
the rising and falling of multiple four-stroke engines revving hard
became audible.

"On me," she said into the comms mike.

The pitch of the motorcycle engines changed noticeably and
soon six riders rode up to the DPV, stopping in a ball of grit.
Engines died and desert silence closed in.

Phoenix Zero-Four, a team of eight CIA Special Activities paramilitaries, all ex US Special Forces and Special Ops, gathered around Nanaster who sat half in and half out of the DPV, leaning casually against an arm of the rollover cage, a tablet in her hand.

"One breather," she said. "From Portland, Oregon, this one. One Omar Al-Haq, alias Gregory James Walford, age thirty-six. Radicalized in 2013, came to Syria with his family via Turkey in 2014." She showed her team the tablet, which displayed a photo of a smiling boy holding up a bearded severed head by its hair. "Walford's kid, aged seven and a half. A highlight from Walford's Facebook page."

No one commented.

"We've got ten points of positive facial recognition. Ninety-two percent."

She called up the confirmation on the tablet, two photos occupying the screen. One, in color, showed a clean-shaven Greg Walford with a football in hand. The other showed him bearded, cradling an RPG in his arms, shot with an infrared camera. Ten fine green lines joined various parts of one facial image with another. The words "92% Positive" underpinned the set.

"Where is he?" asked Luke Eldrich, a.k.a. Gunny, a lean sniper with a supersized mouth and a nose to match, three weeks of dark growth covering his cheeks.

"Two klicks upwind," she replied. "One of seventeen men, all armed, identities and nationalities unknown, except for our breather. Five vehicles."

"What about his kid – Walford's?"

"Says here mother and both sons – also had a ten-year-old – all killed in Aleppo six months ago."

"Gotta be my turn," said Li'l Wilson looking around, a huge African–American from New Orleans, ex Navy SEAL.

Nanaster grinned. "Put your feet up. I got it." *Who doesn't love this job?*

"I'll spot," Eldrich said.

Five minutes later Nanaster and Eldrich were jogging at a medium pace, all necessary loose metal-against-metal items taped to eliminate the sound. The soles of their boots were soft for the same reason, the high ground a mix of flinty grit and loose stones that reflected sound.

Nanaster gave the signal to stop. She checked the tablet, the drone high overhead verifying Walford's presence. Thermal imaging showed sentries posted out as far as 400 yards from the main camp. *They're nervous. They should be.*

Eldrich took the lead. Going into the crouching run, NVGs down, he brought them around so that they would make the approach directly into the breeze. *No crosswind. Thank you.* Nanaster appreciated his thoughtfulness. *Around 800 yards to target. Not overly difficult, but that's a large party of assholes down there. Gonna be no time for a ranging shot. Have to be clean.*

Eldrich got down on the ground and began to military crawl on elbow and kneepads, the carbine carried in the crook of his elbows. Nanaster followed. Several minutes of crawling brought them to the crest of a gentle slope, a wide wadi below. A little less than a klick away, the flickering light of small cooking fires illuminated a number of pickups and other vehicles parked in a rough circle.

Nanaster brought herself up beside Eldrich who was already removing the spotter's high-powered night scope from its container and setting it on its tripod. The tablet containing facial recognition information was on the ground, ready to be plugged into his scope.

She set the M4 down then slipped the Mk 14's strap off her shoulder, swinging the rifle off her back and bringing it into her hands. The weight of it felt good, like holding your child. She got down on the ground, rolled onto her back, removed the scope lens caps, confirmed a round in the chamber, and checked safety. *On.* She rolled back onto her stomach, rested her chin on the stock and her eye aligned with the scope. Nanaster might not have been a sniper in places like Fallujah or Helmand province, but she'd done all the courses, had been taught by the best and had the hands of a micro surgeon – rock steady.

A number of men were visible. She moved the reticle from one head to the next, searching. There was no laughing around this campfire. The faces were serious, vacant or brooding. Two shadows within the shadows moved. Nanaster adjusted the focus a click. Women. In full niqabs. There were, in fact, four of them. One was grabbed by the arm and hoisted onto her feet. Nanaster moved the reticle. It was a man. And this man was special. There was a laser, invisible to the naked eye, projected by the targeting drone, dancing on the side of his head.

"Come to mama," said Nanaster.

Eldrich's voice in her earpiece: "I got ninety percent facial recognition confirmation on breather Omar Al-Haq. Take the shot, Sam."

"Confirmed," she said.

* * *

Anjen Al Masri squatted by the fire. His thoughts were confused. *Perhaps it is like that with everyone,* he thought. *There is so much to say that no one knows where to begin.*

"We should make our way to Dabiq," said Haddi, an Arab from the holy city of Mecca. "Everyone is talking. The Mahdi is coming and the End of Days is upon us."

If I could truly speak my mind, I would say, no, I am going home, hopeful that Allah has spared my home and I have one to go to. I am tired of desert sand, the jump of the gun in my hand, the smell of blood and the lack of sleep. Perhaps if I could sleep, lie down for a week, when I woke I would feel differently. But I am too tired. I am certainly too tired to tell you my secret fears. "Yes, we should do that," he said without conviction.

No one responded. The men ate what little food they had and enjoyed a few moments without battle.

"Tell them, Naashi," Haddi urged.

Naashi, sitting with legs crossed in front of the fire, eating a jar of olives taken from a refugee, ignored him.

"What about you, Omah?" Haddi asked him. "What are you going to do?"

"What every devout Muslim should do," he said, squatting, drawing circles in the earth with the tip of his blade. "Die a martyr's death and spend an eternity in Paradise. That is what we should all do. But in the meantime, I will do as Allah dictates, kill the unbelievers and enjoy the company of slaves." He stood and walked to where the women had been seated. They were refugee women. These were the handsome ones, their apostate husbands, fathers and brothers sent to hell. "You," he said, grabbing one of the dark shadows by the arm and pulling her to her feet. Her wrist was small. She was young, but old enough. "Tonight you will lie with a warrior who fights for Allah's glory. Be grateful –"

The woman screamed and dropped to the ground, Omah's body falling also to the ground. Only now his head was halved – an eye, a cheek and most of the mouth was all that remained. What was no longer on his face had soiled her niqab.

* * *

A muffled *phut* accompanied by a small puff of dust rose from the ground around the barrel of Nanaster's rifle.

A moment later Eldrich, not taking his eye from the scope, said, "Nice shot, boss. A breather no more."

Thirty-four

Ronald V. Small @realSmall
ISIS. Trying to use our Christian symbols against us. SAD!

"Make sure you are in close with the camera," said Al-Aleaqarab. "More than just feel his pain, I want the armies of Rome to smell it."

The operator brought the camera to within half a meter of the president's filthy hand, slicked with blood in various stages of coagulation. The hand shook as if shivering with cold, but it was not cold.

"Get his feet too. I want everyone to see his feet. I want them to know this is no trick. And do not forget his face. If he cannot be recognized this will be for nothing. When you make the video, you can put it all in. Show me when you think you are finished."

The two film crews assured the Scorpion that of course they would do all of this. Nevertheless, Ortsa berated them. "Do you not know how to operate a simple camera?" He clipped a sound recorder across his head. "This is a great honor, to be here at the beginning of the end. What is wrong with you? When the Mahdi speaks, listen and do as he says."

"Ortsa, enough. I am not the Mahdi," the Scorpion admonished him.

"Amir, all of us have read the passages over and over. Al-Baghdadi lied. *You* are the Mahdi. It has to be you! Who else but the Mahdi purifies the world with a great battle? This is the word of Allah, may his name be praised."

Al-Aleaqarab had heard the men whispering this among themselves. Truly, this was not an honor he sought. Mohammad, who had received the words from God, proclaimed the Mahdi's coming, the prophesized redeemer who would usher in the End of Days and rule until Judgment Day. And yet he, Temurazi Kvinitadze Sumbatashvili, was just a man. He was not even of the Qurasysh tribe favored by Allah to rule all Muslims, as al-Baghdadi was, the deceased leader of Ad-Dawlah al-Islamiyah gone to Paradise. He could not be the Mahdi ... And yet it was also true that his actions were following the sacred texts given to Mohammad by God, not exactly as they were rendered, but close. Was it possible that God so favored him? Was he the Mahdi? Did he not have the codes; the ones that could rain missiles down on the Earth and burn away all apostasy?

A whimper that was also part scream took Al-Aleaqarab from these thoughts. Dark urine ran down the president's leg, down his bloody foot and off the end of his big toe. It made a puddle in the dirt below his feet.

Ortsa waved at the BMW. "Bring it around! Turn on the lights."

The BMW crawled forward, and fixed its high beams on the Scorpion and President Petrovich. The Toyota with the ZPU was also brought up, its powerful spotlights beating back the night. Whorls of dust and motes drifted through the powerful beams.

Al-Aleaqarab read his notes a final time, his lips moving as he scanned the Arabic hurriedly written with a woman's eyeliner pencil on a page torn from the BMW's service manual. He stuffed the paper up a sleeve and faced the camera. "I am ready," he announced.

One of the men made the signal with his hand showing four fingers then three, then two, and then he pointed at the Mahdi.

* * *

The Toyota bounced and then shuddered violently on the ruts carved into the hard, baked earth of the wadi, etched there by the wind. The headlights carved a cone of light into the darkness. The occasional low shrub stood like bones in the brittle white light cast by the utility's LEDs.

"He is the Mahdi," said Jalil. "Everyone is certain of it."

"I am sure as well," Imad agreed.

They exchanged a look, proud but scared.

"What will the Antichrist look like? What have you heard?" Imad asked.

Jalil scoffed at him. "I don't listen to rumors or stories told by women to scare children. I have read the Qur'an and hadiths so I know that he has red skin. And this red, it is the color of blood."

They drove in silence for a while, lost in their imaginings of the end of the world foretold. Eventually, Jalil said, "Crucifixion is not a good death. There is nothing noble in such a death. Give me a sword thrust or a bullet."

"This punishment was chosen by Allah himself for the enemies of Islam. You wouldn't honor your enemies with a glorious death."

"Have you seen the Crusader's hands? The nails pulled through, between his fingers, so they nailed him again through the wrists. He hangs there, no more strength in his legs. He labors for breath as if there is a huge weight on his chest."

"The weight of the unbeliever."

"I wonder if he will die before the appointed time? He seemed strong, but this is a punishment that saps the strength."

A shepherd and three goats suddenly rose from the blackness, causing Imad to swerve violently and wrestle with the steering wheel, bouncing at a steep angle down the side of a wadi. Finally, the Toyota came to a stop. Imad's heart was racing.

"*Astaghfirulaaaah!* You drive like a blind man," Jalil screamed at him

"We, we nearly rolled over."

"Yes, I know. And it is fortunate that we didn't." Jalil looked back over his shoulder, hoping to see the shepherd so that he could beat the man but, beyond the red of their stoplights, there was only darkness. "We are the Mahdi's messengers," he continued. "I don't think Paradise would be happy to see us if we died, our holy task left unfulfilled. Drive more carefully."

Imad put the pickup back into gear, massaged the accelerator pedal and eased the vehicle up the bank of the wadi and onto the flat. "There is no road, that is the problem."

"You are a bad driver – *that* is the problem. How much further?" Jalil enquired. "We don't have all night."

Imad checked the trip meter. "Sixty kilometers. Maybe a little more."

"Just drive. Keep your eyes open!"

"You can drive," said Imad. "I have no love for it."

Jalil glared at him and sank lower in his chair, looking for comfort. They drove in silence a while longer, Imad more cautious now behind the wheel, realizing that the empty desert was not so empty.

A home made from mud bricks with small yards fenced with wood came and went, light shining from a window.

"Stop!" cried Jalil, taking a few seconds to process what he had just seen.

Imad took his foot off the pedal and the Toyota slowed quickly in a field of sand, rocks and bush. "Why? Before you were in a hurry. Now you are not?"

"The house back there. I saw a dish. There was also electric light. Perhaps they have a computer, and also the Internet. We could upload from there."

"We should keep going to Al Hasakah, as the Mahdi ordered," Imad cautioned him. "He was specific about it. We must go to Al Hasakah."

"He wants the video on YouTube – that is the point. If he knew there were closer options, would he still have us drive all the way to a city? Cities can be dangerous. The Kurds rule Al Hasakah. We could be shot or wounded. There could be bandits. What if we lost the thumb drive?"

"He said Al Hasakah."

"Because he believed it to be the closest opportunity to access the Internet."

"I don't know ..." said Imad, wavering.

"Imad, to become a leader, you must lead. Al-Aleaqarab will not know. What does it matter to him? Here or Al Hasakah?"

Jalil's reasoning was sound. "Okay." Imad relented and turned the Toyota around until the house lay ahead, a distant light burning clean and bright behind a curtain. Shortly after, he brought the vehicle to a stop outside. Both men grabbed their AKs and got out. Jalil noted the hum of generator.

"*Assalam alaikum*," said a voice from the shadows. A man stepped into the dim starlight.

"*Wa alaikum assalam*," Jalil replied, mirroring the familiar greeting.

"I heard you stop and turn around. Travelers are always welcome in the home I share with my brother and mother."

"And ten goats," Imad said, counting them as they milled about the small dusty enclosure.

"You are men from the caliphate," he said.

"Yes," Jalil replied.

"Good. You work in the service of Allah the merciful. Come in, be my guests and share in our food. There will be enough for you. I am Nasim Al Badur," he said, leading them to the front door.

Once inside, the air smelt of bread and spices. A dusty old table occupied one corner, a single chair behind it. A computer was open on the desk, the picture of a waterfall and another of a polar bear drifting across the screen. A squat older woman adjusted the full niqab she had clearly rushed to put on, and otherwise ignored the men. On the floor, a man sat cross-legged among cushions, a tray in front of him with bowls of flat bread, a little meat and cheese. Behind him, against the wall, leaned a couple of AKs.

This is my younger brother, Emran," said Nasim. He addressed the younger man. "Emran, these are men from the caliphate. They are guests."

"We are most grateful for your hospitality," Jalil told him. "Do you have Internet here?"

"Yes, my younger brother brought it to the house."

"*Assalam alaikum.*" Emran lifted a hand in a vague gesture of welcome. "You talk about me as if I were not here, brother. I brought the television, too. And the generator that powers it." He aimed the remote at the large television screen that took up almost one entire wall of the house and turned off the sound.

"*Wa alaikum assalam,*" Jalil and Imad replied. Jalil continued, "We are going to Al Hasakah to get news of the world. We saw your dish."

"My computer is there on the desk, if you would care to use it." He motioned at it. "Please ..."

"I thank you," said Jalil and he went to the desk.

"I can tell you a great army of the faithful assembles in Turkey and other lands. They say the signs point to the coming of the Mahdi."

"He is here already," Imad told them.

Emran, who was a little overweight, struggled to his feet with some noisy effort.

"This I did not know!"

"Is there a passcode?" Jalil asked at the computer.

"Emran99. No space."

Jalil tapped the code into the field and the screen showed the browser. "Nice computer," he said.

"You can do anything on it," Emran bragged. "It is quite powerful."

Jalil turned and opened fire on Emran, his older brother Nasim, their mother and the television, until the firing pin clicked on an empty chamber. The three died quickly, making a bloody mess of the wall behind them.

"Stop! Why did you do this!" Imad shouted at him as gun smoke curled from the muzzle of Jalil's AK. "We were their guests.

We were under their protection. You broke the sacred bond. We will both be cursed."

"Don't be a fool, Imad. The Crusader police will hurry straight to the upload source. In Al Hasakah we could come and go and conduct our business unnoticed. Here, we will be remembered. This way, our identities remain unknown." Jalil dug the USB stick from a breast pocket and pushed it into the slot.

"Now we can stay awhile, eat, relax, and no one will be any the wiser."

* * *

"Boss," came Jimmy's familiar voice in my earpiece, "we got an intersection coming up."

Alvin turned the map over and indicated our position with the tip of his ka-bar. It was decision time or, rather, confirmation time of an earlier decision: back to Latakia, north to Idlib, Aleppo and Dabiq, or harder right to Raqqa? "Raqqa it is, but when the time comes we want to find a way around it. Got no desire to tour the main street."

Jimmy concurred. "Roger that, sir."

The road ahead was framed by the opening where the ambulance's windshield used to be. There were no streetlights, the irregular surface was pocked by holes and debris, and the night was heavy with the smell of burning shit, rubber and diesel; the usual perfumes of war. We were approaching a road sign full of bullet holes and other larger projectile holes, indicating the intersection was not far ahead. So here's the thing that surprised me since we'd hit the main road. Where was everyone? Not the refugees, they were everywhere. I meant the combatants. We'd seen two BTRs motoring in the opposite direction, which we avoided by driving slow, Mazool and Taymullah waving at them, but not a single jihadist asshole. So how come, right? No pickups with recoilless rifles in the back, chaperoned with assholes. No racing convoys of

AK-waving assholes. No assholes by the roadside. Just the usual ceaseless flood of despairing humanity taking itself to a place where it believed it wouldn't be shot, burned or tortured by whichever assholes felt like it at the time, or bombed by the rest of the world trying to protect them from said assholes.

As an OSI special agent, essentially a criminal investigator, your job is to deduce the identity of the party or parties involved in a crime, based on the evidence you find, and then you bring him, her or them to a court where a judge, judges and/or jury make the decision about guilt or innocence. Complex, but not something that assaults your sense of humanity. But here, looking at the sullen waves of people shuffling forward, there was only complication mixed with privation and death and assholes. And always the feeling that I should be doing something to help. I guessed that I was doing something – helping to bring this catastrophe to an end sooner rather than later.

The ambulance followed the sign and we lurched hard in the turn. Knowing you can't do anything about the shit you see around you can get to you. Even when you recognize that it can get to you, it still gets to you. Maybe saving the world wasn't so bad after all. I had it good, and didn't know it. Draining, yes, but at least it left me with a smug sense of over achievement.

Images of the family killed by the Scorpion back at the warehouse took over my thoughts. The Scorpion – head and shoulders above the other assholes. And now this asshole had become a supercharged chocolate starfish, waving the captured president of Russia at the world in the hope of unleashing calamitous death and destruction on an unprecedented scale. And on the Scale of Helpfulness, it would be right up there if a bullet could just find its way between said asshole's eyeballs. Like Hitler, right? If only, back in the day, they'd managed to –

"Boss," said Jimmy interrupting my daydream. "You seeing this?"

I felt the ambulance slow and pull over. "What up," I said, snapping out of it. The first thing I noticed – no refugees. For some reason they were giving this place a wide berth. I ducked my head so I could scan ahead and the reason became plain. "Shit," I muttered. Across the road, blocking the way forward, were several burning cars and other less substantial refuse, along with fires burning in 55-gallon drums.

"This is not good," Natasha informed me helpfully. "What does American tough guy do now?" She asked it in that sneering manner you can't get away with unless you're at least a solid nine. She was referring to the maybe fifty or so assholes toting AKs, RPGs and numerous "fittys" – .50 caliber machine guns. Others were waving around ISIS flags, a gutsy call with all the Russians around, let's be honest. This platoon and a half of assholes was maybe 100 yards ahead, shouting and gesturing at us, full of dangerous trigger-happy excitement. I wasn't sure what they wanted, but I was pretty certain it entailed us vacating the vehicles, which I was not inclined to do.

This answered my question about where all the assholes had gone. They'd come here, and probably to other checkpoints, in the hope of killing and extorting their way to a little nest egg to set themselves up in the peace to come. Shooting our way out would be dicey – too many of them, too few of us. And running an ISIS jolly roger of our own up the flagpole and driving through while they all saluted it probably wouldn't cut the mustard. Options were narrow. Shadows in the ambulance began to dance around – assholes driving up behind us, narrowing the options to none. At least, none that were good.

"Boss ..." said Alvin.

"Lock and load," I said into the comms. There was nowhere to go, certainly nowhere to go quietly.

Bo and Jimmy replied, "Roger that," their voices tight in their throats.

"One thing we got plenty of now is ammo," said Alvin, checking his webbing.

"And the other is Spaghetti with Beef & Sauce," I said, placing a couple of magazines on the gurney for rapid access.

"I'd prefer to go with the Colt, boss." Alvin unwound the scarf from his head and replaced it with Kevlar, cocked the M4 and snicked off the safety.

"No, no – I can talk to them," Mazool urged from the front. "I can get them to let us pass. Hand me a black flag. I can do it."

He was serious about it, but I wasn't about to –

A sudden massive explosion picked up the ambulance and dropped it, bouncing and rocking, back onto its tires. Noise, heat and blinding dust consumed our vehicle along with a blast wave that threw me against the roof. As I fell, a second explosion behind us kicked the ambulance sideways and all of us with it. I fell to the floorboards and paper, wound dressings, unidentified plastic and metal flew around inside the ambulance, along with a whirlwind of grit. The frosted windows in the rear doors were shattered, adding crystals of safety glass to the shower.

Beyond the ambulance, flames were everywhere. Tongues of yellow and orange slicing through dust clouds billowing here and there from the percussion of multiple small and larger explosions. Heat radiated through the newly vented rear doors, pulsing hotter with some of the larger explosions. I could feel it as I lay on the floor tangled in rubber tubing, torn sheets, a niqab, used dressings and Alvin's limbs. I felt like I'd been worked over by a baseball bat. My ears rang as Alvin and I got to our hands and knees, Alvin spitting blood. Blood dripped from my nose onto the debris between my hands. It was running down a cheek. I was wounded, but where and how badly hadn't registered.

Though my brains were addled, I could guess what had happened. Hellfire missiles. Two of them. One ahead of us, one behind. The Reapers. Some operator in an air-conditioned booth a thousand miles away had assessed the situation and decided to go kinetic on our behalf. It was a little too close for comfort, but I quietly thanked him or her anyway. Shit would have been trumps otherwise. I happened across my M4 on the floor – after kneeling on it painfully – got up, kicked the rear doors open and fell out onto the road. The dust was clearing and fires burned all around us. Leaning on the ambulance for support, I edged around it, ready to shoot. The pickup came into view. "You okay?" I shouted, my own voice sounding muffled to me, like I had socks stuffed in my ears. For a few seconds – nothing. But then I saw a couple of raised arms and thumbs-up hand signals. Bo and then Igor. The front passenger door opened and Jimmy dropped out as if falling through a trapdoor. Everyone was confused, battered and covered in black oily soot. I approached the Toyota, my ears numb and ringing. Taymullah sat up slowly in the vehicle's bed, bewildered and dazed like a hit and run survivor, as Farib opened the driver's door. Everyone had come through, albeit badly shaken up.

"On me," I said through the comms. If not for the earpiece I'd have had two burst eardrums. Jimmy, Bo and Alvin made their way to me somewhat drunkenly, their silhouettes outlined by oily fires, the smell of barbecue and diesel in the air. Not a great smell. Nothing moved beyond the barricade, which was now scattered, scorched and burning.

"Damn Reapers," said Jimmy. "With friends like that, right?"

"You okay, boss?" Bo came closer. "Half yo' ear is hangin' off. Fuck that shit bleeds, don't it?"

Jimmy gave him a nod.

I was relieved. In the scheme of things, a mangled ear was better than a ruptured eardrum.

"I can stich it," Bo continued.

"Trim the other one the same an' you be Mr Spock, sir." Alvin was grinning. "Live long an' prosper."

Hilarious.

The amusement faded into a frown. "Oh, sir..." he reached forward and picked something off my webbing, a piece of bloody gristle. He held it up. A piece of me.

"Lemme see," said Bo, coming in for a closer look. "Yeah, we hurry I can stitch it back. Won't take more'n five minutes.

Maybe it'll take. Or I can stitch the two halves of what's left – join 'em up. Up to you, boss."

Vanity won. "Okay, put all the pieces of me back together," I told him. We returned to the ambulance, opened the doors and I sat on the back end while Bo readied his OR.

Jimmy said, "There were foreign fighters on these barricades, sir. Saw 'em before the Hellfires came in. Could be some of them were the Scorpion's men."

Bo went to work with swabs, saline, antiseptic spray and antibiotics. That was entirely probable. There had been at least fifty fighters in Al-Aleaqarab's band back at the warehouse, and not all of them had gone off to look for the wounded Russian bird. "Let's go see if we can find some survivors," I said without confidence. Given the devastation, finding survivors was a lottery we'd be lucky to win.

Bo was still working on me with swabs, saline, antiseptic spray and antibiotics.

Natasha, Igor and the Syrians milled around the back of the ambulance, still dazed, wondering what next. Fires raged here and there, but the flames were dying down in places where there wasn't additional fuel, like tires or people, to feed off.

I felt a pulling sensation on the side of my head that stopped when Bo, wearing surgical gloves, snipped a thread with small scissors. "Done," he said, peeling the latex gloves off his hands. "Better'n new. It starts to itch, gonna mean it's healing."

Jimmy peered at my head. "Nice work. Watch for gangrene."

"What if it gets infected?" said Alvin pointing out a third option.

"Probably have to take the whole ear off."

"At the neck, right?" I said. The odds were one in three. I'd had worse and told Bo thanks. Now, where were we? I grabbed my M4 and stood. On the basis that many hands make light work and we were all on the same journey and other clichés, I said, "Work in pairs. We want survivors." I addressed Natasha, who was blackened by the sooty oil covering all of us. "And we want them to stay that way. In fact," I told her, "you come with me."

She shrugged and said, "Yes, this would be my choice also," like she was accepting an invitation for a friendly stroll. A tiptoe through the tulips maybe, except the garden beds here were planted with men, caught in the moment of their death by a firestorm that burned away lips, ears and hair and left them all alike: mouths open in a scream, charred, blackened limbs akimbo. Flames were still licking many of the dead as we picked among them. As for Natasha, perhaps I had done her a disservice. She was as affected by this horror as any sane person would be, stunned and silent as we toured the roadblock's grim battlements, her mouth and nose covered with a rag picked up in the ambulance. Don't get me wrong, I wasn't mourning for these men who, barely moments ago, were our biggest immediate threat. But it is sobering to see so much life snuffed out in a ghastly instant. There are few more gruesome sights than the aftermath of a firestorm, and this was as bad as any of them.

As for recovering survivors, the odds were long. The Reapers' payloads had done the job they were designed to do and a tanker hauling diesel, captured by the jihadists, had added to the conflagration, its contents atomized explosively by the Hellfires, which then cooked off small arms ammunition over a wide area.

I don't know where they came from, or who told them the road was clear, but the river of refugees began to flow again, moving around the roadblock. None slowed to gawk, probably because they'd had violence and death up to their eyeballs.

After touring much of the site, Natasha pulled the rag away from her face just long enough to say, "There is no one."

She meant there was no one left alive, but I kept up with the inspection anyway, working methodically toward a barricade of vehicles near the perimeter of the roadblock where the fires were less intense. Maneuvering around the barricade, I saw three crispy black corpses lying on the ground, smoking, caricature faces stretched into the typical silent shriek. But one of them was moving, rolling stiffly from side to side. Using the sole of my boot against the body, I turned it over. Beneath it lay a man of around thirty, wearing a typical version of ISIS garb, the one that was a cross between Prince-Ali-Fabulous-He-Ali-of-Bagwa and Obi-Wan Kenobi. He was covered in the sooty oil like everyone else, but his bloodshot eyes were bright green, a kind you don't see much in this part of the world. He was sobbing like a lost toddler at a fairground. "C'mon, shoot me," he babbled in an unmistakable accent, which, to be honest, took me aback.

"You're from Queens?" I asked him.

He ignored the question, or didn't hear it. "Hey!" I snapped, getting his focus. "You're American."

"I am Ad-Dawlah al-Islamiyah," he babbled.

In other words, he said he was Daesh – Islamic State, ISIS, the caliphate. "What's your real name?"

"Kill me."

Funny name, right? His accent reminded me of Queens and Al Bookerman's. "Hey - say, 'One Reuben on rye to go!'"

"Kill me."

"Don't wanna play?"

He glanced up at me, a little confused.

"Okay, as far as killing you, maybe we can do you a solid and get around to that," I said. "But first you're gonna have to earn it."

Thirty-five

Ronald V. Small @realSmall
This week I lost five pounds and one notch on my belt!

Slanting rainfall smeared the foyer windows. "Great," Schelly muttered to herself. *Wasn't it supposed to be sunny today?* The cold hit her skin when she came through the revolving door, the rain immediately soaking her stockings to the skin. *Damnit!*

After taking advantage of as much overhead cover as possible, she ran the last 30 yards to the Air Force Ford allocated to her for the duration. "Ughhh." Schelly felt cold and half drowned as she pulled the door shut. Where has this rain come from? *They can put us on Mars, but they can't get the damn weather right.* "What's with that?" she muttered. Moments later the Ford was exiting the lot, its heater and defog warming the cabin and clearing the mist from the windshield.

The turnoff that would take her back to Fort Myer rapidly approached on the Interstate, but Schelly decided to keep on going. Some thinking time was needed to process the mission being re-planned on the hop. *Is the end of the world really nigh?* "Not if I can help it," she said, continuing the conversation with the empty passenger seat.

Schelly took another exit, following a sign that would take her into the city. *The world can put itself on hold for 30 minutes.* DC was a stranger to her, its famous monuments only familiar because of appearances in TV shows and movies.

While programing a route into her phone, she caught a glimpse of a burgundy Cadillac parked in the breakdown lane and a woman lashed by wind and rain, wrestling a spare wheel out of the trunk.

The Ford braked hard, turned into the breakdown lane and reversed twenty yards back toward the stricken vehicle. There was a plain black umbrella lying along the rear seat. Shelley grabbed it, opened the door and stepped into the downpour.

Professor Kiraz Başak appeared from around the end of the trunk holding a jack lever in her hand. "Hey!" Schelly called out. "Need a hand?"

* * *

Schelly felt self-conscious sitting on the couch in a hotel bathrobe, her wet hair wrapped in a towel, but Professor Kiraz Başak had insisted. The freezing rain had soaked both of them to the skin. *Nothing a hot shower couldn't fix.* Schelly's non-secured phone rang. Al Udeid, according to the screen. She reached forward, plucked it off the low coffee table in front of her, and pressed the green button. "Major Schelly speaking."

"Major, Lieutenant Colonel Josh Simmons."

"Afternoon, Colonel." *Colonel Simmons, 42nd Attack Squadron – Reapers.*

"Closer to zero dark here, Major."

"Yes, sir." Schelly felt her heart rate surge. *You wouldn't be calling me, especially this late, unless there was a problem.*

"A courtesy call, Major. Your unit was under duress so I authorized a get out of jail free card for them.

They were in trouble, but everything's now okay? "Duress, Colonel?"

"You were out of contact and we both know that I can't say much of anything over an unsecured line. Everything's fine on that front for the moment. I just wanted to give you a heads up."

"It's much appreciated, sir."

"Not all good news, I'm afraid."

What?

"My assets are winchester, Major. All I can promise is a turnaround that will be as quick as we can make it."

Winchester - your Reapers are sucking fumes and their missile stores are empty, so you're bringing them home. But you'll get them back on station as soon as possible. "Understand, sir. Anything else for me?"

"No."

Shit.

"Major?"

"Sorry, Colonel. Just thinking."

"Best I can do is hawk the situation."

You can get some eyes in the sky, but nothing with offensive capability. Well, I guess that's something ... "Thank you, sir."

"Check sipper. Bunch of intel images there for you. One thing - your unit's dress code has gone all Hajji, makes 'em hard to pick out in a crowd."

"I'll see what can be done about it."

"Good night, Major."

"Night, sir."

Schelly put the phone back on the table. It was easy to lose focus on the reality for the boots on the ground where the situation could go into the toilet in a heartbeat. And now there was nothing riding shotgun for an uncertain period of time. *There's nada you can do, girl. You know the whole operation is held together with duct tape and paperclips.*

"Important?"

"Huh? Sorry?"

"The call."

"No." Schelly tried to smile, but knew it looked forced. The professor was standing at her bedroom door in a robe, her hair also wrapped in a towel coiled up on her head, her skin flushed and pink. *Wow, you have no right to look so good without makeup.* The professor came over and flopped on the couch beside Schelly, trailing an invisible cloud of Arpege. *And you smell so warm and ... well, you smell good.* "Feel better?" Schelly asked her.

"Yes, thanks to you ... Look, there's nothing either of us can do. Everything we can do has been done."

"That doesn't stop me worrying about it." Schelly massaged the bridge of her nose between her fingers.

"Worry will get you nothing but an early grave. Hey, I really want to thank you," said the pProfessor, removing the towel and rubbing her hair. "I thought I was going to get stranded out there on the highway. There was a special nut for the wheel, but I couldn't find the spannerwrench. I called Triple A, but they were engaged."

"No problem. Really."

"Your clothes won't take long to dry. Meanwhile, I have ordered lunch. Do you like pizza? I have it only when I need comfort food."

"Thanks, but I should keep moving." Schelly removed her towel. "Got so many things to check up on." *And I want to get onto sipper and look at those photos.*

"Sitting on top of a computer will not make things go better, nor will it go worse if you are not. Ignore your Protestant work ethic for an hour. I have ordered for us already. Have you eaten? If it eases your conscience, we can talk work."

"Maybe I can spare twenty minutes." *Why am I feeling so self-conscious?* "So ... This is a nice hotel. The NSA treats you well. The Air Force isn't as generous."

"The NSA does not pay for this. I pay for it myself. This makes Washington a little less unbearable, and it can be unbearable."

"You don't like DC?"

"I like the city, parts of it – like the Smithsonian. It is some of the people that are unbearable."

"Like our friend Chalmers?"

Kiraz Başak grinned. "Yes, like him. I think he is one of these people who is promoted only because it is easier to promote than to fire. And then one day this man, he wakes up and finds himself in a job he has no talent for, but now it's too late for anyone to do anything about it because he has risen too high. I am sorry, sometimes my English gets tangled up."

"No, I think you nailed it," said Schelly, grinning.

The professor rose from the couch and glided to the fridge in the kitchenette. "I am having a glass of wine. Would you like one also?"

Schelly assessed the remains of her day. *No meetings, no briefings, but that doesn't mean you get a guilt free pass. I really should go.* "I'd better not. That Protestant work ethic ..."

"Please, I do not want to drink alone. Look, why don't I just pour you a glass and put it in front of you and if you drink, you drink. It would make me feel better."

"I thought Muslims didn't drink."

"Shows you how much you know about Muslims," the professor called out from the kitchenette. "It's the devout who don't drink – like ISIS. The rest of us – let us say a healthy proportion of us – just don't do it in public. Sometimes I think perhaps the fundamentalists need to discover vodka. Could you imagine the Scorpion ordering a martini? He would be more relaxed." The professor giggled like a schoolgirl. "Don't tell anyone I said this. I will deny it."

"Your secret's safe with me, Professor."

"Kiraz, please. Professors have wild gray hair and thick glasses."

"True," Schelly agreed, aware of her smile and the growing sense of comfort. *She's gorgeous* and *charming*.

Schelly's phone chimed, a text. She leaned across and picked it up off the table. It read, *Major Schelly, ADD Chalmers here. We need to talk. You've got my number.* "Speak of the devil," she said.

"Who?"

"Chalmers. His ears were burning. Wants me to call. Doesn't say what about." She put the phone down. "I was tempted to turn on the television while you were in the shower; see what's happened in the world while we've been locked up all morning."

The professor returned with two empty wine glasses and a bottle of chilled Riesling, placed the glasses on the low glass coffee table, filled them, and then took one. She curled up on the end of the couch with her bare feet tucked beneath her. "I was listening to the radio before I had the flat tire," she said. "There have been more stabbings, more shootings, more hit and run attacks ... And this is happening all over the world." The professor shook her head slowly. "More riots in London, Paris, Brussels, Amman, Istanbul ... Muslim countries have it worse, with all of the above plus car bombs and suicide bombers. I am sure the Scorpion will rejoice in the havoc he has caused. The train derailment – the fatalities will climb beyond 200. And the reports from Denver – the mothers and fathers who lost children – it's terrible. And this is only the beginning." The professor found it hard to continue and drank her wine instead – all of it. "It seems so, so personal," she continued. "The world is being attacked where it will hurt the most." She reached for the bottle, poured herself another glass. "You really are not going to drink?"

Schelly took her glass in hand, had a sip. *The least I can do.*

"What about this this Major Cooper? Do you really think he can find the Scorpion?" the professor wondered.

"Honestly? I don't know. But it's all we've got, unless the Russians locate him. Or a random air strike kills him. Or ... there's a lot that could go wrong." *And now there are no Reapers riding shotgun.* "It's a race. At least we have one horse in it."

"Then let us toast our horse's success," the professor said and held her glass to Schelly.

"To success," Schelly said. She clinked glasses and self-consciously drank a little.

The professor leaned forward, topped her glass and Schelly's. "What else shall we drink to?"

"I shouldn't ..."

"My house, my rules. First you will drink up your glass, and then one more toast."

Schelly looked at her.

"I am not an enemy spy trying to get you drunk."

"Well, that's a relief," she smiled and drank the rest of her wine. The doorbell rang.

"Ah," the professor said. "Lunch." She went to the door via her bag to get a credit card, and returned a minute later with two boxes, which she opened and placed on the coffee table. "One is four seasons. And the other is pepperoni. We don't have to eat it all."

"How did you know? Pepperoni is my go to," Schelly said, reaching for a slice. "I filled your glass, but I have to be honest with you, I can't think of anything to toast to right now."

"Then how about – pizza, wine and good company," the professor suggested.

"Okay. I can drink to that." Schelly raised her glass and drank, and as she placed her glass on the table the professor leaned forward and kissed her on the mouth, her lips soft and fragrant, her tongue gentle, persuasive and chilled by the wine.

* * *

Schelly lay naked on her stomach, her feet covered by the clean starched sheets, the professor stroking her shoulder and arm with long manicured nails.

"In the meeting, that first one, I fantasized about you," the professor confessed.

"Really? My first impression of you: glamorous, smart, sexy."

"I like that. And now?"

Schelly turned her head so that the professor could see the glow in her face. "I think I've made my opinion of you abundantly clear."

"Reid Hamilton. He was staring at you."

"I didn't know. Well," Schelly said dreamily, "clearly there was a lot going on in that meeting other than what was being discussed."

"The history of the world, great events – these have always turned on the lusts of men and women."

"Men and women turned on their backs," said Schelly.

"I read a thesis on this. Wonderful reading with a vibrator."

"I can imagine."

"This was not your first time," the professor suggested.

"How do you know?"

"I don't, but it is true, yes?"

"I had – I guess you'd call it an encounter. At college, my sophomore year. Well, it was probably more than an encounter because we encountered each other quite a lot."

"Do you think you are gay?"

"Hmm … I've thought about that. I prefer to think of myself as a healthy woman with no hang-ups, at least sexual ones. Honestly? When I'm with a man, I prefer men. When I'm with a woman, I miss men. At least what a man can bring to the table, if you know what I mean."

The professor pouted. "I am disappointed."

"Don't be. What just happened – is happening – feels amazing. What about you? You're a Muslim who doesn't wear a headscarf, drinks wine, has sex outside of her marriage; sex some of your fellow Muslims would stone you for, or throw you off a rooftop for, or both. What would you call that kind of a woman?"

"Courageous."

"Confused, I would call it."

"I think I like you. And you have skin like warm milk," the professor said, brushing Schelly's bare shoulder with her lips.

"I like you too, and you have a magic tongue," Schelly confessed. "Does your husband know?"

"About my tongue?"

"You know what I mean …"

"Yes, of course he knows. This works for the both of us. My orientation is similar to yours."

"Then the CIA and the NSA also know. They worry about this kind of thing. They believe it makes you open to blackmail.

They probably have the room bugged, especially if you come here all the time."

"I am an academic, so my sexuality is less than important. And I am not scared of being, how do you say … outed. If it happens, it happens. I am beyond blackmail. What about you?"

"Times are changing and so is the Air Force. There's a lot of blue on blue going on … Trust me. I am in no way unique. Now, you're not going to ask me to divulge any secrets, are you?"

"What does your heart tell you?" said the professor.

"It says, 'Don't be ridiculous.'"

The professor traced the curve of Schelly's spine to the cleft between her buttocks. Schelly opened her legs, an invitation, and the professor's finger took it, circling her anus and then moving on to the warm wet lips of her vulva, enjoying the velvety feel of the wetness and the warmth.

Oh god, you know where my sweet spot is. Schelly murmured something involuntarily and moved to increase the pressure where it counted. Her breath caught in her throat. "Yes," she whispered, instantly drunk with the pleasure of it.

* * *

Schelly and Professor Başak sat on the bed facing each other. The professor reclined against the bedhead, one forearm draped over her head.

"I swear you look like you're about to purr." *Your dancing black hair, incredible gray-green eyes and olive skin. Those beautiful full breasts and dark, exotic nipples. Who needs a penis?*

"I am wet just looking at you." The professor sipped a glass of ice water, her movements graceful, languid.

Schelly shook her head and laughed. "The end of the world is nigh. And I am with you and … this is frikkin' nuts."

"Yes, that is a good word for it – nuts."

"Can we get serious for a minute?" Schelly asked her.

"Do you mean can we stop having sex?"

"Yes."

The professor grinned. "As long as it's only for a minute or two."

"I've barely skimmed your briefing notes. Take me through them, the Islamic version of Armageddon, the End of Days."

The professor sighed deeply. "If you insist. Where to start? Okay, the hadiths say that the arch devil, whose name is Iblis –"

"Yes, I remember. He's chained on an island."

"You were paying attention."

"I think I was hanging on your every word."

"Iblis, he waits for the right conditions for the End of Days, the Yawm ad-Din, to make an appearance and cause havoc among men. The Yawm ad-Din will be heralded by signs. And you should know, this is a horror story written to frighten people in 600AD."

"It's doing a pretty good job scaring us today."

"Yes. And then there will be the Day of Judgment – this is also called the Great Massacre, an indication of what is to come. Allah will place all life in the scales, annihilate it and then resurrect it, separating the good who will go to Paradise, and the bad who will go to hell. Leading up to this day, Jesus will appear and help the Mahdi become the ruler of the world. On ascending the throne, the Mahdi will banish all other religions except for Islam, bringing a great peace to the world. He will then do battle with Iblis. With the help of Jesus, the Mahdi will win this battle, but not before his army suffers terrible losses."

Schelly was mesmerized, and a little confused. "Wait ... So the Mahdi wins the battle against the devil and Islam is the only religion on Earth, and it's a time of peace and presumably prosperity. Then what's Allah's excuse for killing everything off in the Great Massacre?"

The Professor wagged her finger. "Please do not look rationally at this."

"Yes, religion, I forgot." Schelly's mind spun. "You mention signs that the End of Days are coming. What are they?"

"Yes, the signs written in the hadiths are plain. There are many of these signs – minor and major ones. The first sign is that Gog and Magog will be released."

"Who are Gog and Magog?"

"Scholars disagree, but they could be the tribes walled off by the Gates of Alexander, that have long since been let loose on the world – Huns and Mongols. Two: Iblis, released from his chains, will walk the world. Islamic scholars believe he has indeed been released, but is invisible to us. The proof of his release is all the mischief, secularism and apostasy in the world."

"We can't see him?" Schelly wondered. "That's convenient."

"The signs from here on become more obvious, even to cynics. Three: The sun will rise in the west. This could be interpreted – *is* being interpreted – as the rise of the hegemony of western culture. Four: This is called, 'The Beast of the Land'. It is taken to mean the beast, Israel, will rise to a position of great power. Few would argue that Israel doesn't pull America's strings."

"I might."

"Five: The Euphrates River will reveal a river of gold that all will fight and die over. This gold people believe is, in fact, oil. Six: Non-Muslims will feast on Muslim lands. This one is self-evident, with the invasion of Iraq and other lands by coalition forces. Seven: The construction of tall buildings."

"What?"

"Yes, tall buildings. Look at every major city. That is one of the signs. Eight: A sinking of the Earth in the east."

"What does that mean?" Schelly was captivated.

"There was the earthquake off the coast of Indonesia in 2004. This caused massive subsidence of the seabed, setting off a tsunami that killed hundreds of thousands across Asia."

"I can see how some people would believe these signs are playing out."

"In fact, many millions of Muslims believe that, yes, we are in the Age of Signs."

"I feel like having another drink."

"Nine: A second sinking of the Earth, this time in the west. Perhaps it could be New Orleans, which sank over twenty feet and was then smashed by Katrina. Ten: Jerusalem will flourish."

"Well that hasn't happened," Schelly observed.

"Have you not heard there is a movement to make Jerusalem the capital of Israel?"

Yeah, okay. "What about you, Kiraz? Do you believe in these signs?"

"There are many reputable Islamic scholars who agree."

"You're avoiding the question. What do *you* think? Are we in the prophesized End of Days?"

"There are other signs – the arrival of the Mahdi and the end of the Hajj."

"The Scorpion. You believe he's the Mahdi of the prophecies, don't you?"

"He has styled himself as the one who will lead the armies of Islam to victory over the armies of Rome. Muslims are not going on the Hajj to Mecca, because they flock instead to Al-Aleaqarab and his black standard. His force will soon number in the hundreds of thousands. Perhaps they will eventually number more than a million."

"And Jesus will appear as the dead arise," Schelly whispered, the unfolding nightmare playing out in the theatre of her mind.

"I will be one of those who will be going to hell for all eternity," said the professor. "I think I need another drink. The prevalence and acceptance of homosexual sex is another of the signs."

"You're kidding?"

"No."

"How did we get to this place? You're a believer in this dark fantasy. It's wholesale delusion."

"Is it a fantasy if people believe and will kill for it? I have no answer. The near demise of ISIS – that, also, is a sign.

"Is there anything that isn't a frikken' sign?" Schelly had the overwhelming sense of being locked in a death spiral. Her non-encrypted cell started ringing. And then the professor's vibrated within the pile of wet clothes on the floor. The two women looked at each other. Coincidence? Unlikely. A chill ran down Schelly's spine as she reached for her cell. *Shit always rolls downhill.* The screen gave her the caller ID – Colonel Gladston. "Major Schelly speaking."

"Jillian. You near a computer?"

"No, sir."

"Use your phone. You need to see what's trending on YouTube and Twitter. It ain't cute kittens."

Thirty-six

Ronald V. Small @realSmall
All terrorists are losers. If you had a TV series, no one would watch it. Your ratings would be terrible.

Jimmy and Alvin returned empty-handed, Taymullah and Farib tagging along behind. Jimmy motioned at the jihadist seated on the ground whose shoulders were hunched, his blackened, shiny head hanging low between his legs. "We got nothin', boss. Looks like he's the sole survivor."

There was something about this guy. "You look familiar," I told him. "Why is that?"

"We here long, Major?" Jimmy asked. "Alvin and I gonna keep a lookout."

"Five minutes," I said. "No more."

The sergeants took a flank each and were swallowed by the night.

I pulled the ka-bar and lifted the jihadist's chin with the tip of the blade. "We met somewhere?"

"Yeah," Bo agreed, pondering it, "I reckon I seen him before too." The sergeant got there faster than me, realization dawning on his face. "Boss, this asshole ... I think he the one pulled them folks from the white Beemer back at the warehouse. You remember?"

I took some water, splashed the jihadist's face then wiped some of the soot off his beard with my forearm. Bo played the flashlight across him. Bo hardened up on it. "He the one all right."

The beard was dirty blond. Yeah, *that* guy. "Hey, buddy, you're not exactly doing the homeland proud, you know that, right?"

"Is he cryin'?" Bo asked. "What's he cryin' about? Cos you lost all your asshole friends?"

Mazool ventured. "He cries not because he lost brothers, but because they reach Paradise before him. They are in Allah's presence, while he has been captured by kafirs and martyrdom has left him behind." He kicked the guy in the leg.

"That why you bawlin' like a baby, asshole?" Bo demanded.

The man turned to look at him with hateful bloodshot eyes..

"What's your name, the one your mother gave you?" I asked him again. No response to that, either. "Check his pockets."

Bo slung his weapon and searched him. After a thorough pat down, he said, "Nothin', boss. All his pockets got holes in 'em. Nothin' in his shoes. Mouth empty. Don't think he's carrying anything in any other cavities either, 'cept maybe a whole lotta stink."

"Gonna call you Bob," I told the jihadist. "Good American name, Bob. Back home the media would call you Jihadi Bob. Suits you."

"My name's Dawar," he sniffed. "My homeland is Ad-Dawlah al-Islamiyah, and you can go fuck yourself."

"Okay Dawar from Ad-Dawlah al-Islamiyah, where is The Scorpion?"

Bob stared straight ahead, the tears having dried up at least. He wiped the snot off his nose with a grubby forearm then blew an air hanky into the dirt.

Natasha was hovering nearby. "He won't talk. That is why I kill the last one," she said. "Let me kill him." She pulled her Yarygin and cocked it. "He will talk. He believes there is no Paradise if woman kills him."

Natasha took a step toward Dawar and he recoiled in fear.

"Put the gun away, Natasha. We kill him if and when I say we kill him. That's the rule, remember?"

"You are soft, do you know that?" she said.

"Call me Cream Puff," I replied.

She bent down and holstered her piece in the top of her boot, and I was glad I didn't have to add a threat to the command. But maybe Natasha had pointed out some leverage we could use. I watched Igor climb up onto a nearby charred vehicle to add his eyeballs to the watch. The big Russian was nervous, and that made at least two of us. There could be other jihadists around and the explosions and fireballs would draw them here. "Jimmy, Alvin. Anything?" I asked into the comms.

"Negative."

"Negative."

"On me," I told them. "Mount up," I said to everyone else. Bob could ride in the utility bed with Jimmy, Alvin and Igor. Right about then is when I noticed Farib and Taymullah looking at Taymullah's cupped hands, the light from the screen of a cell phone illuminating their faces. Shock pretty much summed up their expressions. Maybe because they were getting phone reception.

Mazool exchanged a bunch of words with the teens in Arabic. Whatever was said had Mazool worried. Taymullah handed the phone to me. "Please. You watch."

I took the phone. Yep, two bars of reception – 4G no less. How about that? On screen was the familiar YouTube logo. Intrigued, I pulled my shooter's glove and thumbed the triangle. Following a couple of seconds of silence and a shaky black screen, a heavily accented voice said, "It is written in the Qur'an and hadiths that the armies of Rome shall be defeated by the faithful at the gates of Dabiq. This will come to pass as surely as the sun rises."

The shaky screen suddenly lit up with the hard white beams of vehicle LEDs. In the center stood the Scorpion. He reminded me of a deer caught in the headlights, maybe one that had already been run over a couple of times due to his face being mottled by heavy red scarring and his patchy uneven beard. Even from this distance I could tell the guy needed to take a shower.

The zealotry continued. "On the plains of Dabiq, the blood of Allah's enemies shall drown them and the End of Days will be upon the world and the dead shall rise."

"Who writes this stuff?" I asked Mazool who didn't have an answer and wasn't in the least amused.

"I have captured one of the Emperors of Rome," the Scorpion continued. "I have made a prisoner of his general. I have slaughtered his servants. I have the keys to his weapons of mass destruction. Do not doubt that a humble servant of Allah can bring the Crusader to his knees. I will do this as surely as I have punished Caesar for his crimes against the faithful in Chechnya, Georgia, the Crimea, Dagestan, Syria and others."

The camera operator walked toward the Scorpion, the picture jerking up and down, left and right, but remaining centered on him. Bugs zipped through the light around him like slow moving tracer. When the camera stopped moving, he pointed off to the wings, stage left, the acting about as wooden as any fifth grader's Christmas pageant. The camera lens panned in the direction of the Scorpion's extended claw. I was anticipating maybe some cheesy thunder and lightning effects. There weren't any, but what I did see made the words, "Holy shit," fall out of my mouth. It was Petrovich. At least I was pretty sure it was Petrovich. I'd never seen the president stripped down to his shorts, though I had seen him shirtless in that bear wrestling video that did the rounds. He won that contest. But in this latest film, Russia's Number One Citizen was up against a tree, as in nailed to it, and the tree was winning. Petrovich's hands were outstretched, spikes hammered through his wrists to keep them fixed to the boughs. His feet, too, were nailed to the trunk. Flies buzzed around them, excited. The guy was being crucified and not figuratively; crucified just like that other guy had been – I think you know the one I'm referring to.

Petrovich's wrists were coated in a mixture of flies and blood. The critters were swimming in small rivers of it flowing down the tree trunk below his feet. His body shook with agony.

"The faithful are pouring into Syria and the lands that bound Syria," the Scorpion's voice continued off screen. "Muslims from all over the world come to fulfill the prophecy promised by God. If your government prevents you – burn, maim and kill the kafirs and yours shall be the glory of Paradise and you will sit closest to Allah with your new bride."

The camera panned away from the Russian president, the wreckage of the man a metaphor of the horror that awaited the world, and returned to the Scorpion, a head and shoulders shot. "Journey to Dabiq and join the army of Islam," he continued, ignoring two large flies that landed on his face until they became too brazen and he was forced to dislodge them with a wave. "It is the Mahdi who shall lead you as, through the darkness, the Crusader's own fire rains down on the unbeliever, bringing sunlight. The time has come for all men who love God to pledge allegiance to Ad-Dawlah al-Islamiyah and give of their life for Allah's glory. The End of Days is upon us. Allahu akbar." The image of a gently fluttering black Islamic State flag ended the video.

I struggled to articulate what I had just seen. It was on YouTube, which meant it was probably breaking the Internet. I could see links to other posted Scorpion vids, two others in fact, both less than a couple of days old, the ones the Quickstep major had mentioned – Major Schelly. I played them through, one after the other. After watching them, any doubt I may have had about the contribution I could provide, evaporated. I had a job to do here, the one I was trained for and had practiced enough on a daily basis to be reasonably adept at: to track the Scorpion down and do it fast, just as if he was Air Force personnel gone AWOL. And here's where the job spec departed from my day to day. I also had to kill him. I handed the phone back to Taymullah and saw that Natasha had been watching the video over my shoulder, her hand covering her mouth in shock.

"Bo, you confident with that UAV?" I asked him.

"Yessir. Charged and ready to go."

"Then let's get it up and see if we can't avoid any more surprises."

* * *

Schelly dropped her phone on the bed, got up and gathered her clothes. *Shower.* She headed for the bathroom.

"Are you okay?" the professor asked.

Schelly laid her clothes on the vanity, opened the shower door, but then her mouth filled with saliva, catching her by surprise. *Oh my god.* She turned and her hands found the toilet seat as vomit welled into her mouth and gushed into the bowl. Her stomach convulsed again and Schelly leaned there, exhausted. *"Jesus."*

"Can I get you something?" the professor asked quietly.

"No. I'm, I'm fine."

The professor helped Schelly into the glass shower cubicle. "I'm okay. I'll take it from here ... Don't know where that came from." Schelly pulled the lever all the way on the faucet splitter and the cold water that flowed from the showerhead shocked her, but she needed it. It helped the numbness. The images of a person being crucified were not something she ever thought she'd see. Crucifixion may have been a fact 2000 years ago, and growing up a Catholic with a devout mother she had seen enough depictions of Christ on a cross to last a lifetime, but they were symbolic; not real. The true barbarity of crucifixion, what something like that would actually feel like, what it would look like ... the reality was something she had never truly considered. It was confronting. Horrific. *No one deserves to die like that.*

The professor leaned on the bathroom door and turned on the fan to exhaust the steam. "You feel connected to this personally because you are involved. I understand. I too feel responsible, also as a Muslim."

Schelly adjusted the water temperature. "I just don't understand why. I mean, why *that*? Why crucify him?"

273

"This is the punishment dictated by Allah for those who wage war against the faithful."

Schelly mentally embraced the growing warmth and the cleansing of the water as it coursed down her skin.

The professor continued, "The subject is placed on the cross for three days before being killed, so Sharia law dictates, by being stabbed in the heart."

"Death would be a mercy."

"Killing him would cost the Scorpion leverage, and he is not ready. Providing the president's heart is strong, he will survive, but his time is limited. ISIS follows a literal interpretation of the Qur'an and certain approved hadiths. Based on these, Petrovich has three days, no more. And then he will be stabbed."

"I just don't get it. The Scorpion is already achieving what he wants." *Yeah, but you knew he would post more videos. He has to keep pushing buttons. And each one was always going to be more confronting and compelling than the last.*

"This is a warrior zealot, brutalized by a lifetime of war, who offers more proof that he is a man of God. I am sure the symbolism of crucifying a man who leads a Christian nation, this would have been a factor in his decision to choose this punishment. It is somehow worse than decapitation. At least that is quick."

"Is it about recruitment?" Schelly asked, reaching for something tangible.

"It is always about recruitment," the professor confirmed. "As were the beheadings in the early days. This is how ISIS gathered momentum. Now it is time for a new phase in the conflict. The Scorpion has declared war on the Crusaders, the Christian West. He confirms to Muslims everywhere that this is a war fought in the name of Allah. For the Scorpion, there is only one true god, his god, and only one true interpretation, his interpretation."

Schelly stood in the column of the water, her head bent, her hands outstretched against the tiles, welcoming the stability. "It's just so barbaric."

"In the West these practices have ended. But the Saudis practice crucifixion and it is still part of Iran's criminal code. Hamas has also reinstated it in Palestine."

"What does that tell you?" asked Schelly.

"That my religion has been hijacked and used by men for their own purposes."

"Then tell me ... what do female martyrs get when the reach Paradise. It's not virgins, right? Can't be."

The professor took a breath. "It is said they get to marry their favorite husband."

"Really? And what does *that* tell you about your religion?" Schelly turned the water off with a jolt that made the pipes clang. "I feel I need to call someone. I just don't know who. Maybe my mother."

"What about Cooper? He has a phone."

And say what? Hurry up and do your job? And by the way, we don't have your back? Schelly opened the glass door and accepted a towel as she stepped out. "The Scorpion mentioned the Mahdi as if this was someone other than himself. You said you think people believe he's the Mahdi. Why doesn't he just embrace it?"

"To admit to such a thing may cause others to say that he is merely a madman, delusional. There are crazy people in straitjackets who claim to be Mohammad reborn, just as there are many Christs. The Scorpion is not stupid. Something else he said – the pledge. It is written that once a caliphate has been proclaimed, then Muslims must by law pledge *baya'a* – allegiance – to the caliph, who is recognized as a descendant of Mohammad. To do otherwise would be to turn your back on God and die ignorant. And this would exclude you from Paradise."

"Allah is not exactly a forgiving god, is he?" said Schelly as she slipped on her underwear.

"Not as he is worshipped by ISIS, no." The professor moved in close to Schelly, held her face between her hands and kissed her, the warm soft kiss of a lover. "You must trust me, Islam is about so much more," she said once their lips parted. "And that is why there are so many Muslims." She then squeezed past Schelly and opened the shower door. "While I remember, the call I received – it was from Epstein. We have a meeting at the White House."

"Who with?" Schelly asked, examining her face in the mirror. "Can I borrow your lipstick? I love this color."

"Yes, of course. The meeting is with the president."

Thirty-seven

Ronald V. Small @realSmall
Andrew Bunion is a great American, living proof you don't have to
be six feet two to stand ten feet tall.

Bunion held the door open and President Small strode into the
Situation Room, not happy if the pursed lips were any indication.
Epstein, Rentz, Bassingthwaite, Hamilton, Chalmers, the professor
and Schelly all stood. "Admiral, I believe that's my chair," was
President Small's opening remark as he handed his putter to
Bunion. "That's the one I always sit in." He pointed to the chair at
the head of the table. "Someone always wants to be the boss when
I'm not around."

"My apologies, sir," said Rentz, moving, sliding his folders along
the desk.

The president sat, the signal for everyone else to follow suit.

Schelly assessed the commander-in-chief, her first ever meeting
with the man who had a reputation for being, well, challenging.
So far, no surprises. His dark navy suit was expensive and tailor-
made, but that didn't disguise the fact that here was an old
man used to high living and clearly overweight, no matter what
the press secretary had insisted to the media about his BMI.

Bags under his chin seemed to be tucked into his white shirt and held there by his red silk tie, and the folds under his eyes were more like hammocks. Clearly, also, he was wearing makeup. *You might have come straight from a television interview, except the putter says maybe not. But I wear makeup occasionally, so why not the president?*

"What are the Russians saying?" the president asked Bassingthwaite.

The Secretary of State began to fumble his notes as if he'd just been asked to make a presentation on a topic he hadn't prepared for. Eventually he found the relevant email. "Ah, here it is. Yes, Mr. President, sir. They want us to …um … to provide proof that we had nothing to do with shooting down their helicopters. Though god knows how you prove the negative case."

"Well, it's unreasonable that they're blaming us, but if we can show them something?"

"Mr President," Admiral Rentz interrupted. "We absolutely had nothing to do with this, but I wouldn't give them anything, and most certainly not any intelligence."

"Why not?"

"Because anything we give them will indicate something of our intel gathering capabilities – what we can and can't do. And I guarantee you that is at the heart of their demand."

"I would agree, Mr President," CIA Director Hamilton said. "We can't give them anything."

"Are the Russians still at whatever DEFCON, priming their nukes?"

"Danger of War, sir, they call it," said Bassingthwaite, checking another email. Same as our DEFCON Two."

"What are we at?"

"DEFCON Four, Mr. President," said Rentz.

"Then we should match the Russians and go to two, DEFCON Two. What does that say?"

"Mr President, DEFCON Two says nuclear war is imminent,' Rentz advised him. "I would strongly counsel leaving things where they are. That is the best course. We don't want to pour gasoline on the situation."

"I feel we're in a corner being pummeled by everyone," the president said in an aside to Bunion, using his hands in an open-armed palm-up gesture that said, "We got nothin'." Bunion agreed, mirroring the president's gesture. "Well, I don't wanna be caught napping," the president continued. "We go to DEFCON Two." Small glared at Bassingthwaite. "And get me a meeting with Rodchenko." He addressed the room. "Next."

Rentz fumed at the papers between his hands as he shuffled them.

"One more fact you may not be aware of, Mr President," said the SECSTATE.

"What is it?"

"The terrorists have uploaded the Russian launch codes onto the dark web. There's a reference to this in the video." The SECSTATE referred to notes: "'through the darkness, the Crusader's own fire rains down on the unbeliever, bringing sunlight ...'"

The body language around the room reflected instant dismay.

Oh, fuck, thought Schelly.

"So?" enquired the president blankly.

"This will give every digital criminal a crack at infiltrating the launch algorithms."

"The codes say plenty about the Russian system and its protocols," said Rentz. "Their launch system is even more antiquated than our own."

"Do we need to get to the shelters?" Small asked.

"Mr President, CIA believes that while this raises the stakes to some degree, there is no imminent threat," said Hamilton. "We don't recommend releasing this news to the public, though. We don't want to cause panic."

Bassingthwaite mopped. "That's almost funny. You mean *more* panic because there's already plenty of it around. And I disagree in regards to this new information. I think we should release it."

"Why?" Hamilton asked.

"Because if we don't the terrorists will. Try and keep this a secret and we just hand the Scorpion another opportunity to control the narrative and stampede public opinion. We need to release this news and explain that the codes do not actually launch missiles, but merely confirm the president's desire to send them on their way once the decision has been made to launch. In their system, the president gets the final say. Unlike ours where the president has the only say."

Don't remind me, thought Schelly.

"Will the public believe us?" Small asked.

"It's the truth, Mr President," Bassingthwaite replied. "There's no reason not to believe us."

"Except that the terrorists have told them otherwise," said Rentz, weighing in. "And the public seems ever more ready to believe conspiracy over reason and bad news over good – if you can call this qualification good."

Epstein chimed in too. "Isn't the release of the codes onto the dark web something of a capitulation?"

"How do you mean?" asked Bassingthwaite.

"Well, surely it's the Scorpion saying that they can't do anything practical with them, beyond spreading terror, so over to you."

"Yes, okay, but it's a nuanced picture and nuances are hard to sell. They sound like we're dodging the truth."

"Mr President," said Bunion, "may I suggest we have your press secretary release a statement saying the codes are old news and worthless – not worth the paper they're written on."

President Small waved his hand. "Yes, good idea, Andy. At least someone here is thinking."

Epstein handed a single sheet of paper toward the commander-in-chief stamped Top Secret. "Mr President, I have prepared a report. This is where we're at, sir."

"So now I have to read?" The president scanned it. "I don't see my name in any of these words you've written here. So maybe it's irrelevant to me."

"It's just the headline points, Mr President."

"So here's what I don't get," he said, ignoring the briefing note. "We have the best military, the best people – everyone knows that – but this Scorpion guy keeps posting videos and getting away with it. And these videos, the whole world is watching them. And meanwhile we kinda know where he is and we've got drones flying all over the place, but we can't find him? The guy's got Russia's nukes in his back pocket! He's got how many fanatics massing at the borders ready to join him in some crazy battle? We got numbers? Anyone?"

Reid Hamilton checked his own briefing notes. "The current estimate is 80,000, growing at over 30,000 a day with no signs these numbers are tapering off."

Small thumped the table. "We should be all over this guy by now. Am I the only person in this administration who gives a damn about this? Where's the fucking SEALs, for Chrissakes, or are they all off doing movies? I can call generals. You want me to call generals? I can send an aircraft carrier. I can call on phenomenal power." The president paused to take a breath, and also to properly land his displeasure. "And you know," he began again, "I've got all kinds of people in my ear because of this new video. My Christian friends are very concerned. It's like any minute I'm gonna get a call from the pope asking me what the fuck, right?" He turned to Bunion. "Jesus, Andy, you've seen this fucking video. Fucking crazy, right?"

Bunion nodded, deeply concerned. "Fucking crazy, Mr President."

Small took a sip of water from a glass in front of him. "And then there's what people are saying on television. This whole End of Days thing. It's fake news, right? The dead people rising up? I'm like, seriously?"

"Mr President, I am Professor Kiraz Başak."

"Oh, and you are?"

"Defense Intelligence, currently working with the CIA on terrorist profiling."

"Okay." The president clasped his hands in front of him and sat back. "Nice. Someone who is prepared to step up. I like that."

"Mr President, ISIS believes any view of the Qur'an, other than the literal one, is apostasy. They believe wholeheartedly in the Qur'an's apocalyptic prophesies as they are written."

"So, what are you saying? I'm not gonna see my grammy walking down the street with Jesus?"

Someone chuckled.

President Small thumped the table again. "I'm serious. I never liked her and I don't want her back." POTUS let his displeasure sink in. "I don't get it, we had ISIS on the ropes. How did we get here to this place?"

"Mr President, if I may?" the professor asked.

Schelly wrenched her eyes away from the president. *Yes, please do, Kiraz. I don't know how you manage to look so perfectly cool and collected.*

"Continue," President Small said.

"In the Qur'an and hadiths it is written that, as the End of Days approaches, the forces of Islam will be almost wiped out. This has happened – or I should say is happening. Beating ISIS militarily only confirms to these fundamentalists that we are indeed in the End of Days."

"But it's bullshit, right?" Bunion insisted. "The End of Days thing is not real. Can't be. I mean, people coming back from the dead?" He made a dismissive sound and waved his hand to underline it.

"Many hundreds of thousands of Muslims believe it is very real, as the Qur'an is the word of God and God does not lie."

"Is it written that the President of Russia will be shot down, captured and crucified?" the president asked.

"No," the professor replied. "But it is proof to all Muslims that the Scorpion is a powerful man. It is being said that he is the Mahdi, the person who will lead Muslims to victory over the West. Whether this is true or not, he is certainly someone who has recognized an opportunity and seized it."

"Yes, I can see that. Look, what you're saying is scary, but you're very calming in the way you say it. I like that." The president nodded at Basak appreciatively. "That's a tremendous quality. If you don't mind me saying, I like what you're wearing too. It's business-like, but feminine. A lot of women can't pull that off." He turned to Epstein. "I don't need to read this." He pushed the briefing paper toward her. "Now, I've sat back and let you get on with it," he said to no one in particular. "Do you want me to micromanage? I don't wanna be telling you how and when to do stuff, do your jobs. Do I have to fire people and get new people on it, cos I'm wondering, right?"

The body language around the table was uncomfortable to say the least. Epstein rasped, "Mr President, as you know, we have a team on the ground, a mixture of Army Special Forces and Air Force Special Operations. The best. We have relayed your expressed orders to that team and they are hunting down the Scorpion as we speak."

"Good. Very good. And where are we at with that?"

"Sir, we have the officer here who runs the team – Major Schelly."

The president looked at no one in particular. "Where?"

"Mr President, Major Schelly, sir," she said and gave the president the briefest of smiles. It was only then, it occurred to Schelly, that the commander-in-chief seemed aware of who was actually present in the room, other then the professor and perhaps Bunion. Up to that point, with those exceptions, it had just been a collection of faceless warm bodies.

President Small gave Schelly the once-over. "Major, eh? I thought we'd at least have a colonel supervising a big operation like this."

"Let me assure you, Mr President," said Admiral Rentz, "Major Schelly is eminently qualified, having managed the assets we have in the field for several years. She is a fine officer. None better."

Nice of you to say, thought Schelly.

The president shrugged, less than a hundred percent convinced on that score, but, turning to Bunion, he said with a leer, "I'm not sure about the effectiveness – I'd prefer a colonel at least - but we certainly have one of the best looking teams working on this, right?" His eyebrows jumped up and down a couple of times, in case Bunion had any doubts on his appreciation of Schelly and also the professor.

WTF? Schelly gave Epstein a glance, but the SECDEF bunted it with a deadpan expression.

"Major Schelly is it?" the president asked her.

"Yes, sir."

"Okay, over to you Major. Where are we at?"

"Mr President, a short time ago, local Syrian time, in the hunt for President Petrovich, a small unit of US Special Forces and Special Operations, assisted by Air Force drones, stormed a major roadblock in the north of the country." Schelly aimed the remote at the screens and a number of before and after shots of the barricade were presented. "Details are light on at present but this team also managed, on an earlier occasion, to secure two Russian nationals who accompanied President Petrovich on the downed helicopter."

"Impressive," the president said with a smirk at Bunion suggesting to Schelly that POTUS was less interested in what she said than how she looked saying it. *If there was a shelf, you'd be asking me to reach up and get something. Or bend over and pick something off the floor.*

She continued, "Our unit, callsign Quickstep 3, is currently making its way further to the east, into the area where we believe the Scorpion is likely to be holding the president and also General Yegorov."

SECDEF Epstein gestured to Schelly that less would be more.

"These are the only details we have at the moment, Mr President," Schelly said, taking the hint. "But this is a drama unfolding hour by hour. We hope to be able to bring you more concrete information soon."

"Tremendous presentation, Major ... Major ..." he clicked his fingers, impatient.

"Major Schelly," she told him.

"Major, what makes you think you know where the Scorpion is?"

An intelligent question. Maybe you've been listening after all. "Sir, CIA can best answer that."

"Thank you, Major. Yes, an excellent presentation. What's your first name?"

"Ah, Jillian, sir."

"You look more like a Roxanne to me. Jillian is kinda like an old matron or something. Keep up the good work, though."

Schelly stole a glimpse at the professor and received the barest of frowns, a line that appeared in the middle of her forehead and just as quickly vanished. It was a don't-worry-we-'re-in-this-together-frown and it reassured Schelly. The president turned to Director Hamilton. "Reid, the major has thrown to you."

"If you don't mind, Mr President, my new Associate Deputy Director Bradley Chalmers can best answer the question. Bradley has personally been coordinating the CIA's end."

The president's attention span was clearly waning. "I'm a very busy man." He glanced at his watch. "Do you know how busy I am?"

"Mr President, sir," Chalmers began with altogether too much zeal. "Let me start by saying that I've been a big fan of yours from the beginning."

Schelly tied not to let the disdain show. *And you think POTUS can't spot a brownnose when he sees it?*

The president beamed. "Thank you. We've been trying so hard to make America number one again, where it should be. It's nice to be appreciated."

Schelly blinked. *Are you kidding me?*

"Sir, my pleasure, sir."

"What's your name again?"

"Bradley Chalmers, Mr President, sir."

God almighty.

"So, Bradley, you were saying?"

"Mr President, we've been working closely with the Defense Imagery Management Operations Center. DIMOC is of the opinion that this latest video was not shot in the same place as the first two videos." Chalmers aimed a remote at a screen and various stills of the Scorpion with the desert stretching away behind him played in slideshow. "Sir, that's important. The Scorpion went out of his way in the first two videos he posted to make us believe they were shot in the same location but on different days. He wanted us to think that he was staying put somewhere out in the desert, so that we'd concentrate our search for him there."

Old news, thought Schelly.

"Three locations were identified as his possible camp, but, of course, he moved. In the third video, uploaded this morning, every effort has been made to conceal the background. That's because this is the place where he actually is right now, and intends to stay, at least for a while."

Yeah, three days, max.

The president shifted in his seat, scratched his head with a finger and then meticulously smoothed over the hole that had opened up in his comb-over.

"However, did anyone notice these guys photo-bombing the Scorpion throughout the video?"

Screens around the room filled with the image of large compound eyes and a hairy proboscis.

"What's that?" President Small asked.

"A sand fly, sir. A critter by the name of phlebotomus papatasi."

"What?"

"Phlebot –"

"Okay, I have the Chinese waiting. Germany is having a tantrum about something, as usual. What I want to hear is, can we rescue Valeriy Petrovich?"

"Well, sir, I'm getting to that if –"

The president raised his hand. "Stop. Yes or no?"

Chalmers wasn't sure which way to turn.

"Brody? It's Brody, right?" the president asked.

"Bradley, Mr President."

"Well? Can we?"

"We have some ideas, sir."

"Ideas? They've turned the guy into fucking Jesus. Don't you people get it?" President Small shouted. "There are riots in Moscow. They are burning pictures of me. Perfectly good pictures. It's very, very bad. They have raised their alert level, we have raised ours." He rose from the table, shaking his head and buttoning his coat. "The fake news media want a bone so I'm telling them we got some tremendous leads on President Petrovich's whereabouts. We're expecting a result very, very soon. America has a reputation. An unbelievable reputation. It's my job to protect that reputation. Next time we meet on this, I only wanna see you and you," he pointed to Schelly and then Professor Başak. "And I wanna hear some good news." The president went to the door, opened it and walked out.

Bunion followed the commander-in-chief to the door and paused, his back to the room. He said, without turning, "Not happy, people. Let's try not to disappoint the best president America has ever had." He left the door open as he left the room.

Thirty-eight

Ronald V. Small @realSmall
America's intelligence services keep the world honest. Where
would we be without them? In a very very bad place.

Schelly and Professor Başak left the Situation Room together into
fast-moving people traffic, most of which was head down concentrating on cell phones and hurrying through the corridors on the
business of the United States. "That was interesting," the professor
ventured after a couple of minutes of silence.

"Interesting covers a lot of territory," Schelly replied. And
then, after a little consideration, "So, what outfit are you going
to wear?"

"Outfit?"

"Yeah, you know, when we meet with the president next? I'm
thinking a super short skirt, pigtails and bangs. He's that kinda guy
– into the schoolgirl thing. You – I'm seeing a nurse's uniform with
a stethoscope and a whip."

A smirk escaped from the professor, but she quickly got on top
of it. Sotto, she said, "Stop. You are making me horny."

Schelly shook her head. "That whole thing back there ... crazy."

"Major!"

There were other uniformed officers in the corridor from all four services, but Schelly knew the call was for her. It was Chalmers, breaking into a trot behind them to catch up. "He's all yours," the professor said as the associate deputy director closed in.

"Thanks a lot."

The professor smiled. "I will call you."

"You'd better," Schelly replied. Their hands brushed and she felt an electric charge in her groin and then the professor was gone, merged with the traffic.

"Gee, that went well, don't you think?" Schelly ventured when Chalmers arrived beside her.

The ADD countered, "He shakes things up. That's what he does."

"I'm shaken up. You don't have a problem with what just happened back there?"

"I'm sure he was just fooling around. You don't have a sense of humor?"

"Because now is the perfect time for a laugh."

Chalmers sighed heavily. "Look, we need to talk."

"So you said."

"What's your problem?" he asked her.

"No problem."

"Can we go somewhere?"

"What's wrong with here?"

"It's not exactly secure."

"*I* feel secure."

"Let's walk," he said. "You got a car?"

"Why?"

"We can go for a drive."

"I don't think so," Schelly said.

Chalmers stopped for a moment, scratched his forehead, and then set off again. "Okay, seems we got off on the wrong foot. Or maybe ended up there. Y'know, I thought we had a thing in that first meeting."

"A thing?"

"Yeah. You know …"

"There was no thing. If that's what you wanted to talk about then –"

"No, it's not," he said. ""Someone at the Company may have come up with something to help your boy."

"Cooper?"

"Well he ain't *my* boy."

"He's ours, Associate Deputy Director. Remember? The good ol' US of A?

"Don't be so naïve, Major."

"Interesting history between you and Cooper," said Schelly.

"You checked up on me?"

"No, I was checking up on Cooper. You were collateral."

"Whatever you think you know – that isn't the story."

"After what Cooper found, you're lucky they didn't throw you in jail."

"Those files are redacted, Major, so you can quit with the fishing. They locked up the guilty party – my boss. I was just doing what I was told to do."

"Following orders. That defense didn't work at Nuremburg for the Nazis."

"You are seriously gonna go *there*?"

Schelly glanced at her wristwatch. "Look, this is highly entertaining, but I've got work to do."

"All business. Okay, fine. I sent a few items of interest to you. As I was about to inform the president, we may be able to narrow the search."

Schelly stopped. "How?"

"Sand flies."

"So all that back there was actually leading somewhere?"

"The flies feed on rotting meat. They're a problem in Syria. Dead bodies get left lying around after the fighting. No flies in the first two videos, but all those flies in the most recent video place the Scorpion near a population center. As we all suspected – he moved.

Fighting broke out several days ago in Mamit, a town close to the Turkish border, ninety miles west and a little north of the point designated Position Alpha. It's all in the stuff I sent you."

"When did you send the files?"

"Just now."

"Sand flies." Schelly was still processing. "And this came from …?"

"A contact at Medicins Sans Frontiers. The flies carry leishmaniasis, a flesh-eating disease. Targets children, mostly. There have been outbreaks in those towns I mentioned."

Flies? "It's a long shot," Schelly said.

"The Scorpion is going to be moving toward Dabiq, not away from it. Those towns are between Position Alpha and Dabiq."

Still a hell of a long shot, Schelly thought.

"Major?"

"I was thinking … putting it together."

"Makes sense, right?"

She exhaled. "Professor Başak believes Petrovich will be kept alive for three days, after which they'll kill him."

"Where'd she get that from?"

"The Qur'an."

"Mumbo-jumbo."

"Not according to a quarter of the world's population."

"Tick-tock then. What else you got to go on?" he asked.

Not a lot. "We're working on some angles …"

"Okay, well, share and share alike." Chalmers stopped short of the exit doors.

Something gnawed at Schelly. "How long have you had this information?"

"The fly thing? A couple of hours. Maybe less."

"You texted me before the crucifixion video aired. So whatever you wanted to talk to me about, it wasn't about flies."

Chalmers glanced up and down the crowded corridor, but no one appeared to be paying them any attention. He moved to the side, out of the human freeway of people in a hurry. Schelly, intrigued, followed. Under his breath he said, "Your unit is not the only asset we got incountry."

"What?"

"You've heard about Phoenix?"

"Rumors," she said.

"We don't want US nationals coming home from Syria with certain skills. So we're cleaning things up before the whole Syria thing ends in tears. We're not the only country doing it."

"Why are you telling me?"

"Cooper gets into trouble, as he no doubt will, there may be backup. Just let us know where he is."

"I'll consider it." *And now that I've considered it, no fucking way.* "A question for you, Associate Deputy Director – you and Cooper. What was it about - back at the beginning?"

"Oh, that?" He snorted. "His girlfriend. Well, we ... You know ...," he smirked. "She might've been his fiancée at the time. Or about to be."

You are every kind of gross. "Anna Masters."

"You have been doing your homework. Listen, there's all kinds of stuff you know nothing about – and you'll never know because it's above your pay grade."

Asshole.

Chalmers's smile broadened into a leer. "As for Masters, she was only human."

I just want to take my fingers and poke them in your smug beady eyes.

"Major, in regards to Phoenix, I'm telling you because I want to help."

"Really. Are you sure you're not telling me because you want Cooper to get caught in the crossfire?"

"Shit happens in the desert, Major."

Chalmers turned to go.

"Wait – you know something's going to happen out there and you're taking credit in advance."

"Now what kind of a person do you think I am, Major?" he said, leaving Schelly alone at the building's exit.

Thirty-nine

Ronald V. Small @realSmall
Tonight, dinner was KFC. America has the best fast food in the
world. No wonder everyone wants to live here.

Al-Aleaqarab stood at the mouth of the cave, darkness all around,
first light still many hours away. The air at his back was cool and
smelt of wood smoke and unwashed men. The air off the desert in
front was clean and still warm, but it would chill during the night.
The stars above burned bright, joined now on the horizon by a
crescent moon, the sliver of curved yellow light against the velvet
blackness as sharp as a blade. The sight of it warmed the Scorpion
and he whispered the verse, "Of this fierce glow which love and you,
within my breast inspire. The Sun is but a spark that flew and set the
heavens afire." He wondered how Allah might greet him in Paradise.
Will I be seated at his right hand, known by all as the Mahdi?
What will my new bride look like? Will I meet Mohammad? He
sighed. There was much that he would have to do to earn his place
among the most renowned martyrs. *Is Allah watching?* Al-Aleaqarab
shook his head. *How easy it is to make the mistake that God has*
any of the weaknesses of Man. Allah is all knowing, he reminded
himself. *He knows everything that has passed, and everything that*

294

will be. *That is what it is to be God. Allah knows the outcome of his endeavors. And what the outcome will lead to, and what the outcome of the outcome will bring and so forth, forever and ever and on and on.* Al-Aleaqarab breathed. It made him a little giddy just to ponder what omnipotence might be like.

One of his men brushed past him, murmured something respectful, and his brief presence brought Al-Aleaqarab down from the stars. The man made his way to a collection of scrubby bushes at the base of a rock ledge, and urinated. And the stress of the not knowing came back to Al-Aleaqarab. *What was happening in the wider world? Are the reports true of an army growing along the Turkish border? Much could happen in a day. Will the West meet the armies of Islam on the plain of Dabiq? When will the Antichrist reveal himself? When will Jesus come? Have I been foretold? Is it possible that I am actually the Mahdi? What will the final battle look like?* He pictured the plain around Dabiq, hundreds of thousands of men and machines clawing and tearing at each other like ferocious ants fighting to the death. And once more, he felt overwhelmed.

The Scorpion left the cave mouth and walked up the hill, picking his way through loose scree to where another finger of rock provided enough protection for some low trees and shrubs to survive the elements. Arriving slightly breathless, he saw two men standing guard here. Al-Aleaqarab ignored them as he walked past, their greeting respectful. His attention was focused on what was around the next bend in the rocks. He came around the corner and saw the man nailed up in the tree. The doctor was there, too, he noticed.

"Thalib," the Scorpion said, his voice low.

"Amir, I did not hear you coming," the doctor replied, removing the stethoscope from his ears.

"Which is why you are a doctor and not a guard. How is the Crusader president? Does he live?"

"He lives, Amir. He has weakened, though."

"Will he survive the full three days?"

"Three days is a long time, Amir. I do not know. Much will depend on his will. If it is strong, yes. If not?" He shrugged.

"What will kill him? Loss of blood?"

"He will suffocate, Amir. It is hard for him to breath and, as he loses strength, it will become harder still. He must drink."

"See that he does."

"Yes, Amir."

"What of General Yegorov?"

"The general is much recovered. He is taking food now and his fever has dropped."

"Bring him here, to the feet of his lord and master."

"Amir, I do not recommend it. He is still weak."

The Scorpion said nothing in reply.

"Yes, I will bring him immediately."

* * *

Phoenix Zero-Four arrived downwind from the south – six on dirt bikes, two in the support Desert Patrol Vehicle. They parked their transport, left one of their number to guard it, and jogged the remaining 500 or so yards across the flat gritty, rock-strewn ground to the coordinates.

"This is the place," said Gunny Eldrich's voice through his comms.

"Breach and secure," Sam Nanaster said into the mike. The bright green flare in her NVGs told her there was an electric light source inside the home. Out here, that was unusual. She flipped up the goggles. "Go easy, Gunny. We want breathers."

"*No Johnny Rambo shit," was the Company's message – not exactly SOP.* She gave a mental shrug – orders were orders.

"Roger that," said Eldrich, his voice in her ear.

Something there, in shadows near the house. She flipped down the NVGs. Small four-legged creatures. "Movement, southeast corner. Goats."

The team went about its work silently.

And then. "The door was open, boss. We're clear. No breathers."

A minute later, Nanaster was inside with two of her men. Three bodies on the ground, dead from gunshot wounds. A large flat screen TV – smashed - shared the floor with them.

"Deceased a couple of hours, no more." Gunny leaned over the bodies. "My guess - wrong place, wrong time."

Hard to disagree with that, Nanaster thought. She glanced around. *Television, internet, an Apple laptop – unusual.* The computer was also on the floor, open, stomped on and kicked, the screen hanging from one hinge, the keyboard depressed into the frame. "Waste of a good MacBook Pro," she said. *Someone did that for a reason.* "Bag it." *Breathers lie, computers don't.* "So, what do we think happened here? Any ideas?"

"You're the ex-cop, ma'am," said Gunny.

There was food scattered around among spent AK brass casings. Two AKs were undisturbed, propped against a wall. "You wouldn't get many guests out here. Hard to sneak up on this place. My guess, the occupants were taken by surprise by people they invited for dinner. Maybe they knew 'em, maybe not." *They practice a form of* Pashtun melmastia *and* nanawatai *here – being a good host and giving asylum to strangers. This one looks straightforward, but the Company sent us to this place and wanted prisoners, so maybe not straightforward at all.* "Look for vehicle tracks," she said.

"Got 'em," said Li'l Wilson's voice through the comms. "A small truck, one bald tire. Probably a pickup. ISIS vehicle of choice. Two occupants wearing treaded boots – worn tread. Followed the vehicle tracks a hundred yards to the east. Nothing left to follow after that. Two sets. One incoming, one outgoing. Whoever they were, they came, did what they needed to do, then split."

"Maybe they wanted to catch a movie and didn't like the ending," she said looking at the remains of the television. And then, "Okay, let's pack it up."

"What's next, boss?" asked Gunny.

"Catch some zees and then, Raqqa."

"The usual."

"Got an asshole from Nebraska needs whacking."

"Boss," said another voice in Sam's ear – Ronan, the unit's RTO back at the DPV. "Transmission from Ops Command. We're to hold until further notice."

Nanaster asked, "What about Raqqa?"

"That's the message we got, ma'am. That's it."

* * *

The moon and the stars provided enough illumination for the two men making their way with some difficulty up the hill. General Yegorov was limping heavily, using the doctor for support. He heard the Scorpion call out, "General, I see you have recovered from your wound. Come join me. Let us talk about the future."

The Scorpion came down the hill several paces to meet them. "Here, allow me," he said, offering his shoulder to lean on in place of the doctor's. To the doctor he said, "Wait nearby. When I am done, you will take him back inside."

"Yes, Lord." The doctor gave a slight bow as Al-Aleaqarab took the weight of the general.

"Only a little further, General," Al-Aleaqarab informed him. "The doctor has looked after you well. Your wound is healing. You cannot not say the men of Ad-Dawlah al-Islamiyah do not give succor to their guests."

The general didn't reply immediately, concentrating instead on every step, each of which was accompanied by a grunt he couldn't stop himself from making. Catching his breath he said between gritted teeth, "What do you want?"

"To brief you, General. Much has happened in a very short while. Here," he said, guiding Yegorov onto flatter ground. "Not much further."

The general kept his eyes on the rock-strewn dirt in front, carefully assessing the ground, his foot pulsing with intense discomfort. A fall would induce searing pain.

"Here, now. We have arrived," the Scorpion informed him.

General Yegorov stopped and secured his balance. He lifted his head and seemed to wonder for several seconds whether he was experiencing a dream. In front of him was a naked man on a cross, his body and head hanging in a familiar fashion.

Al-Aleaqarab read the confusion in the general's face. "Yes, this is real," he said.

Yegorov gaped speechless at the scene that confronted him.

"He is alive," the Scorpion continued. "This is the punishment for enemies of Islam, and the criminal must be alive to be punished. Death will come, and then punishment will continue with an eternity in hellfire."

"Why?" was the only word the general could manage, his throat constricted with revulsion.

"Why the president? Why crucify him and not you? Your president is a symbol. A powerful symbol. But you have something more valuable to us now – practical knowledge, an intimate understanding of your country's war fighting assets and technologies; how they are deployed, the command structure, the strengths and the weaknesses. I am sure you would also have a considerable knowledge of the capabilities of potential opponents: Europe and, of course, the United States. As the world prepares for the final battle, this knowledge makes you far more prized than a mere symbol." He motioned at the president.

"You are ... insane," said Yegorov with not enough strength in his body to shrug off the Scorpion's hand resting on his shoulder.

"My life belongs to God, as does yours. But you deny this simple truth. You allow yourself to be blinded by trinkets and values and ambitions, all of which are as worthless as dust. In my eyes, it is you who have lost your mind. And you have also lost your soul."

"I will give you nothing, tell you nothing."

"If you do not cooperate, your president's suffering will be increased. His own eyes will beg you to cooperate, even if he is in too much pain to speak."

"You are a monster," Yegorov whispered.

"I am not the one who has created the instruments of mass destruction used to ransom the world for my own benefit. I am just a simple warrior who serves Allah's will."

The general stared up at Petrovich. Would it be better to cooperate and reduce his suffering than to be responsible for the deaths of countless thousands of his own countrymen? Was this just a nightmare? "You have brought this on yourself," Yegorov said under his breath at Petrovich, a man he had long despised.

"You have something to say?" the Scorpion asked.

The general ground his teeth, a surge of hate and anger for the man on the cross. He said no more, choosing instead to recall their last moments in the helicopter.

The Hind flew low over the remains of Latakia on your orders, low enough to fill the helicopter with the smells of death and devastation. That's what you wanted. With pleasure on your face, you looked down on our air force's handiwork, at the sea of broken tiles, wood and cinderblocks.

It pleased you that the few buildings teetering among the rubble would require complete demolition; the homes, shops, hospitals and schools all blown to dust. You delighted in the fires burning here and there, yellow flames snatched and torn by the wind. "We need the body count for the people back home," you said into the headset mike.

"Yes, Mr President," I replied.

"Have the numbers broken down."

"There will be collateral casualties, President Petrovich. Women and children."

"General, need I remind you that boys grow into men who avenge their fathers, and these women are the factories of terrorism, their wombs turning out new fighters to replace the

ones gone to hell. Have we learned the lessons of Chechnya, or haven't we?"

"We have learned, President Petrovich."

"Good."

Rapid pounding vibrations, like beats in a drum solo, came up through airframe. Something caught my attention, a freshly made hole in the aircraft's skin, just above your head. Another burst of small arms ground fire peppered the Hind's armored underbelly, which you acknowledged with a stamp of your boot, "She is not called the Flying Tank for nothing, eh?"

Your helmet was stowed under your feet. How stupid! And yet I gave you what you wanted: a grin that said you were a man of unrivalled courage.

"Tell the pilots to recirculate the air. The smell of burnt terrorist is like perfume to me, but I have had enough of the sweetness for one evening."

I relayed the order to the flight deck.

"The air force has done good work here," you told me. "I am looking forward to congratulating our pilots personally. You have made arrangements for this?"

"Yes, President Petrovich." I knew what you meant by "arrangements" – to ensure cameras were on hand to record the occasion.

What drives your need to prove your balls are always the biggest in the room? You are short. Is that it? Or is it just vanity? The cameras, always the cameras, on the lookout for another YouTube moment to join the horse riding, the motocross jumping, the deep sea diving, the mountain climbing, the bear wrestling ... If only Russia knew that the bear's claws had been removed, its teeth filed and its ass shot full of drugs. And wouldn't they also like to know that the rumors are true - that you are not averse to conquering women in much the same way. You like them dead to your touch, so say the whispers.

You asked no more questions, so I put my head back and closed my eyes and then we were spinning and the world was on fire ...

General Yegorov stared up at the broken figure on the cross and a hidden smile spread across his lips. *And now I am sure there is another video of you to join all the others on YouTube.*

Forty

Ronald V. Small @realSmall
President Petrovich is a wonderful person. The nasty rumors about
him are fake news. He could easily be an American.

"Accompany the captive back to the cave," Al-Aleaqarab
instructed Thalib. The Scorpion left them and strode down the
hill, occasionally sliding on the loose surface, aware of the cooling
desert air on his skin and in his nostrils. It was like a drink of
cool water – refreshing. The doubt he had felt earlier was gone,
replaced now with a sense of Allah's will and the certainty of
his own destiny. The President of all Russia, the persecutor of
Muslims in so many lands, was so utterly within his power that
he had crucified the man in the manner of the minor prophet Jesus
Christ, and this was now being shown to the world. He tingled at
the thought. These images would surely goad the Crusader armies
to come and fight. And when they did, General Yegorov would
help him defeat them. What of his own army of the faithful? Was
it massing still? His doubt about this had faded too, replaced
now with an eagerness for news. His plans had been hurriedly
formed once the bounty of the Hind had been discovered and
secured, the pieces fitting together with a perfection and purpose

that suggested divine intervention. Who else but God could create such opportunity for him to exploit? Would Allah then desert him? No. He shuddered with the joy of it.

A sudden twinkle of vehicle lights across the plain below caught his attention and lifted the Scorpion from his reverie. Men on guard duty ran to rocks providing the best combination of protection and lines of fire. The vehicle was on its own, approaching from the east. Al-Aleaqarab climbed a bluff and watched the vehicle's progress. It turned toward their position, the headlights turning off and then on again several times. It could only be his two fighters returning from Al Hasakah. *News!* The Scorpion jumped from the rock and hurried to meet them, the night carrying snatches of the noise of a surging engine climbing the ridge.

"You are early," he said when the driver's door opened.

"Yes, Amir. We drove quickly. We knew you would want the video uploaded as soon as possible," said the tall one whose name was Jalil.

"And we wasted no time returning, Amir," the short Arab said as he got out and released two bleating goats tied to a rail in the pickup's bed.

"Your name is Imad," the Scorpion told him.

"Yes, Lord. I am humbled that you would remember."

Al-Aleaqarab was also surprised that he could recall it, the man having done nothing memorable in battle.

"It is incredible, Lord," Jalil enthused. "Twitter, Facebook and all the news services speak of nothing other than the End of Days. The words of Allah, sublime and mighty, are on everyone's lips. Inspired by your deeds, the faithful in every country on Earth are waging war on the kafirs, killing them with trucks, bombs, knives. In America a train was derailed, killing many; the children of kafirs are also being slaughtered. There is much fear and panic that their empty, godless world is collapsing. The kafir media have also begun to talk of the signs and the coming of the Antichrist. Cities all over the word are discussing measures should there be a nuclear attack."

Al-Aleaqarab worked hard to keep his rapture hidden. "What of the armies of the faithful? What talk of the Crusaders committing their forces?"

"Amir, Russia blames America for the capture of their president," said Jalil. "There is much conflict. The whole world is aflame. Thousands upon thousands arrive every day at the borders of Turkey, Jordan and Lebanon, a flood of true believers drawn from the four corners of the Earth, ready to fight and wash away the stain of Rome. There is much talk of you also, Amir. They say, as we do, that you are the Mahdi who will defeat the Crusader. They wait for you to lead them. They wonder when the Antichrist will appear."

"You have not answered my question. Will the armies of Rome meet us on the plains of Dabiq?"

"I feel there is no doubt of this, Lord," Jalil replied. "Certainly once they see the fate that has befallen their Caesar."

This wasn't what The Scorpion had hoped to hear. He was after confirmation that America, Russia, Europe – the West – was sending armed men and machines to do battle at the place appointed by God. But then surely the video his men had just uploaded would goad them to fight. A warm glow of triumph spread through Al-Aleaqarab's limbs. "What is the attitude in Al Hasakah?"

"This city is one of many that is behind us, Amir. Without question."

"Did you talk to anyone there?"

"No, Amir," said Jalil.

"Then how do you know the city has pledged itself to the caliphate?" he asked the short fighter whose name had again slipped from his memory. "You tell me."

"Graffiti, Lord," the short one assured him. "It is everywhere in praise of the deeds of the Mahdi."

"Graffiti is written in protest. If the city is with us, then why do they write graffiti?"

"I do not know, Amir. We talked to no one – saw no one."

"What about in the Internet café. There was no one there?"

"Everyone was asleep, the café closed," Jalil assured him with a sideways glance at the short one.

Something was not right about this. The Scorpion could sense it. Had he not survived countless attempts on his life from the Americans, the Russians, and any number of ambushes and skirmishes? "What of the owner of the Internet café? Did you not see him?"

"The hour was late," Jalil said. "We broke in. No one saw us."

"And these two goats?" he asked motioning at the animals leashed to the short one with old rope.

"We stole them, Lord."

The Scorpion noted the unease of both men. The short one, his eyes in particular displayed ... was it guilt? Certainly this guilt had nothing to do with the goats – the men had always taken whatever they needed, be it animals, comfort or slaves.

"Jalil," he said to the tall Arab who had done much of the talking.

"Yes, Lord?"

"You have done well. You may go."

"Yes, Lord." Jalil turned and motioned to his friend. "Imad, let us –"

"No, I said *you* may go. Imad, it is you I wish to have some further words with."

The Scorpion noted Jalil's reluctance to leave. And Imad's nervousness had increased markedly. He wondered what might be the cause of it.

Forty-one

Ronald V. Small @realSmall
Once you are dead, you are dead. Don't even think about coming back. That would be very bad.

Deputy Ignatius Folkstone cruised at thirty miles an hour down the darkened backstreet of Macon, Georgia, not thinking of anything much in particular. His shift began at 6 pm, but while it was now closer to dawn than to midnight, he was feeling reasonably fresh. Certainly that's what Deputy Folkstone would later tell the sheriff. Some folks didn't like the graveyard shift, but he was okay with it. The world was mostly quiet at this time. You could sleep away part of the day and still get plenty of time in the sunlight to have a life. And his wife, Jeanie-Belle, was an ER nurse at the hospital also pulling the night shift. They had no kids, so the arrangement worked.

So far, this particular night was no different to any other. Macon was a large town rather than a small city, and reasonably wealthy too. Sure, there was drug-related crime, a little gun-related crime, the odd break-in, domestic altercations and the town had its fair share of road accidents, especially out on the Interstate, but the nasty, violent crime that featured in places like Atlanta? Macon was spared that.

Sometimes Deputy Folkstone actually wanted something to happen, just to make things a little more interesting. But as Jeanie-Belle would say, "Careful what you wish for." Sound advice right there.

The dispatch radio had been quiet for twenty minutes or more. Absolutely nothing going on. So Deputy Folkstone, enjoying the night, searched the airwaves for some tunes as he cruised the streets. Just background music. Some country. *Shania Twain, if I'm lucky.* He turned the receiver on, scouted the waves, and ...

The deputy slammed on the brakes.

The tires screeched horribly.

The front end of the car dove.

A figure caught in the glare of his headlights bounced off the grille. It then whirled away into the night.

Folkstone got his heart under control, parked the vehicle at the curb and turned on the patrol vehicle's emergency lights. Where the fuck did that come from? What was that, anyways? Was it a man? The clothing. It was old and ragged. And the face ... it was ... it was ...

His hand shaking, Folkstone reached for the radio mike. *What are you gonna call in, exactly?* He hooked the mike back on its cradle. *You're a sheriff's deputy, Ignatius Folkstone – so get out of the goddamn vehicle and investigate.* He opened the door and climbed out, one hand holding a flashlight, the other resting on the butt of the firearm on his hip. There were no overhead lights on the road, the crowding darkness stabbed by the patrol vehicle's brilliant flashing red, white and blue LEDs. He switched on the patrol vehicle's search beam, swept the shadows and saw ... nothing. He heard nothing. The night was dark and still and – *the face!* It suddenly came back to him like a repressed memory. Now it seemed the ghastly nightmarish features were burned onto his mind. Its lips were gone, exposing brown and blackened teeth. The nose was deeply pockmarked and partly dissolved off the face. And worms snaked from deep, dark green holes in its cheeks. The face, he realized ... it was ... *rotting!* He'd never seen anything like it, at least not in real life. At the movies, maybe. "What the hell was that?" he said to himself. Deputy Folkstone kept his hand on the butt of the holstered Glock and kneaded his palm against the hard plastic, just for the reassurance of it.

He moved to the front of the vehicle and played the flashlight beam across the hood and grille, looking for any sign of impact. There was none, he was relieved to see.

"Patrol Zero Five, Patrol Zero Five ... Hello ... Ignatius?" said the voice over the radio dispatch, making the deputy jump. "Can see here you're over on Lite'n'tie Road, aren't you? You wan' pick up?"

Deputy Folkstone reached in and took ahold of the mike. "This is Iggy, Irene."

"You all right, Iggy?"

"Of course I'm all right. Why do you ask?"

"I dunno ... there's something in your voice."

"I'm fine."

"You don't sound fine."

"Irene – you call for some reason?"

"There's been a disturbance over at the Cedar Ridge Cemetery," she said. "You wan' go over an' take a look?"

Deputy Folkstone shuddered. "Um ... what sort of disturbance?"

"Had a couple of complaints. Maybe just kids. Y'know ..."

Kids. "Okay, I'm on it. Over."

"You sure you're okay?"

For Christ's sakes! "Over!" Folkstone hung up the mike, unnerved but also annoyed. He gave the darkness one more fruitless sweep with the search beam and climbed back behind the wheel. *You don't know what you saw,* he reassured himself. And then aloud, said, "Maybe just dust on the damn windshield."

Cedar Ridge Cemetery wasn't far. A couple of minutes drive, no more. He arrived in the parking lot. His was the only vehicle. The place was, well, dead. Deputy Folkstone got out of the car with the flashlight.

The night was still. No breeze. And no starlight or moon either. Deputy Folkstone went for a walk, the skin on his scalp tight and prickling. There was some rustling among the bushes, which made him jump. But thinking about it, the air smelt of raccoon piss and whatever it was ignored his call to come on out. Soon he was walking along rows of gravestones, but still nothing to report. Folkstone swept the flashlight back and forth. There! Was that someone walking off into the night? "Hey!" he called out, taking a couple of steps forward. And that's when he stepped into midair and fell wholly six feet into a pit of soft earth.

Deputy Folkstone yelled. He wasn't sure what he yelled. Maybe it was more like a random yelp, the sort you made when you dived into the ice-cold water of the Ocmulgee River in winter. Finding air under his boot instead of solid ground had taken him completely and fearfully by surprise. He smelled the fresh earth as he bent down to retrieve his flashlight. Under his feet, rotted mulch. And the smell. Was that putrid flesh?

He sprang at the side of the hole, scrabbling for a foothold. The earth was pliant – loose. It took him several long seconds to climb out, his arms and legs a blur of movement, his heart in his mouth, his skin crawling, the whole experience giving him the creeps.

Finally, his feet back on solid un-churned ground, the deputy stood up straight, swept the flashlight across the ground and realized that there were many holes like the one he'd just fallen into, and many overturned gravestones too. Piles of freshly dug earth were all around him. "Oh, Lord," he said. If he didn't know better, Deputy Folkstone would have said that the dead had dug themselves right out of their graves.

Forty-two

Ronald V. Small @realSmall
The fake news has been having a field day. Do not be CONNED by journalists. They are terrorists by another name.

Schelly sat up, surprised. *Was I asleep?* She rolled her neck back and forth. A full hour had passed since she'd lain down on the couch, just to rest her eyes. The lump in the middle of the mattress, right on her hip, had woken her. The hotel room at Fort Myer was more comfortable than the couch in her temporary office at OCJS, and so was the bed there, but it was too far from sipper access and the situation was moving too fast. There had been no choice but to move her things into the office at the Pentagon, to be near the secured computer terminal.

She got up and poured herself another mug of burnt percolated coffee, and called up some real-time intelligence on her computer, otherwise known as Fox News. Rioters on the streets in Moscow were burning the Stars and Stripes. Cars were torched in the streets, windows were smashed and Molotov cocktails were being hurled at lines of riot police attempting to protect private and public property. The US Embassy was under siege, but the building in downtown Moscow was well protected. Schelly shook her head. *How can they believe* we *did this to Petrovich?*

311

The next story: a wall of teddy bears and soft toys over ten feet high and fifty yards wide had formed at the scene of the bus crash that had killed so many children. Parents, relatives and friends mourned with compete strangers at the site of the tragedy and Schelly felt her own eyes well with tears of sorrow and anger.

And then there were the events taking place on the Turkish border with Syria. She clicked on the video report, which began with low altitude overhead drone footage showing thousands of men on one side of a fence, mobile armor on the other.

"They've come from all over Europe and the Middle East," said the reporter, the picture cutting to a man with a microphone standing beside a Turkish battle tank. "Muslim men of all ages streaming into camps like this one on the Turkish side of the border with Syria, north of Dabiq. Camps which are well and truly under-resourced to cope with the numbers. Food is scarce and tempers are fraying. The Turkish army has been called out to contain the growing horde, but this carries its own risks. Weapons were smuggled into this particular camp, a recent skirmish wounding two Turkish soldiers. But still the government here treads carefully. Mass demonstrations in Ankara and Istanbul, and other capitals of Muslim countries, in support of the battle they believe has been foretold in the Qur'an, are destabilizing the status quo. Push too hard and their own regimes might topple ..."

Schelly breathed deep and closed the computer. *Get back to work.* She climbed up on the couch to get a better perspective of the whole spread across the floor: photos, ground maps and other intel taking up all available space. The multitude of seemingly unrelated intelligence, key amongst it reports of localized sand fly infestations; World Health Organization assessments on the spread of the flesh-eating disease cutaneous leishmaniasis; weather updates of wind speed and direction in northern Syria; high altitude photos covering the ground where the Scorpion and his captives were believed to be hiding, an area of around 530 square miles.

A knock sounded on the door.

"Who is it?" Schelly asked.

Goldman's head appeared through a crack.

"Idris," she said.

"Ma'am, you have a visitor."

She glanced at her watch. "Really?"

"It's DC, ma'am. CIA Associate Deputy Director Chalmers. He said it was urgent."

Schelly's eyes went to all the intelligence laid out on the floor and Goldman read her concern.

"You can use my office, ma'am," he assured her. "It's small, but no less secure. I'll be out for 30 minutes. Will that be enough?"

"Thanks, Idris." She gave him her warmest smile.

"No problem, ma'am."

When she walked into the yeoman's office, Chalmers was already sitting in the chair, one foot up on the desk. "You're up and hard at work, Jill. Good to see." He took his foot off the table.

"Yes, sir." *What did you expect?*

"No need to be overly formal. Call me Bradley."

"Yes, sir." She leaned back against the wall opposite the desk.

"Still all business are we? Fine. This is not a social call anyway. A couple of hours ago one of our teams recovered a laptop. Thought you might like to know." *Why is every conversation with this guy like extracting a splinter?* He continued, "It's the laptop the latest video was uploaded from, the one starring President Petrovich."

It was as if two electrodes had suddenly zapped Schelly's heart. "You're sure?"

"Digital fingerprints don't lie, Jill. Seems the Scorpion or his minions, whoever used the computer, also took the opportunity to do a little internet surfing – Al Jazeera, BBC, CNN, Google – looking for news on jihadist activity across the world, in particular any news on the forces building up that the Scorpion will be calling on, and whether our own president is going to come out swinging at Dabiq. All of which tells us that the Scorpion is getting sloppy."

"Sloppy?"

"Careless. The previous videos were uploaded in Raqqa. As we all believe, the Scorpion chose Raqqa to make us think he was in that general area, while he was nowhere near there at all. But this latest video was uploaded from a different location - from a farmhouse."

A farmhouse ...

"Out in the middle of nowhere. You can interpret this a number of ways, but our two favorites are that the Scorpion is on the move and is now too far from Raqqa to access the city. But top of the list is that just maybe he was in a hurry and ..."

Schelly felt a tingle run up and down her spine. "... and the farmhouse is close to where he's hiding out."

"There ya go."

"Can you send me the coordinates?"

"Check your sipper."

"Thank you."

"Thank me over dinner."

"I thought you said this wasn't a social call."

"I'm multi-tasking."

"And I'm gay."

"And I'm CIA. You don't think I know your dirty laundry?" Chalmers stood and took a couple of steps toward her. "I guess we could invite Professor Başak. You never know, right? Things might get interesting."

What the hell? "Are you passing this information – these coordinates - to your Phoenix teams?"

Chalmers hesitated. "This is not a game of Marco Polo, Major. Just because you've called me out over a program I have nothing to do with -. that doesn't sideline me."

"A Phoenix team hits Quickstep 3, we'll both know how that happened."

"I don't know what you're talking about." He took another step toward her, leaned forward and placed a hand against the wall beside her head, patently inside her personal space."

"We done here, Mr Associate Deputy Director?" said Schelly, refusing to be intimidated. *Asshole.*

"I'll call you." He pushed back off the wall, opened the door and left.

Schelly exhaled and considered calling Kiraz. But at this hour the professor would be asleep, or maybe not given that sleep seemed to be a dirty word in Washington. *And anyway, there are more important things to think about than personal outrage. You've got men in the field who are under-resourced and under-briefed, there's a president hanging on a cross, millions are on the brink of war, and now this CIA Phoenix bullshit.*

Nevertheless, the news about the laptop was potentially a major break. Schelly returned to her office. She opened the operations folder on sipper and clicked on a new file just added. Overhead images showed a small, mean farmhouse, its coordinates around thirty miles due west of Position Alpha. If the hypothesis held that the Scorpion would be moving closer to Dabiq, to where his army was mustering, his hideout would have to be somewhere further west of the farmhouse. In that case, the search area was instantly reduced by at least two thirds.

She pulled the WHO records again, looking for reported clusters of leishmaniasis, and cross-referenced those against battle reports. Ghasaniyeh fitted the profile. Medicins sans Frontiers had reported a sand fly infestation in the town. Ghasaniyeh lay to the south of Ayn El-Arab, a town on the border where fighting had broken out. Satellite weather reports had the prevailing winds coming from the north, which would bring the flies. Checking maps, Mamit, a border town mentioned by Chalmers, was in the same area. Crosschecking intelligence surveys confirmed that both Ayn El-Arab and Mamit were Sunni towns and assessed as being strongholds of ISIS sympathizers.

Schelly felt a familiar tingle way down deep. *This is where you are, isn't it? You're somewhere here.* Topographical maps revealed an area of ridges and valleys around seven miles south of Ghasaniyeh gored by the erosion of ancient wadis. There were several tiny hamlets in the vicinity located around fourteen miles east of the Euphrates River. The area was roughly equidistant from Raqqa and Dabiq and formed the northern-most point of a triangle up near the Turkish border. *A perfect place to get off the grid, and yet still close enough to the strings if you need to pull them.* The search area was around fifteen square miles. *A large area for a single team to cover, but doable.*

The satisfaction Schelly felt was short-lived. Chalmers and his Special Activities Phoenix hit squads - they had access to the same information. And indeed Chalmers had already pinpointed Mamit. Perhaps he'd already come to the same conclusions. And then there were the Russians. They weren't stupid, as well as being highly motivated. Every scintilla of their enormous military and intelligence resources would be employed in the hunt for their president. All of which potentially put Cooper and his men in quite a few lethal crosshairs. And those crosshairs were much more likely to find their target if Schelly directed Quickstep 3 to the much reduced search area. But what choice did she have? Schelly folded her arms tight against her body and looked down at the map, now with a small circle on it drawn in red. It was a hell of an hour to be phoning the United States Secretary of Defense, but as Schelly saw it, what choice did she have?

Forty-three

Ronald V. Small @realSmall
America wins because we are born winners. It's in the water. If you
are an American stand up and say, "I am an American. I win.
That's what I do!"

Bo was hunched over a screen, his default position pretty much
ever since the supply drop. Looking over his shoulder, I asked him,
"What are those multi-colored blobs?"

"This shit's insane, boss. They're rodents," he replied. "Heat
signatures."

The RQ-11 Raven drone was buzzing around above our heads
at around 1000 feet, orbiting in a one-mile radius centered on our
vehicles. At that height, it could see five miles out across the desert
floor. And what it could see at the moment was rats, none of which
carry AKs, wear suicide vests, or are looking for a place in Paradise.
Reassuring on one level, but not at all helpful in our search for the
Scorpion. I was starting to hope for some jihadist action because
the desert was feeling vaster and emptier every time we stopped and
found absolutely nothing. Not even refugees.

I walked over to Dawar, who was sitting cuff-locked with his
hands behind his back in the bed of the Toyota utility, his head

317

hanging low. So far, he had decided to act like the desert and reveal zip. So I had decided no more Mr Nice Guy. "Natasha!" I called. The Russian reluctantly got out of the ambulance and joined me at the utility. My fellow American lifted his eyes, but only when I cocked my Sig and handed it to the Russian. "There's no safety," I told her. "Just squeeze the trigger. The action is tight. Takes a few pounds of pressure. You might need to use two hands."

"You want me to shoot?" she asked, confused.

"Yeah." I gestured at Dawar. "In the head. Make it a clean shot. No need to make him suffer unduly. Through an eye or maybe the temple, or through the ear."

"You do not need to tell me where," Natasha said. "Finally, you grow pair,"

I felt like shaking her and saying *a* pair, but there's a time and a place.

"What?" said Dawar, suddenly animated. "No, wait!"

Natasha aimed the pistol at Dawar, pulled the trigger and the gun went off with that seriously loud bang at close quarters that always makes me jump these days.

Dawar was surprised to find himself still alive. And Natasha was surprised as well, having just shot a hole in the side of the Toyota instead of blowing Dawar's lights out.

"Why did you do this?" she asked me angrily, my hand having pushed the gun to the side at the last instant.

The answer seemed obvious to me, and it had nothing to do with her refusal to use articles in her speech. I said to Dawar, "Next bullet is yours, asshole. Killed by a woman. Fuckin' embarrassing, right? No Paradise for you – not unless you tell us where the Scorpion is."

"That's torture," Dawar pointed out. "Congress has outlawed that shit."

True, though the press said the commander-in-chief was ambivalent about torture. Be that as it may, as it currently stood, I was breaking every rule in the book, at least the one that said threatening to kill a prisoner in cold blood unless they talked was a no-no. This could get me court martialed. But here's the thing. You have to break some eggs if you want to make an omelet, right? And the omelet in question here was finding a criminal holding the world to ransom so that I could kill him in cold blood. So, the circumstances were extenuating, if you get my drift.

"So sue me," I told Dawar, and motioned at Natasha to line up his head for round two. "As I told you when we met, Natasha here killed our last prisoner and the thing that concerned her most about it was breaking a fingernail, so I know she has it in her to do you. And now, as she has just demonstrated, you also know she has every intention of pulling the trigger *when I tell her to.*" This last bit I said as much for Natasha's benefit. "If you don't give us something useful, bub, she will shoot you dead and there'll be no dewy-eyed virgins for you, if that's what you're looking forward to."

"I don't know anything," he blubbered, his eyes shifting from Natasha to me, and back again.

"I don't believe it."

"I got separated when Al-Aleaqarab picked up Petrovich and the others at the crash site. I don't know where he is."

"He must have set out contingency plans, in case his fighters got separated."

"Yeah, coz you pick up a Russian president every other day."

"Leave the sarcasm to me," I told him. The nerve, right?

"Our base was a warehouse back at Latakia, but that got overrun by Russians. I wasn't there at the time, but I heard about it."

"And what have you heard about where your boss might have gone since? What's the word on the jihad-barricade-checkpoint-street?"

"They say he has brought the Crusader to his knees."

"Who?"

"The Crusader – that's what we call the West."

Right. Like I said, who writes this stuff? That aside, Dawar may have been correct about the effect the pictures of a crucified Valeriy

Petrovich were causing around the globe. No doubt assholes everywhere were seeing this as some kind of rallying cry. Meanwhile, I was getting nowhere. "Shoot him," I told Natasha.

She smiled and raised the gun.

"Wait, wait ... Up north, up north, somewhere close to Dabiq. That's the rumor."

Maybe he really was concerned about being shot by a woman. Yet another example of inequality between the sexes right there, if one were looking for it. I put my hand on the weapon again. "Keep going," I told him.

"They say he hasn't crossed the Euphrates yet. He's waiting for his forces to build up."

"Whereabouts is he, exactly?"

"No one knows. But he's not hiding in plain sight, not like bin Laden did. He's not in any town or city. No time to organize a safe house. Our retreat from Latakia was a rout. Our intention was to die fighting. Al-Aleaqarab will be somewhere in the desert."

"He'll be worried about being spotted from the air," I said, thinking aloud. "Any caves you know of in the general area of 'up north'?" I gave him some rabbit ears.

"No." He shook his head. "Haven't been in that part of the country."

I've questioned enough criminals in my time to know when someone's telling the truth. And also when they've said everything they've got to say. Press too hard beyond that point and you get embellishment.

I put my hand out to Natasha. "Thank you," I said, meaning, hand over the piece. She shook her head at me and pushed it into my hand with as much displeasure as she could muster. I checked the weapon, made sure a round was up the spout and –

An explosion made me jump about a foot sideways. Again. But this time Dawar was sprawled across the Toyota's bed, his brains all over the paintwork, the rest of him twitching. Natasha checked her own weapon and replaced it in her boot, happy in her work.

"What? What the fuck?" I yelled at her.

"Everything he was going to say, he said. But this wasn't enough. So, now he cannot go to heaven. And he cannot claim to authorities he was tortured by you. I do you favor. I know your system. It needs to grow pair also."

"But why the fuck did you kill him?"

"I tell you why just now. Also, you do not know these people like I know them. They are all like Chechens. You cannot trust them. You cannot trust anyone who loves death more than life. These pigs murdered my twin sister in Beslan. You remember that? Beslan? The school? These Chechens, they take the school, they make explosives in the classroom and the gymnasium. All the children are going to be killed, so what choice does government have? Spetsnaz, tanks, they move in. Much gunfire. Some children live. My sister, Irina, is not one of them. This is why I join army. This is why I do this." She gestured off hand at what was left of Dawar.

Everyone has a story. But this was another of hers I wasn't buying. Either it wasn't entirely genuine, or there was more to it. "I thought Beslan was part of the Chechen fight for independence."

"What would you know?"

"Didn't the Russian army do most of the killing?"

"You believe everything CNN tell you?"

No, not since around the year 2003. Fair enough. I gave a mental shrug and let it go. I didn't want to get sucked further into her backstory. And what could I do about the very dead Dawar? He was a terrorist, so who cares, right? But something Arlen told me niggled: *Don't take this the wrong way, but your normal is kinda fucked up from pretty much every perspective except your own.* I pictured him saying it, like it was somehow not a positive aspect of my personality. I looked at Dawar, at least what was left of him shaking against the bodywork, and I felt … nothing. Truthfully, I wasn't even angry with Natasha, although I was annoyed that she had disobeyed my order. That's what I was pissed about – not that she had killed someone's son, possibly someone's father, in cold blood. Nothing I could do about it though, not now. And maybe she was right about having done me a favor. I could see Arlen, arms folded, shaking his head at me. Do me a favor, Arlen, and go back to your Power Point preso. "I have a question for you, Natasha," I said, feeling calmer.

"*Da?*"

"Why are you so angry?"

"I just give reason."

"Maybe that's what motivated you to join the military, but not–"

"How do you know? Did terrorist kill your sister?"

"I'm an only child. Can't you tell? Look, I'm not asking you about your personal history. You told me what happened in the helicopter, but there's something else. I've got this feeling and it's telling me to keep pushing you. You'd rather stay with us and look for Petrovich than go back to your own people and join their hunt for him. I don't think it's because you like us. So, what are you not telling me?"

"Everything. I tell you everything."

"Natasha, c'mon. What really happened in the helicopter? Actually, I believe you about the what. Let me rephrase. *Why* did it happen?"

She looked at me, squinting a little like she was trying to understand the point but not quite getting it. "Why do you care? What does it matter? The bodyguard, he blew up helicopter and it crash." She opened her hands out as if to say, "I have told you this already. There you go - you got it all."

But I didn't have it all, and that was the point. "Natasha, it's not enough to know that a thing has happened. People want to know why a thing happened. We're not down with uncertainty, randomness. When we know why something happened, it gives some control over the universe, makes us believe that we can maybe stop a thing happening the next time."

"You want to know, because you want someone to blame. You can't blame the universe. This is your stupid American culture. Shit happens. You know this expression?"

"Yeah, but more often than not the shit gets a helping hand. You told me one of Petrovich's security detail blew himself up. I'm not down with the whole Islamic terror sleeper thing. Before your suicide bomber is tasked to close protection duty for the President of Russia, the FSB is going to know more about him than he knew about himself."

My pocket began to vibrate. The satellite phone. "Don't go away," I told her, and walked several paces out of earshot before I thumbed the green button.

"Major Cooper," said the voice on the line. "Major Schelly."

"Major. We still on a first name basis?"

"Vin. How's that?"

"There you go. What's up?"

"Good news and bad news," she said.

"Love it. Gimme the bad. I eat bad for breakfast."

"Right, well, the Reapers had to bug out."

"What?"

"We've got a Predator coming online soon, so we can keep eyes on you, but it's winchester."

"So, there's no one watching us at the moment?" I asked.

"No, unfortunately, right now you're on your own."

I was relieved. Video footage of Natasha whacking a prisoner while I stood right beside her wouldn't look so great in any kind of enquiry, should one ever be called. I covered my relief on this score by saying, "Hey, you saw what we came through a little while back, right? Those Reapers saved our bacon." Everyone knows how important it is to save bacon.

"Yes, that's why no Reapers is the bad news."

"I'll just tell the enemy to back off for a while. At least until we're ready to blow them up again."

Clearly uncomfortable about our bacon swinging in the breeze, the major changed subjects.

"We see that your identification strips are covered by scarves and other non-military clothing. The Russian woman is a blonde. Easy to spot by eyes in the sky. Maybe you could ask her to leave her hair uncovered."

"Not advisable, Major," I said. "You know how they feel about exposed hair round here. Don't want my men driven to the heights of passion. You were saying something about good news?"

"We've been able to narrow the search area considerably. You're no longer covering northern Syria and half of Iraq."

"Don't make it too easy for us, Jillian."

The voice on the line – an attractive voice, and I pictured an attractive face to go with it – then proceeded to give me the background: a rundown on sand flies, a flesh-eating disease and a few other pleasant details besides, along with map references for a grid pattern search covering a much smaller area of wadis two to three hours drive, terrain permitting, a little northeast of our current position. "Anything else," I asked her at the appropriate time.

"Bradley Chalmers," she said.

"One hell of a guy," I replied.

"Really?"

"If you like complete tools, he is the full set of wrenches," I told her. That got me a laugh. I was liking Major Schelly more and more.

"I have to tell you he, or rather the CIA, is operating hit squads in Syria, taking out US nationals."

"I heard the rumor."

"Well, I can make it official for you. It's no rumor. Operation Phoenix."

There was a pause in the line, and it told me a lot. "And you think Chalmers wastes enough time thinking about me that he might try and have me whacked?"

"It's possible," she said.

No, it's probable, I thought but kept that to myself. "Chalmers is insecure, narcissistic and vindictive."

"He bears a grudge against you."

"That's the vindictive part, and the feeling is mutual. Why should he have it all to himself, right?"

"Only the difference is that you're not the one in charge of black ops death squads operating with impunity who can do your dirty work for you with absolute deniability."

"Now you're just sugar coating it."

"Look, I've asked the Secretary of Defense to get me the names and communications details of every unit leader, so that I can call them up and advise them of your area of operations."

"Good luck with that."

"I'm confident."

"And if you do manage to reach them – which I doubt – you'll also be telling them exactly where the barrel is that the fish they're looking for are swimming around in."

"Of course I've thought about that, but we're trying to avoid a blue on blue here. The only defense Chalmers's hit squad would have, if you were to be, well, whacked, is ignorance of your presence in a given area. I'll be taking away that defense, and letting them know Air Force Special Operations is watching."

I could see the reasoning, but it didn't stop that fishy feeling. "What about President Petrovich?"

"A video was posted earlier today. They have crucified him. Literally."

"I've seen it," I told her.

"What?"

"Yeah. On someone's iPhone. Two signal bars."

"Wow," she said, clearly as impressed as I was by the phone service hereabouts.

"I know, right?"

"Well, there's a strong possibility that Petrovich may already be dead, though there is expert opinion that the Scorpion will keep him alive for three days. If that's the case, then he doesn't have much time left." She then said, "By the way, the Russians are reasonably convinced it was a US missile that shot Petrovich down, so they're not happy with us."

"Do they have the same map coordinates you've just given me?"

"I don't know – we haven't supplied them. But arriving there is a matter of deduction. If we cracked it, we have to assume they will too."

"Great."

"The commander-in-chief is counting on you. He asked me to deliver that message personally."

"Please tell him I'd like a pay rise."

"Vin, around 100,000 men on the Turkish border are waiting for the Scorpion to lead them to a final victory over the West, or the armies of Rome, as they call them. He has, almost overnight, become something of a messianic figure to millions of Muslims, who fully expect he will usher in the End of Days when the dead will rise and walk the Earth. He is being called the Mahdi – an heroic character straight out of the Qur'an ... Sorry, that's all a bit much to take in, and probably irrelevant, the point is, the Scorpion ... He absolutely can not be allowed to join this horde and be seen to be fulfilling the Qur'an's apocalyptic prophesies. His army will then almost certainly advance into Syria to reassert the caliphate and a coalition response will have to follow. And that could galvanize previously moderate Muslims the world over to take up arms. And if you want to ice this cake, the Scorpion has also had the Russian nuclear launch confirmation codes uploaded on the dark web."

I was thinking, "Just another day at the office, Major," which was trite so I said nothing.

"I'm giving you the overall strategic end game, as we see it," Schelly said, filling in the silence. "Now it's pretty much over to you."

To which I replied, "Just another day at the office, Major." Okay, so I said that because, frankly, I just couldn't think of anything else to say other than, "don't worry", or, "it'll all work out fine", both of which were even further along the trite scale.

Also, I wasn't feeling super confident that it would work out or that she shouldn't worry, because I, for one, was worrying like hell.

The call ended. I pocketed the sat phone and took a deep breath. At least now we had a focus – somewhere to start the search. Natasha had returned to the ambulance and was sitting in the front seat. The moment with her was lost. She saw me walking toward the ambulance and turned away, confirming it. But we had time. Natasha would keep. My sense was that whatever lay at the heart of her reluctance to share was pivotal to the cascade of shit my team and I were being asked to clean up. I found my pack in the back of the ambulance, removed the trenching tool and passed it to her through the passenger door window opening. "If you can kill 'em, you can bury 'em." By way of further explanation for burying the body, I added, "Rats."

Her eyes flashed some more of that Russian fury my way, but she still got out of her seat with the spade. Surly compliance was better than getting the bird flipped in my face, which I'd fully expected. She went to work with the trenching tool on a shallow grave, the earth mostly sand and stones, as the horizon began to lighten with the coming of a new day.

"Bo," I called out as I walked over. "What have we got?"

"Same as before, Major. Just the pitter-patter of little rodent feet."

The coast being clear, I called a briefing with my guys and gave them the picture. A messiah to track down, a massive army ready to march, a probably deceased president on a cross, every overweight pimply hacker in every basement in the world having a crack at launching Russia's nukes, the possibility of a CIA hit squad targeting us, Russians closing in, and something about dead people coming back to life, which was handy if you were in the Russian president's most likely present state.

Forty-four

Ronald V. Small @realSmall
He calls himself the Scorpion. Why would you name yourself after
an insect? So dumb!

"Caesar grows weaker by the minute," the Scorpion said to the
camera lens, behind him Petrovich's bare rib cage was rising and
falling with effort, the man's slight paunch slick with blood, sweat
and desert dust. "He lives still, but for how much longer is the will
of Allah the Merciful."

The jihadist operating the camera came out of the medium
close-up, pulling back and widening the shot to show that there
were now two more men crucified either side of Petrovich, their
wrists and feet nailed to ancient, gnarled trees, the limbs of which
seemed twisted and contorted, a silent agony in sympathy with
the men.

The Scorpion continued, "Caesar now shares his pain with two
others. They too have proven to be enemies of Islam. Confirm to the
world that the armies of Rome will meet the faithful on the plains
of Dabiq, this being the will of Allah as written, and your president
will be freed into your care. Allahu akbar." The Scorpion gazed
serenely into the camera lens for some seconds and then snapped at

328

the camera operator, "Enough. Do what you must to the edit, but do not waste time."

"Yes, Lord," said the cameraman and hurried away.

"Ortsa," Al-Aleaqarab beckoned and the young Chechen came to him.

"What do you wish of me, Amir?" he said.

"Tell me, what do the men say of these two?" He motioned at the men now accompanying the President of Russia on his most unpleasant journey.

Ortsa gestured at the man on the left. "That one – Imad. He was well regarded. The other one, Jalil, not so much. They are now both despised for what they have done."

"Take two fighters with you to Raqqa and upload the video to YouTube from there. It is most important that you go nowhere else to do this. We must confuse the Americans and the Russians."

"What of our encampment here, Lord? Do we stay or leave?"

"It is a consideration. These two fools have put us all at risk by not journeying to Al Hasakah to use the internet there. We cannot tolerate laziness and stupidity." Ortsa's question required some serious contemplation. Were soldiers from the West already journeying to this area, led there by the DNS address of the computer used to upload the previous video? Al-Aleaqarab had not survived so many years of war through incaution. And yet there were laws that had to be adhered to. It was stated that a man must be crucified for three days and then stabbed if he still breathed. Three days in the one place at a time of war when you are no longer certain of your location's security was a long time. And yet the West was often ponderous and slow to react. Here in this cave was refuge, and yet ... "Go quickly to Raqqa. Find also men who have pledged *baya'a* to the caliphate. Bring them here. We will move from this place soon and then we will call to our flag the faithful gathered at the borders. When we move, it must be with strength. Go."

"Yes, Lord."

***

Sam Nanaster watched her men. Breakfast time. They seemed relaxed, eating MREs. No one bathed or washed. Survival meant smelling like the desert and the fighters who populated it. Scents carried on the wind, Hunting 101. Proctor and Gamble could get you killed. No one smoked, either. Not so unusual in a highly motivated, committed unit like this. And anyway, if you smoked it would have to be the local tobacco – *dokha* – a pungent nicotine-rich blend that could give you cancer from 100 paces.

Li'l Wilson was doing sit-ups, counting down from 300. Soon he would move on to pushups – fifty on each arm – a morning ritual.

Nanaster turned around slowly. The farmhouse they had inspected before dawn was a bump on the hard, flat tan line that marked the curved circle of the world. All around, for as far as she could see, was blissful emptiness. Sneaking up on someone here took some talent and experience. And the right time: mostly between the hours of twilight and first light.

A drone was up, providing early warning of any movement – there was none – which made this a moment of relaxation before the day's business was attended to: making sure the wrong people never made it home, not even in a bag. *Home.* She snorted. *Where is that anyway?*

She dug the fork into breakfast, put it in her mouth and chewed. Spaghetti with Beef & Sauce. Her least favorite. The meat tasted like minced cork and the sauce defied description. Splashing sriracha sauce on it helped. She didn't hold back on the sauce. This food needed a lot of help.

"Sam," said Ronan, his voice in her earpiece. She glanced over at the DPV. The sergeant was sitting on the back of the desert racer the CIA gave them as a command vehicle, the words "Boot Hill Express" written in large white lettering against the olive paintwork. He gestured at her with a brief wave. "Morning."

"Morning, Ronan. Sleep okay?"

"Yes, ma'am. Like a baby."

"So you were up every two hours with a soiled diaper?"

"No, ma'am. The, er, proverbial baby. The one that sleeps through."
They come in that version?

"And you?"

"Like a log, thanks." *Liar. You haven't had a decent night's sleep in a long time. Not since … well, you know when.*

"Like the one headed for the sawmill?"

"Touché," she smiled. The pleasantries out of the way, the RTO informed her, "Just had our early morning wakeup call from command. Big news."

"Do tell."

"The President of Russia has been captured by ISIS."

"What?"

"Yeah. His bird came down somewhere east of Latakia."

"Shit." *Latakia is not in our field of operations. That's a relief. Gonna get real ugly in that part of the world. The Russian CSAR will be tearing the place apart searching for him.* "Couldn't have happened to a nicer guy. Any instructions for us on that front, other than a heads up?"

"Nope. Just an FYI. Gonna be another ground hog day for us. Map references for some place up north. Four nationals. Priority Alpha. Extreme prejudice."

Four breathers? That's a high concentration. "They with a bigger unit?"

"No information on that, ma'am."

"Guess we'd better roll."

"I'll pass the word."

Nanaster returned to her breakfast and a few moments of further contemplation. The patrol had been outside the wire for nearly three weeks chasing breathers who'd turned their backs on Uncle Sam. Three weeks was a long time. The team was fatigued. Mistakes loved fatigue.

* * *

I decided to change things up, give Natasha and me a break from each other, and sat in the Toyota's bed with Jimmy, Alvin, Igor and Mazool, headscarves pulled across our faces to keep out the rooster tail of dust thrown up by the vehicle. The going was slow on account of all the wadis running west to east across our path, bumping down one side and up the other. The ambulance got itself bogged to the axles in fine sand and dirt a couple of times, and had to be towed out before we'd motored more than a couple of miles into the desert. The sun was already high, the light dazzling and the heat creeping toward the intense end of the scale. Summer was on the way.

The men bouncing around beside me in the Toyota looked like jihadists: headscarves, waistcoats, combat pants and AKs. I wore the same fancy dress. When in Rome, right? Especially in broad daylight. The fact that we were a racial potpourri mattered little in a country that had been a Mecca for assholes from the four corners of the planet for much of the civil war. And if we were stopped by remnants of Islamic State, we had plenty of their black flags we could unfurl to put their mind at ease. Simplistic, but we didn't have a lot more to work with. If things got too complicated, our only answer would be to flick our selectors to full auto.

Bo's drone was up, orbiting 500 feet above the vehicles. It was impossible to see with the naked eye, even when you knew where to look. Every now and then I asked if he'd picked up anything, but, so far, negative on that. I knew he'd inform me the moment there was something so the question was a waste of breath. Maybe the drone hadn't picked up anything because it was a dud. Okay, so I'll admit to being a little nervous. The picture Schelly painted presented odds that were – let's call 'em asymmetrical. "We nearly there yet?" I asked Bo over the comms.

"Averaging around twenty miles an hour, boss. Got a ways to go yet."

In other words, quit bugging me. I looked for a distraction. There was one sitting right next to me: Igor. His shoulders kept bumping me as the Toyota rolled slowly across the uneven landscape. He had a lot of shoulder and they took up plenty of room. "Hey Igor, what is it with you and Natasha? You don't see eye to eye. How come?"

No response. I gathered that he was looking at me, at least his head was turned in my general direction, but actual visual contact was not easy to verify given his eyes were behind sunglasses shrouded in shadow thrown by his headscarf. And, of course, there was the language problem. "Natasha. You no like. Why?" I said butchering the English for him.

He nodded his big head, which I took to mean that he agreed with the statement, though it could have been the up and down movement of the Toyota's suspension doing all the agreeing.

"What is it between the both of you?" I persisted. Igor's noggin moved like a bobble head. "The way you guys are with each other, something's gone on, right?" Still nothing. Maybe he was deaf, or had sand in his ears. There was plenty of it about. I tried another tack. "Tell me about Petrovich? You traveled with him. What's he like?"

"He good man, and not good man," he said finally.

Okay, so we'd established it wasn't sand, but I was right about the language barrier. "Good and bad?"

"*Da.*"

Progress. "Why was he good?"

"Strong leader. Make decision. Good for military."

"And with cute, furry creatures? How was he with them?" I asked. Igor looked at me. I think.

"He liked to ride stallions bareback, move battle tanks around the board and annex small, defenseless former Soviet satellites. That much I know. Was there, y'know, a softer side?"

"Serzhánt Novikova tell this."

I wondered how much Igor knew about Natasha and the president. "Were she and Petrovich ... bad? Bad individually.

Bad together?" Define bad? Unlikely. We were barely half a step above sign language. I was grasping. I rephrased. "Were Natasha and the president lovers?"

"Lovers? *Nyet. Nyet* lovers."

"Why would Natasha say they were if they were not?" I asked him, a stream of consciousness question. The fact that she would lie about something like that made no sense.

"Did President Petrovich like Natasha?"

"*Da.* Natasha, she ..." He held out his hands like he was feeling a couple of melons, squeezing them for ripeness. This universal signing crossed all language and cultural barriers. Petrovich thought Novikova had great melons. Check. No argument there.

"What about Natasha? Did she have feelings for the president?"

"Feelings? What is?"

"Did she like him?"

"No like. Ask Natasha."

This was an interesting departure from Natasha's story. Why claim they were trading fluids when they weren't? A question for the serzhánt. Moving on, I asked him, "Why were you traveling with the president?"

"Fighting. I teach."

He seemed to relax now the questions were moving away from Petrovich and Natasha.

"You were teaching Petrovich to fight?"

"*Da.*"

"What sort of fighting."

"Ju-jitsu. He want make video."

I recalled the manner in which Igor had pacified Mazool. According to Natasha, Captain Russia here already had a big rap with the folks back home. And Petrovich was a narcissist fond of posting videos of his machismo on the World Wide Web. A friendly match between the Russian commander-in-chief and the cage-fighting Spetsnaz hero of the Crimea was definitely his style. "Was Petrovich an okay fighter?"

He rocked his big hand from side to side, which I took to mean no, not really.

I was sure the YouTube video would have told a different story. And there we were, back at the beginning. "Natasha says one of Petrovich's bodyguards blew up the Hind. Geronimo, I think the man's name was," I said, impressing myself with my memory. "You agree with that?"

He frowned the frown that says I don't know what the hell you're talking about.

I gave it another crack, using my best Russian. "Um, Geronimo … sovich? Something like that?"

He brightened. "Geronosovich. Arkady Geronosovich."

Okay, you wanna split hairs with me, fine. "There you go," I said, "Geronosovich."

"*Da.*" He pointed to the M26 grenades attached to my webbing. "Bodyguard. He use this."

So we got there with the name, and what Geronimo used to blow it up with. "Natasha said Geronosovich was an Islamic terrorist."

Igor's face split into a wry half grin. "*Nyet. Nyet* terrorist. *Nyet* Islamic."

Okay, so this was also interesting. Another divergence from Natasha's story. "Serzhánt Novikova told me Geronosovich said, 'Allahu akbar' before detonating the weapon." That, in my book, tended to suggest fairly heavily that the would-be assassin was, at the very least, leaning towards Islam.

"No terrorist," he repeated. "Natasha. She know … You ask."

If Geronosovich wasn't a terrorist, why'd he blow up the president's bird, killing himself, and a bunch of others in the process? Igor believed Natasha had the answer. Somehow now that we were going on a hunt for President Petrovich, this was becoming important to the snooping side of Cooper I'd left behind at Al Udeid. Someone was lying and I didn't think it was Igor. At least, not about this. Igor was lying about other things: specifically why he wanted to hang out with my team and me rather than rejoin his comrades. I'd already asked the question. He said his money was on us beating Mother Russia to finding Petrovich, or words to that effect. Really? Sure, the US has a reputation for having the best surveillance gadgets, but I knew our technological limitations. And I was pretty sure, whether they were prepared to admit it or not, the Russians did too. No, Igor was hanging out with us for a different reason, but what was it?

"Boss," said a voice in my ear – Bo. "Company, three o clock."

I looked out to our right. Over on the horizon were faint specks. "What have we got?"

"Bedouins. Folks riding camels, anyway. They're packing Kalashnikovs."

I pictured his drone buzzing them – the 21st century circling the 6th century armed with AKs. Actually, the rifles weren't relevant. A carbine here was like underwear back home – everyone wore it. A shriek underscored by a thunderous rolling boom disturbed the monotony of the Toyota's labors. Fighter jets - two of them from out of the east, flaps down and a couple of hundred feet off the deck. Sukhoi SU 27s, a.k.a. Flankers, the Russian version of our F-15 Eagle, painted three-tone gray-green camo. They passed close, the pilots banking hard to eyeball us. "Wave!" I shouted above the racket and we gave them a brace of gestures sans middle fingers. Okay, mine was raised, but the ambulance with its big red crescent would hopefully give them a solid reason to ignore us. Were these Russians an advance search party or was this a chance meeting between them and us? Did they have coordinates for the same search area? If so, how far behind them were the Hinds, BTRs and legions of Spetsnaz? Whatever, the sudden arrival of these Sukhois was a reminder if I needed one that the Pentagon had given us a tall order – to find Petrovich before the Russians did. With any luck, the Kremlin and the White House were right now patching up their differences and we could just stand back and let their military do its thing, find its commander-in-chief, kill the Scorpion and then we could all go back to a world that almost made vague sense.

Who was I kidding?

Forty-five

Ronald V. Small @realSmall

Today I hit a hole in one. Nothing in life provides more satisfaction.

The Russian ambassador lowered himself with some care into the chair.

"Ahh," he said, the ubiquitous grunt disguised as an expression of appreciation, "the famous desk."

Secretary of State Bassingthwaite presented the old GRU colonel with a generous tumbler of Iordanov vodka with rocks. "Mikhail Ivanovich?"

"It is early ... "

"Breakfast of champions."

The ambassador was easily convinced. "*Spasibo*. Thank you." The ambassador accepted the drink with the enthusiasm of a man half perished from thirst accepting clean water. Then, leaning forward, he ran a hand along the front edge of the desk and said, "Donated by the British Queen Victoria to President Hayes in 1880. Beautiful."

"It's not so nice." President Small, seated behind the desk, was dismissive. "I have one in my office back at the tower. It has solid gold knobs. Worth a lot of money."

"Ah yes, but this one is made from history – used by many presidents, fashioned from timbers recovered from the Arctic exploration vessel, HMS *Resolute*. What momentous events it has witnessed."

The president said, "Who knew, right?"

"You did not know this?" The ambassador was surprised.

Bassingthwaite jumped in. Clearing his throat, he said, "Thank you for agreeing to meet with us, Mr Ambassador."

"I like the Oval Office," Rodchenko said, taking in the surroundings with a measure of awe.

Looking around, President Small offered, "It's small. I have much bigger offices all over. But this is a symbolic place. A very powerful place. It intimidates a lot of people."

"Is that why you invited me here," Rodchenko wondered, "to intimidate me?"

"No, please, Mr Ambassador," said Bassingthwaite. "We asked you here because President Small –"

"I can speak for myself," the president admonished him.

The SECSTATE smiled thinly. "Of course, Mr President."

"I asked you here," the president continued, "to tell you that the American people are very anxious about Valeriy's … ah, predicament … and I wanted to assure you personally that we had nothing to do with his helicopter being shot down, which was very terrible, very grave, and to say we will do anything we can to help find him – *are* doing whatever we can to find him – and bring these terrorist criminals to justice, because they are very bad people and we need to hunt them down and kill them all until every single one of them is dead."

Bassingthwaite examined the old colonel's scarred and battered face and, as usual, got nothing. It was the perfect face for an ambassador or a gambler – completely impossible to read.

Rodchenko rolled the rocks around his glass, taking time to consider his response. "Mr President, our own investigators have recovered missile fragments from the helicopter accompanying President Petrovich. They have determined that this missile was made in Turkey."

Bassingthwaite was visibly relieved. "So not one of ours."

"It was an FIM-92A Stinger missile," Rodchenko replied.

The SECSTATE went pale.

"What is it?" the president asked, wondering at the sudden silence.

"The Stinger is made in Turkey under license by Roketsan, Mr President," Rodchenko informed him.

"So?" President Small's shoulders were hunched up around his ears, the significance of this news failing him.

"The Stinger is a Raytheon product, Mr President," Bassingthwaite informed him, sweat beading on his forehead, one of his worst fears realized.

"But Turkish, right? Not one of ours…"

"Technically, it is 'very much one of yours," Rodchenko pointed out. "Turkey put them into the hands of anti-Assad fighters. This the Turks did in secret, but they did it with your permission and your blessing. Turkey was merely your proxy. We know this because, of course, we have our own sources. We protested. We warned you through back channels that these missiles would put our pilots at risk, which you assured us would not happen. But of course weapons are captured, and they leak from this group today and pass into the hands of another group tomorrow. Allegiances there shift like the wind. And now our president is shot down and captured and ISIS has crucified him for the whole world to see. This is an insult to all of Russia – to see our president treated this way. The country is united in anger at your betrayal of friendship –"

"Now wait just a minute," President Small said, outraged.

"A betrayal, Mr President. Nothing is clearer to us."

"Mr Ambassador, there seems to be some misunderstanding here," Bassingthwaite said. "You're saying that your president's helicopter was shot down by a missile? Our sources –"

"Misunderstanding? Did not your own president just say he wanted to assure me personally that you had nothing to do with his helicopter being shot down?"

"Sir, witnesses on the ground at the time reported that a missile shot down only one of the helicopters. An internal explosion of some kind disabled President Petrovich's helicopter, rather than a missile."

"Witnesses? You have witnesses? Were these witnesses soldiers? Your soldiers? Were they, indeed, the very soldiers who shot down these helicopters?"

Bassingthwaite was suddenly aware of the trap he had just stumbled into, and silently cursed his own foolishness for doing so. "I can assure you, Mr Ambassador, that the United States was not involved in this terrible accident and its outcome in any way."

"That is not how it seems to us. President Small, you and President Petrovich were friends and then you were not and then you were, back and forth – a most confusing dance. And now President Petrovich is brought down in the presence of your own soldiers and given to ISIS. There is a faction in the Kremlin that considers this an act of war. You have seen the protests. The riots. There is much anger."

"War between our countries would be unthinkable," Bassingthwaite reminded him, his legs feeling weak. The special operations unit in Syria had confirmed that Petrovich's helicopter had been taken out not by a missile but by other means. The missile attack on the second aircraft was merely opportunistic. The Hind just happened to be in the wrong place at the right time. He sat, relieved that there was a chair under him. "Mr Ambassador, I must insist that there seems to be some confusion here. It's probable that your president's helicopter was sabotaged."

"Sabotage? You have evidence of this?"

Bassingthwaite was not going to get caught a second time. "No, but –"

"No, no evidence. But we have evidence of this missile."

The SECSTATE wondered if he should inform Rodchenko that two Russian citizens had been recovered from President Petrovich's helicopter. *But that would likely open another can of worms – why hadn't he, Rodchenko, been informed; why hadn't these citizens been turned over to Russian forces; were they in fact being held prisoner by US forces; were these soldiers the so-called witnesses; were the Russian citizens being held by the very unit that attacked the president's helicopter?* No, Bassingthwaite decided. *Best to follow Director Hamilton's advice and not give the Russians anything. Maybe the president and I have given them way too much already.* Instead, he pointed out again, "Open hostilities between our two countries would be unthinkable."

Rodchenko responded, "Then tell me why your forces have moved to DEFCON Two?"

"We raised our alert level because you raised yours," President Small insisted.

"We raised our alert level because of these events. Terrorists have our president, along with our most senior general and the codes for our nuclear weapons, codes now released on the dark web. This is a catastrophe of global proportions. What did you expect would happen, Mr President? You Americans never seem to understand that when you do these things, there are consequences beyond what you can predict."

"But, I insist - we haven't done anything," said Bassingthwaite, aware that he sounded shrill.

"You know where our president is being tortured – the location."

"What? No. If we knew, we would inform you immediately! We would not keep that information to ourselves."

"I think you are not telling me the truth."

"Are you calling me a liar?" Bassingthwaite's gorge was rising.

Rodchenko turned to the president. "Did not your own press secretary announce that your military had solid leads? What solid leads are these?"

Bassingthwaite could see instantly how this statement would look to the Russians.

President Small said, "In fact, Mr Ambassador, she told the press we are doing everything that we can to help find Valeriy and bring the Scorpion to justice."

"And what, may I ask, are you doing in that regard?"

"Everything we can."

"We think you have done more than enough." Ambassador Rodchenko drained his glass, leaned forward and placed it on the desk on a coaster bearing the seal of the President of the United States of America. "Truly excellent vodka." He stood and looked around. "You are right. This office really is quite small." He ran his hand along the desk and appeared to pity it. "And now we have said everything that needs to be said. I must go and make my report."

"Mr Ambassador," Bassingthwaite beseeched.

Rodchenko put his hand up, the signal to stop. "Enough, please."

The SECSTATE went to get the door as the ambassador moved toward it on joints that were plainly giving him grief.

"No need." Rodchenko waved him away. "I can let myself out."

"I trust you will continue to protect our embassy in Moscow," said Bassingthwaite.

"We will do everything short of firing on our own people. Please see that your marines stationed within the building exercise the same restraint. Good day."

The door closed behind him. Bassingthwaite let out a long breath, not realizing he had been holding it.

After a few seconds, President Small said, "The nerve of that guy. But I think he likes me and trusts me. What do you think?"

Bassingthwaite blinked. "I'm, I'm sure that's true, Mr President. Nevertheless, it may also be the wisest course to pull our team out of Syria – the one searching for President Petrovich. There is too much risk of a misunderstanding."

"Well, I disagree. If we find Valeriy, and find him alive, the Russians will be enormously grateful. Those are some pretty important bargaining chips right there. No, we need to keep some skin in the game. Think of it as a business deal, if you can."

"The Russians will shoot our people on sight and claim it was our fault."

President Small shook his head and looked at the SECSTATE as if he had no grasp of the situation at all. "Never gonna happen, Ed. Our SEALs are the best in the business."

Forty-six

Ronald V. Small @realSmall
Evildoers beware! America's best weapons are its people. And we
have over 300 million of them!

This was the hard part. Major Schelly had called everyone, written up
everything, and now there was nothing left to do but hurry up and
wait. She considered calling Colonel Simmons at Creech and asking
whether the Reapers were back on station, but the colonel had enough
to occupy his time without having to field nuisance calls from her. If
the killer drones were flying overwatch, then great, zero more to do.
If not, there was still nothing she could action to change the situation.
Simmons knew the score. Quickstep 3 had the highest priority.

So, to pass the time, Schelly monitored the BBC, NBC and so forth.
The world was in meltdown, but most of what they reported was
repetitive regurgitation, some speculative and the rest unnecessary,
even unhelpful, the reporting cycle sifting through the backstories of
victims of the violence. However, the story just hitting her Twitter feed
had Schelly's full attention. The link said, *End of Days. Today's the
day.* She clicked on it.

It was the lead news story breaking on *NYTimes.com*. Reports
were coming in from all over of graveyards being disturbed – in

the US, this had happened at Macon and Savannah, Georgia; in Parsippany, New Jersey; Eden Prairie, Minnesota; and Clarkstown, New York; in Canada it had happened at a cemetery in Moose Jaw, Saskatchewan; in England, Surrey was the hotspot and half-a-dozen cities in other countries around the world – including, France, Germany, Australia and New Zealand – had experienced much the same thing. It was being called the "End of Days Phenomenon" because the graves appeared to have been disturbed *from the inside*, "as if the dead within had burst out" according to reports.

The *NYTimes.com* article said eyewitnesses were claiming to have seen corpses walking along city streets. They described it like seeing a scene from the cable show, *The Walking Dead*. Whole towns were in panic. In Macon, so the report said, sheriff's deputies had been issued with axes, presumably if bullets failed to do the job, and were staking out the city's graveyards. The Macon Sheriff, Sheriff John Carter, reportedly said that this was being done to "ease the public's mind and put the dead back where they belonged".

However, a protest group in Macon had announced through its Facebook page that it was determined to spare deceased loved ones the indignity of being hacked to pieces when they rose, and would form "a living shield" between the sheriff's deputies and the dead. At other graveyards, there were reports of welcoming committees for "the newly returned", as a spokesperson had termed them, with stalls set up with weird selections of food and drink – everything from plain water to bourbon to pound cakes to sheep brains. Religious fundamentalists were having their say. The Christians were preaching that the newly returned heralded the imminent arrival of Jesus and that non-believers had better repent their sins, or else. Muslims agreed that Jesus was on the way and that non-believers had better convert, acknowledge that there is no god but Allah, or suffer the fires of hell for all eternity.

All manner of groups were springing up on social media discussing various aspects of this confronting phenomenon, from the potential biology of the newly returned, to the implications of the existence of "the soul", to the more practical concerns of healthcare for these undead and whether or not they presented a biological hazard to the living. Other less worldly groups argued over whether the undead would come together as an army to fight the living alongside Jesus, as stated in the Qur'an. And speaking of Jesus, how might Jesus arrive? On a donkey, on a cloud, in a Tesla? Would he be of the Jewish, Christian or Muslim faith? And what would he look like? Would he have the appearance of a young hippie in his prime, with a dark beard and long dark hair, just as he had been back in the day, according to various shrouds and religious artworks. Or would he have the countenance of an old guy, one who had been dead for over 2000 years? Others argued that he'd never died in the first place. The discussions raged.

"Whaaaat?" Schelly said aloud several times as she reviewed the sudden outpouring stirred up by the Macon Sheriff's department. Had the world gone completely and utterly batshit crazy?

A tone sounded, alerting her to a new tweet, this one from CNN. It contained the irresistible link, "Macon Sheriff denies dead are rising". She clicked on the link and was shocked to see that the story featured a grainy black and white image taken from surveillance camera footage. It showed three longhaired, tatty people of indeterminate age walking through a gate. The caption read, "Cameras catch the dead leaving cemetery". Schelly blinked. "No fucking way!"

Another tweet arrived. The *LA Times* had written this story up under the headline, "Zombie Apocalypse unleashed". Schelly absorbed the tabloid shock tactic and went back to the *NYTimes.com*, her preferred source.

Hungry for details, as were over three million people currently reading, according to the rolling counter, she read the article that extensively quoted Macon's Sheriff Carter from a press conference just held. Logos on microphones crowding the sheriff indicated that a large media scrum had attended this event, including journalists and stringers from all the wire services. Scrolling down revealed the picture of a fat, graying, late middle-aged man in a sheriff's uniform contained within a frame overlaid with the familiar blue and white "play" icon. She clicked on the triangle.

Sheriff Carter leaned forward into the microphone on the lectern and read from a statement. "The Bibb County Sheriff's Department received a call from residents in the area of the Cedar Ridge Cemetery, complaining of a disturbance – bottles breaking and whatnot – at around 2 am last night," he drawled. Several grim-faced deputies flanked the sheriff, a couple of them nodding confirmation as their boss recounted the details. "A deputy was dispatched to the scene. He found no one present at the cemetery, but the graveyard had been all dug up in places, with numerous tombstones overturned.

"We expected this to be the work of vandals. Checking surveillance camera footage proved difficult as there are no cameras in the graveyard itself, though there was a camera in a nearby parking lot.

"The footage showed over a dozen persons, what appear to be a mix of males and females in old worn clothes, coming from the graveyard and walking through the lot.

"Over a dozen graves appeared to have been disturbed. We conducted a search for these – we're calling them suspects – but so far the search has proved fruitless. That is all I can tell you at this time."

The sheriff and his deputies then walked away from the lectern as journalists burst into a chorus of shouted questions: "There are many cemeteries in Macon. Have any others been disturbed?" and, "Do you think corpses have actually risen from the dead?" and, "Is it true you've issued your deputies with axes?" and "Do you think this is the start of the End of Days predicted by the Scorpion?"

The sheriff found at least one of these questions irresistible, and stopped to growl an answer at the reporter concerned. "Hell, corpses rising from the dead? C'mon, I'm not saying anything of a kind. Something's going on here, and looks like at other places too. We just don't know what it is. And no, I have not issued my deputies with axes. I don't know where that's come from."

The sheriff then continued his journey out of the room until one reporter drawled, "Is there any truth to the rumor that one of your deputies actually struck one of these zombies with his patrol car, Sheriff, ran into him with enough force to kill him? I heard that the man then ran off. Is that because he was already dead? Can you explain it, sir?"

This almost caused a riot with the gathered reporters surging toward the sheriff and his deputies and demanding more information.

The sheriff put his hands in the air in an attempt to calm the mob. "No, I can tell you there is no truth in any of that. Our investigations are continuing. We will keep you informed."

Here the video ended.

"Oh, man," said Schelly, shaking her head.

It was obvious from the Twitter alerts pouring into Schelly's phone from the major news services that the world believed the sheriff was confirming precisely what he denied he was saying: that the dead had crawled their way out of the ground and were walking around. The predictions made in the Qur'an and stated by the Scorpion were coming true.

Where are they walking to? Schelly wondered. *Are they going all the way to fucking Syria?* She reached for the phone and called the professor. "Jill," Kiraz said when she picked up. "I was about to call you."

"Hi, have you seen the news?" Schelly asked her.

"You mean the video?"

"Yeah, the video of dead people supposedly leaving their graves."

"What?" Evidently, the professor was unaware of it.

It was clear to Schelly that they were talking at crossed purposes. "Kiraz, what video are you talking about?"

"The latest from the Scorpion. What video are *you* talking about?"

An incoming call cut across her conversation with Professor Başak. It was Secretary of Defense Epstein. "Oh, I have to take this." she told the professor. "Call you back?"

"Don't worry about it, I will see you soon."

349

"Okay," Schelly replied, frowning, and a little confused. *Did we make plans to get together? I don't think so.* She thumbed the button, accepting the incoming call from the SECDEF. "Morning, Madam Secretary."

"Major, where are you right at this minute?"

"At the Pentagon, ma'am."

"The president wants an update. The Situation Room. Get here as soon as you can with whatever you can bring."

Forty-seven

Ronald V. Small @realSmall
Do not doubt our strength and determination, Mr Insect. You
don't want to pick a fight with us. That would be tremendously
stupid.

Hakim had not slept for fear that Zuti may be lying injured
somewhere, unable to free himself. Much of the village had
searched tirelessly, but Zuti seemed to have simply disappeared.
That was not altogether unheard of, but it was unusual. There
were whispers that perhaps he had been abducted by some warring
faction and pressed into soldiery. Or abducted by slavers and sold.
Hakim didn't believe these stories – he refused to believe these
stories. Zuti was out there somewhere, he just needed to be found,
and quickly. He carried water but he would have drunk it all long
ago. Thirst was the biggest enemy in the desert.

Zuti was his oldest boy, the one who looked most like his mother,
the mother who had died giving birth to Nur, his youngest. Hakim
loved his son and so he searched all the places they took the herd
with his second son, Labib, calling Zuti's name. Sometimes fear and
desperation filled Hakim's eyes with tears as the hours slipped by. It
was Labib who was strong and told his father not to worry.

But then, while searching one of the areas frequented less by the goats due to its sparse feed, Labib saw a lone goat standing on a rock ledge. He recognized the animal, for it had a large white blaze on a coat that was mostly black. He ran and captured it. The goat was collared and, on closer inspection, it wore Hakim's mark.

Hakim and Labib called Zuti's name as he led the goat in and around the base of the shelf. Soon they came upon three other goats that were living, and one that was dead, its flesh picked at by carrion birds. The goats did not need to be tethered and happily followed them, Hakim and Labib's voices familiar to them, along with their smell. Labib wished the animals could speak, because surely they would know where to find his brother.

Coming around a finger of rock, Hakim saw a mound of smaller stones set in a pile. It was manmade and unfamiliar, a new feature. They approached it, a natural inquisitiveness driving them, and then the mound of stones seemed to shudder and move as, disturbed by their sudden presence, many rats, beetles and other insects began to pour from out of the earth, between the stones. Above, a carrion bird circled and Hakim found himself saying, "*La la la – la 'iilah la ...*" *No, no, no – no, God, no ...*

The father tore at the loose stones, tearing them down. Soon he saw a white shroud beneath them, and there was dried blood on it and the pain in his chest made breathing almost impossible: "*La, la, la!*"

The last of the rats ran from the shallow depression as Hakim scooped up the body he knew was that of his son, the boy's hand and arm with many pieces of flesh torn away falling from the loosely bound shroud. Hot tears ran from his eyes and the pain of the loss was like a hand around his throat. "*La, Zuti, la...*" he cried softly, nuzzling the bundle hugged tight to his chest.

Forty-eight

Ronald V. Small @realSmall
Today Ronald Small Jr. bought five hotels and got the best price.
Very proud father!

Secretary of Defense Epstein and Professor Başak were already seated at the polished ebony conference table. It seemed to coalesce from the darker regions of the vast Situation Room. The feeds from assets around the globe were silent. The unnatural quiet reminded Schelly of an empty sports arena between games.

"Major. Thanks for getting here so quickly," Epstein said in her now familiar smoke-and-booze-scarred voice. "Traffic from Maryland is a bitch this time of day."

"Morning, ma'am. Wasn't so bad – the traffic." Schelly placed her briefcase on the desk and pulled out the chair beside the professor, who looked up at her with a quick smile.

"Major."

"Professor." *Hi, how are you? Love that combination you're wearing – pearl silk blouse with pleated orange skirt and black lacquered heels. God, you smell like heaven.*

Collegiate pleasantries exchanged, Schelly sat behind her briefcase and released the locks, which gave a satisfying *thunk*.

"Kiraz was just saying she doesn't think you've seen the Scorpion's latest effort," Epstein said.

Schelly organized her notes. "No, I haven't. Tried to get it up on my phone on the way over here, but it wouldn't load."

"It's only just hit the usual outlets." Epstein's fingers tapped a touch screen in front of her. A wall monitor flickered, stirred by a sudden burst of electrons, and a picture materialized. It showed a balding man with graying wisps of hair in his mid-sixties – General Yegorov – on his knees in the dirt. In front of him was a compact suitcase attached to a chain and handcuff – the Cheget. Immediately behind him were three men, stripped naked to the waist, their wrists and feet bolted into tree limbs denuded of leaves to make the arrangement appear more symbolically cross-like. A fold in a towering rock formation framed the scene, the colors muted in the pre-dawn light.

Three men crucified together … That picture looks familiar, thought Schelly, who was again struck with the ancient brutality of crucifixion.

"The terrorists are getting more artful with practice," Epstein observed, "and also more careless. Note the terrain. They appear to be in some kind of shallow ravine – a cleft in a rock formation. We're working with the folks at DIMOC to locate this topography within our revised target area. We're hopeful of a match."

"Madam Secretary, unfortunately, until the next satellite pass we have no way of contacting Quickstep 3."

"Oh …"

The door flew open, Andrew Bunion holding it wide for President Small, who strode in like a man who believed taking big steps made him appear dynamic. "Have we found him?" the president demanded, coming to a stop at the conference table.

"Good morning, Mr President. Valeriy Petrovich? No," Epstein replied. "But we believe we're close." Her eyes flicked for an instant at Schelly. "The good news is that he appears to be alive in the video just posted to YouTube. We believe it was shot only this morning."

The president glanced over and saw the still frame on the monitor. "You got the video loaded? Play it."

Epstein tapped the control screen and the images on the monitor moved, the focus on the kneeling General Yegorov pulling out to a wider shot as Al-Aleaqarab walked into the picture and stood beside the Russian. Gesturing with a deformed claw clutching the now familiar curved blade he used as a pointer, he addressed the camera, "I speak to all leaders of the Crusader nations. One of your own, a great Caesar, will soon be dead, given to the Hellfires for all eternity, unless you agree to send your armies to meet the faithful at Dabiq. Time is running out. Only you can spare him. You must decide."

The Scorpion then looked behind him, up at the unconscious president. "It is written that the crucified must be stabbed in the heart after three days, freeing him from torment. Allah the Merciful commands this, and so it shall be done."

Al-Aleaqarab then went back to Yegorov and crouched beside him, the camera framing both men, the Russian's head bowed. "In the meantime, Caesar's general has been most helpful with our battle plans. His knowledge and assistance will help us sweep your Crusader armies from the Earth. The purity of the one true faith will then be the flower that blooms in the desert and spreads across the world, uncontested. Do not forget that Caesar's weapons of mass destruction are also mine to command." The terrorist picked up the briefcase with the knife under its handle, then set it down again. "The End of Days is coming. Soon the Antichrist will be among us. The moment draws nearer with every breath Caesar takes."

The camera panned closer in on Petrovich, his chest heaving like a frightened bird's. And there the video abruptly finished.

"Well he's a determined sonofabitch," the president said. "You have to say that for him." He turned to Bunion. "I still really like your idea, Andrew. Get 'em all in one place and nuke 'em. I can't believe this guy wants to come up against the best military in the world. It would be a hell of a battle. The greatest battle the world has ever seen. Win something like that and you'll go down in history."

As a monster, thought Schelly, horrified. *Surely you can't be serious.*

The professor was also clearly less than comfortable about the president's continued enthusiasm for what would be slaughter on an unprecedented scale.

"It's nice to see you again," the president said, smiling at Schelly.

"Huh? Oh, thank you, Mr President," Schelly replied, suddenly aware that the commander-in-chief was staring right at her. "It's ... it's great to be here." *What the hell do you say?*

President Small turned toward the professor. "And nice to see you again, too."

"Thank you, Mr President," the CIA analyst said with a respectful nod.

"I like your shirt. It's nice, very feminine," he told her. In an aside to Bunion, he conferred, "Do we have the best-looking intelligence types, or what?"

What? Again? Did you just lick your lips at Kiraz? Why are we here?

"I like your red braces, Mr President. They match your red tie," the professor replied, playing the game.

And your eyeballs, thought Schelly.

Small continued, glowing. "Do you think so? I believe they look business-like and also very very presidential."

"Mr President, if I may offer an opinion of this video?" the professor cooed, leading him back to the business at hand.

"Yes, of course. That's why we're here."

"The Scorpion continues to prey on the religious iconography of Christianity, the default religion of what he calls 'the Crusader nations'. He is hoping we will find this an offense, an insult, and that it will goad us into the response he desires, and which he states is the final battle between the faithful and the armies of Rome."

"But we're smarter than that," the president told her.

Hey, a minute ago you were gonna nuke them, thought Schelly. *I'm confused.*

"Religion – both Muslim and Christianity – is the bedrock on which he builds all of his communications," the professor continued. "With a religious fanatic, who undoubtedly sees everything through the prism of his faith, it is not unexpected. And now, as you can see, there are three men crucified on the hill. This is no mistake. If you remember, there were three men crucified on the hill – two thieves joining Christ. Interesting also that the Scorpion references a crucified victim having to be stabbed after three days on the cross."

President Small appeared to be hanging on her every word. "Yes, very, very interesting." He turned to Epstein. "Do we know where the Scorpion is? Can we get him? I want to get him. And I want cameras on hand when we get him."

"Obama had cameras when he took down bin Laden," Bunion reminded him.

"We gotta have cameras there," President Small reiterated.

"Mr President," said Epstein. "The CIA believes, interesting though it is on a psychological level, that the iconography is a diversion. This video was hurriedly shot and edited for one reason and one reason only – so that it could be posted from a location far away from the Scorpion's hideout – Raqqa in this instance. His last video was posted from a location close to his current hideout – we don't know how they made such a mistake, but mistake it was. It's CIA's view that this video was shot purely for our benefit – to make us believe he's someplace other than where he is. Yes, three men are now crucified instead of one, but the video essentially contains no new information, no new demand. But the terrain is clearly visible. It's not flat, non-descript desert. It has form and feature, geology and geography. There's a chance this video will lead us right to him."

Except that the Scorpion might already be on the move, the thought struck Schelly. *That would be a good reason not to be too concerned about giving away my location if I were the Scorpion.*

The president was nodding with some satisfaction. "Andy?"

"I think we may be getting somewhere, Mr President. At last."

Professor Başak appeared troubled. "Madam Secretary, if I may?"

"Of course," Epstein replied.

"The Bible says Christ was on the cross for less than a day – nine hours – before he was proclaimed deceased. Just prior to this, the Bible tells us, the Centurion Longinus, who used his spear, stabbed him in the side of his chest. It is clear that the Scorpion uses religious precedent when it suits him to do so. We believed he would keep President Petrovich alive on the cross for three days, and he is telling us this. But if Christ can be stabbed after just nine hours on the cross, perhaps he thinks the Russian Caesar can be, too." The professor concluded, "That tells us two things. We believed the Scorpion would have to stay in the one place for at least three days, to give him time to lawfully, at least in the eyes of God, crucify the president. But if he feels that nine hours is enough, the president was probably stabbed shortly after this video was made and the Scorpion is now on the move. I fear, if the aim is to recover the Russian president alive, we may already be out of time."

Schelly found herself nodding in agreement to the professor's conclusion. *You read my mind, girlfriend.*

"Of course, we're only speculating. Whichever way you look at it, time is of the essence," said Epstein. "Recovering the president alive is an aim. But the priority now must surely be to prevent a rendezvous between the Scorpion and the many thousands of Muslims on the Turkish border who have pledged their support to his cause. And then, of course, there is the significant goal of recovering the Cheget. Major?" Epstein said with a gesture at Schelly.

Schelly pulled the map from a tube, unfurled it on the table, and placed empty water glasses at the map's four corners to stop it rolling up. "We believe the Scorpion is, or was, in this area." The president got out of his chair and came over to stand beside her, flooding the immediate area with cologne. Using a red Sharpie as a pointer, she said, "This line here is the Turkish border. This is the Euphrates River. Here, as you can see, is Dabiq, and this is Raqqa." She removed the Sharpie's top and drew an oval shape on the map to the right of the Euphrates, the location roughly equidistant to Dabiq and Raqqa. "This circled area is around fifteen square miles. He's somewhere here. Or at least, he was here this morning, local Syrian time. With luck, he still might be." She drew a cross through the circle. The graphic resembled crosshairs in a gun sight.

"And where are our forces?"

"Here." She drew a small circle. "Moving north."

"How many we got?"

"A team of four."

"That's it?"

Epstein reminded him, "Mr President, the team that took out bin Laden wasn't much bigger."

The president digested this. "Cameras?"

"We'll try, Mr President," Schelly told him. "We should have drones – Reapers or Predators – on station."

"We have spoken with the Russians," the president told them. "They believe this whole thing with Petrovich was our doing, right? So unfair."

"Delivering Valeriy to them alive might be the one chance we get to put the world back together," Bunion said, staring straight at Schelly. "We're counting on you."

"Yes, sir," she said with less conviction than was required. *And I'm counting on a guy most believe is a liability and who I think the CIA is gonna try to whack.*

"Next point on the agenda, Mr President," Bunion reminded him.

"Yes, the disturbing reports in the news," he said, changing gear. "Dead people coming back to life."

"We're still trying to verify those reports, Mr President," said Epstein. "There has to be an explanation."

"But these reports are coming from all over," said the president, deeply concerned.

Bunion added, "We've had discussions with several senators and congressmen who are more than a little alarmed. What do we do with criminals who have received the death penalty and had their sentences carried out? Do we kill them all over again? Will they stay dead a second time? What about all our war dead coming back? What about the pensions we pay their families? We'd have to ask them to repay that money. From how far back will these dead return? I mean, how old will they be? Are we gonna have Civil War dead walking the streets? Will they still be fighting their battles? Will the returned dead have memories of their lives before they died? What do these newly living dead eat? Do they have heartbeats? Are they technically alive? Will we have to redefine what dead actually means? I gotta tell ya, church leaders are going crazy. We worship Christ because he came back from the dead, but if this becomes a commonplace event, where does that leave Christianity? Where's the miracle? These are just some of the questions being asked."

Schelly found herself bewildered.

"There are reported sightings of the Antichrist," the president reminded them. "The Antichrist – sounds like a title for a horror movie. They say he has red skin – like, seriously blood red skin, not like sunburned. The question is, where is Jesus? I mean, there are people claiming to be him, right? How do we know when the real Jesus arrives?"

"Maybe he'll perform a miracle, Mr President," Bunion suggested.

"There'll have to be tests," the president said. "I could ask him to walk across the pond – the one in front of the Washington Monument."

"Walking on water. Good idea, sir."

"I think so."

"Anyway," Bunion continued, "the more we hear about these things in the media, the more the random attacks against civilians from radical Islamists increase. All these reports just embolden more acts of terror. Do we consider censoring the news?"

Schelly had no answers, and was about to say so when the professor counseled, "Mr President. We have all heard these stories about the dead rising and fulfilling the Qur'anic apocalyptic prophesy, and certainly these are strange times with a man claiming to lead the world's Muslims to a final battle against the West, a battle foretold over 1600 years ago. But we have not seen one of these so-called undead properly examined, in a medical sense. This phenomenon is new and far from thoroughly investigated. Let us hear what the experts have to say before we jump to conclusions."

The president seemed somewhat reassured. "Good, yes. Good advice, Professor. You are not just a very pretty face, are you?" He stood. "Andy?"

"Agreed, Mr President."

"Well, please keep me informed. These more intimate meetings work well. What do you think?" he asked Bunion.

"Yep," he said, "works for me."

"You're all doing a tremendous job. Tremendous," the president continued. "But we need to win this. A win win win for America. We're a winning country. The greatest. And let's not forget – cameras."

President Small grinned, changed his look to a scowl. He then stood and walked out, Bunion in his wake.

"I have to get going also," said Epstein. She glanced at Schelly as she packed. "Anything happens with your team in the desert, I want to be the first to know. What about those Reapers? Can we really get eyes on?"

"Yes, ma'am, but it won't be Spielberg. Nothing at ground level."

"We'll take what we can get." The SECDEF slid a small piece of paper the size of a Post-it across the table toward Schelly. "There's a name and a number. You have need-to-know, but the security protocols are sketchy. I can't tell you whether you're allowed to have this or not. Best I can do."

Schelly palmed the folded slip. "I didn't get this from you, ma'am."

Epstein smiled briefly and picked up her briefcase. "Professor, Major ..." She gave them both a nod and headed for the door.

Once the SECDEF had cleared the room, Schelly said, "Despite what you just told the president, you're worried, aren't you?" She rolled up the map and fed it into the tube.

"The signs, remember? They all point to the same thing. And now with the stories of the dead rising."

"But you said –"

"Forget what I said. I fear it is upon us."

"The End of Days?"

"Yes."

"But you're a professor. An academic. How can you believe in this stuff?"

"With everything that is happening, how can you not believe? I will be judged." The professor looked genuinely scared. "They will throw me from a rooftop and I will spend an eternity in hellfire."

Schelly placed a hand on the professor's shoulder. "If that's what happens, Kiraz, I'm gonna be right there burning beside you, holding your hand."

SECSTATE Bassingthwaite walked in. "Where's the Secretary of Defense?" He was on edge, one hand on a hip, the other on his forehead. "I was told she was here."

"She just left, Mr Secretary," Schelly replied. *What's happened?*

"The most technologically advanced country on Earth, but when the phone's switched off ..." He paced left and right as if considering his next move. "You see her, tell her I'm looking for her."

"Yes, sir." Schelly stood.

"Be among the first to know, Major. The entire 20th Brigade of the Turkish Army has just now deserted and gone over to the Scorpion's army. Over a hundred tanks, plus armored vehicles, self-propelled guns, anti-tank weapons ... A lot of those tanks are old, but a tank's a tank."

"Shit," Schelly blurted, stunned. And then, realizing that she had said it and not just thought it, she added, "Sorry, sir."

"No," Braithwaite replied, "I think that about sums it up. One brigade goes over like that, others will follow. This will be the thin edge of the wedge for sure."

Forty-nine

Ronald V. Small @realSmall
Your days are numbered. You know who I mean. We will squash you with a boot made in America by real Americans.

Almost nowhere to hide out here, Captain Nanaster thought. There were no valleys, forests or cities on the Hamad, a vast billiard-table flat plain of grit and rubble that covered most of Syria to the east and northern Iraq. Tunnels were an option, but tunnels required cooperation, organization and time. So, for the most part, there was not even a rock to crawl under. *Makes my job easier.* She swept the horizon with high-powered binocs and saw plenty of heat haze rising off the ground, but little else. "I got nothing," she said and sucked water from the Camelbak.

"Same, boss," Li'l Wilson reported, checking all the feeds from the drone high overhead.

"Let's see what the Company's got for us. Ronan?"

The RTO staked out the portable antennae, the backend comms unit already connected. Once the uplink confirmed a solid connection, the download took only a few seconds.

"Four breathers. Priority Alpha," Ronan said, reviewing decidedly poor quality stills photographs of four US citizens. "Hard to make out who they are. You wanna look?"

Nanaster took the images and flicked through them. Yeah, poor quality. So what? Ultimately, it would be the data downloaded to their software that would confirm their ID. She handed back the photos. *Priority Alphas – what had they done to deserve that? Males, three white, one black. All early-to-mid thirties. What makes a man throw in his life to fight a war on a foreign shore for a cause as brutal as ISIS's?* Nanaster just couldn't figure reasons good enough. But there had to be something, because so many men had left families, friends, communities and their histories behind to fight for it. Maybe it was something in the religion or the ideology, a hook that jagged some part of the brain. But whatever that something was, Nanaster couldn't get a hold on it. It wasn't as if the land they fought for was worth all the blood. The area ISIS had staked out was a harsh and unforgiving place, almost impossible to scratch a living from. All it had was a population who could be taxed and extorted for revenue, but little else. Ultimately, though, the questions mattered little. The mission was simple: to ensure these bastards, who had killed and raped their way across two sovereign nations for the last four years, never got to bring their poisonous knowledge home. Priority Alpha meant these guys were the worst.

She glanced at the accompanying intelligence. It was scant, just names and aliases: Bo Baker, alias Mohammad bin Mohammad, from Tennessee; Jimmy McVeigh, alias Ali Al-Bakr, from Brunswick, Georgia; Vincent Smith, alias Kareem Al-Waleed, from Washington DC; and Alvin Leaphart, alias Raamiz Al-Jafar from El Paso, TX. The four men were in the company of three unidentified Syrian Army deserters who had taken up with ISIS, plus two other unidentified nationals from Chechnya, one of them a woman. That last fact was unusual: a woman fighting within an otherwise all-male ISIS unit? Nanaster hadn't seen that before. Was she someone's wife? Someone's slave? Poor quality photos, poor quality information. The intel might be in error. More than possible. Nanaster let it go – Uncle Sam's beef was not with other foreign nationals. "Where are they?" she asked.

"Close, boss. The last intel available had them in an area around forty clicks north."

Nanaster scanned the horizon again. Clear. "Okay. We'll get to the general area. Start a grid search from the south when we get there."

"Sounds like a plan."

"Pass the word."

"Yes, ma'am."

* * *

The voice in Al-Aleaqarab's mind was a warning. It was a voice he listened to because it had kept him alive while so many friends and comrades had fallen. The voice told him that it was time to leave the cave. *It has provided security, but we could also be trapped here. There is safety in mobility, provided we have numbers in support. Ortsa should return from Raqqa well before nightfall. How many fighters will he bring? Everyone must be ready before Asr.* "You and you – Ramis, Ehab," he said pointing at two men lying on the ground, trying to sleep. "Now is not the time to rest. Get up, gather the men." The two veterans leapt to their feet, excited and awed that the Mahdi knew them by name. "Pass the word that we must be ready to leave this place before afternoon prayer. Go now."

Ramis and Ehab circulated first among the fighters in the cave, which was soon buzzing with activity.

The only question Al-Aleaqarab had concerned Petrovich and the other two. "What to do?" he said quietly. *May Allah give me the wisdom to choose.*

At the very back of the cave, lit by flashlights, the doctor was leaning over the remaining wounded fighter. The Scorpion went to him. "Thalib, how is our wounded little scorpion?"

"Lord," the doctor replied with a deferential bow of his head, "he sleeps now, but he is much better. When he wakes, I will be getting him up."

366

"I am pleased to hear that Allah was not anxious for his arrival. His time will come. In the meantime, we will need every soldier for the battle to come."

"Yes, Amir," Thalib replied.

"Have you seen President Petrovich recently?"

"No, Lord. I was about to visit him," the doctor said. He grabbed his stethoscope from atop a footlocker of diminishing medical supplies.

"I will join you," said Al-Aleaqarab. The two men walked through the cave, which was now alive with activity. "Perhaps you have not been told. I have just now warned the men that we are leaving after Asr," the Scorpion explained.

"I am ready to go when you command it, Lord."

The Scorpion did not acknowledge him, already lost in his own thoughts and less than interested in small talk. The sun's power was undeniable once they left the cool of the cave and the light caused both men to squint. A right turn, a climb up a steep incline of scree that caused them both to sink to all fours to prevent a backwards slide to the bottom, and then another right turn brought them to a small copse of stunted trees. The shapes of three men suspended off the ground were immediately visible, as was the gentle moaning of the two men most recently nailed up.

"How much longer will he live?" the Scorpion asked the doctor with a gesture at Petrovich.

Thalib went forward, removed the stethoscope from around his neck, fixed the buds to his ears, and listened to the pulse behind the ankle. "He may live another day, but not unless he has water. He has lost a lot of blood. Also, Lord, some diluted vinegar would be a tonic."

"If we take him down?"

"He may live, but equally he may die. There is no way to be sure. Perhaps he has reached the point of no return."

The Scorpion considered this. "See that he drinks your tonic. And what of these two?"

Thalib did not listen to their hearts. "These two put you at risk with their stupidity. They are young and strong, Lord. They will live many days."

"They have been punished for nine hours or more, yes?"

"Yes, Lord."

"Then they can be killed – a knife through the heart. I would make it quick so as not to make them suffer unduly."

"You are most merciful, Lord. Strike them not between the fourth and fifth rib, but up through the belly." Thalib demonstrated on his own gut. "Enter here, under the rib cage, then thrust up through to the vena cava."

One of the men, the tall one, Jalil, opened his eyes and, between breaths, said, "Thank you, Lord."

"Do not thank me, dog," the Scorpion growled. "You will not be going to Paradise." He turned to the doctor. "I will kill them before afternoon prayers."

* * *

Captain Sam Nanaster. That was the name jotted on the slip of paper, but according to the databases that Schelly had access to there was not, and never had been, an officer commissioned in any of the four services by that name. Apparently, though, Captain Nanaster was now working for the CIA, leading a team running around Syria whacking US citizens. Or, more to the point, whacking US-born jihadists.

The slip Epstein had passed her also included a series of digits: the exit code for the United States, the country code for Syria – 963 – and an eight-digit number series. Schelly dialed the numbers and heard the familiar tones of a satellite phone out of range, plus the standard recorded voice informing her of such. She dialed again. Same result.

Great. Now what?

A satellite phone didn't necessarily mean instant communications with someone anywhere in the world, despite the sales and marketing

BS. Russia had a virtual armada of satellites parked above Syria, but the US did not, and none of the civilian call providers had geosynchronous communications satellites covering Syria and northern Iraq. To get a connection, the phone on the ground had to have a line of sight connection to at least one satellite. It was for this reason that Quickstep 3 was uncontactable except for two ten-minute windows.

The CIA Phoenix team, however, would undoubtedly have 24-hour radio communications with some off-the-grid CIA signals base in the region, but not even Epstein had access to that.

Schelly stared at the map and wondered what the hell was going on. She dialed another number because, what the hell, there was nothing else she could do.

"Lieutenant Colonel Simmons speaking."

"Colonel, Major Schelly here."

"Oh Jill. Just about to call you. You beat me to it."

"What's up, sir?"

"Your boys are about to get squeezed by Russian forces. There's a company-strength unit headed their way."

The bottom dropped away from Schelly's guts. "Where is Quickstep 3 now, sir?"

"Coming up on the designated area."

"The Predator is still with them?"

"Indeed it is."

"Sir, can I get a live feed patched through to the president's Situation Room?"

"You get the authorization, Major, I'll get you the patch."

* * *

"We're here, boss," Bo said, his concentration fixed on the Raven's control box. The unbroken plain of the Hamad for once had a little more going on than usual. The ground ahead was rough, broken and gouged by numerous deep wadis. For another, there were people here. And goats, lots of goats.

"Okay," I replied. "Pull over."

The pickup and the ambulance stopped on a slight rise, the last of the hot, dry flat desert and the start of the hot, dry lumpy desert. I jumped down from the pickup's bed, along with Jimmy, Alvin, Igor and Mazool. Taymullah and Bo climbed out of the cabin. Natasha, who had been driving the ambulance, closed its door and walked over with Farib.

"Okay," I began, "we have fifteen square miles of terrain to search. Bo has set up a grid pattern in quarter mile increments. The Raven will circle above and provide lookdown overwatch for a mile-and-half radius all around. We don't want any surprises."

This received unanimous nods.

"The area has a number of villages and the drone tells us there's a fair bit of animal husbandry going on – goats and goatherds. Where possible, we stop and ask if anyone has seen our unit. The story is that we've become separated, insha Allah, Allahu akbar, que sera, sera, and so forth. Our long-lost unit is Al-Aleaqarab's, so we'll be flying ISIS jolly rogers. Taymullah, we've got a few of those lying around, right?"

"*Nem fielaan,*" he said.

"What?"

"*Nem fielaan.* I am sorry - yes."

"Right. Mazool, what's your acting like? I need you to be our leader, driving out front."

"The leader would not drive."

"Farib, Taymullah, which of you two speaks enough English to translate for us ignorant Americans in the second vehicle?" The two Syrians glanced at each other. Taymullah raised a hand. "In that case, Farib, you drive for Mazool. Taymullah, you're with me in the ambulance. The rest of you, cover up with kitchen towels and make like ISIS fighters – be aggressive arrogant assholes and take as many slaves as you want."

Jimmy smirked.

"Mazool, a reasonable plan?"

He shrugged. "What of the Russian?" He was looking at Natasha.

"What about her?"

"She cannot fight jihad with men."

"We're an equal opportunities unit," I told him.

"No. Women cannot fight with men."

Taymullah walked over with some black cloth draped over an arm, and handed it to Mazool.

Mazool insisted, "She must wear this." He held it up. A niqab. "She can be your wife."

"You're scaring me," I said.

"She can be a slave."

"I was joking about that."

"I am not," he replied.

Natasha came over, sensing she was being discussed.

"We're all going to a fancy dress party," I told her, pointing out elements of my own Ali Baba costume. "The theme is 6th century chic. What do you think?"

"You want me to wear this?" She screwed up her nose at the robe Mazool held up, and then took the fabric and smelt it. The look on her face said this was probably a job for Tide Odor Rescue. "*Nyet.*"

"You'll put it on if we need you to put it on," I said. "That's a commandment." I could have said, "That's an order," but I was warming to the whole slave thing. Then, feeling guilty about how much I'd enjoyed that, I told her, "It's not just for your safety, Natasha. It's for ours too."

"Like all men, you are pig," she replied.

"*A* pig," I told her, this being a good time and place.

"Major, none of us speak Arabic," Alvin pointed out. "What if we are stopped? We can't just say Allahu akbar every time we're asked a question."

I didn't see why not. That seemed to be the only words Islamic terrorists knew. Care for a cup of coffee with cream and sugar? Allahu akbar.

"You are American jihadists," Mazool said, "new to the fight. Say, 'Assalamu alaikum' when you meet someone. It means, peace be upon you. If they say this to you, reply with 'Wa alaikum assalam', which means upon you be peace."

"Get in first and you won't have to remember the reply," I suggested.

Alvin and Jimmy repeated the words to fix them in their heads.

I said, "Do we say that before or after we start shooting?"

"What if we find Scorpion?" Natasha asked.

"I'm glad you asked," I told her, "because that's simple. One," I held up a finger. "First we enquire nicely about returning President Petrovich, and then two ..." I held up a second finger, "We kill him or arrest him, whichever is easiest at the time. To save confusion in the short term and everyone a pain in the ass in the long term, the former is the preferred option. Next?"

"And after that?" Mazool wondered.

"You go back to Latakia with the thanks of not one but two grateful nations – America and Russia – and we skedaddle for Turkey as fast as our turbocharged Toyota can take us. You can keep the ambulance."

Bo informed me, "Boss, we'll need structured breaks. Got four batteries for the Raven. Each takes forty-five minutes to charge off the vehicle for twenty minutes of flying time. So we can have the Raven in the air more or less continuously, long as we time it right."

"Well, just let us know what you need and when you need it."

"Yessir," he replied. "Where do you want to start the search?"

"We're at the south end of the designated search area. We don't know where the Scorpion is gonna be, but he's eyeing off Dabiq where this motherfucker of all battles is supposed to happen, so we can reasonably assume he'll be traveling east, heading for that. Who knows, maybe the Scorpion has already left. So, I say we skirt the circumference of the search area, come at it from the east, put ourselves between Dabiq and the search area, and work our way further east." No one had any objections to this line of thinking.

"Everyone needs to stay locked and loaded. But no one ..." I shifted my gaze to Natasha, "and I mean no one, goes kinetic unless I give the signal."

"What is signal?" she enquired.

"You'll know it when I give it."

A short while later, once Bo had landed the Raven, swapped out the battery for a fresh one and relaunched it, and with black flags flying, we started the search going from village to goatherd, looking for the Scorpion. The ambulance bounced over terrain more suitable to a four-wheel drive. Of course, almost none of the people we asked had seen shit, the earth apparently swallowing the Scorpion whole, though one goatherd said he had heard he'd gone this way, pointing east, and another thought he'd gone that way, pointing west ... Meanwhile, one wadi looked like every other wadi. This was a good place to get lost in and, if it wasn't for Bo's drone, we might have done exactly that.

So I settled in and had a talk to Natasha, who was feigning sleep in the back of the ambulance. She was lying on her side, one breast almost falling out of her flight suit, the zipper too low for anyone's good. "Hey, Natasha, you awake?" I asked her. "Natasha ..." A couple of heaving breaths, which almost popped that breast completely free, and her eyes fluttered open. "Um ..." I said and pointed in the general direction of her chest. While she reorganized things, I said, "Igor and I had an interesting chat." Interesting how the word interesting has become a major weapon in the armory of the passive aggressive.

"That is nice for you," she said, waving at a persistent sand fly orbiting her face.

"You and Petrovich, and the bodyguard detonating a grenade were the general topics of discussion."

"And?" she said, opening her hands out with a shrug of her shoulders, hitting me with a little passive aggression of her own.

A worthy interrogation technique back when I was in the OSI: the suspect sits in a chair in one corner of the room while the interviewer begins question time sitting more or less in the opposite corner, but on a chair on casters. As the interrogation progresses, the interviewer gradually inches forward, toward the interviewee, building pressure, not just with the questions but with proximity to the suspect so that, ultimately, the special agent is suddenly in the suspect's face when the big question is asked. The pressure of this two-pronged attack cracks open the nut, an admission of guilt spilling forth. In the back of the ambulance, however, the only object on wheels was the gurney and that wasn't going anywhere. So I improvised and changed positions, sitting on one end of the bench with Natasha down the other end.

"Tell me," I continued. "How come the grenade blew a hole in the side of the Hind, but you and Igor escaped without so much as a scratch?"

"Yes, I think about this also," she said, the volume of her voice raised above the ambulance's labors as it ground over the rough terrain in low gear. "He hold grenade like this, in front of him." She demonstrated, her hand in front, close to where her belly button would be. "He wear ... how do you say – armor."

"Body armor."

"*Da*. Body armor. Igor, General Yegorov and I, we sit beside president. When Geronosovich stand, we are behind him, like so."

I guessed that made some sense. Russian body armor was a quality item. If the grenade detonated with the armor between the explosion and the spreading anti-personnel fragments, that could explain why some people survived the blast while others didn't. If Geronimo's intention was to kill everyone, he made a mistake there. Perhaps he thought the grenade would kill the Hind first and the ensuing crash would tidy up the loose ends.

I brushed a couple of sand flies out of my face and came in a little closer. "You told me Arkady Geronosovich was a terrorist."

"*Da*, terrorist. He blow up *vertolet* ... gelikopter."

"Terrorist?" I said, sliding in closer still. "No, I don't think so. And I don't think you and Petrovich were lovers."

"Igor tell you this?" she asked, a furrow down the middle of her perfect forehead.

I had moved in for the kill, sitting beside her, angled toward her, the big question that needed to be asked locked and loaded. I even had a theory, which I was prepared to test. "Why would you say you were having an affair with Petrovich if you were not? And why would you claim the president's bodyguard was a terrorist if he were not?"

Natasha was breathing hard. I knew this because I was practically sitting on top of her. I was about to spring the big one on her. At the same time I was also considering that that zipper of hers must be made of titanium to withstand the intense pressure behind it. At this precise moment she leaned forward and kissed my mouth hard, her tongue lashing out and wrestling mine to the mat. I pulled back, breaking the suction, which is when she grabbed my hand and placed it on her breast.

Wow. I should have used this interrogation technique on her sooner, when we weren't bouncing over wadis. "That's enough," I said. "After you've told me everything – the truth – then and only then can you have your way with me." No, actually, that's what I thought. In truth, what I said was a stumbling, "Um ... What ... What are you doing?" My hand was still on her breast when I said it because, well, it was a hell of a breast. She smiled at this reaction of mine, as if she'd won a kind of victory. Perhaps she had. I got my hormones back under control at that point, removed my sweating paw and told her, "Geronosovich didn't yell Allahu akbar before detonating the grenade, did he?" There it was, the big question. It wiped away her smile, which had become more of a smirk. I was about to press the point and suggest an alternative parting statement when she was saved by Bo, whose voice in my ear said, "Coming up on a village, boss. Over the next rise. Something's going on there."

Dammit! Serzhánt Novikova and her zipper would have to wait. The niqab was on the floor. I picked it up and handed it to her.

"Put this on," I told her. "No argument. If anyone asks, you're Mrs Cooper – lucky you." To Taymullah, I said, "Stop here." I switched on the comms and told Bo, "I'll come to you. Let's take your toy in for some close-ups."

A short while later Taymullah and I walked over to the Toyota, the Syrian teenager's back covered in flies – fat, well fed ones. "What have we got?" I asked Bo as I arrived. He offered me some space under a towel, out of the sun, so that I could get a little contrast on the drone's control screen. "What's going on, do you think?" I asked him.

"Dunno, Major," which, translated meant, "You're the officer. You tell me."

Men and women were running down the narrow street, following a donkey pulling a cart. "What's in the cart?" I asked. "Take a look."

Bo bought the Raven and its camera in closer. There was nothing to see. At least, nothing we could see. Whatever it was, it was covered in a dirty blanket and clearly distressing the village.

"We need to do down there and find out what's up," I said.

We parked the vehicles, flying black flags, on the edge of the village. I left Jimmy and Bo behind along with Farib, Igor and Natasha, while Alvin, Mazool, Taymullah and I strolled the main street, a dust-blown track that stank of goat with top notes of human shit. Many of the women were wailing. The fact that there were women on the street, mixing with men, was unusual. The wind was up and the flies were fierce little fuckers, biting any and all exposed skin. We saw a tight group of men consoling several sobbing women whose age was indeterminate, because, like all women, they were shrouded in full black niqabs.

I instructed Mazool, "Find out what's going on."

Two teary-eyed young boys caught my attention, standing beside a couple of morose adults whose AKs drooped at the ground. The taller boy, who I guessed was probably around ten years of age, had a nasty open wound on his cheek playing host to a herd of sand flies. They were gathered at the edge of the ruptured flesh, drinking like horses bent over at a trough. The boy's smaller companion had a much larger, even more grotesque sore on his leg, and more flies. That had to be the wasting disease Major Schelly had briefed me on – leish-something-or-other – carried by sand flies. This village fit the major's profile like a glove. Was the Scorpion close? If so, how close?

Mazool returned, coughing the dust and the flies out of his lungs. "The deceased is a boy, brother to those two," he said after spitting noisily on the ground and then indicating the kids I'd already noted being eaten alive. "He was shot in the back of the head and buried under rocks. He had been missing for several days. Many of his goats came home without him. The village searched for him. His father and brother found the grave."

"Who do they think killed him?" I asked.

Mazool shook his head. "No one knows. Death is no stranger in this small village, but children here die from disease or accident, not bullets. This is not Latakia."

A kid shot in the head, and in the area supposedly hosting the Scorpion. Coincidence? It might be, except that I believed in coincidences like I believed in pixie dust. "Can you convince them to take us back to where the body was found?"

"I will try."

"Tell them ISIS will avenge his death."

"I have told them they are very lucky. He is now in Paradise."

"And they bought it?"

"It is true."

"Right." If it was true then the kid had to share it with all those assholes who were there because they blew up innocent people, which would take a lot of the shine off it in my book. Mazool went off to ask around for a guide while I loitered with Taymullah and took in the local color, which was basically a monotone of black niqabs and men dressed in dirty beige pants and smocks, with a few dusty goats and a brown donkey. It was a mean, hard existence. It wasn't impossible to see how the promise of an eternity spent sitting around a fountain with virgins eager to become trollops would be seductive.

Mazool returned with the kid whose cheek was dissolving, and his father Hakim, a painfully thin man with skin the color of an old tobacco pipe bowl and teeth worn down to yellow stubs. Hakim seemed able to talk without moving his lips. I called up Bo over the comms and the vehicles met us at the end of town. The older kid, whose name was Labib, Hakim, Mazool and I climbed up on the bed of the Toyota. Labib directed Farib through a maze of ancient wadis that had eroded the bedrock until, eventually, we pulled up at a pile of rubble beside a small depression in the flinty earth. I noted several hunks of rubble were partially stained black with sunbaked blood. This was the place.

Hakim and Labib were clearly upset to be at the hurried gravesite, hugging each other, both weeping tears that ran down their shirtfronts. It was hard not to be affected by their grief. All these people had was each other, their goats, and their belief in Allah. Not a lot, really.

I left them to it for a while and took in the area, which was utterly deserted, a little flat ground at the base of a heavily eroded rock shelf.

With Mazool interpreting, I eventually asked Labib if he knew the area well.

"Yes," Mazool said. "The three brothers would come here all the time."

The surroundings were dry, like everywhere else, but some vegetation was managing to grow where the deeper fingers of rock met the desert floor. Vegetation meant moisture. I asked if the boys brought goats here, and the answer was yes. Goats need more than food, as do jihadists. "Ask him if there is water nearby."

I didn't need Mazool's translation. Labib nodding his head was enough.

"Where?" I asked.

After Mazool asked the question, the kid said a couple of words and pointed up the hill.

"What did he say?"

Mazool looked at me, excitement in his face. "He said, 'in the caves'."

Fifty

Ronald V. Small @realSmall
America does not torture people. But if you're a terrorist and we catch you, life will be very very painful for you.

Li'l Wilson lowered the binoculars. "Four of them, Sam."

"What are they?" Nanaster asked.

"Mil twenty-fours."

Hinds. "Gotta be carrying at least a platoon of Spetsnaz," said Nanaster. "Question is, what are they doing out here – same time, same place as us?"

"Could be something to do with their missing president."

"Could be."

"They'll know we're here for sure," Ronan added.

The helicopters were tracking low over the desert a couple of miles away, across the plain. There would also be some high altitude lookdown overwatch – a drone, a satellite, or a high-flying MiG. The Hinds would know they weren't alone in this part of the desert – that was a certainty.

"We're headed in the same direction," Ronan continued. "We'll cross paths for sure."

No one wanted to be anywhere near the Russians when they were carrying out a mission. They played a little too fast and loose with dumb ordnance for anyone's liking. And with ISIS holding their president, they'd be extra juiced.

"Better to be loud and proud, boss," Wilson said unnecessarily. "Don't want there to be mistakes."

Nanaster nodded and held her hand out for the glasses. Wilson passed them across. The Russians had no beef with the US Phoenix program, or any similar programs conducted by other nations, if only because a few less terrorists in the world suited everyone. However, it would be safer to go in after the Russians were done and gone. *They might even do our job for us. Might. Be helpful to know exactly why they're here.*

"What do you wanna do, boss?" Ronan asked. "You wanna wait?"

Nanaster considered the options. Wait - ordinarily, that's exactly what they'd do, but not this time. "Our breathers are Priority Alpha. We have to make sure. Let's get the drone up, see where those Hinds set down – they might continue north for all we know. Meanwhile, we got a job to do."

* * *

The look-down feeds from the Predator illuminated several large screens with moving real-time footage, provided in both the visual light and thermal ranges, from altitudes ranging from 51,000 feet to fifty feet. The resolution at fifty feet was astonishing and still amazed Schelly given that the bird itself was loitering at close to its ceiling at 50,000 feet above the desert floor. You could read the nametag on a uniform. The feeds were overlaid on terrain features provided by ground-mapping databases so that assets could be tracked against ground features in all weather and light conditions. Other screens transmitted data from the Predator's various sensors, both flight and environmental, to deliver a total and accurate picture of every second of ground activity. It was getting on towards dusk and, when the sun went down, the imaging would switch to low light, delivering pictures in outline rather than in solid color, lending a ghostly feel to men and machines alike. There, was however, no sound. And when the tracer started to fly and men began to die, Schelly knew from past experience that the utter silence would simply add to the terror. She wrung her hands unconsciously. *In space, no one can hear you scream.*

"It would be helpful to know who's who," said Epstein, squinting up at a screen.

Schelly agreed, but there was nothing she could do about it. She could, however, set the scene. "Madam Secretary, I can't point out individuals because the unit's fluorescing strips are obscured. But making up the numbers are the two Russians, plus the three fighters from the Syrian Democratic Forces. It seems the group has also now picked up some local villagers and they're taking them somewhere. Why, I don't know."

A door opened somewhere and in walked Andrew Bunion, on his cell. He motioned that everyone should just continue what they were doing, as he muttered into the phone.

"So that's what we're looking at here?" Epstein asked, momentarily distracted along with Schelly. They returned their concentration to a screen displaying the view from one hundred and fifty feet overhead.

"Yes, Madam Secretary."

"No sign of the CIA's meddling?"

Schelly ran her eyes across the screens showing various resolutions. There were heat signatures all over the place – human and animal … For all she knew some of those signatures could be a Phoenix unit. It would be impossible to know until the shooting started.

"Did I hear the Company's name mentioned?" Chalmers asked as he strolled into the Situation Room. "Oh, Madam Secretary. My apology. I didn't see you there. Mr Bunion …"

The president's special advisor nodded acknowledgement, put his hand over the phone and said, "The president."

Schelly glared at Chalmers. *How did you know about this? What is it about you that reminds me of hair oil?*

"Ah, Associate Deputy Director Chalmers," said Epstein. "Good of you to join us. I really don't want to see a SAD team in the area. Things are complicated enough."

SAD, as in CIA Special Activities Division. That's appropriate, Schelly thought.

"Ma'am, with respect, and as I have stated to Major Schelly on numerous occasions, those operations are well outside my purview. I have nothing to do with that program."

"Thank you, Mr Chalmers, but we all know how these things work."

"Madam Secretary, I'm ... I'm at a loss," he said.

"Take a seat, why don't you?"

"Thank you. I will." He walked over to Schelly. "This one taken?" he asked, a hand on the seat beside her. Schelly ignored the question. He was going to sit there anyway. "We can watch history in the making, eh?" he said, almost but not quite nudging her.

Touch me, jerk, and I'll break your arm. Six bright green triangles entered the search area from the southwest, diverting her attention, each triangle dragging a small box of information with it. "The Russians, Madam Secretary. Six Hind helicopters."

"If the Kremlin truly believed their president was somewhere here," Epstein observed, "they'd be directing thousands of assets to the area."

"Yes, ma'am," Schelly replied. *But they arrived at the same conclusion I did, at least with enough conviction to divert at least these assets north. Let's see where they set down – if they set down* ... Schelly shifted her eyes to a monitor that showed the view closer to the ground as the helicopters altered their heading to a more westerly course. The Hinds flew on steadily for several minutes. "They've landed outside the town of Ghasaniyeh, a little over seven miles to the northeast of Quickstep," she said, her stream of consciousness finding voice.

Bunion set the phone down in front of him, folded his arms and scowled up at the screens.

"Plenty of separation," Chalmers observed, full of confidence.

What are you so self-satisfied about? The CIA deputy was amused about something. Schelly just knew, even from the minimal dealings she'd had with this guy, that his good humor spelt trouble for Cooper, if not his mission. His personal issues with Cooper required failure for Quickstep at the very least, and to hell with the rest of the world. Schelly scribbled two words on the pad in front of her and angled it towards Chalmers.

"Marco Polo?" he said.

Yeah, stick that shit where the sun don't shine, asshole. You know I know Phoenix is your baby. They had better not show up.

Footsteps on the hard flooring alerted Schelly to a new arrival – Ed Bassingthwaite, on edge as usual.

"What is it, Ed?" Epstein asked him.

"A word," he replied and took the SECDEF to a far corner in the darker recesses of the room. His hands were thrust deep in his pockets, and his shoulders hunched.

Bunion watched them, his scowl unchanging.

Hearing the agitated murmur between them, Schelly wondered what the problem might be, but only for a moment. Quickstep was on the move again. A number of unidentified heat signatures appeared on the screen, moving in fast from the west. Vehicles – pickups. "Who's that?" she heard herself ask. Her eyes flicked to the screen with the view from 50 feet. The vehicles were flying black flags – ISIS.

Bassingthwaite finished his impromptu meeting with Epstein. "Have we found the Russian president?" he asked Schelly, dragging her attention from the monitors.

"No, sir."

"Well, we'd better." With those three words the SECSTATE left, in a hurry to be somewhere else.

Schelly glanced at Epstein, whose look of general concern seemed to have risen to a new level.

"It's the Russians," said Bunion, silent till that moment.

"You know about this?" Epstein asked him, massaging her temples. Bunion nodded.

The SECDEF turned to Schelly. "Hackers on the dark web are using the Cheget codes as a template to crack the Russian nuclear defense network algorithms."

"We predicted this would happen," said Bunion. "We're doing it, too. It's a hell of an opportunity."

Epstein continued. "Yes, but now the Kremlin is threatening to take their nukes offline completely, effectively shutting them down."

The expression on Schelly's face must have suggested she was thinking that might be a good thing, because Epstein added, "The Duma is concerned that we might take this opportunity to launch a first strike, while they're defenseless. Maybe if the shoe was on the other foot, that's what they would do to us. Maybe they've gamed this out, who knows? The point is, Russia has not been exposed like this since the Cold War began back in 1947. The Joint Chiefs believe the level of paranoia is such that there's a very real threat the Kremlin may launch a pre-emptive strike against us, before they shut down their nukes. Rodchenko, the Russian ambassador, says his people are convinced this is some kind of grand plan we've cooked up, starting with the take down of President Petrovich, to wipe them out once and for all. Did I mention paranoia?"

Schelly was flummoxed. "Whaaat?"

"Yes, so I hope your people on the ground are good, because things could turn black and crispy around here if they're not."

Bunion's phone rang. He picked it up. "Yes, Mr President ..."

Schelly caught a glimpse of Chalmers's face out the corner of an eye. His smirk had been replaced with a look of uncertainty, but there was no pleasure in it for her. Things were getting worse moment by moment. This was further confirmed with a review of screens showing the changing situation on the ground in northern Syria. Yet more idents were entering the picture, these were closing with Quickstep 3 from the north. The Hinds had landed and were now taking off, heading east – backtracking. The number of moving figures on the ground suggested the helicopters had set down close to fifty combatants. A cold dread spread into the pit of her stomach. *Spetsnaz.*

Fifty-one

Ronald V. Small @realSmall
If you leave America to fight with the Scorpion, we will send the
rest of your family to Syria whether they want to go or not.
WATCH OUT!

The day was coming to an end, which was a relief because it
was one of those days, the sort you wished you'd stayed in
bed and missed. I don't know what we were thinking. Actually,
that's not true. We were thinking caves in the area meant this
was the perfect place for the Scorpion to hole up. We were
also assuming that the murder of the boy shot in the head
for reasons unknown was somehow connected – that he had
wandered into the path of the world's most wanted man and
paid with his life. The boy's mysterious death, the flies, the flesh-
eating disease, the search area, the caves ... Pixie dust, right?
The Scorpion was near – had to be.

I heard Bo say, "We got company coming from the west. Vehicles."

"What?" I replied, the news unexpected. "How far? When?"

"Sorry, Major. They're close – minutes away." Bo explained,
"Had the Raven at a low altitude. I missed 'em."

"What sort of vehicles?"

"Pickups. Tangos."

I turned to Mazool. "Tell Labib and Hakim to go. Right now."

Mazool acted quickly and the two Syrians made a run for it.

I squinted into the fading light. We had flags, but not as many as the approaching vehicles. It was as if a large murder of crows was flapping toward us across the desert.

I reorganized the towel wrapped around my head to better hide my face and the fact that I was wearing battle comms. "*Assalamu alaikum*," I said into the mike by way of reminder, and Alvin replied, "*Wa alaikum assalam*," which surprised me. "Thanks, Alvin," I said, and then added, "Look happy, everyone." A shadow stood beside me; Natasha, all in black, only her eyes visible. She didn't look happy. Maybe black wasn't her color.

Mazool grabbed a fistful of the niqab and pulled her several paces behind me. "A wife stands behind her husband," he whispered hoarsely.

None of your fancy pants equality nonsense in the 6th century, right?

Five pickups rolled in, all Toyotas of varying age. They were loaded to the gills with fighters armed with AKs, rocket launchers, pistols, swords and the most eye-wateringly pungent body odor imaginable. The pickups swept around us and squealed to a stop, enveloping us in a cloud of grit.

Mazool took the lead, raising his AK to the sky and shouting "Allahu akbar" with much excitement. This proved my earlier point about two words for all occasions, but I held off pointing out I told you so. You often have to put a sock in it around here. Anyway, I followed his example, which my guys, Taymullah, Farib and Igor also emulated. Shouts of "*Assalamu alaikum*" and "*Wa alaikum assalam*" were given and received. Happy, happy, happy ... The jihadis jumped down and we all hugged, united by religious insanity, unwashed funk and so forth. And then we all stood around looking at each other with varying degrees of suspicion while Mazool and Taymullah spoke to the leaders.

Two fighters walked past Natasha and me to check out the ambulance. They walked around it, kicked the tires like half-hearted buyers, and returned to their vehicles, eyeing off Natasha like she was some Victoria's Secret model. She was, but how the hell did they know that given she was completely hidden within a badly fitting black bag?

One of these fighters looked at me with a grin and said something. I nodded and grinned right back. I think he spoke Dutch, which is double Dutch to me. He was dark, but didn't look particularly Middle Eastern, and that reassured me. These were foreign fighters. That would make the fact that there were Americans present far less significant.

Mazool came over to report. "We are in luck. Those two jihadi," he said, trying to hide his excitement, motioning casually at two filthy fighters. "They are the Scorpion's men. The man on the left. His name is Ortsa, a Chechen. I spit on the ground with disgust.

"Hold off on that for the moment," I advised him and waved at a fighter staring at us.

Mazool continued, "He says they went to Dabiq to bring back these men, more fighters to accompany the Mahdi to the great battlefield."

"You're starting to sound like one of them, Mazool," I told him.

"It is necessary. I told them we have become separated from our fighters, and have gathered up other jihadi who have lost their units in the fighting. We are to join them, and bring the Mahdi to his army, which has gathered on the border north of Dabiq."

"What's a Mahdi for you?" I said.

"I am sorry? What's the Mahdi?"

"No, no ... Wassamaddaforyou, get it?"

He looked at me.

"Forget it," I told him, waving it away. "If you were from New York, you'd be slapping me on the back."

He still looked at me.

"Okay," I said. "Where were we?"

"The Mahdi is the one chosen by God to defeat the Crusader armies and bring about the End of Days. It is written in the Qur'an. They say the Scorpion is the Mahdi."

I knew all that, but whatever. Moving on, I asked him. "You believe that rubbish?"

"No, but there are many, many thousands of fighters crossing into Syria from Turkey who do believe. The Scorpion must be killed. If we do not, the world will change."

"I liked you from the start, Mazool."

The Syrian went off to poach a cigarette and a light and maybe a little soldierly scuttlebutt from a couple of fighters. Bo told me over the comms, "Boss, had to let the drone go. Couldn't risk recovering it with these pricks around."

"Forget about it," I murmured. "Uncle Sam will take it out of your pay when we get home. Mount up, everyone. We're following these cocksuckers to the promised land." I caught Alvin's eye. He motioned a subtle acknowledgement and made his way to the Toyota with Jimmy and Igor. Minutes later we were all on the move, following the dust cloud ahead, which slowed and began to climb. I'll admit to excitement. Or maybe fear. Sometimes they feel like the same thing. Whatever it was, my heart was thundering along and I was sweating, but also cold. No one spoke. I couldn't think of a single joke to lighten the moment, though I was thinking that Natasha could be mistaken for Mrs Vader, Darth's boss.

Less than five minutes later, we stopped beyond the fingers of an ancient deep and steep wadi that had carved its way through solid rock. All around us, standing on overhanging ledges and rounded boulders, were more fighters cheering and raising AKs above their heads. A couple of idiots fired rounds skywards, as they do.

It was then that I saw him. The Scorpion. You couldn't miss the ratty, patchy beard or the hands that wouldn't look out of place presented on a bed of ice in a seafood buffet. There was the opportunity of a clean shot as he walked among the fighters newly arrived at his hidey-hole. He was clearly revered. If he'd had a ring on his finger he'd have presented it to be kissed. Maybe if he had fingers, he'd have a ring. A couple of fighters did the next best thing and kneeled in the dirt and kissed the hem of his robe. Perhaps I should have killed him right there, but I didn't. Actually, we should have punched his ticket way back at the warehouse. It could have been done. We'd identified him and he was a legitimate target. It's something I've thought a lot about since.

Checking bona fides was not on the Scorpion's agenda. His fighters weren't concerned with background checks either. There was a rush to get moving, a war to start. No one knew we were Americans, and if they knew they probably would have cared less. The fighters had come from all over – Indonesia, New Zealand, Russia (Chechnya), Georgia, Canada, England, Scotland, the Netherlands, Germany and Italy. And, of course, there were a whole lot of Sunni Arabs from various countries. All of them had left their lives behind to take up jihad. What were a few Americans in amongst all that? It was the perfect Petri dish for a cancer of US servicemen to hide in, ready to turn malignant when the opportunity presented. The only question: would the opportunity present itself or would we have to create it?

Fighters poured from a dark hole in the rock. Think cockroaches swarming from a drainpipe. More group hugs and I-told-you-so-Allahu akbars.

Mazool, who did the circulating on our behalf, returned to say that we would all be leaving soon, just as Al-Aleaqarab turned and pointed at a couple of nearby fighters, as if to say, "You and you ..." And then his claw moved on to Mazool, Alvin, Jimmy and me. "You, you, you and you ...Come."

"He wants us to follow him," Mazool informed us.

"What about Natasha?" I said, thinking aloud.

He could see the problem. She was the only woman here. Leaving her alone among a large group of lawless assholes who considered women property could be asking for trouble. And not necessarily just for Natasha, who had proven to be a stone-cold killer. But then again, I had no idea why Al-Aleaqarab picked us.

"Bring her," he suggested. And then to Natasha he added, "But you must walk behind."

The black bag hid Natasha's reaction, which was helpful, because underneath I was sure it was all one big raised middle finger.

I considered all this and decided it would probably be better if she stayed behind, out of sight. I moved to Bo and said, "Take Igor and provide Natasha some close protection. Keep a low profile."

He nodded.

And so a group of around ten of us followed the Scorpion up the hill. My trigger finger was itchy as hell. He was right there, eminently killable – a bullet to the brain stem. Again, I should have, but didn't. After a couple of minutes of climbing a scree slope that kept falling away beneath my feet, we found more solid ground and turned toward the rock faces. Coming around a deep cleft I was confronted with the biblical scene of three men crucified on a hill. All three were naked but for their underwear. It was like a scene from an Easter pageant, but without the bunny. When I got a little closer to the three crosses, which were ancient, gnarled desert trees stripped bare of foliage, I admit to being sickened by it. All three men had bled profusely from where the bolts were driven through wrists and feet, as well as from their noses and mouths. The skin and muscle around the wounds was festering and raw, weeping pus. They had also let go their bowels and bladders and were covered head to toe in filth and flies. Buzzards hopped around on nearby rock shelves, expectant. The area stank worse than a busload of jihadists, which was saying something. The agony all three men were suffering, or had suffered for every single moment of their torture, was evident. They hung limp from the bolts. Were they all dead? They looked dead. No, at least one of them was alive – the victim in the middle moved his head. His arms were tied to the boughs so that his bodyweight wouldn't rip flesh and bone through the bolts securing his wrists and feet. I couldn't see his face, because his chin rested forward on his chest.

"Jesus," I heard someone say softly in my earpiece. It was an exclamation of surprise and dismay, nothing ironic about it.

The Scorpion stopped, and considered the men up on their crosses for a moment. He then drew a knife and walked to the man on the right, a tall guy. He was young, mostly bone and sinew. Without any ceremony or delay, the Scorpion inserted the long blade he carried up through his abdomen, slowly, methodically, further and further, until the victim gave a final moan and slumped forward. Now he really was dead. Al-Aleaqarab walked to the second man, the one on the far left-hand side, and killed him the same way, slipping the knife in slow. No rush. No emotion. Just deliberate, orderly, unhurried, psychotic.

Withdrawing the knife blade, he wiped it clean in his hand, which had also gathered up some of his black clothing. One of the jihadists went to the men the Scorpion had just murdered, pulled a stethoscope from over his shoulder, put the buds in his ears and held the business end to each. He gave a nod to the boss, confirming death, I guessed. It was a strange spectacle. I wondered why we were there until fighters fastened ropes around the boughs holding the remaining victim, who I figured had to be President Petrovich, while another jihadist with a tree saw made quick work of the trunk supporting the Russian president's torment.

Minutes later, we were carrying the man, still nailed to his rudimentary cross, down the hill, where we loaded him into the back of a pickup. Wherever we were going, we were taking him with us.

Fifty-two

Ronald V. Small @realSmall
Attention Mr Scorpion, Jesus will not be walking with your dead. Everyone knows he's on OUR SIDE.

Major Schelly had ripped off a hangnail. And now that finger was hurting like a bitch, as well as bleeding. The feeds playing out on numerous screens showed that Quickstep had been absorbed by a larger group of ISIS fighters, which had taken place without a gun battle. Schelly was at a loss to understand how the unit had managed to pull that off. Quickstep, along with this much larger group of ISIS fighters, had then driven a short distance to ...

"Oh my god," said Epstein as men spewed from the side of the rock. "Is that a cave? Have they found ..." The thought trailed off as the feed she was viewing moved on, somewhat aimlessly.

Bunion was back on his cell, muttering, but with more urgency.

"The Predator's pilot doesn't know who to follow," Schelly surmised. There were a lot of fighters down there and no way to identify friend or foe. She picked up the phone to Creech and Colonel Simmons. Shortly after, individual idents were painted against every warm body. And in other news, she informed Epstein, those two Reapers were finally inbound. Meanwhile, the feeds continued to drift silently over the fighters at various altitudes, Schelly hoping to pick up something familiar so that she could have the Predator lock onto an individual.

"Which one is Cooper?" the SECDEF wondered.

"I don't know, Madam Secretary," she admitted. *Everyone's wearing a goddamn towel over their head, or a hat. No fluorescent strips. No comms. Fucking nightmare.*

"What's that?" said Chalmers, pointing up at a screen.

Schelly's eyes shifted to that view. It was a group of men carrying someone between them, arms out wide, feet together. "Oh, lord. That's, that's Petrovich," she said before she knew it was true, but only because it couldn't be anything else. Shifting to a view at a lower altitude showed that the man was still affixed to a rudimentary cross. They'd cut him down and were carrying him somewhere.

"Jesus fucking wept," murmured Epstein, her eyes flitting from one screen to another, trying to take it all in. "There!" she said, pointing. "Look. The hands. Isn't that the Scorpion?"

"We got a Predator up there," said Bunion. "Blast that son of a bitch. We may never get another opportunity."

What! US servicemen were down there. Her men. The president's chief advisor was telling her that they had done their job and were now surplus to requirements. "Sir, the Predator is unarmed," she said quietly. "And President Petrovich has a heat signature. He's still alive. Hit them with Hellfire missiles and we'll be murdering him. Also, sir, you do know we've got people down there?"

"They're soldiers. They knew the score when they signed up."

The tips of Schelly's ears burned, a white-hot anger rising through her.

"Mr Bunion," Epstein said, keeping her tone neutral. "They are Americans. We don't blow up our own people. We need to give them time."

The advisor picked up his phone and dialed. "Time to do, what?" he said, waiting for the call to connect. "They're heavily outnumbered. Four against – how many? Your team has located Petrovich and the Scorpion. They will be commended for that. But there's a bigger picture - averting World War III." He glared at Schelly. "This is the price of command, Major. If you can't take the heat, there's the door." He indicated over his shoulder. "Anyway, as you pointed out, re the Predator, ending this now is not an option."

The president's chief advisor's willingness to incinerate US servicemen troubled Schelly more than a little. Four Hellfire missiles would soon become available. What then?

"ISIS, they're loading up," said Chalmers. "Gonna be on the move at any time. Where are your people, Major? Cooper and the rest?"

They're down there somewhere. And they're our *goddamn people.* "I don't know," she said honestly.

"What are those idents coming in from the southeast?" asked Epstein. The monitor directly behind them held the SECDEF's attention.

What now? Schelly turned and saw another potential storm of bad news heading Quickstep's way. She tasted copper. The bleeding hangnail was back in her mouth and she'd made it far worse.

* * *

According to Mazool, the Scorpion's reinforcements, the ones we'd run into, had raced across sixty miles of desert in broad daylight without incident. Hard to believe, but there you go. For them to have survived the trip, I figured most if not all of Russia's assets had to still be congregated in the area generally to the east of Latakia, where the president's helicopter went down. The advent of NVGs, which turned night into a bright green-lit day, meant attempting the same run under the stars would advantage the Scorpion's enemies - the rest of the world.

I could see the Scorpion's quandary. Option one: head for Dabiq now and risk it. Option two: head for Dabiq after sunrise and risk it and lose ten hours.

A couple of the Scorpion's long-serving fighters threw a cover over Petrovich and then climbed up onto the utility bed beside him, their AKs locked and loaded along with their battle faces. The jihadist with the stethoscope climbed up too as the Scorpion's lieutenants began shouting at the rest of us to get our shit together. Apparently the Scorpion was going with option two.

I told my guys I would meet them back at the ambulance.

There were a lot of vehicles in this convoy. Thirteen all up. A nice juicy target for an A-10 or Hind gunship. The pickup with the familiar four-barrel ZPU made an appearance and motored slowly down the lineup, heading for the rear of the column. A fearsome weapon, that, but it would be first on the target list of any self-respecting Warthog pilot. I noticed the white Beemer was here too, the one we'd seen at the warehouse and, later, departing what was probably the area of the helicopter crash. That had to be the Scorpion's car. Fancy that, the same car my ex-wife and our marriage counselor who is now her husband drive. Figured, right? Just seeing it sitting there unattended, minding its own business, made me want to key it. "Oh, man," I said, the idea hard to shake. Remember what I said about the Air Force and getting your kicks?

I headed over to it, faking battle readiness. It was unlocked. Not surprising. I couldn't imagine the Scorpion parking, thumbing the alarm fob – *chirp-chirp* – and then running off to wage a little jihad, secure in the knowledge that his Bavarian sports limo wouldn't get itself boosted in the meantime. I took my ka-bar, glanced in the window and ... hey, was that a briefcase attached to a chain and handcuff on the front seat? "Shee-eet," I said, opening the door. Finders keepers, right?

A short while later, I made my way back to the ambulance, creeping along the wadi with a certain briefcase carrying the launch confirmation codes for the destruction of the entire Earth several times over tucked under my arm. Natasha was watching on, a big black bag, as two men loaded a wounded jihadist onto the gurney. Job done, the orderlies ran off.

"You saw president?" she asked behind me, her voice muffled by the *khimar* covering her head.

"Yeah," I told her, stuffing the briefcase in the bottom of the trash bag containing soiled, blood caked bandages.

"He is alive?"

I nodded. "Unfortunately for him."

"Where?"

"Up the line," I nodded in the direction. "Three vehicles ahead of a white BMW."

And that was pretty much the exact moment a rocket streaked down from out of nowhere and buried itself in an ear-splitting fireball that engulfed the lead vehicle in the convoy. Suddenly, everyone was running everywhere, taking cover where they could find it, including me. Another rocket hurtled down on the column from out of the night, missed the ZPU, and exploded under an old Landcruiser, flipping it onto its roof. Green tracer began to zip down from the heights like bars of laser light, accompanied by the sounds of multiple semi and full-auto cracks and rattles.

"Gotta be the Russians," I said into the comms, the green tracer a sure tell. Major Schelly's hunch had been right. They'd figured out the puzzle and here they were, same as us. Spetsnaz, most probably. But how many? And they'd have night vision for sure, which would put the ISIS fighters at a huge disadvantage. We had four sets of NVGs between us, but couldn't use them. Walking around with those on our heads would instantly blow our cover.

The Scorpion's men began to fan out, working in pairs and threes. Panic was non-existent. I had to hand it to them, they were well trained. They were also highly motivated as well as being hardened by years of combat. Finally, on the plus column, they cared less about dying, which made them fearless risk-takers. Nevertheless, in the minus column, they were outmaneuvered in both the areas that counted most: the opposition held the high ground and ISIS had no idea what they were facing. The amount of fire raining down made me think the folks we were tagging along with were in a lot of trouble. And the Russians would be calling in reinforcements.

For the Scorpion, the jig was almost definitely up.

"Who do we kill, boss?" Jimmy asked.

Good question. The Russians were trying to shoot us dead, which meant we were entitled to protect ourselves. Except that the Russians were supposedly our allies here and who knew where Americans knowingly killing Russians would lead ... At the very least to a court martial and a long stay at Leavenworth. We could start shooting the ISIS fighters, but they were the only force standing in the way of the Russians trying to kill us. The rules of engagement I'd read didn't cover this scenario.

"Just sit tight," I replied.

The ZPU burst into life, its .50 caliber barrels spewing death into the teeth of the tracer coming down the hill at us. Every tenth round was bright green tracer. The display was almost hypnotic. Green zips flew from those four barrels in gentle arcs that mostly ended in sudden ricochets that speared off at crazy angles, the lights sputtering like doused fireflies swallowed by the night. The tracer was slowly walked across the hillside, the ZPU operator firing in short bursts. Several distinctive RPG explosions boomed high within the upper rocks and ledges, lighting up the Russian positions with fire, beacons for the ZPU.

I watched a jihadist backlit by one of these fires pull the pin from a grenade and cock his arm for the throw, which is when the thing in his hand detonated and he disappeared for good inside a cloud of dust and shrapnel. Must have been a captured Russian F1 grenade. Hate the damn things.

The incoming fusillade seemed to fade a little, which exhorted the ISIS fighters to press harder, and so they advanced; moving, running, their charge championed by the ZPU, which suddenly fell silent. And I saw why as something took the head clean off the man with his finger on the trigger.

The ZPU's fearsome racket silenced, there seemed to be a sudden lull in the fighting. But that was an illusion as, up in the rockery, there was a lot of hand-to-hand going on, punctuated by the odd scream and staccato blasts from carbines and pistols.

I glanced over my shoulder to check six, and also to see what Natasha was doing ... Gone. Where had she gone to? "Has anyone seen –"

At that moment a Russian helicopter – of uncertain variety but let's call it a Hind – arrived with all guns blazing, cutting off my question as I dived for cover. The cover, beneath a utility, was completely ineffectual as the Hind's twenty-three millimeter rounds could turn vehicles into metal confetti, the utility two car lengths in front of the one I cowered beneath a case in point becoming shredded, burning scrap after a three-second burst. The helicopter made one pass and disappeared into the blackness, but it would be returning.

"Anyone seen Natasha?" I asked the comms.

"Negative," came several replies.

She was dressed all in black, which around here on a moonless night was perfect camouflage. I heard the *thump-thump* of rotor blades somewhere near, the tone of the sound changing as the aircraft turned hard, somewhere close. I figured the next pass would more than likely bring it down the line of vehicles, which meant it was time to move. I pushed myself out from under the utility and ran at a crouch until I fell into a low wadi. I wouldn't have to tell my guys to do likewise. They did this stuff for a living.

"Boss," I heard Alvin say. "That you?" He added, "On your right."

I saw movement, and then it congealed and became a man, running at a crouch toward me, a distant fireball illuminating the silhouette of a US soldier, sans head protection. Alvin had ditched the local threads. Maybe it was time we all did likewise. The irony of being mistaken for a jihadist and shot by the Russians wasn't lost on me.

Back to Natasha. A tank driver would have to know how vulnerable we were to an attack from the sky. I hoped she had found cover, wherever she was. Nothing I could do about it. Her survival, and Igor's too for that matter, was in their own hands. As for that helicopter firing its fool head off, the Russian Air Force's motto seemed to be "No care and no responsibility"." They had to know this was the Scorpion and his band they were shooting up, which also meant there was a good chance their own president was somewhere on the ground they were strafing with complete abandon.

"Major." It was Jimmy, appearing from out of the night on my left, bringing Farib and Taymullah with him. Breathing hard, he said, "Reckon we just let 'em slug it out. Then we can move in and pick up the pieces."

Me? I'd be happy to let those pieces pick themselves up.

"Bo," I said into the mike. "What's your status?"

Silence.

"Bo."

"Boss, his comms are sketchy," said Alvin. "Loose connection somewhere. Or maybe low batteries. He told me he was going to look for Natasha. Igor is missing too, right?"

I nodded.

The gunship returned, its second attack running down the line as I thought it would. That's when the ZPU started up again, hammering away at the perfect target: an object at low altitude approaching head-on. Four barrels spitting fire reached out for the helicopter with hundreds of hot lead and pyrotechnic rounds. They sparkled and danced as they were absorbed by the bird's approaching airframe. The Hind appeared to dip its head in the withering fire, its own guns falling silent. And then it nosed up, climbing, rotor blades pounding the night air accompanied by the symphony of an engine destroying itself. That familiar *thump-thump* didn't disappear off into the night as I hoped, but continued, changing pitch. Damaged or not, it was coming back to try its luck a third time.

The ZPU had to be the Hind's next target. Kill or be killed. I heard someone yelling above the gunfire in a language I didn't understand. Taking a peek over the top of the earth berm I was crouching behind, I saw the Scorpion aided by Ortsa, the Chechen, standing behind the ZPU's steel armor plate. Al-Aleaqarab was screaming at the top of his voice, spittle flying from his mouth, the weapon's barrels swinging around for another crack at the inbound enemy.

But it was not to be. The Scorpion didn't get off a shot. Three rockets streaked in from out of the blackness, the helicopter standing off, out of range. Two exploded short of the ZPU, but the third detonated beneath the Toyota's engine and the whole area suddenly boiled within a ball of orange flame that lingered on the ground for a couple of seconds before rising skyward.

The heat and the concussion of the blast rolled past me as the Hind flew by overhead, dipped, went into a corkscrew dive and flew into the side of a rock face. A thunderous explosion followed, with multiple secondary explosions – ordnance cooking off. As it fell to earth, the fireball bulged with each of these explosions like it was breathing, alive and growing. And then it crashed into a ravine with a cracking boom.

Meanwhile, the ZPU's usefulness as a weapon had come to an end. Small fires were left burning and I saw one of those fires crawling slowly away, trying to pull another man along with him. "Cover me," I said to Alvin and rolled up and over the berm.

Fifty-three

Sam Nanaster watched the fireworks through the eyepiece of a night scope, the occasional flare blinding her with green light.

"The Russians and ISIS slugging it out. Looks to be roughly platoon-sized units squared off," said Ronan lying in the prone position, the stock snug against his cheek and shoulder, his eye glued to an eyepiece.

Couldn't be related to President Petrovich, Nanaster considered. *If the Russians thought he was down there, they'd bring up a whole division.*

"Lotta lead being thrown around. Who's winning?" Li'l Wilson asked, his voice in Nanaster's comms. He was down range on higher ground, in her three o'clock position - part of Bravo team.

"Looks pretty even at the moment," Nanaster replied. "Wait, maybe not for much longer."

The distinctive sound of rotor blades reached them before the Hind appeared in their night scopes. The firefight was less than 700 yards away so the cracks and booms of small arms fire and anti-personnel explosions were barely dulled. The Hind came into view, flying a perpendicular course across the lineup of vehicles. Air support would quickly turn the tide in favor of the Russians.

"Got a bead on any of our breathers?" Nanaster asked, moving the crosshairs to another ISIS fighter.

"Nope," Li'l Wilson told her. "But got a good feelin' they's down there somewhere."

Nanaster settled the crosshairs of the scope on another fighter who had taken cover. No face recognition hits. *Next...*

* * *

"Is that your Phoenix team?" Schelly demanded in Chalmers's face, her arm outstretched at the monitor. The Predator had picked up eight new idents, a group that had arrived from the south, and all carried the appropriate fluorescent strips identifying them as American.

"Major. How many times do I gotta tell ya ... ?" He folded his arms and leaned back.

"Did you manage to get through on the number I gave you?" Epstein asked.

Schelly took a deep breath and tried to calm down. "No, Madam Secretary." She turned to Chalmers. "Anything happens to Cooper, Mr Associate Deputy Director ..."

"Are you about to threaten me, Major? If so, I'd think very carefully before I –"

"Okay, let's all take a step back," said the SECDEF. "Everyone's under a lot of pressure here."

"Shhh," hissed Bunion. "I can't hear the president."

Schelly's attention returned to the screens. It was almost impossible to figure from the display what was going on down there. The Russians had engaged the Scorpion's outfit, but what about Quickstep? Had it been drawn into the fighting? And if so, on whose side? And where was Petrovich? And the Scorpion? Both had been lost in the confusion. Without intel from the ground, it was impossible to get any context. There was also now the presence of a mysterious unit of Americans. Schelly's guts churned. She had a bad feeling about this.

* * *

Al-Aleaqarab was still alight when I reached him. I kicked dust and dirt over the flames to extinguish him, his beard and hair singed back to the skin. The guy he was trying to drag along, Ortsa, was as dead as a stone. I grabbed a handful of the Scorpion's clothing and pulled him down into the wadi. He was unconscious and still smoking a little so I took a couple of mouthfuls of water from the Camelbak and spat it over his face and hands. His skin was black and blistered, his eyes closed and he smelt of barbecue and charred funk. But he was alive.

Alvin made his way along the wadi to help pull the Scorpion along by his collar. Reaching Taymullah and Farib, we stopped.

"That's the Scorpion?" Alvin asked, a little disbelieving.

"That's him," I confirmed.

"Don't look like such a big deal."

"No."

"I don't think it's a good idea to let him live, boss. They killed bin Laden. Best thing they could've done. Solved a lot of problems."

I nodded. All this was going through my mind too. But at least we had the option. Capturing President Petrovich had kick-started a global movement of jihadist hatred and violence. Maybe capturing the Scorpion would shoot that same movement in the foot. Following that logic, maybe shooting him dead would do the same to the whole End of Days bullshit, and avoid any of the moral dilemmas that would no doubt result from having the guy imprisoned somewhere awaiting trial, bleating about us respecting his human rights. I pulled my pistol, cocked the hammer. What stopped me was a voice in my ear. "Boss," it said – Bo.

"You okay, Sarge?"

"Yessir. Go … tasha an … gor. You'd … etter co …"

"Where are you?" The transmission was sketchy, the way a loose connection cuts off some words and not others, but I got the gist of it.

"With Pet … ich. We're a ways … d … wn … column … vehicles."

"Coming to you."

I told Alvin to keep his eye on the Scorpion, and ran forward at a crouch along the wadi, the vehicles more or less lined up beside it. Meanwhile, on the higher ground, the firefight between the jihadists and the Russians continued, diverting attention from the convoy. I had the sense that, without air cover, the Russians were being whittled down. But it wouldn't be long before reinforcements arrived. I wondered why they hadn't turned up already.

When I reached Bo he was keeping Natasha and Igor at bay with his M4, shifting his aim from one to the other. And then I saw that Natasha, in the back of a pickup, had a gun pointed at Igor. Beside her in the bed of the pickup was Petrovich, still nailed to the cross, but he was semi-conscious, his head rolling around. Igor also had a pistol in a two-handed grip, the muzzle aimed at Natasha. "What's going on?" I asked Bo.

* * *

"You sure that's him?" Nanaster asked. There was a group of people in and around that pickup. There was something in the pickup – maybe a person – but from their angle it was impossible to tell. Maybe it was a wounded fighter. One of the people in the pickup was a woman, wearing the full black niqab complete with a *khimar*, and she was pointing the pistol at a big motherfucker of a jihadist. "You go, girl," she said softly to herself. "I'm sure he deserves it."

"Yeah, boss," said Li'l Wilson. "Got fifty points on a facial match here. Ninety-three percent certainty it's Mohammad bin Mohammad formerly from my own patch of paradise – Tennessee. It's him."

Fifty points is all we need. "Take the shot," Nanaster ordered.

* * *

"Take hand off knife," Igor instructed Natasha. He motioned at me. "Tell him."

Natasha's hand was on a knife? I checked the scene again. Yeah, Natasha had a gun in one hand, pointed at Igor, and her other hand gripped a knife handle, the blade embedded almost to the hilt in President Petrovich's shoulder. I'd missed that detail. Fresh blood poured from the knife's entry wound. She twisted the handle, which elicited a gurgle from deep within the president's throat.

"What are you doing?" I asked her. Okay, as questions go not one of my best because "torturing the president" was the obvious answer, but I was taken aback. Somehow I knew her actions were connected to the reason the bodyguard blew up both himself and the president's helicopter. And I remembered I had a theory about all that, I just hadn't expected to be dredging it up right at that moment, not with a firefight raging in the hills around us, the world's most wanted man black and smoking in our custody and questions about how we might get the fuck outta Dodge starting to prick my consciousness. But, in regards to the scene that confronted me now, one thing was absolutely clear. I told Natasha, "I get it. You wanted to stay with us because if you went back to a Russian unit, doing what you're up to right now would not have been possible." I thought about this an instant longer, then asked her, "What did Petrovich do to you?"

"Three, four time … He rape me," she said and gave the knife a twist, which prompted another gurgle from the president.

"I stop her," Igor said. "I stay for this."

"You knew this was Natasha's intention?" I asked him.

"*Da.*"

"Then why the hell didn't you say something?"

"This for me," he said. "Not you."

First and foremost I was happy to see Bo still alive and kicking because his silence over the comms had made me fear the worst. So I could check that box. Next. "Your president's bodyguard blew up the helicopter not because he was a jihadist," I said to Natasha, "but because he was your lover. He didn't say Allahu akbar when he pulled the pin, he said, I love you."

Igor smiled a twisted, complicated smile that was impossible to decode. "*Da.* Tell him," he said.

"Yeah, tell me, Natasha. Who knows, I might have Bo here shoot Igor so that you can go right ahead and do to Petrovich whatever it was you intended to do." I said in an aside to Igor, "I wouldn't really let him shoot you, but I think she knows what I mean."

Igor ignored me. "Tell him."

"The president would put drug in food for me and Arkady Geronosovich. When we sleep, he would rape me in bed beside Arkady. He did it many time. I believe it is nightmare, but he become rougher, and I wake up bleeding from ... from many place. Not nightmare, real. Arkady believe I am lying, having affair with president. I did not tell him truth because I find hard to believe, you know? The general – General Yegorov – warn me about president, but I do not listen ..."

Until it was too late. "Go on," I told her, "give that knife a twist for me." I turned to Igor. "What about you, Starshina? You gonna pull the trigger?"

"My duty to protect president. I fail before. Now I do not fail. I swear oath."

President Petrovich was clearly an evil motherfucker of the first order, as well as being vain and narcissistic. Igor's sense of duty to him was misplaced, oath or no oath. Maybe vodka had rewired his brain.

A gunshot nearby made me flinch. "Shit!" The shooter – it was Mazool. "Mazool!" I snapped. "What the fuck!" He lowered the AK. I looked around. What had he been shooting at?

"Ahh! You kill him!" Natasha shrieked, a small hole in Petrovich's chest where there wasn't one just a few seconds ago. "You steal this from me!"

"No," Mazool shouted right back at her. "This was *my* duty. Duty for my mother, my sister, my brothers. All dead from Russian bombs – his bombs." Mazool dropped the AK at his feet like he had no use for it anymore. He looked at me. "If you would allow it I would cut his heart from his chest."

No one moved. Mazool quickly gathered he was not going to be granted that particular wish. He shrugged and said, "I praise Allah for giving me this bounty. Allahu akbar."

Thus, suddenly, the main reason for our presence here was no longer relevant. "Thanks a whole bunch, Mazool," I said. "My unit was supposed to rescue this guy."

Mazool shrugged. Plainly, the Syrian could care less, except that he said, "God bless America. You have helped me avenge my family."

Okay, so he'd evened the score for a lot of folks. Good for you, Mazool. The folks back home would be less than pleased. "What about you, Igor? Natasha?" The two of them were still pointing weapons at each other.

What was done was done. Nothing any of us could do about it now. The starshina lowered his weapon.

Natasha had different ideas. She pulled the knife from the president's shoulder and stabbed him in the chest a few times, just to make sure his corpse knew how she felt. Maybe Mazool's extra request had given her the idea. As for Mazool, I motioned to him that he should make himself scarce – Natasha had a temper.

I took a moment to reassess. The fighting up in the rocks was almost done, the shooting sporadic. From the shouts of "Allahu akbar" coming down from the heights instead of tracer, it wasn't hard to guess who'd won. Pretty soon they'd be withdrawing to their vehicles. We couldn't be here when they did, and neither could the Scorpion, dead or alive.

"Okay," I said, unwinding the scarf from around my head, "time to rejoin the air force and bug –"

I didn't get to finish the sentence. I heard a zip that ended in a wet slap and, out the corner of an eye, I saw Bo's head get turned inside out and completely disappear in a small geyser of spray.

"Bo," I said, confused about what I thought I just saw. And that's all I know because my own world was suddenly filled with a blinding flash of white light and ...

* * *

"That's a confirmation on Vincent Smith from DC, alias Kareem Al-Waleed," said Ronan. "Ninety-five points of ID."

"Nanaster's scope lingered on breather number one, confirming the kill. *Nice. A good clean shot.* She pivoted the scope a few degrees and picked up Ronan's target breather, Vincent Smith. A scarf obscured the man's face. Nevertheless, the screen informed her that there were indeed ninety-five points of identification confirmed. *Magic what technology can do these days.* "Take the shot, Ronan," she said, her voice low.

"Roger that."

But as Nanaster watched, Smith removed his headscarf, revealing his face.

Nanaster blinked. *It's not possible. It's, it's you!* "No!" Nanaster yelled suddenly, slapping her hand on Ronan's barrel as it jumped with recoil.

"What the hell?" Ronan was incensed.

"Shit, shit, shit." Nanaster peered into the scope, squashing her eyeball up against the lens, unsettling the instrument on its tripod, the image dancing around the black hole inside the scope that framed the image. Smith had fallen, but that's all she knew, as a vehicle and people's legs obscured whatever had happened to him. *Did we kill him? Shit, did we fucking kill him?*

"Boss, you blew my shot," Ronan complained, showing more annoyance than he probably wanted to.

Nanaster, still hunting around the area with the scope, said, "Fuck, Ronan, I damn well hope so."

"What's ... what's happened?"

"There's been a terrible mistake," Nanaster snapped. "Ours ... SAD's ... I don't know. Kareem Al-Waleed from DC, right? Formerly known as Vincent Smith?"

"That's him."

Al-Waleed alias Vincent Smith. *Oh my god!* "Bravo team! Stand down. Immediately! Confirm!"

"Standing down, Sam," snapped Gunny Eldrich, Wilson's spotter. "What's up?"

"We just shot and killed two Americans," she said. "Our kind of American, not the bad kind. On me, warp speed. Bring up the DPV. Do it now. We're going down there."

* * *

Men were fighting and dying on every display. It had been impossible to tell who was who, but as the fighting progressed, it was evidently ISIS that was grinding out the upper hand.

"It's safe to say this has been a useless exercise," said Chalmers sitting back, hands behind his head.

Schelly took her eyes off the displays for a moment. "Why do you say that?"

"Just a hunch."

"Quickstep brought us to Petrovich and the Scorpion."

"We don't know that. Not yet."

"Your Phoenix team is advancing on the jihadist's vehicles. Are they going in to mop up now? Is that what's happening?"

"Major, I keep telling you ... "

"Chalmers?" Epstein said, weighing in.

"Madam Secretary," he assured her. "I swear to you, this is nothing to do with me."

Schelly pictured a man caught in bed by his wife in the act of fucking his mistress, denying that he is fucking his mistress.

Up on the displays, a spreading white light that was so hot it seemed to fuse the very pixels of the screens themselves into molten glass suddenly and silently obliterated the entire hillside.

Schelly's mouth was agape in horror.

"Orders. Direct from the commander-in-chief," said Bunion. "No more Scorpion, no more war. Good job everyone." He stood and thumbed a text on his phone as he walked from the room.

Fifty-four

Ronald V. Small @realSmall
Burger King does the best fries and everyone knows it. Deal with that, Fake News.

Phoenix Four raced to the convoy of ISIS vehicles, into the teeth of the distinctive smells of a hard-fought desert battle that rolled outward from the source: the smells of explosives, broken rock, dirt, urine and shit. Nanaster's heart was in her mouth, a lump constricting her throat. *No way. It just couldn't be ...*

The DPV took air over the crests, as did the dirt bikes. The firefight all but concluded, the fighters would be coming down out of the hills at any minute and there was no time to lose, but the Phoenix unit's approach would be tricky. The American force on the ground there wouldn't know who Nanaster and her team were. There was a real risk of blue on blue incidents. Nanaster's only choice as they sped across the desert was to fire off an M125, a distinctive star cluster flare used by the US Army, which would also alert ISIS to their presence. The flare was duly fired high into the black night, and five bright green stars began to float slowly earthwards on parachutes. The signal was the best Phoenix Four could do. It was the only thing they could do. Nanaster hoped like hell it was enough.

413

Ronan was the best wheelman she had ever worked with, an experienced racer in Southern California before he'd enlisted. He took the approaching berm at an angle, but found some raised ground that wouldn't send the vehicle over the edge fatally unbalanced. The following drop into the wadi was sickening, but the landing was textbook, and soon the convoy of parked ISIS vehicles was in sight. And so far, they had attracted no incoming fire.

"There," said Nanaster, pointing at the utility. "Pull up short."

"Yes, ma'am."

A little further and Ronan hit the skids. The other guys on their bikes slid to a halt beside the DPV, but Nanaster was already running.

"Stop!" said a voice from the shadows.

Nanaster didn't need to be told twice.

"You got two M4s aimed at your head," the voice drawled. "Saw your flare. You got ten seconds. Talk."

"Major Sam Nanaster, Special Activities Division, CIA. We're here to help with the evac. You got casualties?"

"You know that, or are you asking?"

Nanaster thought about her answer, and decided there was no point making things more complicated. "Asking."

After a few seconds of consideration, the voice replied, "We, we got no damn passwords to exchange and our comms are all gone to shit, so we're gonna trust you. But it's a conditional trust until I say otherwise."

"Fair enough," said Nanaster. A man rose from the shadows and walked toward her. She asked him, "Got a name and rank, soldier?"

"Sergeant Alvin Leaphart, United States Army, Special Operations Group. And yeah, we got casualties."

Leaphart looked her over and then signaled to the shadows. One of them stood.

"That's Sergeant Jimmy McVeigh, US Army," Leaphart told her.

Nanaster followed the sergeants to the man down. There was no light to see by, but he was clearly not an ISIS fighter and neither were his two surviving men. A huge relief swept over her when she felt his pulse. It was strong, but the head wound was bad. How bad, it was difficult to tell. The round had creased his skull, and no doubt it was cracked. Her next hope was that there'd be no lasting brain damage. She looked down on him, read his nametag. "Cooper." Where had the intelligence come from that led their team to this point? They had just killed a US serviceman, and almost killed another. How could such a terrible error pass through the system? Nanaster was at a loss.

The voices of the ISIS fighters carried on the night air were getting louder and closer. Time was short.

"Let's get him off the ground."

"Ma'am, got an old ambulance back there," said McVeigh. "No medical supplies to call on, though."

"Let's take him there. We've got a full medical kit."

Nanaster's men lifted Sergeant Bo Baker's remains and followed Sergeant McVeigh. She bent down and took a handful of the wounded man's webbing.

"Stop," said a woman's voice. "*We* carry him."

Nanaster looked up. The woman in the niqab. *The accent ... distinctive.* "You're Russian," she said, somewhat confused.

"*Da,*" the woman replied. Her face was no longer obscured, the niqab's hood removed. It was a beautiful face, even angelic, but also strangely fierce. Nanaster stood back as the Russian, and a monster of a human being whom Nanaster recognized as the man this niqab-wearing Russian woman had been pointing a gun at not five minutes ago, took hold of the wounded man's shoulder. Three males who looked Syrian, and who acted like they were part of this team, took the wounded man's legs and all of them carried him gently down into the wadi where the depression provided some cover.

And then, suddenly, the whole side of the hill disappeared in an explosion that was almost volcanic. The enormous percussion shook the earth and knocked everyone to the ground. The heat flash was unbearable and Nanaster, on her knees, found herself panting, starved of oxygen, the smell of her own singed hair in the back of her mouth. She thought she had been spirited through the gates of hell itself.

Almost as quickly the heat was gone, moving out across the desert with the shock wave. Nanaster managed to lift herself up. *Jesus, Hellfire missiles.* Their signature was unmistakable. Someone sitting in the comfort of an air-conditioned control booth who-knew-where had fired them. Had the intention been to save them, or kill them? If it was to save them, the wadi had done that, along with the line of vehicles, a shield which was now mostly burning. Up on that hill, survival would have been impossible.

* * *

Several vehicles were spared from the explosion, protected by the lay of the land and other vehicles that had taken the brunt. One of these was the ambulance. The Russian woman wouldn't let Nanaster anywhere near Cooper while she cleaned the dirt and the blood away from his face and head.

Are they lovers? Nanaster wondered while she prepared a shot of antibiotics, and another of morphine should it be required. She climbed in the back of the ambulance to administer the drugs and looked down on the man's face. Her heart stopped beating – his eyes were open. Was there recognition in them? He stared up at her.

His Adam's apple worked up and down as if loading words into his throat like cartridges racking into a twelve-gauge. But then he slipped back into unconsciousness, the words left unsaid.

Fifty-five

Ronald V. Small @realSmall
Air Force One now has a putting green WITH REAL GRASS!
Next president, you're welcome!

It was a nice day, but not for a funeral. No day is good for one of those when the person being sent off is a man in the prime of life, which has ended violently and to no purpose. A detachment from the United States Army 5th Special Forces Group (Airborne), Bo's outfit, came to see him off. There were a lot of folks there on that sunny day, standing on the hill at Arlington National Cemetery. I didn't know many of them. Bo was married, but they hadn't gotten around to having kids, so I guess that was something. I introduced myself to his wife, whose name was Jo. Bo and Jo. BoJo, they called themselves. Every couple needs a name. Jo was pretty – tall and shapely with intelligent eyes and a great booty. It's a funeral, but you still take note of these things. Well, I do.

Seven men fired into the sky three times, drilled to within an inch of their lives to do it right. They did it right. Not sure that's the kind of send-off I want when it's my time. I'd rather folks get drunk and tell jokes. Bad ones. The kind I tell, apparently.

Okay, so I'll confess here that I didn't feel great about the way this operation had gone, and I was mulling it over as I stood in the sunshine with Sergeant Alvin Leaphart and Sergeant Jimmy McVeigh, listening to the preacher talk about God and sacrifice and His bountiful blessings and all the associated bullshit about resurrection and so forth. Religion, what got us into this mess.

The Russian president was dead, killed by ISIS so the official story went. There was no concrete evidence of US involvement, other than a desperate attempt to rescue him that had failed. He had a great big fucking funeral, though – horse-drawn gun carriages, booming cannons, a million flags at half mast, parades up and down Moscow streets, thousands of mourning citizens and a legion of unknown women who wished they'd had the chance to kick him square in the nuts. Or maybe cut them off. Petrovich would be pleased to know that his funeral is now a YouTube video.

The Russians got their general back. General Yegorov had suffered a little wear and tear that he would no doubt have nightmares about for the rest of his life, but he was otherwise okay. My team pulled him from a cave while they were mopping up the last of the Scorpion's followers. I was seeing stars at the time. The Kremlin also got its Cheget back, but the significance of its return was purely symbolic. The entire Russian nuclear launch system had to be ripped out and a new one installed. They're still working on that. And still threatening us with a pre-emptive strike. Better hurry. North Korea might beat them to the punch. Or China. Take a number, right? I wouldn't be at all surprised if the outfit that won the tender to design and install Russia's new system was a dummy CIA company. Thinking about it, is there any other kind of CIA company?

And, on the subject of the CIA, Associate Deputy Director Bradley Chalmers send me a get-well card. We both know he hoped infection would set in. And it still might. There's a small titanium plate and other bits and pieces of hardware in the space between my ears now. I'm hopeful of being able to receive radio transmissions if I tilt my head just so. Chalmers – he has a lot of explaining to do, something he has so far neatly sidestepped. I don't like where he is, sitting up there high on the totem pole, but I can't do anything about it. Although I am hoping the universe gives me the opportunity sometime in the future to push him off because, where he's sitting at the moment, it's a hell of a long way to fall.

Bringing the Scorpion back alive, I am told, was a blot on my copybook. He was meant to die on that hillside and a lot of people were surprised when he was flown to the States cooked medium rare, but still among the living. It had been my intention to end his days, I had even cocked my weapon to put a nine-millimeter full stop on his life, but, as they say, shit happens. Currently, there's a fight over what to do with him, where to imprison him. And, as I personally foretold, there are a bunch of people bleating about his civil rights. Gotta laugh. Nevertheless, the Mahdi, as he was but is no longer being called, has been paraded around the media in bandages and prison orange, and because of this has lost all his shine in the Islamic world. The so-called army of the faithful on the Turkish border melted away almost immediately news of his capture was splashed around the globe. The Turks were thrilled to get their tanks back.

Meanwhile, the imams have been telling anyone who'll listen that Al-Aleaqarab was an imposter because the apocalypse he promised didn't happen. But don't you worry about it, they insist, the real one will be along any time soon. Why? Because it is written in the Qur'an. Seems everyone loves a good Chicken Little story, apparently even Mohammad.

As for our commander-in-chief, the less said the better. I really don't want to think or talk about him, just like I don't want to think or talk about the guy who killed John Lennon. Some people don't deserve consideration. And also, around here, you never know who might be listening.

Last on the list of details, the phone SIMs we recovered from the Scorpion's fighters on the hill overlooking the warehouse were turned over to the Military Intelligence and the NSA. Don't know what they contained, and will never find out.

The preacher finished his sermon about the awful choices God has to make, taking those we love to a better place. And it made me think. Let's say there is a God. He has to have one fucked-up sense of humor, right? He set up three competing religions on the one patch of turf, and then gave one of them all the gas. Laughing all the way to the pearly gates, I'm sure. If that doesn't tell you what we're dealing with, you've got no sense of the ridiculous.

But, my mind has been wandering. Back to Bo's funeral. "Amen," said the preacher and this was repeated by most of us standing around the coffin, which was then lowered into the ground. Jo picked up a handful of dirt and sprinkled it on the casket. A line of people followed her example and then we were left to our own devices.

"Major," said Sergeant Leaphart. He saluted me, I gave him one back, and then we shook hands. "I'd do it all again, boss," he said. "Well, maybe not all of it." There was a motion at the mound of dirt inside the ropes. "What I mean is, if you decide to go round again, put in a word for me."

"Me too, boss." Sergeant Jimmy McVeigh saluted and we shook. He asked me, "You gonna come to the wake?"

I'm not a fan of wakes, at least not until I discover where the good scotch is stashed. "I'll be there."

"We'll have a drink then," he said.

"More than one, I hope."

"Yes, sir. Thanks, Vin."

First names. A serious break of protocol between enlisted man and officer. It made me feel good.

We stood there for a moment. "This was a tough break, sir," Alvin reassured me. "Not your fault."

I knew that, but when one of the guys in your unit gets whacked you ask yourself what you might have done different. Especially when, as I said, Bo lost his life to no good purpose.

McVeigh, Leaphart and I couldn't shake, because we'd already done that, and doing it twice would feel weird, so the parting at the graveside felt awkward. I stood there, watching people go and just thought about stuff.

"Major Cooper? Major Jillian Schelly."

The major stood in front of me.

"Major Jillian Schelly," I said to give myself some time to frame an intelligent response. "At last we meet."

"At last."

"Back when I was incountry, I tried to put a face to the voice," I said.

"How did you go?"

I examined the spray of freckles across her nose and the full heart-shaped lips. I thought, out of ten a solid eight-plus, but I said, "I think I pretty much nailed it."

"This is Professor Kiraz Başak," Schelly told me, introducing the exotic creature in a fitted black pants suit standing beside her. No uniform, so therefore a civilian. "The professor worked on this with me." Amend that to CIA, or maybe Defense Intelligence.

"Major Cooper," she said.

"Professor," I replied and took her proffered hand.

"It is a pleasure and an honor to meet you," she said, which took me by surprise.

I might have mumbled something because what do you say to something like that when you know you don't deserve it? I defaulted to, "Good of you both to come and pay your respects."

"How are your wounds healing?" Schelly asked, her eyes searching my head.

"I'll be fine."

"Whoever did your ear has done an amazing job. You'd never know."

I nodded. "Yeah." Maybe Bo missed his true calling. "Are you going to the wake?" We could have just the one drink and have a chat, or maybe have the whole bottle and all leave together.

This was one handsome couple. As I said, it's a funeral but you still take note of these things and it would be difficult not to note either the major or the professor.

"No, I don't think so," said Schelly. "I'm sorry. I'm truly sorry about Sergeant Baker."

"He was a good man, a good solider. I liked him."

"I wanted to visit you when you were in hospital," Schelly said, "but I couldn't get away."

"I wasn't lying in bed asking myself, 'Now where's Major Schelly?'"

She smiled. Nice smile.

I have a radar that's sensitive to body language and it was telling me Schelly wanted to say something, but was finding it difficult.

"I've seen your file, Vin. I feel I know you really well, but of course you don't know me at all."

Not much I could say to that.

"I just wanted to say that you and your team did an incredible job," she continued. "I ... we ... the professor and I ... We just wanted you to know that."

"Yes, incredible," the professor reiterated.

"Thanks," I said. Sure you don't want to go have that bottle? We started to walk down the hill, towards the vehicles, most of which were leaving. "There something else you wanted to say, Major?"

"I'm sorry?"

"You've got something on you mind. At least, I think you do."

"Yes," she said, real awkwardness taking over. "I just thought you might have questions."

I did. "The Phoenix team that pulled us out. A woman led it. Major Sam Nanaster, according to the guys in my unit. What can you tell me about her?"

"Not much," Schelly replied with a glance at the professor. "Except that you're asking the right question."

"A Phoenix team would make her CIA."

"Yes."

"A straight answer," I said. "I could get used to those."

"I'm sorry, Major. It's classified. I think you know the drill."

I did. "I'd like a photo of her, see what she looks like. I think I remember her face, but I might have been dreaming."

"You know that's against the rules, Vin," she said with another glance at the professor. We stopped at my car. "This yours?" She asked. "I like old cars. A '68 Impala, right?"

"You know your old shit beaters," I said. "I had a Canadian Pontiac Parisienne. Swapped it for this baby."

"Good trade." Something seemed to prick her memory. "Oh, I wanted to ask you ..." She produced an envelope from the leather satchel under her arm, opened it and extracted a photo of the dusty white BMW, the one the Scorpion had stolen. She had a question. "Did you do this?"

"Who's asking? The insurance company after me?"

"No. But you did that?"

The Scorpion called himself a religious leader just like the pope. His ride had a name, so I figured Al-Aleaqarab's wheels needed one too. I looked at the photo again, the words scratched into the paintwork with a ka-bar went all the way to the metal – "Assholemobile." I said, "Keying a car isn't as easy as it looks, y'know. The s's are tricky, hard to get the curve going."

She smiled again. It was still nice. "I thought you might have done that." She handed me the envelope. "Anyway, souvenir."

"Is that what you wanted to ask me?"

"Yes."

Really? That's it? I doubted it, but I had the impression that now we were done because she held out her hand to shake.

"Thank you, Vin, and good luck."

"Thank you," said the professor. Another handshake.

Final smiles and goodbyes from Major Jillian Schelly and the professor and they walked off together towards a burgundy Cadillac.

I got into the Chevy, fired her up, put the radio on, and called up the address for the wake on my phone. The news was playing on the radio, the craziness still unwinding from The-End-of-Days-When-The-Dead-Shall-Rise-And-Walk-The-Earth. I couldn't believe folks actually fell for that shit. Proving my point, the Sheriff from Macon, Georgia, was giving a press conference. A group of kids from Georgia State University had been charged with "trespass, vandalism, and criminal mischief" for the desecration of graves at the Macon Cedar Ridge Cemetery. Other charges of "conspiracy to commit criminal mischief" were pending. Seems the kids from Georgia State had used Facebook to organize attacks of similar nature on an international scale, at cemeteries from New Jersey to Surrey, in England. They were members of some global zombie club, according to the sheriff, and were inspired by the apocalyptic mythologies in the Qur'an. Apparently the kids thought that what they'd done – instigate the "End of Days Phenomenon" – was cool.

I was sure their bravado vanished when they heard there was a massive fine to pay as well as the threat of imprisonment in a federal correctional institution hanging over their heads.

I punched the button a couple of times until I found a tune I liked, in this case Fogerty singing about a bad moon rising. Seemed appropriate. It was about then that I noticed the envelope with the photo of the Beemer sitting on top of it wasn't empty, the edge of another photo poking out beneath the flap. Curiosity got the better of me. I pulled to the side of the road and a burgundy Cadillac drove on by. I shook the photo onto the passenger seat. It was a head and shoulders shot – Major Sam Nanaster standing beside a desert patrol vehicle. It was not a great shot – grainy, and a little out of focus. Even so ...

"Jesus," I said aloud, took a deep breath and then let it out. Was it possible?

The moment in the ambulance came back to me. Lying on my back, my head ringing, when I opened my eyes and saw her face. I thought later that maybe the memory was the figment of a brain addled by a bullet's graze. This photo suggested otherwise. Maybe the Sheriff of Macon had gotten it wrong. Could be that at least one person had risen from the dead after all.

Epilogue

Ronald V. Small @realSmall
Nobody in the history of this country has ever been better at the military than me. Nobody. No one. So amazing.

"'If anyone here objects to this marriage, speak now or forever hold your peace," said the celebrant.

Crickets spoke up, which didn't count.

A few more words, the ring, a kiss, and it was done. Marnie Masters, Anna's sister, was now Mrs Marnie Wayne.

Weddings. Put it this way, I like them a lot more than funerals.

The bandages had been off a month. My hair had pretty much grown back. The sun was shining. And my toes were digging into the sand lapped by the warm waters of St Bart's.

"Here," said Natasha, putting the drink in my hand. "Is vodka."

Of course it is. "Thanks."

Natasha? Yeah, we were doing each other. She looked me up when I was in recovery. Go figure. A pain in the ass in Syria and here she was, a long way from being a pain in the ass. And now we had two weeks on this island together to discover that it was never going to work out between us. So far those acts of discovery were taking place three times a day.

426

With the wedding ceremony over and the temperature rising, dresses were coming off and swimsuits were getting pulled on. Beach weddings beat the hell out of church weddings. Natasha peeled off the elegant blue sheath she had wriggled into this morning and, lo, beneath was a sheer, backless one-piece, also blue. We're talking dynamite. Care for a little more discovery?

She handed me her drink and said, "I go in. You come too. We swim out past boat and do it like fish."

Now there's bait you don't often get to bite – we were clearly on the same wavelength. "Give me a minute to finish my drink and I'm there," I told her.

"Hurry," she said, and we kissed, a kiss that tasted of vodka, which I could get used to.

Natasha skipped down to the water. It was hard not to stare. It was also hard to believe she could kill someone as easily as sneeze. She grabbed Marnie's hand on the way through, and Marnie grabbed Arlen's, and the three of them ran into the water.

"Vin!" Arlen shouted. "C'mon!"

I waved, fully intending to join them, until I noticed that the person who had been watching the wedding ceremony from the old boats stacked under a tree over yonder was still watching. There can be too much watching. Now that I was focused on this person, I could see it was a woman. The wedding party was in the light and she was backed into the shade, so that made her hard to see, on top of which she wore a wide brimmed hat, increasing the shadow coefficient. But, somehow, I had a feeling she'd placed herself just so, knowing that I'd see her and that curiosity would bring me over.

My heart started to race as I came nearer, and for a few reasons. She was sitting on an upturned dinghy, wearing shorts, a T-shirt and a Redskins cap. Reason one, that's my team. Reason number two, her hair was tied in a ponytail, but it fell over one shoulder and I'd recognize that hair anywhere. Reason number three, there was a bottle of Glenkeith beside her. And everyone knows that's my brand, right?

I climbed up on the boat, sat beside her and tossed the vodka in my glass onto the sand. She replaced it with a couple of shots of single malt. I needed it.

"She's gorgeous," the woman said.

"Marnie's a beautiful bride," I replied, deflecting. "And the short blonde bob really suits her."

"Yes, it does, but I mean your girlfriend."

"Yeah, she is beautiful, but she has a problem with articles."

"That's Russians for you," she said.

"Are you jealous?"

"I'd be lying if I said I wasn't, but I also know I have absolutely no right to be."

"No, you don't." I took a mouthful of single malt and embraced the burn. "You died," I told her.

"Did I?"

"Maybe you don't remember. I was holding you in my arms at the time. And then I went to your funeral."

"Me too. It was nice."

"There has been a lot of talk about the dead rising. Did you get to meet Jesus? What's he like?" I took another big mouthful of Glenkeith, the pulse racing in my temple, and hoped my drink wasn't shaking too noticeably.

"Vin—"

"You have a lot of explaining to do, Major Nanaster. You know that, right?"

"Yes. I promise you, it's a hell of a story."

"It had better be." I polished off my drink. "So…is there a Mr. Nanaster?"

"What do you think?"

"I don't know what to think," I told her honestly. "What do I call you? Major Nanaster? Sam? What?"

"No, Vin. You ..." She took my spare hand and turned to look at me, I figured so that I could see how much it meant. "*You* can call me Anna."

CPSIA information can be obtained
at www.ICGtesting.com
Printed in the USA
LVHW110107031120
670544LV00005B/14